THE FIGHTERS

JOHN TURNER
From the waste of war he'd made a life for himself—a life that threatened soon to end. But before it was all over, he had to find the three friends who'd faced—and defeated—death and prison with him years before.

DUGGIE BRENT
The paratrooper had killed a man in a barroom fight. The answer to a single question would decide his fate. Was it an accident of war—or murder?

DAVID LESURIER
For a black soldier kissing a white girl there was only one sentence. But not if he himself could carry it out first.

PHILLIP MORGAN
The flyer turned beachcomber seemed least fitted for the battle of life. But it was he who'd found both love and fortune in a place far from home.

Also by Nevil Shute:

MARAZAN*
SO DISDAINED*
LONELY ROAD*
KINDLING*
ORDEAL
LANDFALL
AN OLD CAPTIVITY
PASTORAL*
MOST SECRET*
VINLAND THE GOOD
A TOWN LIKE ALICE*
ROUND THE BEND*
THE FAR COUNTRY*
THE BREAKING WAVE*
BEYOND THE BLACK STUMP*
ON THE BEACH*
THE RAINBOW AND THE ROSE*
TRUSTEE FROM THE TOOLROOM*

Published by Ballantine Books

THE
CHEQUER
BOARD

NEVIL
SHUTE

BALLANTINE BOOKS • NEW YORK

ISBN 0-345-32174-X

This edition published by arrangement with William Morrow and Company, Inc.

Manufactured in the United States of America

First Ballantine Books Edition: February 1968
Third Printing: May 1988

'Tis all a Chequer board of Nights and Days
Where Destiny with Men for Pieces plays:
  Hither and thither moves, and mates, and slays,
And one by one back in the Closet lays.

Rubaiyat of Omar Khayyam
EDWARD FITZGERALD

I saw Mr John Turner first on June the 25th last year. He came to me on the recommendation of a general practitioner at Watford: I have the letter before me.

DEAR MR HUGHES,

I should be grateful if you would make an appointment to see a patient of mine, Mr John Turner. Mr Turner has been suffering from attacks of vertigo and fainting: I have been attending him consequent on a fall which he suffered in the Strand Palace Hotel, when he was unconscious for some minutes. I have found some apraxia, and the sight of his left eye appears to have become subnormal in recent months. In view of a severe head injury which he incurred in the year 1943 I feel that an intracranial lesion may be at the root of his trouble, and it is upon this diagnosis that I would like you to see him.

Mr Turner is married, but has no children. He is in some branch of the food business, and lives in a style corresponding with an income of £800-£1,000 per annum.

Yours very sincerely,
V. C. WORTH, M.B., B.S.

Mr Turner came to see me by appointment that afternoon. The first thing I noticed when my receptionist showed him in was the scar. It stretched as a deep indentation from a point about an inch above the left eyebrow up into the hair on the crown of the head, over four inches long. It was a deep cleft in his forehead, red and angry-looking.

The rest of Mr Turner was not very prepossessing. He was about forty years old, with a fresh complexion and sandy hair, going a little bald. He had a jaunty air of cheerfulness and bonhommie which did not fit in well with my consulting room; he was the sort of man who would be the life and soul of the party in the saloon bar of a good-class pub, or at the races. He was wearing rather a bright brown suit with a very bright tie, and he carried a bowler hat.

7

I got up from my desk as he came in. "Good afternoon, Mr Turner," I said.

He said, "Cheerio, doctor. How's tricks?"

I smiled. "I'm all right," I said. I motioned him to the chair before my desk. "Sit down, Mr Turner, and tell me what you are complaining of."

He sat down with his bowler on his knee, and grinned at me with nervous cheerfulness. "I'm all right," he said. "You won't find much wrong with me, doctor. May want a bit of a tonic. You know," he said confidentially, "this wound on my napper frightens people. I tell you, straight, it does. Every doctor that I go to gets the wind up and says I ought to see a specialist. They'll none of them touch me. If I want my corns cut, they say I ought to see a specialist." He laughed heartily. "I'm not kidding you. They get the wind up."

I smiled at him; one has to create confidence. "Does the wound give you any trouble?" I asked.

He shook his head. "None at all. Throbs a bit, now and then. The only trouble I get is at the hairdressers' when they come to cut my hair—it don't half fox them." He laughed again. "Not that I've much to cut, now."

I pulled my pad towards me. "Let me get down the preliminaries first," I said. He gave me his age, address, and occupation; it seemed that he was a flour salesman. "Cereal Products Ltd.," he said. "I went to them in 1935, and then went back to them again after the war."

I picked up the letter on my desk and glanced it over. "I see that you told Dr Worth about attacks of giddiness," I said. "Do those come very frequently?"

He said, "Oh no. Might be two or three in the last month. They don't last long—just a few seconds, or maybe half a minute." He laughed nervously. "Sort of make you feel you want to hold on to something. I think I want a tonic, doctor. I told Dr Worth . . ."

"Yes," I said, writing on my pad. "How long since you had the first of those, Mr Turner?"

"I dunno. Couple of months, maybe."

I glanced again at the letter. "Dr Worth says that you had a fall in the Strand Palace Hotel," I said. "How did that happen?"

"Well," he said, "it was like this. We have to do a bit of entertaining in my line—it all goes on the firm, you know. Well, to cut a long story short I was in the American Bar last Thursday with Izzy Guildas and another Portuguese—Jew boys, you know, but good types all the same—and I suddenly passed out cold. Fact, I'm telling you. I passed out cold, and fell down off the little stool onto the floor, clean out. When I came to I was in the lavatory lying on my back on the floor with somebody splashing water on my face, and my collar all undone. I wasn't half in a mess, I tell you."

I said, "How long were you unconscious, Mr Turner?"

"I dunno. Maybe three or four minutes."

I made a note on my pad. "When you came to, did you feel any pain?"

"I had the hell of a headache. I was sick, too."

"What time of day was this?"

"About eight o'clock in the evening. We were just going to have dinner. I was looking forward to that dinner." He laughed.

"What did you do? Did you see a doctor in the hotel?"

He shook his head. "I sat about in the lavatory for half an hour or so till I felt better, and then I went home by underground and went to bed. The wife made me stay in bed in the morning and see Dr Worth."

"I see," I said. I made another note. "Had you been drinking heavily, Mr Turner?" I asked. "Forgive me for such a question, but I have to have the facts."

He laughed again. "I been tight often enough not to mind talking about it, doctor—you ask anyone who knew Jackie Turner in the war. But, matter of fact, I hadn't had a lot. I had a couple of pints at lunch, and then nothing tell we went to the American Bar that evening. I had one dry Martini, and Izzy was just ordering the second round when I passed out."

"That's quite moderate," I said.

He took me up. "I wish you'd tell that to the wife. She don't half carry on about the beer I drink. But I think beer's best. I started to lay off spirits the thick end of a year ago. I got a sort of throbbing, so I stick to beer, mostly."

I made a note. "You get this throbbing with whiskey, say, but not with beer?"

"That's right."

"Where is this throbbing, when you get it? Under the wound?"

"No—sort of right inside."

I made another note. Then I passed him the silver box of cigarettes; he took one. I lit my own, and absent-mindedly slipped the lighter back in my pocket as I glanced over my pad.

"Were you very tired that night?" I asked.

He looked up at me quickly. "Funny you should ask that," he said. "I was just about all in. I dunno when I felt so tired."

"You'd had a very heavy day?"

He shook his head. "I'd not been doing much. I think I want a tonic. A good, stiff tonic, doctor—that's what I need. I told Dr Worth 'that's all that's wrong with me,' I said."

"Do you get this feeling of exhaustion very often, Mr Turner?"

He did not answer; he was fumbling with his lighter. The cigarette was held between his lips. He had taken the lighter from his jacket pocket with his right hand and held it for a moment as if to strike it with his right thumb, but his thumb did not move. The little finger waggled to and fro instead. Then he took it in his left hand, and with some difficulty rotated the knurled knob and made a flame, and lit his cigarette. "I'm sorry," he said. "What was that you said?"

"I asked if you felt tired very often."

"I do sometimes. I didn't used to. I'm a bit run down."

"Are you left-handed, Mr Turner?"

He stared at me. "No."

I said, "I saw you had some trouble with your lighter. Let me see you light it again."

He pulled it out of his pocket. "You mean, light it with my right hand, doctor?" He was flushing a little.

"Yes. Can you do it with your right hand?"

He said awkwardly, "Well, I always used to, but it doesn't seem to go, now." He was fumbling with it. "I don't seem able to put my thumb on to the knob."

"How long have you had this trouble with it?"

"I dunno. Couple of months, perhaps."

I did not want to frighten him. I said, "All right; never mind that now."

He stared at me uneasily. "Rheumatism, that's what it is. I knew a chap once lost the use of every finger on his hand —every bloody finger, doctor—all through rheumatism. He got it right by taking Kruschen salts. Every morning he took salts, much as would go on a sixpence. He never had no trouble since."

He paused, and then he said, "I got some salts last week,

and I been taking them." He glanced at his thumb. "It's much better than it was. It's only the lighter I can't seem to manage."

"I'll make a physical examination of you in a minute," I said. "First of all, though, tell me about that wound. You got that in the war?"

"That's right," he said.

"Mortar?"

He shook his head. "It happened in one of them aeroplanes. Twenty millimetre. It burst right in front of me; right inside the cabin."

I made a note. "You were in the Royal Air Force in the war?"

He shook his head. "I was in the Royal Army Service Corps. I was on my way home from Algiers," he explained, "by air. In 1943, that was. We come by Gib and then straight from Gib to the U.K., four of us, in a Hudson, with a crew of three. A Jerry jumped us over the sea somewhere around Ushant, a JU-88. He had four goes at us, but he couldn't get us down. Over and over again he come at us, and his shells bursting on the wings and in the cabin every time. I got put out on his second run, so I didn't see the end of it. They said some Spitfires came and drove him off."

In the quiet peace of my consulting room I made my note. "You got back to England all right, then?"

"In a manner of speaking," Mr Turner said. "The second pilot made a belly landing in a field by Penzance. There was him and me and another chap all in hospital together when I come to. That's all that there was left, out of seven of us."

I wrote again on the pad. "What was the hospital?"

"Penzance General Hospital."

"That is the normal civilian hospital, is it? Not a service hospital?"

"That's right. They took us to the nearest one there was."

I made another note. "Who operated on you?"

There was silence. I glanced at him; he was troubled, evidently distressed that he could not remember. I tried to help him. "Was it a civilian surgeon?"

He looked up. "It was an Army doctor, a major. I know his name quite well. I had it on the tip of my tongue to tell you, case you wanted to know. But I can't say it now."

"Try and think," I said. "It's rather important to get all the records of your case together."

11

There was a long pause.

"Never mind," I said at last. "Do you remember what he looked like?"

"Oh, aye. He was a young chap with sandy hair like me, rather thin. He knew his onions all right. The sister and the matron said he made a rattling fine job of me. Well, he did, now, didn't he?"

I smiled. "I should say so. Do you remember the date when this happened?"

"End of September 1943," he said. "I dunno the day."

I made another note. "That's good enough. I can find out all I want to from the hospital." I glanced over the notes that I had made on my pad, and then got up. "Now will you please take off your shirt, Mr Turner, and let me have a look at you."

He got up and took off his coat. When it came to un-buttoning his waistcoat the same functional disability of the right hand became apparent; he had to use the left. I stopped him, gave him a pencil, and told him to sign his name on my blotting pad. He could do that all right. The disability seemed to be confined to certain familiar actions, such as unbuttoning his clothes or lighting the lighter. For these familiar actions he had no control over his fingers.

Apart from that, I did not find much physically wrong with him. Reflexes were normal. Blood pressure was rather higher than it should have been, but that might have been due to anything. Heart, lungs, stomach seemed to be quite all right. When I came to examine his eyes with the ophthal-moscope, however, I found the disc of the left eye to be blurred and pinkish. That was the only physical sign of real trouble that I found. On giving him an eye test I found the vision of that eye subnormal in all ways.

I let him put on his clothes, and we sat down again.

"Well, I think you'll have to come into hospital for a few days, for examination, Mr Turner," I said. "I want to take some X-ray pictures of your head, and we can do a lumbar puncture for pathological examination at the same time. That's quite a simple matter."

He said, "I'm all right, though, doctor?"

"That's what I'm trying to find out," I replied. I leaned towards him. "Look, Mr Turner—you know as well as I do that you aren't quite right at present. So far the symp-toms are not serious. There is the slight functional dis-ability of your right hand, lighting the lighter and button-ing your clothes. We've just found that your left eye isn't doing much to help you see; of course, you didn't notice that. Added to that there are the giddiness and fainting, and the exhausted feeling that you get. There's some reason for all this, you know. It may be that something under that wound of yours requires a little attention. You'll have to come into hospital for a week for observation."

There was a long pause, "Okeydoke," he said at last. "If that's what's got to happen—well, that's that. When would it be, doctor?"

"I'll have to see when I can get a bed," I said. "You'd like a private ward?"

"How much is that?"

"Six guineas."

"I suppose so," he said. "Be nicer if the wife comes to see me."

I nodded. "I'll fix it up as soon as I can," I said. "Probably in about a fortnight. I'll write to Dr Worth and tell him what I can arrange."

"I'll tell him what you said." He stared down at his hat for a minute, and then looked up. "You'd be able to see splinters and that in the X ray?" he said.

"Were there any splinters left in the wound?" I asked.

He said, "I think there was. I don't think they got 'em all out. They was too deep in."

"I see," I said thoughtfully. "Oh yes, they'll show all right. If any of them are giving trouble, that may show too."

"They wouldn't, after all this time, would they?" he asked.

I got up and pressed the bell on my desk. "I hope not, Mr Turner," I said. "But that's what we've got to find out."

He went away, and in the evening I wrote to the War Office about surgeons in the Penzance neighbourhood in September 1943, who might have operated on him after that crash. In a few days they sent me an answer. At that distance of time they could not identify the surgeon, but they gave me a list of five names of R.A.M.C. officers stationed in the district at that time who were of sufficient seniority to tackle such an operation, any one of whom might have done it.

One of them, Major P. C. Hodder, struck a chord of memory. Percy Hodder had been a medical student in the London Hospital under me in 1943. I remembered him particularly because of his great interest in the brain. He had been a thin, sandy-haired young man. I turned to the Medical Directory and looked him up; he had got his F.R.C.S. in 1938. Percy

Hodder was probably my man. He was now practising in Leeds.

I sat down and wrote to him.

Three days later I received an answer.

Dear Mr Hughes,

I remember the case of Captain Turner very well; I did the operation at Penzance about the time you mention. I doubt if we could locate the X-ray photographs now, and my own case records were destroyed by enemy action in London at the time of the V bombs.

So far as I can remember, I had to leave several splinters in the brain matter as the immediate operative danger to the patient in their removal seemed greater than the risk that they would create trouble later on. I am not, therefore, greatly surprised if trouble has developed.

I shall be in London on Tuesday next, and could look in to see you at your rooms in Harley Street at about five o'clock if that would be convenient for you.

Yours sincerely,
P. C. Hodder

When we met in my consulting room he said at once, "If it's the Captain Turner I remember, he's had some years of useful life. I never thought he'd live to make old bones."

I described the man to him, and his apparent injury.

"That's him all right," said Hodder. He thought for a minute. "So far as I remember," he said slowly, "there were seven or eight metallic splinters or fragments in the cerebrum. I know I left three of them in, as being altogether too deep-seated to be tackled. As it was, the patient very nearly died of shock; we had a great deal of trouble in saving him after the operation. I didn't think he'd live. After that, I didn't think he'd recover all his faculties. But he did. I saw him some months later, and he seemed to be completely normal."

He went on to tell me in some detail where he thought the other splinters were. The more I heard of it, the less I liked it. The man was older now, and less able to resist operative shock.

"Not a very good prognosis," I said at last.

He shook his head. "I wouldn't like to try to get those out, myself," he said. "Would you operate, sir, in a case like that?"

I said slowly, "I doubt it. That is, assuming that the pres-

14

ent X ray supports your memory of where the pieces are."

"I think you'll find that fairly accurate," he said. "I remember this case particularly, because of all the circumstances."

"You mean the crash?" I asked.

He hesitated. "Well, yes, there was that. But he and two others were prisoners awaiting court-martial, in a detention ward. Did the patient tell you that?"

I said drily, "No, he didn't."

He said, "Well, that's what they were. There was an armed guard on the door of the ward."

"He told me that he was on his way home from Algiers," I said. "It is not helpful when the patient tells you a pack of lies. It just wastes time."

"Well, that was true enough," said Hodder. "They were sent back from Algiers. There was a load of four or five of them. This man Turner and two others were wanted for some black-market racket in London, selling Army stores, I think. They were found out when they got drafted to North Africa. Turner was the only one of that lot who came through the crash alive. Then there was a paratrooper up for murder in a London pub. The D.A.J.A.G. sent them all back for trial in England in this Hudson, the one that got shot up and crashed."

"Nice party," I said. "How many of them survived the crash?"

He wrinkled his forehead in thought. "Three or four, I think; but they weren't all my patients. They weren't all prisoners, either. One couldn't have been a prisoner—the second pilot—the one who crash-landed the machine. He had a broken thigh; an R.A.F. doctor was treating him. I think he was taken in with the rest of them, and not moved when they put the guard on. I think there were four altogether. There was the pilot, and Turner, and the paratrooper, and the Negro. That's right. Four."

"A Negro?" I asked.

He nodded. "There was an American Negro soldier in the ward, who'd cut his throat. He wasn't one of the party from Algiers. The hospital put him in with them, in the same ward, because he had to be under guard and he was too bad to be moved."

"What did he want to cut his throat for?"

"I forget—some civil offense or other. The American military police were chasing him. He went into an air-raid shelter and cut his throat. But he didn't know anatomy."

15

I returned to the subject in hand. "I'm taking Mr Turner into hospital for examination," I said. We stood together for a few minutes longer, discussing what I meant to do with him and talking generally about the case. "I'll drop you a line later on to let you know what happens," I said finally. "But I doubt if it will be very satisfactory, from what you tell me."

"I wouldn't lose much sleep over that," said Hodder. "I've not got a lot of use for people like Mr John Turner, myself."

"No," I said thoughtfully. "They make a lot of trouble and they don't pay much dividend."

I did not see Turner again till just before the X rays, and then only for a few moments. I got the photographs and the reports from the pathologist and house surgeon that afternoon, and after my consultations were over for the day I sat down with the photographs at the stereoscope. As Hodder had said, there were three metallic fragments. Two were sizable pieces not far below the dura. It might be possible to get at those if necessary, though there was the gravest danger to the patient in such an operation. The third was very small and much deeper in the cerebrum; it was surrounded by a darker infusion of the negative in the immediate vicinity. It was quite inoperable.

I sat for half an hour studying this thing and trying to think out ways and means of dealing with it. I did not want to be beaten, even in the case of Mr Turner. But presently I put the negatives and the reports back into their envelopes and said quietly to myself, "Well, that's that." I stubbed my cigarette out, put on my hat and coat, and went home.

I slept very badly that night. At the age of fifty-eight one does not normally lose sleep over a patient, but I lost sleep over Mr Turner. I wanted to do something for him; wanted to very badly. I had a queer inverted feeling that because this little black-market racketeer was a man of no account, the case called for the very utmost limit of my skill. I put that down with diffidence because it looks absurd on paper, but that's what kept me awake. I could not sleep for running over in my mind the possible combinations of operative and anaesthetic technique, of palliative operations and of neurological treatment. I got out of bed once and went down to my study to look up some recent German work on intracranial fibrosis. I read German rather slowly,

16

and stayed down there for an hour. Then I went back to bed, and slept a little before dawn.

I saw Turner next morning in his ward at the hospital. I took the X-ray photographs along with me. The sister showed me into his rooms; after a perfunctory examination I sent her away and sat down in the chair beside his bed.

"Well, you've got three metal fragments in your head still, Mr Turner," I said. I pulled out the negatives and showed them to him; they were quite clear without the stereoscope.

"Gosh," he said. "Is that me? I don't half look a guy."

"The prettiest girl doesn't look any better, taken in this way," I said. I picked out one of the pictures. "This one is the side view—this shows it best. These white things are the metal pieces. These two high up, there, and that one farther in."

He was interested. "Where would they be on me, doctor?" He put his hand up to his head. "Somewhere here?"

I laid two fingers on his head. "The first two, here and here. The third one about two inches down, under here."

I showed him the other views. He looked at them carefully and quite intelligently. "Is this third bit the same stuff as the others, doctor?" he asked presently. "I mean, those two are sort of clear-cut, but this one looks all fuzzy."

I nodded. "That's the one that's giving you your trouble. I should say that that is fibrous matter forming round the piece of steel."

He glanced at me quickly. "Something that oughtn't be there?"

"Yes," I said. "That is my own interpretation of these photographs. To some extent it is supported by the pathological report."

He said weakly, "Well, that's bloody good fun."

There was a short silence. "Would that be what makes me feel tired, doctor?" he asked at last.

"I think so," I replied. "It would account for that and for the disability of your right hand. It would account for the fits of giddiness and fainting, and for your eye trouble. In fact, it fits in with most of the symptoms that you've got."

He said, "I suppose this means I've got to have another operation."

I was silent for a moment. "I'm a surgeon, Mr Turner," I said at last. "I've been operating all my life, and mostly on the head. What I have to tell you now is that there are limits to the things that operative technique can achieve. If

17

you have your leg cut off in some accident, the surgeon cannot operate and give you a new, wholesome leg. In the case of the cranium there are similar limits. There are some operations that one does not usually attempt." I paused, and looked him in the eyes. "I've got to tell you, Mr Turner, that I think this is one of them."

The slight grey on his rather florid face showed that he understood me. "You mean that if you tried to get that bit out, I'd die?" he asked.

I said evenly, "I've given this a lot of thought, Mr Turner. I have to tell you that I could not undertake such an operation with any expectation of success." I paused. "At the same time, you must understand that that's only my personal opinion, the personal opinion of one man. If you feel you would like to have another surgeon examine you and study these photographs, I should be very pleased to arrange it for you, or to co-operate with anyone you choose. Because one man admits defeat, it doesn't mean that everybody else does, you know."

He said, "You're the best in England on this sort of thing, aren't you, doctor? That's what Dr Worth told me."

"Oh no, I'm not," I replied. "There are other people here in London just as experienced as I am. You could see Mostyn Collis, for example."

He said, "Well, what's going to happen if you leave it alone, the way it is? Will it get any worse?"

I said, "It doesn't have to get worse, but it may. I can give you certain palliative treatment that may arrest the lesion. That means it may heal up of itself and give you no further trouble."

"Does that often happen?"

I shook my head. "Not very often, in my experience. I have known it to occur, though."

He asked, "How often?"

I thought for a moment, and then I said, "Perhaps one case in ten improves under the sort of palliative treatment that we can apply. Not more, I'm afraid."

"The other nine get worse?"

I nodded.

He whispered again, "Bloody good fun."

There was a long silence in the little ward. A fly buzzed on the window pane, the knob at the end of the blind cord tapped on the window, the bright sun streamed in; from below came up the noise of London traffic. I sat by his bedside waiting for him. It's best to give the patient plenty of time in a case like this. It's all one can give.

At last he said, "If it goes on getting worse, doctor, what's it going to mean? What's it going to be like?"

I knew that was coming, of course. I, too, had had time to think. "You say you first noticed this about six months ago," I said. "The disability, so far, is not very great. I can't estimate the actual rate at which it will progress, you know."

He said impatiently, "Yes, but what do you think, doctor? I mean, I've had it, haven't I?"

I said, "I should say that there might be a progressive loss of faculties, Mr Turner. You might be able to carry on your normal life for another six or eight months, but these attacks of fainting will grow more frequent. You ought not to drive a car again. Generally speaking, I think you must expect all the symptoms to increase as time goes on."

He said quietly, "After that, I'll die."

"We've all got to do that, Mr Turner," I replied.

CHAPTER TWO

I wrote to Dr Worth after I had explained his position to Mr Turner in the hospital. I said,

Dear Dr Worth,

I have examined Mr John Turner, and I have consulted with Mr Percy Hodder, who as a major in the R.A.M.C. performed the original operation on Mr Turner in 1943. I have considered the pathological report resulting from a lumbar puncture, and the X-ray photographs of the cranium, which I enclose with the radiologist's report for your information.

You will see that there are three metallic fragments still lodged in the cerebrum; I have indicated with an arrow the one which I consider to be causing trouble. In my opinion, no operation could be undertaken with success to remove this fragment. A lesion in this vicinity is consistent with the apraxia and vertigo from which Mr Turner suffers, and with a marked papilloedema of the left eye which is apparent on examination with the ophthalmoscope.

I have known cases of this sort to remain static for many years and even to improve, but this is not the normal course. I should expect that all symptoms would increase in severity, resulting in death within a year.

I should like to see Mr Turner again in about four months' time. In view of the wartime nature of his injury and his general position, I should waive any further fee.

Yours truly,
HENRY T. HUGHES

Mr Turner left the hospital while I was writing this. He went by underground to Piccadilly Circus and put his bag into the cloak room. Then he walked up Shaftesbury Avenue and turned into Dolphin Street, and to the Jolly Huntsman. He went into the saloon bar; it was only about noon and there were few people in the place.

"Morning, Nellie," he said. "Gimme a pint of bitter."

The barmaid, a cheerful woman about fifty years old, drew a tankard and wiped the bottom of it with a cloth, and passed it to him across the counter. Mr Turner took it from her, swallowed a quarter of it, and slipped on to a stool. He smacked his lips. "First I've had for a week," he said with satisfaction.

"You don't say," said the barmaid mechanically. "Elevenpence. You haven't been around here lately."

"No," said Mr Turner. "What's more, I won't be around at all after a bit."

"Going away?" she enquired idly.

"That's right," he said. "Going a bloody long way." He lit a cigarette, fumbling awkwardly with the lighter in his left hand.

"There's no need to swear about it, anyway," she said.

Only a man can know the help that barmaids give to men in trouble. "Sorry," he said. "But you'd swear if you was me. I just come out of hospital. They say I'm due to pass out in a year or so. Kick the bloody bucket."

She stared at him. "No . . ."

"Fact," he said. "I'm telling you what they just told me."

"But why? You don't look ill to me."

"It's this conk I got on the old napper," he said moodily. "It's gone bad on me, after all these years."

"Lord," she said. "You got to have an operation, then?"

He shook his head. "There's bits of shell inside going bad, or something. They can't operate, they say."

She said again, "Lord . . ." and then, uncertainly, "I don't suppose they really know, Captain Turner. I mean, doctors say all sorts of things. Friend of mine, she thought she was going to have a baby, and the doctor said so too, but she never. They was all wrong. I expect they're wrong with

20

you. I wouldn't worry my head about it, long as you feel all right."

He took a drink of beer. "I don't feel so good, sometimes," he said quietly. "They done all sorts of things to me in hospital; I reckon they know, much as anyone can do."

There was silence.

"What are you going to do, then?" asked the woman gently, at last.

"I dunno—I got to think it out." He blew a long cloud of smoke. "Got to go home and tell the wife, first thing of all. She don't know nothing about it, yet."

"Didn't they tell her nothing at the hospital?"

"She never come to see me in the hospital," said Mr Turner briefly. "I was only in a week." He paused, and then he said, "We don't get on so well—not like I thought it would be, one time. I don't reckon this is going to mean much to her, except she'll have to start and think about a job again."

"She'll be terribly upset," the barmaid said softly. "You see."

"Maybe," said Mr Turner thoughtfully. "I dunno." He swallowed down the remainder of his beer. "Got to see the firm, too, sometime, I suppose."

"I wouldn't tell them while you can go on working," said the barmaid shrewdly. "Some firms turn funny, you know. Ever so mean they can be, sometimes."

"We get three months' pay, I think," said Mr Turner. "Sick pay, I mean. Of course, you don't get the commission . . . I don't know as I want to go on working though."

"No?"

"Well, would you? I mean, what's the sense in going on?"

"Well, I dunno," said the barmaid. "You got to do something."

"I dunno what I want to do," said Mr Turner moodily. "I dunno that I want to go on selling flour right up to the end. I'd sort of like to chuck it up and do something better 'n that, even if there wasn't any money in it. After all, it's not for long."

"You don't want to chuck up the job and then find you get well again," said the barmaid practically. "I don't think any of these doctors really know."

"You don't want to pack up at the end and find you done nothing but sell flour all your life, either," said Mr Turner.

He pushed his tankard to her across the bar. "I must be getting along."

"Want another?" she enquired.

He shook his head. "I got to go back and have it out with the wife," he said. "She don't like beer." He slid off the stool, and grinned at her. "All be the same in a hundred years," he said quietly. "That's what I say."

He went out into the busy, sunlit street. He had intended to telephone from the nearest box to his firm, Cereal Products Ltd., and possibly to go into the office that afternoon. On the pavement he hesitated, irresolute. He did not want to go into the office; he wanted to think for a little before going back. He bought an evening paper and walked slowly down towards the Circus again, and turned into the Corner House and had a steak and chips with another pint of beer.

By three o'clock he was at Watford, on his way home. He lived in a small detached villa in a row, No. 15 Hyacinth Avenue. It was a fairly pleasant little house, one of many thousands around London, with a small front garden with a cyanotis tree and a larger back one with a lawn and a laburnum tree and rose bushes. He let himself in with his latchkey, and called rather gruffly, "Mollie?" The empty house echoed back at him; he did not call again.

He went out moodily into the garden. The lawn needed cutting, but he did not feel that he could tackle that. In that suburban place of gardens it was pleasant, that warm, sunny afternoon. He did not know a great deal about gardens. His work had made great inroads on his leisure time; so many evenings had to be spent late or entertaining buyers from the provinces that he had never taken seriously to gardening. There was always something more important to be done, the sheer, insistent business of living that stood before the things he would have liked to do. A jobbing gardener came in one afternoon a week to do the garden for him.

He stood looking at the roses; they were coming into bloom. He stooped down to smell one; it had a fragrance wholly alien to the world he knew. He straightened up, and then stooped down and smelt it again. "Be nice to have a lot o' them," he muttered to himself, and his mind travelled to a vision of a rose garden between tall trees without a house in sight, a quiet place with crazy paving and a fountain, a managing director's garden. And then he thought that he had better make the best of what he'd got, that next year's roses would not interest him much.

"Takes a bit of getting used to," he said quietly to himself.

He went back into the house and fetched a deck chair from the cupboard under the stairs, and took it out and set

22

it up under the laburnum tree. It would be nice, he thought, to sit in his garden for a little and look at the flowers, a thing that somehow he had never had the leisure for. He took the Evening Standard with him; within ten minutes it was draped across his face, and presently he slept.

He woke at about five o'clock, aware in some way that his wife was coming down the garden to him. He brushed off the paper and sat up. "Hullo," he said, with no great cordiality.

She said, "Hullo. You got back?"

"Aye," he said. He did not get to his feet, but rubbed his hand over his face. It was for her to make the first approach, he felt. She had not been to see him in the hospital.

"Did they find anything wrong with you?" she asked.

"I dunno," he said briefly. "I'm not going to die next week, anyway."

She said a little scornfully, "Well, that's something off your mind."

"Aye," he said. "Been to the pictures?"

"I went with Mrs Kennedy," she said. "It was ever so good."

He nodded. He liked the pictures well enough, although he had not her devouring passion for them. She was eleven years younger than he, only twenty-nine. She still lived in the dream world of romance, and flew to it at every opportunity as an escape from her realities. He could not follow her; the true world was more real to him, and more interesting. That made a breach between them, increased by the many occupations of his work and by her idleness. At one time she had been a typist in his office; they neither of them realised how much she missed the work.

"Been busy this week?" he enquired. He was bitterly resentful, deep inside him, that with so much time to spare she had not been to see him in the hospital. He had paid for a private ward for that reason only, and he had been lonely there; he liked plenty of company, and would have been happier in a public ward with many other patients.

"I been over helping Laura most mornings," she said defensively. "She can't do much."

Laura was her sister, and about to produce an infant. She lived at Bushey, not very far from them, and she was a thorn in Mr Turner's flesh in that she was a constant excuse for all the errors of omission that his wife fell into. Whenever the dinner was not cooked, the beds unmade, or the house dirty, it was because Laura wanted help. This had

23

been going on for some time now because Laura produced a baby regularly once a year, and Mr Turner was getting very tired of it indeed.

"Well, put the kettle on and let's have a cup of tea," he said, "—if you've got time for that."

She flared out at him, "That's no way to speak to me, after being away all week."

"If you'd found time to come 'n talk to me in hospital during the week," he said evenly, "you might have got talked to better. Now go 'n put that kettle on, unless you want me to go out."

She stared at him for a minute, and then walked slowly to the house. Mr Turner sat on in his deck chair in the garden, the great wound in his forehead throbbing a little. The sordid little quarrel had upset him. He wanted to get rid of all that sort of thing. In a short time now he would have to slough off all experience, both good and bad; since everything must go soon, he wanted to get rid of the bad first in order that he might be left free to enjoy the real and the good. He wanted to get rid of Laura, and the quarrels with his wife, and the office routine. He did not want to go on nickering after small commissions. He did not want to be mixed up again in the sly, illegal deals in pastry flour for East End confectioners that had proved profitable for him in the post-war years. He had some money saved. He wanted to lay off the business of petty earning now and do something different.

He had about three thousand pounds in savings. He had never told his wife the extent of these riches because they had been amassed in a variety of dubious ways; only a small fraction came from legitimate saving out of his income. Full of ideals gleaned from the cinema, she was so rude about his way of life in general that he could not bring himself to tell her how he had built up their joint security, and now things had reached that pitch between them when he did not even want to tell her what he had achieved to safeguard them in sickness or old age. He knew that three thousand pounds would not go far to meet her needs after his death. Safely invested, after income tax it would not provide her with much more than a pound a week; she had been making five pounds a week in the office when they married, and five pounds ten by the end of the war, when she had retired from work. She could earn that again if she went back to office life; she had not treated him so well, he felt, that he need fear to spend his money for the sake of giving her another pound a week on top of the five or six that she could earn.

The little bell rang from the house; he heaved himself up from his chair and went in to tea. She had laid it in the dining room, tea and cold sausages, and salad, and bread and jam, and cherry cake. They usually had it cold in the summer; in winter it was a more generous meal, with a hot kipper or bacon and eggs. Supper was a light meal that took place when they wanted it.

Mollie was already seated when he came into the room. He sat down heavily and forked a sausage on to his plate; she passed him his tea and he buttered a piece of bread. "What about a run in the car afterwards?" she said.

He considered this. He had a little ten-horsepower Ford in the garage by the side of the house, seven years old; he liked driving it. It was one of their chief relaxations, marred only by the destination of their journey. She would have liked to drive out into the country and sit in the sun in some beautiful place and read a book like girls did in the pictures. He liked to drive for an hour to some country pub or roadhouse and drink beer in an atmosphere of smoke and laughter and good company.

"All right," he said. "Might end up at the Barley Mow."

"Lord," she said, "can't you ever get away from beer?"

"That's enough of that," he said. "I don't mind doing what you want to first, and after that we do what I want to. Otherwise, we better go out separate." He paused. "What were you thinking of?"

She said, "I wanted to go out somewhere in the country and pick flowers."

He glanced out of the window at their roses. "Want any more flowers? There's flowers everywhere this time of year."

"Wild ones, I want," she said. "Hawthorn and violets and forget-me-nots, and them sort of things."

"Okay," he said. "Go out past Hatfield, 'n then come home by the Barley Mow."

She said, "All right, if we've got to."

He slit his sausage up the middle carefully, and spread a little mustard on it. "One thing," he said casually, "you better drive."

She stared at him. "Don't you want to?"

"Not much," he said. "I don't feel like it."

She said, "I'm not going to drive all the way—you can't see the country, driving. I'll drive back from the Barley Mow. I'd better do that anyway."

He said irritably, "You'll drive all the way, or we don't go at all."

She said, "For the Lord's sake! Why won't you drive some of the way?"

He said angrily, "Because the specialist told me not to. That's why. If you think I like being driven by you, you're very much mistaken."

She stared at him. "Told you not to?"

"That's right. Not till I get rid of these giddy fits I been getting."

"How long have you not got to drive for, then?"

"I dunno," he said. "Till I get rid of them, I suppose."

She said no more about it, and presently they went out in the car. He sat smoking cigarette after cigarette beside her, watching the arterial road slide past. He was feeling stale and tired and upset by the slight combat with his wife; so little time was left that it was bitter that it should be marred with quarrels. He sat moody by her side, trying not to flinch each time she cut in between two vehicles; he would have to get accustomed to that if he went on motoring, he thought.

She turned presently from the main road and went on through the byways; they knew the country within a radius of thirty miles from Watford very well from afternoon joy-riding. She drew up presently beside a water-splash in a small lane; there was a maytree in red bloom not far away beside the stream.

"Be nice to have a bit of that," she said. "It'd look lovely in the drawing-room vase."

They got out of the car and walked across the field to the tree. He had a very blunt penknife that he knew for a bad tool, but he had no means of sharpening it at home, and if he had the means he would not have had the time. One day, when he had achieved leisure, he would like to have a proper little workshop with a grinder and some hand tools, in a shed in the back garden, perhaps. But that meant time, and when you were out late most evenings there was hardly time to think about a thing like that let alone do it.

With his blunt penknife they hacked off a few twigs of the maytree; the bright clusters of the flowers were thin on the twigs, but Mollie was pleased with them. She gave them to him to carry, and they walked along the hedge for a little time while she looked for cowslips and for violets; he was frankly bored, and presently she agreed that he should sit upon a gate and wait for her.

He sat upon the gate, may blooms in hand, and lit a cigarette. It was quiet and pleasant in the sun, now that he had not got to walk around like a dolt, looking for flowers. It was still, and the sky was blue, down to the riot of colour of the hawthorn and may along the hedge. His eyes fell on the tiny flowers on the twigs that he was holding; they were delicate and perfect, and most beautiful. He realised dimly that there was some sense in what his wife was doing. If you had absolutely nothing else to do it might be possible to get great pleasure out of flowers, though that had never been his line.

Mollie came back presently with foxgloves and daisies and violets and forget-me-nots. He said, "You been buying up the shop?"

She disregarded that. "I think they're ever so lovely," she said. She passed him up the little bunch of violets. "Don't these smell sweet?"

He put his nose to them. "Like that place in Piccadilly," he said. "Coty, or some name like that."

"That's right," she said. "They make scent out of violets. Other flowers, too. I don't think they get it right, though." She buried her face in the flowers again. "Not like these."

"Give yourself hay fever if you go on like that," he said. "What about getting along to the Barley Mow?"

A shadow crossed her face. "If we've got to. But I'm not going to stay there all night."

"They shut at ten," he said briefly. "It'll be quarter-past nine by the time we get there. That long won't kill you."

They drove for half an hour, and drew up at the pub. The Barley Mow is a large modern public house strategically placed at the junction of two arterial roads; it stands on the corner in two acres of grounds, one-and-a-half acres of which is car park. Inside, the saloon bar is a discreet mixture of imitation Tudor oak and real chromium plate; it is warm in winter and cool in the summer, and the place is split up into little corners and alcoves, where a man can tell his friends a blue story without telling every lady in the room. Mr Turner loved the Barley Mow better than almost any other local he frequented.

For one thing, there always seemed to be people there whom he knew. That night there was Georgie Harries and his wife, and Gillie Simmonds with a new girl friend who was on the stage, and fat old Dickie Watson, the bookmaker, with a party. All these greeted Mr Turner—"Jackie, you old sod!"—"What's it to be Jackie?"—"Jackie, you get home all

27

right last Friday? (Sotto voce) Never see anyone so pissed in all my life!"—"Evening, Mrs Turner; got him on string tonight? What'll you take for it?"

It was the atmosphere that Mr Turner loved. He drank pint after pint of beer, while Mollie stood in bright, forced cheerfulness with a gin and ginger, one eye on the clock. Smoke wreathed about them and the voices rose and the place grew hotter and the atmosphere thicker as the minute hand moved forward to the hour. Mr Turner stood red-faced and beaming in the midst, mug in hand, the great wound pulsing in his forehead, telling story after story from his vast repertoire. "Well, this porter he went on the witness stand and told the Court of Enquiry that it was his first day with the Company. The Chairman asks if he see the accident. He says, 'Aye. I see the express run right into the trucks.' The Chairman asks him what he did next. 'Well, sir, I turns to the ticket collector, and I says, "That's a bloody fine way to run a railway!"'" In the shout of laughter that followed, the manager said, "Time, ladies and gentlemen, please!" and turned out half the lights. One by one the company went out into the cool night air; starters ground in the car park, and light shone out in beams, and the cars slipped off up the road to London.

At the little Ford, Mollie said acidly, "Good thing I'm driving you, after five pints of beer."

"Four pints," said Mr Turner. "I only had four." The air was fresh on his face, the moon clear above him in a deep-blue sky. It was perfect in the night. He felt relaxed, as if all his fatigue and distress were soaking out of him. A week was a long time to go without a bit of a blind.

"It was five," said his wife. "I counted them myself."

He was relaxed and happy, and now she was nagging at him. He turned on her irritably. "What the hell does it matter if I have four or five? I'll have fifty if I want, my girl. I won't be drinking anything this time next year if what they said at the hospital is right."

She stared at him. "What did they say at the hospital?"

"They said I'm going to die before so long."

In the quiet serenity of the night that did not seem very important; it was only important that she should shut up and not spoil his evening. "Now you get on and start her up, and shut up talking."

She opened her mouth to give as good as she got, but said nothing. What he had told her was incredible; and yet it was what she had secretly feared for some time. Beneath her irritation with him she was well aware that his condition had deteriorated in the last six months; he was not physically the man he once had been. Moreover, it was no good arguing with him when he had just drunk five pints of beer; from past experience she knew that much. She got into the car in silence and started the engine; in silence he got in beside her and slammed the door, and they started down the long white concrete road to home.

They did not speak again till they turned into the garage of the little house at Watford, forty minutes later. Closing the doors, she said to him, "What was that they told you at the hospital?" She spoke more gently, having had time to reflect.

By this time Mr Turner was more firmly on earth. It was quiet and still and moonlit in the garden, and it was warm. "Let's get the deck chairs out 'n sit a bit," he said. "I got to tell you all about it sometime, 'cause you ought to know."

They fetched deck chairs from the cupboard under the stairs and set them up on the lawn. Mr Turner lit a cigarette as they sat down. "There's bits of shell inside my head going bad on me," he said. "That's what they told me at the hospital. They give me about another year, as far as they can judge."

She said, "But Jackie, can't they operate 'n get them out?"

"They say not." She had not called him Jackie for some time; it was what his friends all called him, and he warmed towards her. "They say they're too deep in."

She said quietly, "I'm ever so sorry."

He laughed. "Not half so sorry as I am!" He thought for a moment, and then said, "I didn't mean that nasty. But I must say, I got a bit of a shock when he told me."

"I should think so, too," she said.

He sat in silence in the deck chair, lying back and looking at the stars. Vega burned near the deep-blue zenith, with Altair on his right hand and Arcturus to the left. He did not know the names of any of them, but he found them comforting and permanent. They would be there when he and all others like him had gone on; it was good to sit there and lie back and look at things like that.

"It's time we had a bit of a talk about it," he said presently. "I mean, I dunno how long I can go on working. These giddy fits and that, they won't get any better now. Six or eight months maybe; then I'll have to go in a home or something. That means you'll have to start and think about a job again."

29

"I know that," she said slowly. "I was thinking the same thing."

He said, "I got a little money saved, but not so much. It's going to take a bit, seeing me finished off. There won't be much after I'm gone—nothing to make a difference, really." He turned to her. "I'm sorry about that."

"That doesn't matter," she said quietly. "I can brush up easy, 'n get another job."

He nodded. "I reckoned that you could."

She turned to him presently. "What about you, Jackie? Will you go on working, long as you can?"

He said slowly, "I suppose so—I dunno. I got to sort of clean things up—one or two things I got to see about that might take a bit of time. I dunno."

She said, "What sort of things?"

"One thing," he said. "I got to try and find a nigger."

CHAPTER THREE

SHE turned to him in astonishment. "For the Lord's sake," she exclaimed, "what do you want with a nigger?"

It was quiet in the moonlit garden. The scent of roses was around them. In the white light the rows of similar, gabled houses were ethereal, the castles of a dream. The beer still had full hold of Mr Turner, freeing him of repressions and of irritations, making him both simple and lucid.

"You remember that time I got in prison?" he enquired.

She said quietly, "I do."

It had been one of the disasters in her life, that had made her both cynical and bitter. She had a good deal of excuse. She had married a young, vigorous man in her office back in 1939, when war broke out; they had lived together very little because he joined the Army almost immediately. He became an officer and quickly rose to captain, and she was terribly proud of him. Then he was sent out to North Africa.

Within three months he was back in England and at death's door from the wound he got in the aeroplane. When she went down to see him at the hospital in Penzance, she discovered that he was no longer a free man; there was a little matter of three truckloads of Army sugar sold in the black market to be settled first. She knew him for a warm businessman in the office when she married him; she had not known that he was quite so hot as that. He was in hospital for a long time before court-martial; then he got a year's imprisonment and was discharged from the Army, His Majesty having no further use for his services. He came back to her in February 1945, a perky, irrepressible little man in civvy clothes, apparently not conscious of any very great disgrace, and with that huge wound that terrified her till she got accustomed to it. From that time she had been a bad wife to him, and she knew it, and she hated him for it.

"I dunno if I ever told you much about that time," he said. "There was four of us all in the ward together, at that place down in Penzance. Just the four of us together." He hesitated, and then said, "They had a guard, you see."

She nodded. "I remember."

"I'd like to know what happened to them other chaps, the three of them," he said. "They used to come and talk to me. Hours on end, they did."

"Talk to you?"

"They used to come and sit inside the screen there was all round my bed, and talk to me. Hour after hour, sometimes."

She stared at him. "What did they do that for?"

"The doctor 'n the sisters made them do it." He turned to her. "I had my eyes all bandaged up after the operation 'cause they didn't want me to see anything, and they gave me things to stop me wanting to move about in bed. I was lying there all strapped up like a mummy, and I couldn't talk much, either. But I could hear things going on, 'n think about things, too. Funny, being like that, it was. So as the others got well one by one the sisters made them come 'n read a book to me, but they read pretty bad, so most times they just talked. I could answer them a little, but not much. They just kept talking to me."

"What did they talk about?"

"Themselves, mostly. They were a bloody miserable lot— the miserablest lot of men I ever saw. But they were good to me." He paused for a moment, and repeated very quietly, "Bloody good."

"How do you mean?" she asked.

The beer was still strong in Mr Turner. He said, "They were sort of kind. Do anything for me, they would. I reckon that I might have passed out that time, spite of all the doctors and the nurses, if it hadn't been for them chaps sitting with me, talking. God knows they had enough

31

troubles of their own, but they got time for me in spite of everything."

There was a long, thoughtful pause. Presently she said, "What's this got to do with a nigger?"

"One o' them was a nigger from America," he said. "The last one to go out. He was the only one I ever see clearly—Dave Lesurier, his name was." He pronounced it like an English surname. "Then there was Duggie Brent—he was a corporal in the paratroops. And then there was the pilot of the aeroplane, the second pilot I should say—Flying Officer Morgan. We was all in a mess one way or another excepting him, and yet in some ways he was in a worse mess than the lot of us."

He turned to her. "I been thinking," he said quietly, "I never seen any of them from that day to this, though we was all in such a mess together that you'd have thought we might have kept up, somehow or another, just a Christmas card or something. But we never. Well, I got through all right 'n turned the corner. I got a nice house here, mostly paid for, and a good job. Folks looking at me would say I was successful, wouldn't they?"

She nodded slowly. "They would that, Jackie. We're not up at the top, but we're a long way from the bottom."

"Well, that's what I mean," he said. "A long way from the bottom. But that time I was talking of we was right down at the bottom, all four of us, me and the other three. And when I was down there they was bloody nice to me. You just can't think."

"I see," she said.

"I had it in my mind for a year or more I ought to try and find out what the others were doing," he said quietly. "Maybe some of them are dead. That nigger, he was charged with attempted rape, and they give them pretty stiff sentences for that in the American Army. The others, too. . . . But I got by all right—I never starved in the winter yet, that's what I say. We've got up a long way from the bottom, and we've got money for a nice house, and a car, 'n holidays, and after that we even save a little. And I been thinking," he said quietly, "I been a bloody squirt not to have done something to find out about them other chaps, and see how they was getting on. They were bloody good to me when I needed it."

He pulled out his cigarette case, and handed it to her. She took one and he placed one between his lips, and fumbled with his lighter in the left hand, and lit them.

"Well, there we are," he said. In the dim, moonlit garden there was privacy. "I've had it now. In a year's time there won't be no more of me. I don't want to go out and leave these strings hanging loose. I want to find out what happened to them other three, case any of them wants a hand, or something."

She stared at him, bewildered. This was a different Jackie from the one she knew, and she distrusted change. Injuries such as his when they went bad made people funny in the head, sometimes; this business of wanting to look for his companions in the prison ward seemed very odd to her. She tried to head him off.

"They'll be all right," she said at last. "I wouldn't worry too much over it."

"I won't," he said. "I'm just going to find out and make sure they're all right, so as I know."

She said helplessly, "What are you going to do, then? Write a letter?"

"I dunno an address for any of them," he said. "No good writing to the hospital, not after all these years. I'd better try the Air Ministry to get the pilot's address, and the War Office for the corporal, I suppose. I dunno what to do about the nigger."

"You'll never find them after all this time," she said. "How would you ever find a nigger that was in the American Army, after the war, and all?"

"I dunno," he said. There was a long pause, and then he said, "I want to have a try."

She sat deep in thought for a few moments. He was a bit queer, she decided. Clinically speaking, she was right; the obsession was probably related to his lesion. That did not help her in her immediate problem, what to do about it. She knew enough about her husband not to cross him directly; when once he got a fixed idea he held on to it like a dog with a bone. Moreover, for the first time in years she felt he needed her. She said, "What were they like, these three? Was there anything particular about them?"

He grinned. "Only they were all in such a bloody awful mess—like me." He turned his head to her; in the white light she saw the gleam of his great wound. "Like me to tell you about them?"

She said, "Yes."

He got up from his chair. "I'm just going in to spill some of this beer. Shall I bring out a rug when I come?"

It was the first time he had offered to do anything for

33

her in a long time. She said, "Please. It's getting kind of chilly out here; but it's nice."

He went into the house, and came back presently, and handed her the rug. She wrapped it around herself and settled down to listen to him talking. They sat there on the lawn in the warm summer night, in the quiet grace of the moon, and the stars faint in the bright light. It was windless, still, and silent. Around them, in the dormitory suburb, the world slept.

This paratroop corporal, Jackie said, was "a proper card." He was a young chap, not more than twenty, a short, stocky young man with a thick mat of curly red hair; he wore it cut short in the Army style, but even so there was a lot of it. He had the grey eyes that go with it, and like most red-haired young men, he liked a bit of fun.

His name was Duggie Brent. In full, his name was Douglas Theodore Brent, but he considered Theodore to be a sissy name, and hid it up as much as possible. His father was a butcher in Romsey, and a lay reader at the Methodist chapel; when his son arrived, it seemed proper to christen him the Gift of God. In later years his father reconsidered that.

In fact, there was nothing much the matter with Duggie Brent except that he didn't take kindly to the chapel and he took a great deal too kindly to young women. He had a way with them. He had his first girl trouble when he was fourteen, and that was only the first. By the time he was sixteen-and-a-half his father was paying a paternity order for him, and didn't like it. When he was seventeen, in 1938, he joined the Territorials for fun, faking his age; in 1939 the war broke out and he was mobilised and sent to Durham. Every mother of girls in Romsey breathed a sigh of relief.

In the Army they set to work to make a man of him. In that time of war they did not waste much effort in teaching him barrack square drill or dress parades. First they gave him a rifle and taught him how to use it. Then they put a bayonet on the rifle and set him running at a line of sandbag dummies. If you gave the rifle a sharp twist after the lunge, they said, the bayonet came out easily and the wound was a lot bigger.

The next thing they gave him was a Bren gun; he discovered that you could kill a lot of people with that in a very short time, if you got them in open country. In case

34

the enemy were so unsporting as to lie in foxholes, however, they showed him how to use a hand grenade, and how to creep up, covered by his pals, with the Bren gun to lob these in among the Germans in the trench. After that came the Tommy gun, and later the Sten gun, and then he was graduated in the three-inch mortar.

All this was elementary, of course, mere high school stuff. He started on his college course in 1941 at an anti-tank school, where he was taught that much the quickest way to kill the people in the tank was to set the tank and all on fire. He did an interesting and instructive little course on Ronson Lighters. He learned that you could kill a lot of people with a couple of hundred gallons of blazing oil if you went about the matter with discretion and intelligence. After that he did a course of mines and minelaying, and then a very amusing little course in the preparation of booby traps.

In 1942 he volunteered for the Commandoes, and they really started to teach him to kill people. All that he had learned so far, he discovered, was routine stuff and unworthy of a serious student of the art of combat. Any fool could kill a German with a hand grenade which made a noise and woke up the whole neighbourhood; a man who knew his stuff could creep up in the darkness and do it with a knife from behind, grabbing the mouth and the nose with the other hand to prevent him crying out. You had to be careful not to get bitten, but like all these things it was quite easy when you got the way of it. You had to get into the right position; then you just went so, and so, and so —and there he was, kicking a bit, maybe, but very dead.

That was how an average good man who knew his stuff and took an interest in his work would do the job. If you really aimed at the top flights of the art, however, and if you were quick and agile, a knife was quite unnecessary. Duggie Brent went through a course of Unarmed Combat at the end of 1942, where he was taught to kill an enemy with his bare hands. This was the real peak of his military education. By the time he went back to his unit he was able to attack an armed man three stone heavier than himself and kill him with his hands and feet alone in perfect silence.

In 1943 he did so, in the dark outside a public house just off the New Cross Road.

It happened on his embarkation leave, and he was out of the country on a transport for North Africa before the police got on to him. It was a sordid little quarrel between men who had drunk too much to mind their words, after a winter of waiting, exasperation, and irritation with the slow progress of the war. At that time Duggie Brent was walking out with a member of the A.T.S. whose home was at New Cross in the southeast of London. Her name was Phyllis Styles, and she was on leave from her A.A. station in Kent. They had tea together at a Lyons' and then went to the Odeon cinema. They came out of that, arm in arm, at half-past nine, after three hours of delicious proximity, and to round off the evening they went to the Goat and Compasses for beer.

Mike Seddon was an Irish boilermaker who had made the Goat and Compasses his evening's entertainment. The evidence did not disclose how much beer he had drunk before Brent and his girl arrived; moreover, it was not significant, because an Irish boilermaker can take an infinite amount of wartime beer before falling over, and as he regularly took home fifteen pounds in his wage pocket, he could afford it. The bar was crowded thick with people in that last hour, so that Brent and his girl and the boilermaker were thrust close together in a corner with their beer.

It was soon after Brent had transferred to the Parachute Regiment, and soon after the maroon beret had been introduced. Mr Seddon took exception to this sartorial idiosyncrasy. "You young fellows running round in fancy hats!" he said scornfully. "They don't give me no fancy hat to wear. I don't get no fancy hat. No fancy hat they don't give me. And why—" he asked the crowd, raising his voice to the injury, "why aren't they after giving me a fancy hat? I'll tell you. I'll tell you why I don't get no fancy hat. It's because I do a mucking job of work. That's why. That's why they don't give me no fancy hat. Because I do a mucking job of work to win the mucking war!"

There was a laugh. Corporal Brent, beer mug in hand, flushed angrily, and said, "What the hell do you think I do, then?"

The boilermaker was on his own home ground. He came to the Goat and Compasses each evening, and he knew the temper of the crowd and their frustration with the slow building up of war effort. He glanced at the corporal's chest, innocent of decorations. He said, "Ah, well, just tell us now, me boy. Stand up and tell the whole bloody lot of us. What are you after doing now to win the mucking war?" He turned to the crowd. "Sit on his arse 'n polish his buttons

36

in his fancy hat, that's what he does. I do a job of work, I do, but they don't give me no fancy hat."

Brent opened his mouth to say that he was on embarkation leave and shut it again without speaking; there was no knowing what security snoopers might be within hearing in that crowd. He flushed angrily. He was sensitive to the fact that he had been mobilised in the Army for three-and-three-quarter years, and had never been out of England, and had seen no action at all.

"I do what the sergeant and the officers tells me," he said angrily. "I don't have no say."

"Don't do no work, either, in the mucking Army," said Mr Seddon. "Do some of you lads good to come and do a mucking job of work 'stead of walking round with floosies in a fancy hat. A mucking job of work, that's what'd do the Army good."

"You lay off the Army and talk clean," the corporal said furiously. "I got a lady with me."

The girl laid her hand on his arm. "Come on, Duggie," she said, "let's get out of this."

He shook her off. "I'm not going to have him talking that way," he exclaimed. "He's got no right to talk like that!"

"That's right," the boilermaker said, swaying a little, menacing, towards them. "You take him away, in his fancy hat 'n all. Bring him back when he's opened the Second Front 'n I'll give him a pint." He paused a moment to consider the proposal. "Two bloody pints," he said. "Bring him back when he's done a mucking job of work."

The wrangle continued for another few minutes with both tempers rising hot; then it was closing time and the barman moved them firmly out at the tail of the crowd, into the dark street.

There was no moon, and it was pitch dark in the blackout outside the pub. On the pavement the boilermaker stood swaying, fourteen or fifteen stone of him, massive and scornful. "The Second Front!" he sneered. "Sure there'll be no Second Front at all, at all; not till they put some guts into the bloody Army. All the mucking soldiers do is walk round in a fancy hat 'n pick up tarts. Army tarts, in mucking uniform with fancy tarts' hats, too."

The girl said quickly, "Duggie—don't!" She pulled him by the arm. "It don't matter what he says. He's had a bit too much."

He shook her off. "That's right," he said. "Scum o' bloody

Dublin, over here to see what he can pick up 'n tell the German consul, I suppose. The country's fair rotten with these bloody Irish bastards." He turned away. "Come on, Phyl—we'll leave the mugger be."

The boilermaker reached out and aimed a kick at him; the heavy boot caught Brent squarely at the base of the spine, infinitely painful. Duggie Brent had never learned to box like a gentleman; there had been no time to teach him that. Blind with fury and with pain, he swung round and in the one movement flung his fancy hat, the maroon beret, straight in Mr Seddon's face, the opening move in Unarmed Combat, to make your adversary blink and hide from him the terrible kick coming. In the same swing his heavy army boot landed with all his force in the pit of Mr Seddon's stomach. The boilermaker doubled up with pain. Immediately his adversary was behind him, and there was a rigid, steely arm in battledress around his neck, the elbow passing his chin up and back against the pressure of a knee intolerable against his spine. He kicked and beat the air, but his opponent was behind him, fighting in a way that he had never known. His body was forced up against the wall and bent backwards with a fierce pain, and the arm pressing up his chin prevented him from making any but small, choking sounds.

It was certainly the corporal's intention to hurt Mr Seddon, to cause him a great deal of pain. In his instruction, however, nobody had ever told him when to stop in order to avoid killing his man. To overcome the boilermaker he had to put out all his strength; I think in that last moment of fierce, straining tussle curiosity may have entered in. Suddenly there was a crack from the man's back, and he yielded suddenly to the pressure, and gave a great choke, and ceased to struggle. It was a moment or so before Brent realised what he had done.

He released his hold, and the body fell limp at his feet, twitching a little. "Christ!" he said quietly.

He stood for a moment irresolute; then he stooped and felt the man's face. He was still breathing, and the corporal straightened up. He had injured him more than he had meant to, and that was going to mean a bloody row. There were men a hundred yards up the street passing a dim lamp, walking away; they did not seem to have noticed anything. There was nobody else about, but in the near-by public house there were still lights, faint streaks that showed around the edge of the blackout.

He crossed to the girl, standing in the middle of the road. "Come on," he said. "We better get out of this. I hurt him bad."

She said, "Oh, Duggie! We'd better do something."

"Come on out of it," he said. "I'll show you."

He hurried her away and up the New Cross Road until they found a telephone box. In the dim light of his torch he found the number of the Goat and Compasses, and rang them up. A girl's voice answered him. "One o' your customers fell down outside on the pavement," he said. "He's hurt himself, or something. You'd better go and see if he's all right." He slammed down the receiver before she could answer.

In the close intimacy of the telephone box the girl stirred by his side. "That was ever so clever," she said in admiration. "I've never have thought of that. You *are* a one."

He kissed her in the telephone box for a few minutes in the friendly darkness, the boilermaker all but forgotten. Then he took her home.

That night Mr Seddon died in the Miller Hospital at Greenwich. Next day Corporal Brent rejoined his unit. Five days later he embarked for an unknown destination, which turned out to be North Africa. The law caught up with him two months later at a place called Blida, led to him by the unwilling evidence of Private Phyllis Styles. The police had a good deal of trouble with her before she would talk.

He was taken under guard from Blida to Algiers, kept there for a week, and was then sent to England in a Hudson with several other prisoners, amongst them Captain Turner. In the hospital at Penzance he was the first on his feet. All he had suffered were a few flesh wounds from splinters of the same 20mm. shell that had disabled Turner, and a simple fracture of the right arm which he got in the crash landing. By that time Turner had been operated upon and lay inert, with his head swathed in bandages, able to think and understand, and to talk a very little, but with both eyes covered. He never saw Brent at all.

The ward sister had been told by the surgeon that she must keep her patient interested, so she gave Corporal Brent a book called *True Tales of Adventure* and set him down to read to Turner for an hour. The corporal disliked reading aloud and did it very badly; moreover, the true tales were thin, watery stuff compared with the adventures that he had been through. Within five minutes his stumbling voice had flagged. He turned a couple of pages, and read a paragraph to himself.

"I don't think much o' this book," he remarked. "You like me to go on? I will if you say."

The swathed figure on the bed moved one hand weakly from side to side.

"Okeydoke," said the corporal. "I'll ask sister if she's got one with more ginger in it, next time she comes—girls and that. Maybe they'll have a copy of *No Orchids for Miss Blandish*, or one o' them. I could read you some o' that," he said hopefully.

The figure on the bed elevated a thumb.

Brent sat in silence for a minute. "When you get in bad with the police, 'n you get charged," he said at last, "they give you someone to speak for you, don't they? At the trial, I mean. Someone to take your side, who knows the ropes, like?"

From the bed there came a whisper, "You get a lawyer given you, a barrister they call him. What you been doing, chum?"

Confession eases things. Brent said, "I had a sort of fight with a chap, and he died. I didn't mean to hurt him, not bad like that." He hesitated, and then said, "They say it's murder."

In the suburban garden the moon was bright. The night was very clear. "I never even see his face," said Mr Turner, "but I got to know him well enough for all of that. I never heard what happened, or anything." He paused. "I dunno. Maybe he got hung. But I don't think they'd hang a chap for a thing like that, do you?"

His wife stirred beside him. "I don't know," she said. "He killed the chap, from what you say."

"Oh, he killed him all right. No doubt of that."

"Well, if he did, they'd hang him, surely?" She thought for a moment. "If he got off—well then, he'll be making a living somewhere, I suppose."

He said, "I dunno what he could do. The only thing he knew about was how to kill people—he knew plenty about that. He hadn't got a trade, or anything. Labouring—I suppose he could do that." He turned to her. "He was a nice chap," he said, "and we was all there in a mess together."

She did not speak.

"Like to hear about the other two?"

She snuggled down into her rug, pulling it more closely

40

around her. "Go on," she said. "I never heard you talk about that time at all."

He thought of his own trial and prison sentence. "It's not the sort of time one talks about," said Mr Turner, "in the normal way."

Flying Officer Phillip Morgan of the R.A.F. was allowed to get up out of bed for the first time two days before Corporal Brent was removed from the ward and taken up to London to be charged. He should not have been put in a detention ward at all, and this fact was to him a permanent grievance. He was taken from the wreckage of the Hudson with a broken leg and three broken ribs and placed with the others in a small ward in the Penzance Hospital. When it became known that the other two survivors were prisoners, a guard was placed on the ward, but there was no other bed for Flying Officer Morgan, so he had to stay there. As an educational experience it was very good for him.

He was twenty-two years old; his school and the R.A.F. had made him what he was. He had no other experience behind him; he was at a loss when faced with any problem for which he had not been trained at school or in the R.A.F. His father had been a bank manager in Kensington and had died when Phil was a boy; his mother was an invalid, and she and his sister lived in Ladbroke Square on the borders of the well-to-do part of London. He spent his holidays in that stultifying place and took no benefit from it. When war broke out, he joined the R.A.F. as an aircraftsman. In that service he developed a good deal; he was commissioned in the summer of 1940 and sent for training as a fighter pilot. By the spring of 1941 he was flying Spitfires operationally in England. He survived that tour of operations and did three months' ground duty; in 1942 he did another tour in North Africa and won the D.F.C. After two tours on fighters he had a choice of occupation; he chose Transport Command, with some vague idea of fitting himself for a job in civil aviation after the war. It was in this capacity that he was flying as second pilot of the Hudson.

He was a callow and ignorant young man, but he could fly an aeroplane very well indeed. He reached the coast of Cornwall on that summer afternoon at an altitude of seven hundred feet, and losing height rapidly with one engine stopped and the other gradually failing. Behind him in the

41

cabin there were dead and dying men; in the seat beside him the captain of the aircraft sat slumped and dead, and falling forward now and then on to the wheel, so that Morgan had to struggle with the body with one hand and fly the aircraft with the other. Beside him flew two Spitfires of the flight that had put down his assailant; they flew with their hoods open, the pilots turned towards the crippled aircraft that they were escorting, powerless to help. And yet, their very presence helped. Phil Morgan was a Spitfire pilot first and last; he loved Spitfires, and their presence was a comfort to him in his difficulties.

At the point where he crossed the coast the cliffs are nearly three hundred feet high; when he came over the fields he was not much more than four hundred feet above them. There were airstrips in the vicinity, but he had so little altitude and he was losing height so fast that he did not dare to turn towards the nearest one; he knew that he would lose more height on a turn. He would be down in any case within a couple of minutes; he must land straight ahead of him within the next five miles. In that undulating country he had little choice of field; the one he chose was bordered by a stone wall at his end. It was only about two hundred yards long, nothing like long enough for a Hudson even in a belly landing, but the far boundary appeared to be a hedge and beyond that there was another field. The Hudson touched down belly on grass fifty yards before the hedge, which slowed her somewhat before hitting up against the stone wall that the hedge concealed. When Flying Officer Morgan woke up he was in hospital, and in the bed next to him was a Negro soldier of the U.S. forces. He took that as a personal affront.

He poured out his troubles to Captain Turner when he came to see him for the first time. By that time Turner's right eye was uncovered and he could see a little with it, though it was very bloodshot and the light hurt it if he kept it open long; for this reason the screen was still kept around his bed. Flying Officer Morgan could talk to Turner in the semblance of privacy; though he knew the Negro could hear every word he said, the screen made it private conversation.

Almost his first words were about this urgent topic. After exchanging names, he said, "I say, old man, do you know there's a bloody nigger in the ward with us here?"

Motionless in his bed, Turner said, "I know. Brent told me. He's here now, is he?"

"He's right in the next bed to me. I think it's the bloody

limit. I'm going to write a letter to the Air Ministry about the way that I've been treated here, and put it in through my C.O."

"They looked after me all right," said Mr Turner.

Morgan said, "Well, I know, old man, but it's a bit different for me." He hesitated for an instant, and then said, "I mean, after all, there's no reason why *I* should be kept under guard. I mean, it's a bloody insult having a sentry on the door of your ward. And then to put us in a ward with other ranks—it's a bit thick, even if they are crowded. We ought to be in an Officers' Ward, we two. And then on top of everything to put a bloody nigger in with us; it's too bad! I told the sister so, and the doctor too."

"What did they say?"

"The doctor was bloody rude. Said this was a civilian hospital and we were all here on sufferance. Said if he heard any more about it he'd tell the R.A.F. they'd got to come and take me away, whether I was fit to move or not. I wish to God he would. That's no way to look at it, is it?"

"Bloody shame," said Mr Turner mechanically. "What's the nigger doing here, anyway? He wasn't with us in the Hudson, was he?"

"No—he's stationed somewhere near here, with the American Army. Went into an air-raid shelter and cut his throat, just near the hospital here, because the Military Police were after him for something or other. Now he's come out all over boils and carbuncles and things, and runs a temperature all the time. Septicaemia, or something. That's what they say, but I think it's V.D. All niggers have V.D. You want to watch out, old man—don't you let them give you a cup or anything he's used. The mugger oughtn't to be in this ward at all. He ought to be in a lock hospital."

He paused, and then he said, "He offered me a paper the other day that he'd been reading and breathing all over. I soon put him in his place."

He, too, was set to read the *True Tales of Adventure* to Captain Turner and, like Corporal Brent, he found it heavy going. "I wish they'd let us have a copy of 'The Aeroplane' or 'Flight,' " he said. "If we were in a proper R.A.F. hospital instead of this stinking hole we'd have all that, and probably the American ones as well."

He went into a long dissertation on the merits of the Spitfire versus the Mustang, which sent Captain Turner into a quiet doze. He had no conversation whatsoever beyond aeroplanes, except a queer hotchpotch of schoolboy prejudices.

He referred to all foreigners as Dagoes, and deplored their moral habits with a frankness of speech that was novel to Mr Turner, who had not had the benefit of an English public school education. He affected superiority to these Dagoes on account of their low standards of life, and he affected superiority to the Americans because they made too much money. He thought money grubbing was frightfully bad form, never having had to grub for it himself. He was not a fool, but he was wholly undeveloped, and his commission in the R.A.F., which had conferred on him the status of an officer and a gentleman without much effort on his part, had bred in him a curious snobbishness. He was childlike in his ignorance of many things, and as pathetic as a child in his blunders.

Once he said, "Are you married?"

"Aye," said Mr Turner. "I got married when the war broke out."

"I suppose you knew her before the war?"

"Worked in the same office, we did," said Mr Turner. "Then we started going out together, evenings, 'n after a bit we got married. October 1939, that was; just before I joined up."

"Really?" The boy stared at him in wonder. "It must have been funny working in the office with her."

"I dunno. It was darned distracting."

"Most people meet girls at a party, don't they?" said the pilot. "That's how I met Joyce. And what a party! At the Bull, in Stevenage, it was. We were all as blind as bloody bats."

"Are you married, then?" asked Mr Turner. The boy seemed so young.

"I'm married," he replied. "I got married just over a year ago, at the beginning of my second tour." There was a faint tone of pride in his voice.

"Fine," said Mr Turner. "Got any kids yet?"

"Oh no," the boy said. "Joyce isn't one of those. She's got her work, you see. She's on the stage. She's awfully good, really."

Mr Turner said, "Got her photograph?"

Morgan was very pleased. He went hobbling across the ward and fetched his wallet from the drawer of the bed table, and brought it back with him, and showed Mr Turner the photograph beneath a sheet of cellophane. Mr Turner took it in his hand and held it sideways to the light, and looked at it with his sound eye. It showed a very luscious

44

and provocative young woman, with downcast eyes and long hair flowing around her bare shoulders.

He gave it back to Morgan. "I think you're a very lucky chap," he said. "She's perfectly lovely."

The boy was pleased. He took the photograph back and studied it himself. "She is, isn't she?" he said. "She's more beautiful than that, really—it doesn't do her justice. Everybody goes mad about her." He hesitated, and then said, "Of course, she's been married before."

Mr Turner was amazed. "She has?" The girl seemed so young.

Morgan nodded. "She was married to an awfully good friend of mine, Jack Stratton. He went for a Burton over France last year. Joyce was frightfully cut up about it, of course—it was terrible for her, poor kid. She was only twenty then, and she's had an awfully rough deal in her life. Jack was a jolly good friend of mine, and we knew he'd want me to look after her, so we got married two months later before I went out to Egypt."

Captain Turner thought enviously that it was grand when duty to a friend turned out like that. "So you're her second husband," he said. "Well, I never!"

The boy seemed a little confused. "Well, as a matter of fact, she was married before that," he said. "I'm her third husband, really. She was married first of all to a chap in 73 Squadron who bought it when they were operating in France back in 1940. She's had frightfully bad luck. It's always the best people get the worst luck, isn't it? I wonder why that is?"

He was worried about an illegal package that he had concealed in the rear fuselage of the Hudson. "There's a stowage rack for parachute flares up in the roof, just above the little hatch in the bulkhead, aft of the gun bay, right in the rear fuselage," he said. "I put it there. But it'll be gone by now. Some wretched Ack Emma will have got it. It's too bad."

"What was it?"

"Perfume that I got in Algiers, and some lipsticks, and powder, and four pairs of silk stockings, and some silk." He hesitated, and then said, "With a girl like Joyce, you've got to treat them right, you know. I mean, she's accustomed to pretty things, and she feels awful if she can't get them. I mean, she can make herself look so stunning, she's just got to have the things." He brooded for a minute, and then said, "I wish I hadn't told her I was bringing her some stuff. Now I've got nothing to bring."

"You're bringing yourself back alive. That's something."

45

"Oh—yes. But she wanted some Coty."

Turner learned that they had only lived together for a fortnight, in the Piccadilly Hotel, before he had been sent out to North Africa on his second tour. Since then they had been together for half-a-dozen week-ends only. "She's got her work, you see." Her work was playing the part of the chambermaid in "Smile Sweetly, Lady" at the Grafton Theatre. She had to speak three lines, smile, and exit into the bedroom.

Flying Officer Morgan wrote a letter to her every day; a long letter, scribbled in pencil in an irregular, unformed hand. But he never seemed to get a reply. He talked about it once. "Of course, there's nothing wrong or anything like that," he said, "but she doesn't like writing. It's about three months since I got a letter from her. It's just the way you're made, you know. When she does write, they're frightfully nice." He showed Turner a little dog-eared sheaf of letters in his wallet, very few. "I carry them all around with me everywhere I go, and read them over and over again till they pretty well fall to pieces." He examined his treasures. "I must get a bit of stamp paper for this one."

Turner asked once if she was coming down to see him at Penzance, but he said, "Oh, I don't expect so. She's got her work, you see. She couldn't leave that, could she?"

Mollie had left her job to come and see him, but Mr Turner said, "Well, no; I suppose not."

Phil Morgan did not often get a letter from his wife, but his friends wrote to him from time to time. Two days before he left the hospital he came to talk to Captain Turner, troubled. "I do wish people wouldn't write things like this," he said. "It's absolutely all right, of course . . ." He handed Turner one sheet of a letter:

. . . and we had a wizard time. We couldn't get anywhere to sleep in London because you have to book a room weeks ahead now, so we rang up Joyce and she said we could come and sleep at her flat. She had a chap called Bristow there, a two-striper from 602 Squadron, and he said he had given up looking for a bedroom in London now and he always went and slept with Joyce, in a manner of speaking, of course. We got some sausage and stuff from the NAAFI and cooked supper about one in the morning, and Bristow had a bottle of whiskey and I had one of gin so we were well away. We all felt like death the next day, but it was a good party.

Captain Turner read this through; the exposed portion of

his face was a poker face. "Nothing in that," he said. "It was kind of friendly of your wife to look after your friends."

"I know . . ." The boy turned to the letter in his hands. "There's only just the sitting room and the bedroom," he said at last.

"Well, that's all right. Your friends wouldn't do anything you wouldn't like 'n go and write to you about it."

"Oh, it's not them." He hesitated. "It's this chap Bristow."

"What about him?"

"Well, he's got a lot of money, and he can give her things—furs and things I simply haven't the money to get. He's awfully kind. But . . ." He hesitated, and then said, "The poor kid's had such a packet of losing husbands, she sort of feels she's got to be safe, whatever happens. If I'd gone for a Burton on my second tour, or any time, I think this chap Bristow would be Number Four."

"I see," said Captain Turner thoughtfully.

"It's all perfectly all right, of course," said Morgan. "It's only that she's so attractive people go mad over her. It's not her fault that happens."

"Of course not," said Turner.

Two days later Phil Morgan was discharged from hospital. "I wish to God I hadn't lost that parcel," he said. "I don't like going up to London with nothing for her. She gets such a lot of presents . . ."

In the moonlit garden his wife stirred beside Turner. "Well, that's nothing," she said. "Actresses and that, they've got different standards."

"Actress, my foot!" said Mr Turner. "She wasn't an actress at all, not till they brought in conscription for women and she had to get a job." He turned to her. "You remember, we went to see 'Smile Sweetly, Lady'? The chambermaid—she hadn't got much to do."

Mollie nodded. "Irene Morton wore a lovely pyjama suit. You remember them pyjamas? Ever so lovely they were. Silly sort of play, though. We went on and had dinner at Frascati's. Remember?"

"Aye," said Mr Turner thoughtfully. "Good evening, that one."

He glanced at her. "I sort of worried more about Phil Morgan than either of the others," he said. "He was married to a bitch that didn't care a sausage for him. But a chap can butt his way through all that sort of trouble."

He paused. "It was sort of—there was nothing *to* him,

if you get me," he said. "There he was, twenty-two years old, and not a thought in his head beyond the perishing aeroplanes. Might have been a kid of ten. Got himself in a bloody mess through marrying a bitch like that, and probably go on getting into mess after mess, unless he got killed in an aeroplane first. But I reckon he was too good for that. He was good at flying; the only thing he was good at. I dunno what would have become of a chap like that. He just knew nothing, absolutely nothing at all."

His wife said, "Well, I dunno. People get more sense as they get older and get settled down in jobs. What about the nigger?"

"Aye," said Mr Turner, "he was the last one. I was much better when he got up. There was just the two of us left in the ward then, and the guard on the door just the same." He paused, and then he said, "Funny thing about that chap," he said. "He didn't talk like a nigger at all. He talked just like any other Yank soldier—better than most, maybe."

"Pretty simple, I suppose," she said. "I mean they don't know much, do they? I don't suppose you found much to talk about with him."

"Well, I dunno," he said. "We got along all right."

She glanced at him, puzzled. "Was he a proper nigger, then?"

"Oh yes, he was a nigger all right. Sort of milk chocolate colour, he was, with black kinky hair. He'd got some white blood in him, I should think, but not a lot." He paused. "Quite young, he was—only about twenty."

By the time Turner was allowed out of bed, the screen had been taken away from around him and the whole of his face was uncovered. He still had a dressing on the wound, but he was sitting up in bed and taking notice of things. He had spoken once or twice to the Negro before, but their beds were on opposite sides of the room, and that made conversation difficult for Turner with his wounded head and for the Negro with the deep wound in his throat. It was not until Lesurier was up and in a dressing gown that they were able to approach each other sufficiently closely for easy talk.

Turner said, "How does it feel, now you're up?"

The Negro said, "I don't feel so good right now. Say, if I'd known that cutting your throat gave you septicaemia, I sure would have made a job of it."

"Or else not done it at all," said Turner.

The Negro paused for a moment in abstraction. "Well,"

he said at last, "that would have been another way." He turned to Turner. "Now I'm up and around, if you want anything, Cap'n, just say."

"Righto," said Turner, and went on reading his paper. He could not read continuously at that time, or for very long; it made his eyes ache and he had to stop. The Negro also had a paper and copies of the "Stars and Stripes" and "Yank," but most of the time he sat in sad, thoughtful abstraction in a wicker chair, or stood in silence looking out of the window at the pleasant, undulating Cornish country scene. In the middle of the afternoon Turner said, "What about a game of draughts? Can you play draughts?"

The other roused himself. "Surely, Cap'n." He got up and fetched the board and the cardboard box that held the pieces. "You know," he said, making conversation, "back home we call this checkers."

They set up the board on Turner's bed, and arranged the pieces.

"Where's your home?" asked Turner, also making conversation. "What part of the States do you come from?"

"Nashville," said the Negro. "Nashville, in the State of Tennessee."

Turner thought for a moment. "That's over somewhere in the West, isn't it? Or is that Texas?"

"No, *sir*. Tennessee is in the South, between the Lakes and Florida. Not right South like Mississippi or Louisiana, just halfway South."

"I see," said Turner, not much interested. "Been over here long?"

"Four-and-a-half months." They began to play.

"Do you like it over here?"

"It's a long way from home, Cap'n," said the Negro quietly. "You get to feeling sometimes that you're quite a ways from home, and then you get lonely. But most of us colored boys like England pretty well."

Presently Turner asked, "What do you do in Nashville? What do you work at?"

"I got a job with the Filtair Corporation."

"What's that?"

The Negro glanced at him, surprised. "Why, that's quite a business, Cap'n, back in Nashville. They got over five thousand hands working now, with war contracts. Make air cleaners for autos and trucks and tanks, and airplane engines, too." He paused, and then he said, "My Dad, he's been with them over twelve years now. That's a long while to be with one corporation in the States, specially for a colored person."

"What does he do there?"

"Runs the print machine, making the blueprints from the drawings. He's a draftsman really, makes a darned fine engineering drawing. We lived up in Hartford when I was a lil' boy, and he worked there as a draftsman. Then we moved back down South because his pa died and Grandma needed looking after. But I guess there's difficulties in the South you don't get in Connecticut. Yes, my dad works in the print room." He said that he had been sent to the James Hollis School for Colored Boys in Nashville.

The ex-draughtsman had given his son as good an education as a coloured boy could get.

"Pa wanted me to be a draftsman too, and I did the course at school, and I liked it well enough. But then when I left school I couldn't get a start nohow. No, *sir;* not in Nashville!"

"Why not?"

The Negro looked at him. "Things is mighty funny in some states," he said quietly. "In Filtair, colored people don't do drafting. I guess if I'd gone up to Hartford I'd have got a start all right, but Ma was poorly, and not much money, either. I got taken on as a garage hand at Filtair; it's all colored in the garage. Then I got to drive a truck for them, and then they put the filters on the Type 83 Bulldozer for desert service, and I got to driving that around sometimes for experimental trials. Then when I got drafted they found I knew how to drive a bulldozer so they put me into a construction unit." He thought for a minute. "I guess I'd have been in a construction unit anyway," he said. "They don't send us on combat service."

In the winter of 1942 he had been moved across the Atlantic; he was stationed for a month or two in Northern Ireland with his unit. An airstrip had been needed in the region of Penzance. By March 1943, his construction company, with three others, was working on a hilltop just above the little village of Trenarth, four miles from Penzance, levelling the fields, breaking down walls, demolishing farmhouses, making roads and runways.

Trenarth is a little place on the railway, at the junction of the main line and the North Coast line. It is a place of about a thousand inhabitants, with a small market square, a church built in the year 1356, and a public house. The construction companies were all Negro except for a few white technicians;

50

the impact of fifteen hundred coloured soldiers on this little place was considerable.

"I like Trenarth," he said. "I guess we all do."

There were some misunderstandings to be cleared up when they first arrived. A party of white American surveyors from the Eighth Air Force had come first to pick the site and mark it out, and they had told the village about the blacks who would arrive in a few days. They said that the Negro soldiers who were coming were rather primitive, and that the villagers would have to be both careful and tolerant. They said the Negroes could speak little English and did not understand the use of lavatories. When they were hungry, they would bark like a dog, and they had small, rudimentary tails concealed within their trousers, which made it difficult for them to sit down. Having drunk their beer and marked the site and had their fun with perfectly straight faces, the surveyors went away, and left the village in perplexity.

Old Mr Marston, the gardener at the vicarage, raised the matter in the White Hart one night. "I asked Mr Kendall if it's true what they were saying about these black soldiers that are coming," he said. "About them barking when they want their victuals. He says it's all just a story they were telling us, to get a rise out of us."

"Aye, that's right," said Mr Frobisher, the landlord of the pub. "They was just pulling our legs. Negroes don't have tails, not any that I heard of."

A mournful little man who worked as a porter at the station said, "Well, I don't think they was pulling our legs at all. Very nice and straight they spoke to me, they did. That corporal, he said this lot come straight from Africa. Africans, they are—that's why they can't speak English. There's rum things happen in Africa, believe me."

The consensus of opinion was that the stories were improbable, but that it would be prudent to maintain a strict reserve when the visitors arrived.

The story reached the Negro soldiers very quickly. In the March dusk, after their evening meal in the rough camp they were making on the bleak hilltop, a few coloured men walked down into the village. They came in a little party, smiling broadly. As they passed each villager they gave a realistic imitation of a pack of hungry dogs. They thought it was a great joke, and barked at everybody, in tones varying from Pekinese to bloodhound. By the time they reached the White Hart, the village had come to its senses; in the bar they were accepted as interesting strangers to whom was owed some sort of apology.

"They were real friendly, right from that first evening," said Lesurier. "They made us feel like we were regular fellows."

It was not only that the villagers were conscious of their own stupidity. At that time there had been a great deal of prominence given in the English newspapers to the assistance America was sending in Lease-Lend, and this assistance was obvious to everybody in Trenarth in the increasing numbers of American tractors, trucks, and jeeps to be seen in the streets. Like others, Bessie Frobisher, the buxom daughter of the landlord, had half believed the stories she had heard about the Negroes, and felt in a dim way that she owed recompense to these black, soft-spoken, well-behaved strangers in the bar. So she got out her electric iron, which had not functioned for a month, and brought it into the bar and put it on the counter, and said, "Can any of you mend an iron?"

Sergeant Sam Lorimer picked it up in his enormous pink-palmed hands. "Sure, lady," he said, "I can fix that for you." He turned it over, examining it. "It don't get hot no more?" he asked.

She said, "It doesn't get hot at all now. It used to be ever so good. It's a job to get anything mended now, you know."

He called across the bar, "Hey, Dave, lend me your screw driver?"

Lesurier lent his screw driver, and with that and a jack-knife they disembowelled the iron on the counter while the girl watched, picked up the broken thread of filament and made it fast, and re-assembled it. They tried it in a lamp socket and it got hot at once.

"It's all okay now," said Lorimer, "but the filament won't last so long—it's kind of rotten. It gets that way as it gets old."

"You can get new parts for irons like that," said one. "I see them that day we was in Belfast."

"That's so," said Lorimer. "Maybe we could get one in Penzance." He passed the iron back to Bessie. "Well, there you are, lady. It's fixed right now, until it goes again."

She smiled at him. "It's ever so kind of you to take the trouble," she said. She turned to her father. "Dad, this gentleman's mended my iron, and it works beautifully."

She used her normal language without thinking anything about it, but each Negro within hearing caught the word

52

"gentleman" and stiffened for a moment in wonder. They certainly were in a foreign country, a long ways from home.

Frobisher passed his hand over the iron to feel its warmth, and turned to Lorimer. "Aye, it works all right," he said. "Will you take something on the house? A glass of beer?"

The big Negro hung his head, smiling and confused. "Well, that's real kind of you, mister," he said.

Within a few days the boys were fixing everything. They liked fixing things. They fixed the leg of the settee in the saloon bar, and they fixed the gate leading to old Mrs Pocock's cottage garden. They fixed the Vicar's Austin Seven, and they fixed the bit of wall by the war memorial, that a truck had knocked down. They fixed the counter flap of Robertson's grocery shop, and they fixed the wheel of Mr Penlee's dung cart. When Penlee gave them tea with all his family in the farm kitchen, as some recompense for what they had done to his cart, they were so overwhelmed that they turned up next Sunday in a body and limewashed his cow house.

They fixed everything that needed fixing in Trenarth in a very few weeks. In a country that had been at war for over four years, with every able-bodied man and woman called up for industry or for the forces, their presence was a real help to the village; the people liked them for it, and for their unfailing courtesy and good humour. They were well paid by English standards and they brought prosperity to Trenarth, which was a factor in their favour, but more important was the willing work they did; England in wartime had plenty of money, if little to spend it on. Some of them were gardeners in civil life, and used to come up shyly and ask if they might work in the garden, asking for nothing but the pleasure of tending flowers. Some of them were farm hands, and wanted to do nothing better in their spare time than to help the land girls clean the muck out of the cow houses. Inevitably they were asked in to a meal as interesting and honoured guests, and equally inevitably they would take the farmer's daughter or the land girl to the pictures in Penzance.

They had a grand time in those early days. They used to bring a couple of trucks down from the camp on Saturday afternoons to pick up the girls, and drive off to Penzance to the pictures in a great merry party, thirty or forty black young men and as many white girls, all laughing and jammed together in the great trucks, having a fine time.

The Vicar, Mr Kendall, held unconventional views on most of the controversial subjects in the world, which no doubt accounted for the fact that at the age of fifty-three he had progressed no further than the living of St Jude's, Trenarth. He stood with Mr Frobisher one afternoon, watching one of these expeditions as it started off, and said, "We'll have a few black babies to look after, presently."

Mr Frobisher rubbed his chin. "Well, I dunno," he said. "It's the girls' own business if they do. Colour apart, I like these fellows well enough, I must say."

The Vicar nodded. "I'd rather have them than some others of our gallant Allies," he said darkly.

It was in that halcyon time that Private David Lesurier became acquainted with Miss Grace Trefusis.

Miss Trefusis worked behind the counter in Robertson's grocery shop, where she spent all day making up little ounce and two-ounce parcels of rationed foods. She was nearly seventeen years old, a pretty, dark, reserved girl who had grown up late and never had much truck with boys. Lesurier, at the age of twenty-two, had played and danced with various mulatto and "high yaller" girls back home in Nashville, but had very seldom spoken to a pure white one. He was shy of Grace, and very much attracted to her at the same time.

He saw her first at Robertson's, where he was buying cigarettes. He could buy better cigarettes in the canteen up at the camp, but it pleased him to go into English shops and buy; it gave him a feeling of competence in a foreign land. From that time on he bought all his cigarettes at Robertson's, in single packets of ten, that necessitated many visits.

In spite of this assiduity, he did not get on very fast with Grace. With a sixth sense she knew he came to see her. She was shy of him and did not want much to be seen about with a black boy. As he was equally shy of her and never asked for anything except, "Ten Players, please, ma'am," she had little difficulty in keeping him in his place. But from his many visits, a queer, tenuous little friendship came into being. She grew accustomed to him and his shy "Ten Players, please, ma'am," and sometimes she smiled at him. She was very young and pretty when she smiled.

Up on the hilltop the Negroes did their work efficiently and well, accelerating their own departure. In six weeks the strip was paved and usable by airplanes of the U.S. Army Air Corps. Half the Negroes were moved on to other work in other places; the remainder were set to putting up prefabricated huts and ammunition dumps, and making roadways. In their place came the first detachment of the Army Air Corps to take over the new strip.

For a week all went well. The white American soldiers mixed amicably with the Negroes, using the bar of the White Hart on friendly terms with them and chi-hiking with them in the street. By the end of the week, however, the detachments were of about equal strength, and a stir of uneasiness was agitating the whites.

Girls were the first and main trouble. Every eligible girl in Trenarth by that time was walking out with a black soldier, for the very good reason that there had been nobody else in the vicinty to walk out with. The white troops found to their concern that every girl was dated up by a Negro. Socially this was no great matter, for there were too few girls in Trenarth to go round in any case and there was a large camp of A.T.S. not far from Penzance willing and anxious to be taken out by the Americans. Amongst the new arrivals, however, there were a small proportion of whites from the "Deep South," to whom the feminine vagaries of Trenarth were genuinely distressing.

Corporal Jim Dakers, from Carthage on the Pearl River, in Leake County, Mississippi, gave expression to his feelings in the bar of the White Hart one evening.

"You'd think these English girls would have more sense of decency than to go walking with a nigger," he proclaimed. "What kind of a dump is this, anyway? Their folks should give them a good whipping. If they don't, well I guess there's other folks that will."

His companions said, "Aw, lay off, Jim. You're not in the South now."

He said, "It sure burns me up to see the niggers getting out of hand this way."

Behind the bar the English landlord stood mute, faintly hostile.

There were other irritations, too. Ninety-five per cent of the white Americans of the Army Air Corps were quiet, well-behaved, and tactful, but unfortunately the remainder were more vocal. Corporal Stanislaus Oszwiecki, from McKeesport, Pennsylvania, considered that municipal affairs were run better at home. He returned to the bar from a visit to the urinal, and said:

"Say, what do you know? They ain't got no sewer here. Just a kinder soak pit, 'n an earth bucket." He turned to

Mr Frobisher, the landlord. "Say, didn't nobody ever tell you guys about modern sanitation?"

The landlord took his pipe out of his mouth, and said slowly, "You'll find all you want in the town and cities in this country. It's not necessary in a place like this." He spoke quietly and with restraint, because he was sensitive about the lavatory accommodation of the White Hart. As soon as the village got a more adequate water supply, he meant to alter things.

"For cryin' out loud!" said Corporal Oszwiecki. "He says proper sanitation ain't necessary. Say, you guys want to brush up your ideas if you're ever goin' to stand up to the Germans. Look what they done to you before we came—" He drew his breath in sharply—"Boy, did you see Plymouth! You British want to get around some 'n get some modern notions. The U.S. Army pulled you through last time, 'n it'll pull you through this time. But we ain't comin' over every twenty years whenever you get into trouble. No, *sir!*"

The landlord sucked his pipe and said nothing. A couple of white American privates got up quietly and walked out into the street. It was quiet and peaceful in the ancient village street under the moon.

At last one said, "Stan got a little lit up."

The other said, "I certainly hate hearing that kind of talk. It's not right, and it don't do any good, either. And here's another thing. It don't do no good speaking about 'niggers' in front of colored boys."

"That's right," said the other. "Back home we never talk about a 'nigger' unless we want to start a row. We always call them colored folks, or maybe Negroes."

It did no good at all in Trenarth, nor did the growing feeling between the white and Negro soldiers. When Colonel McCulloch of the U.S. Army and of Columbus, Georgia, arrived to take over the command of the new station, he found a tension between whites and blacks, the blacks encouraged by the sympathy and friendship of the British villagers. The South has always provided a considerable proportion of the regular officers of the U.S. Army. Colonel McCulloch was a good officer, determined to pursue the war seriously, making the best of the personnel under his command.

"Reckon these colored boys got just a mite above themselves before we came," he said. "We'll have to put that right."

To put it right, he set himself to re-impose the policy of segregation that had always worked well in the Southern states. He sent for a detachment of Military Police experienced in the segregation policy. It was not his fault that these policemen were all white and mostly from the South. He held a meeting with Captain Deane, the Negro officer in charge of the black troops, outranked him and beat him down on every point. Then he sent his secretary, Lieutenant Schultz, to see the landlord of the White Hart. As it was a formal call, Lieutenant Schultz wore his mosquito boots.

Schultz explained his business. "The Colonel feels that friction may arise if the colored troops use the same places of recreation as the rest," he said. He was a big, earnest young man. "Back in North Ireland there were quite a few cases of trouble, especially where troops used the same saloons. We had to make arrangements there for separate accommodation, same as we do at home, and the Colonel's going to do that here."

"Aye?" said Mr Frobisher.

Schultz said, "I've been telephoning to Paddington station, and the railroad company is fixing things so that the refreshment room up at the station stays open till ten o'clock, serving drinks the same as you do, starting Thursday. The Colonel says that, as from Thursday next, the Negro troops go to the refreshment room."

"Not much of a place for them, that," said Mr Frobisher slowly.

"Not for you and me, maybe," said the lieutenant, "but it's all right for them. You ought to see the places most of them come from back home."

"Aye?" said Mr Frobisher slowly. He was thinking hard.

Schultz was young and inexperienced; to him the way seemed easy. "Well, from next Thursday you won't serve any colored soldiers in this place," he said; "only whites. I guess you'll probably be glad to see the last of the black boys, won't you?" The landlord did not answer. "Anyway, you won't serve them any more."

Mr Frobisher said slowly, "I'll serve who I like."

There was a momentary pause. The lieutenant quickly realised that there was something here that he did not fully understand. He thought for a moment, and then said, "The Colonel sent me down to tell you what we're going to do, the way we'd get co-operation. We don't any of us want friction, fights, and such-like, in this place."

"There's been no friction here," said Mr Frobisher.

"We've had the coloured boys here six weeks now, and never a cross word, let along a fight. Why can't you let things be?"

"It's what the Colonel says," said Schultz, "that they must use the refreshment room from Thursday on."

Mr Frobisher took the pipe out of his mouth and drew himself up, dignified in his shirt sleeves. "I've been here twenty-seven years," he said, "and my father before me, and never a question of the licence or a complaint from the police. I say who I serve here, not your colonel. If I say I serve the coloured boys, why then, I serve the coloured boys, and that's all about it."

Schultz was nonplussed. "I can't go back and tell the Colonel that," he said. "You want to think this over a little, maybe."

Mr Frobisher said, "I've been thinking while you've been talking. I don't want to cross your colonel. If you feel there'll be fights if your white soldiers go on coming here along with the black boys, well, let the white boys go to the refreshment room, and let the black ones keep on coming here. That's what I say."

The lieutenant stared at him, dumbfounded. "Say, Mr Frobisher," he said, "we couldn't do that. That's the worse accommodation of the two!"

"Well, then," said the landlord, "let 'em both keep coming here. There won't be no fights in my house, I can promise you that. Twenty-seven years I've held this licence, and I wouldn't have done that, I can tell you, if I let the men get fighting."

"I don't think the Colonel will agree to that," said Schultz. "He wants to get things like we have them back at home."

"Well, he's not at home now, and that's a fact," said Mr Frobisher. "He's in Trenarth, and maybe we've got different ways to what you have at home. I don't want to make no difficulties for you people, but if I stopped serving any man here in this country because I didn't like the colour of his skin I'd soon lose my licence. That I would. I don't stop serving blacks until the licencing justices say different. Not while they behave themselves."

The lieutenant realised that he was up against a very stubborn man. "Well," he said, "I'll just have to go back and tell the Colonel what you say. I guess he'd better stop off when he goes through this afternoon and have a word with you."

"Aye," said the landlord affably, "ask him to look in. Maybe I'll have thought of something by that time, something else we might do."

That happened in the morning, and if Colonel McCulloch had been able to look in that afternoon before the views of Mr Parsons got around the neighbourhood, it would have been a great deal better. Unfortunately, he was detained and did not come till the next day.

Ezekiel Parsons was eighty-six years old. He had been a farm labourer in his day, and had never been further from Trenarth than Penzance. He could not read or write, and he was very deaf. Trenarth was the universe to Mr Parsons; he classed persons from villages ten miles away as foreigners equally with those from foreign countries. His wife was long dead and his family dispersed. He lived in a single attic room on the old-age pension and a small allowance from his children, and sat in a corner of the public bar of the White Hart every day, morning and evening, from opening till closing time. It was his one amusement, to sit there and watch the people. He was the oldest inhabitant, and he had long white side whiskers.

He was well known to Jerry Bowman, the driver of the brewer's lorry delivering the casks of beer. That morning Jerry stood the old man to a glass of mild, and asked, "What do you think of all these Americans in Trenarth, Mr Parsons?"

The ancient piped in his old quavering voice, "I like them very well; oh, very well indeed. We get on nicely with them here. I don't like these white ones that are coming in now, though. I hope they don't send us no more o' them."

It was too good not to be repeated; it ran round both whites and blacks that afternoon. It got to Colonel McCulloch as a good story in the evening. He did not think it a good story at all. He thought it was a very bad story indeed, and he thought about it all night.

Bright and early the next morning he sent for Lieutenant Anderson, chief of his detachment of Military Police. Lieutenant Anderson came from Little Rock, Arkansas, and had served there in the police; he knew a good deal about "niggers."

The Colonel said, "Say, Anderson, we're heading straight for trouble with these goddam niggers. They've been here alone too long, and they've got the whole darned countryside with them."

Lieutenant Anderson said, "I guess that's right, Colonel. They been here alone too long, and they've got uppity."

The Colonel said, "That's right. Mind, we got nothing to complain of yet, beyond the fact that they go walking with these darned English girls, giving them ideas. But *I* know and *you* know what's the end of that. They get swelled heads, and then we'll have real trouble."

"That's right, Colonel."

"Well, now, you got to be strict with them. I don't mean go hazing them and stirring up trouble; just—strict. We got to get things back the way they should be. Keep them smart, and crack down on them if they're not dressed right. It won't hurt any if we make a few examples; if you get anything to go before court-martial, for example, I'll see they get the limit. I had some of this before, one time, and I know what can happen if you let it slide. You want to be just, and give them the square deal. But when you catch them on the hop, then you got to be plenty tough."

Lieutenant Anderson said, "Okay, Colonel. I get it."

The Colonel said, "I'm going down right now to sound out this darned saloon keeper, and get that end of it straightened out."

He drove down in his Command car to see Mr Frobisher, accompanied by Lieutenant Schultz. He found the landlord in his shirt sleeves polishing the glasses in the bar, for it was out of hours and the bar was empty.

He said, "Say Mr Frobisher, I understand there's been a mite of disagreement between you and Lieutenant Schultz here over the use of this place by the colored troops. I just stopped off to tell you why we can't have that any more, so that you'd see it from our point of view."

Mr Frobisher said, "Aye?"

Colonel McCulloch said, "Yeah. I've got to run the war around these parts, and I've got to do it with the troops they've given me. They've given me white troops and colored mixed for my command. I didn't ask for it that way, but that's the way it is. Well, when you get a mixed command like that you got to watch out and be mighty careful, Mr Frobisher, or they'll be fighting and shooting and God knows what."

Mr Frobisher said, "Aye?"

The Colonel said, "You got to be mighty careful with these niggers. Maybe you wouldn't know about that in this country. You start and treat them like you would whites, before you know it they'll be thinking they're as good as

60

white, telling *you* what to do. Then you get trouble. There's only one way to deal with this, and that's the way we do it back home and all through the Army. Separate recreation for the colored and the whites. Keep them apart, and then you don't get trouble. Give the niggers a place of their own, and keep them in it. That's the set-up I'm going to have here."

Mr Frobisher said, "Aye?"

"That's right. From Thursday next the niggers use the refreshment room up at the station. They won't be coming in here after Wednesday night."

Mr Frobisher said, "I was thinking, how would it be if your whites used the parlour of an evening, and let the blacks go on in the public bar as they've been doing?"

He led the way and showed them the parlour. It was a small room, rather dingy, with a few texts on the walls. The officers thought nothing of it. "Can't put the boys in a dump like this," said Schultz. Mr Frobisher did not like to hear his parlour referred to as a "dump," but he said nothing.

"That won't do," said the Colonel. "They'd have to use the same passage and the same door. No, from Thursday next the niggers go to the refreshment room."

"How are you going to keep them out of here?" asked Mr Frobisher.

The Colonel said, "I'm hoping we'll get your co-operation, Mr Frobisher. If not, I'll have to put this place off limits to the colored troops and put a policeman outside in the street."

He went away, leaving Mr Frobisher uneasy and resentful.

Late that afternoon Sergeant Lorimer, the big Negro who had mended the electric iron for the landlord's daughter, called for Bessie to take her for a walk. They had fallen into the habit of doing this once or twice a week, after which he would return with her to tea in the parlour of the pub, finishing up the evening in the bar, playing darts.

Outside the pub they met a military policeman. Lieutenant Anderson had his own ways of putting niggers in their place, and he had been genuinely shocked to see so many walking out with English girls. The M.P. said, "See your pass, Sergeant."

He stared at the pass. "Let's see your dog tag."

The Negro expostulated. "Say, what's that for?"

"So's I'll know this pass is made out for you, 'n not some

61

other nigger," said the policeman. "Come on, step on it."

To get at his identity disc, slung round his neck next to his skin, Lorimer had to undo coat and muffler, disarrange his collar and tie, open his shirt and pull out the disc from beneath his undervest. Then, while Bessie waited for him, he had to dress up again.

Twenty yards on they met another military policeman. "C'm on, Sergeant—pass and dog tag." Again Lorimer had to undress on the pavement.

All up and down the street Negro soldiers walking with English girls were undressing on the pavement while the girls stood giggling or irritated and the Negroes struggled with their clothes in sullen fury. After the fourth encounter, Lorimer and Bessie gave up their walk, thus fulfilling the intention of Lieutenant Anderson, and returned to the pub. The girl told her father all about it over tea.

"Sam, here, he was ever so patient," she said. "They was just doing it to be nasty, seemed to me."

"I guess they don't like to see colored people walking with English girls," the Negro said quietly. "They wasn't doing it to nobody except couples."

Mr. Frobisher sucked his pipe in thoughtful silence. "I dunno," he said at last. "Funny sort of way o' going on."

He was genuinely concerned at the turn that events were taking in Trenarth. He was the unofficial leader of the community; the village had a decrepit village hall, an army hut of the last war put up by the British Legion, but the main meeting place and forum for discussion was the bar of the White Hart. Mr. Frobisher had run that bar for very many years, and so had presided over most of the meetings of the village on topics that concerned them all. He felt, inarticulate, that it was up to him to take a lead in this distressing matter that was agitating the place. He was waiting upon events to show him what that lead should be.

Corporal Stanislaus Oszwiecki showed him, that same night. The bar was filled with sullen, irritated Negroes mixed with white soldiers. Corporal Oszwiecki thought this was a good time and place to give his views on the association of white girls with coloured men.

"Say," he said, "you hear what the Snowdrops have been doing up 'n down the street?" He told his companions in a loud tone what had been going on. "Teach these English bitches to go walking with a nigger," he said.

There was a momentary pause. Mr. Frobisher broke it, from behind the bar. "Not so much o' that language, if you please," he said. "If you can't talk clean, you can get outside."

Jim Dakers said, "Say, what kind of a place is this, anyway? It makes me sick these English floosies go around with niggers. I seen them hugging and kissing in dark corners—think o' that, man, hugging and kissing with a nigger!" He turned to Mr. Frobisher. "Say, mister, this town stinks. Stinks of nigger."

Three white American soldiers got up and walked out in silence.

Mr Frobisher slammed down a jug upon the counter. In the silence that followed the sharp rap he said, "If that's the way of it, I'll clear the bloody bar. Outside, all the lot of you—white *and* black. Outside—every American soldier out of this house, unless you want the Military Police called in. Outside, all the lot of you!"

Corporal Oszwiecki said, "Say, what is this? We don't have to go."

Mr Frobisher left the bar and walked out into the street. Before the inn he found a couple of American Military Police. "There's trouble with your soldiers in my bar," he said. "You'd better get every American out of my house, white and black. They'll be fighting with each other in a minute."

The Military Police swung their truncheons and went in. In a few minutes the house was clear but for a few civilians and old Ezekiel Parsons sitting in a corner. In the quiet that followed the departure of the Americans the old man piped, "Nasty fellows, they white ones. I can't a-bear them."

Behind the bar Mr Frobisher sat grim and silent, writing the large letters of a placard on white cardboard, with a paintbrush dipped in ink.

It appeared in the bar window next morning. It read:

THIS HOUSE IS FOR ENGLISHMEN AND
COLOURED AMERICAN TROOPS ONLY

Two military policemen strolled up and looked at it. "Say," said one, "that's not right. The Colonel's going to put out an order that the niggers use the refreshment room. This place is for whites."

They stared at it in silence for a moment. "I guess it's a mistake," the other said. "The landlord's a bit dumb. Look, he spelt 'colored' wrong."

When Colonel McCulloch heard about the notice he knew that it was no mistake. He was down at the White Hart within half an hour. Outside the inn he paused and read the notice before going in. He found Mr Frobisher in his parlour, seated at the table, making out his orders.

"Say, Mr Frobisher," he said, "I hear you had some trouble down here last night."

"Aye," said the landlord.

The Colonel said, "Well, that's just too bad. It's as I said, we've got to fix up separate accommodation. The only thing is, I want the white boys to use this place, as we settled yesterday."

"Aye?" said Mr Frobisher. "Well, I don't."

"Say, what's the matter with the white boys?"

The landlord thought deeply for a minute. "There's nothing wrong with most o' them," he said at last. "Nine out of ten are quiet, decent lads, remarkable like us. The rest of them are kind of quarrelsome and always making trouble. You can't say you'll have one lot o' white soldiers and not the others, though; it's all or none. I never had no trouble with the coloured boys, of any sort at all."

The Colonel said, "When you say the white boys, ten per cent of them make trouble, Mr Frobisher, what do you mean? What sort of trouble?"

The landlord said, "Last night they was picking on the coloured boys—saying nasty things about 'niggers' in their hearing, and that. It was all the whites doing it, never the black boys. I think they was out to make a fight, that's why I cleared the lot o' them out." He turned to the Colonel. "Some of the whites with foreign names don't seem to like anything—nothing you can do will please 'em. They don't like our girls, they don't like the coloured boys, they don't like the beer, they don't like the lavatories, 'n they don't like the English people, either, I don't think. And they don't mind telling you about it. . . ."

"Some of them may have a lot to learn," said Colonel McCulloch. "Quite a lot of them have never been outside the States before." He had not himself, but he did not say so.

"Aye," said Mr Frobisher. "Well, they can go and do their learning up at the refreshment room, 'n come back to this house when they've learned how to behave."

"Now that's what I've come down to talk about," the Colonel said. "We can't have that. We can't give this place over to the coloured boys and let the white boys go up to the

64

station. That's giving the best accommodation to the niggers. You must see that we can't do that."

"I don't know nothing about that," said Mr Frobisher. "You've got your troubles, and I've got mine. I got my licence to think of, that's what I've got—my licence. If I have fights and that, where do you think I'll be? Why," he said, "I bloody near had a fight with one of your white boys myself last night when he calls my Bessie a bitch. If I'd been twenty years younger I would ha' done, licence or no licence." He thought for a moment. "I'm sorry for the rest of your white boys," he said—"the quiet easy ones that don't feel badly about your black lads. But they just got to keep out of this house along with the others. I can't separate 'em out."

"How would it be, though, if the whites came here and we send the blacks up to the station? That's the way we want it," said the Colonel.

"Have that corporal with the foreign name in my house again? Not likely," said the landlord. "I'll take the blacks."

Colonel McCulloch could not make him alter that decision and returned ruefully to the camp up on the hill to take the matter up in correspondence with his general. The notice stayed in the window.

That evening Mr Frobisher refused to serve white soldiers at all; as the barroom was crowded with pleased and jubilant Negroes, there was not the trouble that he had anticipated. The White Hart became firmly established as the recreation centre of the coloured soldiers, the white troops had to go to the small, ill-lit, badly furnished waiting room, and relations between white and black deteriorated rapidly.

It was at this time of tension that Dave Lesurier made his pass at Grace Trefusis. For some time now he had thought of little else but Grace. It was clear to all the Negroes that they would not be much longer in Trenarth. If Dave were ever to consolidate with Grace, he would have to get on with it; he had no time for the long courtship that he knew, instinctively, would be the right approach. He had been courting Grace now for a month, and he had still got no further than, "Ten Players, please, ma'am."

For a week he had been trying to advance to his next stage, which was "Say, Miss Grace, would you care to take a little walk one evening?" But he had been unfortunate; each time the shop had been full of other people and the girl had herself been busy, though not too busy to smile as she handed him his cigarettes. He knew that she would not agree to walk out with him if other people were in hearing; he would have to wait his chance to say his piece until they were alone together. And he got no chance.

Grace lived with her parents in a cottage near the railway; her father was a signalman at the junction box.

Standing about in the square one evening at about six o'clock, hoping for a glimpse of her, Dave saw her going with a friend down to the Village Hall; she recognized him, and smiled at him as she passed. It was sufficient to keep him rooted there for four hours till, in the moonlight, at about ten o'clock in the evening, she came out on her way home. And she came alone.

He crossed the road, and met her in a quiet corner by the gate that led into the yard of the White Hart. He was repeating his line to himself as he crossed the road, because he was very nervous—"Say, Miss Grace, would you care to take a little walk one evening?" But when he was face to face with her at the quiet corner he forgot his words.

He stood in front of her, and said, "Say, Miss Grace, . . ." And then he stopped.

She said, "Oh, it's you." She smiled at him, a little nervously.

He said again, "Say, Miss Grace, . . ." And then he stopped again, because it suddenly seemed silly to ask her to take a little walk with him one evening, at ten o'clock at night. And because he was uncertain what to do, and because he had to do something, he put his arms round her and kissed her.

For a moment she yielded, too surprised to do anything else. For a moment he thought that it was going to be all right. Then fear came to her, irrational, stark fear. When she was a little child somebody had given her a golliwog, a black doll with staring white eyes and black curly hair, dressed in a blue coat with red trousers. It had terrified her. Whenever she saw it she had screamed with fright so that it had been given to a less sensitive child. Now at the age of seventeen the same stark fear came back to her. What she had been subconsciously afraid of all her life had happened. The golliwog had got her.

She started to struggle madly in Dave's arms, to free herself. She cried, "Let me go, you beast. Let me go." And she cried quite loud.

Chagrined, and already ashamed, he released her. He said, "Say, I didn't mean . . . Miss Grace, I guess I did wrong . . ."

But she was gone, half running, sobbing with emotion and with fright.

At the corner she ran full tilt into Sergeant Burton, of Montgomery, Alabama, and of the U.S. Military Police, who had heard her cry out and was coming to investigate.

He said, "Say, lady, what's the matter?"

He was fat and forty and comfortable—and white. To her at that moment he was all security. She sobbed, "There was a nigger there. He caught me and started messing me about."

Sergeant Burton said, "These goddam niggers!" and blew his whistle. He shot around the corner with surprising agility for so large a man, still whistling as he went. As Grace stood for a moment slowly composing herself, two other Military Police shot past her, heading for the whistle. A jeep came screaming down the road in intermediate gear, driven by a third. With a screech of tyres it braked to a standstill beside her, and two more policemen tumbled out.

The girl was comforted by all this evidence of support, and yet at the same time she was distressed. She had started something and she didn't know what. Around the corner there were men shouting, and then one re-appeared and whistled again. Men came pouring out of the White Hart. American soldiers, white and black, appeared from everywhere. Grace turned from them, still weeping a little, and walked quickly up the street towards her home. She could not bear to be questioned about what had happened.

Around the corner Dave Lesurier had to act quickly. He was bitterly chagrined and disappointed at the blunder he had made. As he heard what Grace had said to the sergeant, he realised that he was in a very serious position. He came, if not from the deep South, from far enough south, and all his youth had been conditioned by tales he had heard of Negroes being lynched and murdered horribly because the whites believed they had assaulted white women. Most of the tales that had conditioned him were quite untrue because such things grow in the telling, but Dave Lesurier could hardly be expected to know that. To him, at the moment, there was real danger that if the mob got him, a bonfire would be made outside the White Hart and he would be burned on it alive. He must get the hell out of there.

He dived into the yard behind him and flung himself over the wall into Mrs Higgins's back garden; over the next wall into Polherring's timber yard; from there he gained the back alley, and looked cautiously around. There was a clamour in the direction from which he had come, but they did not seem to be following him. He heard continuous whistling, and the sound of jeeps. And then, to his dismay, he heard shouted orders sending all American troops back to their camps.

He knew that he must rejoin them immediately and go back to camp with the crowd. He had not heard Grace tell his name; he did not know if she even knew it. If he could catch up with the crowd and mingle in with them he might escape; to stay in Trenarth and go back alone later meant instant detection. It never occurred to him for one moment to walk out and give himself up and tell the truth, that he had given the girl a kiss, so what? He had not hurt her, and he had not meant to hurt her, but it never crossed his mind that anybody would believe him if he said so. He must get the hell out of it.

He edged along the alley towards the end that led into Sheep Street; from there he could gain the High Street and mix in with the crowd. When he was still in the alley he heard voices of men in the street twenty yards ahead of him. He ducked back into the deep shadow of a wall as two corporals of the Military Police ran up, stopped, and peered down the alley towards him. He crouched deeper in the shadow.

One said, "Block this one—you stay right here, and block this one, and keep a lookout up 'n down this street. I'm going on around the block. We got him somewhere in this block."

"What's he done, anyway?"

"Raped one of these darned English girls."

"Gee! They've had it coming to them. Is he armed?"

"I guess not. Might be, though. If he don't stop on a challenge, better let him have it." He ran on.

Peering out of the deep shade, the Negro saw the policeman at the end of the alley pull out his service automatic and cock it, to bring a cartridge to the breech; he moved close to the wall and stood there, vigilant, alert, the gun ready in his hand.

Very gently, inch by inch, Lesurier moved back along the alley, keeping flat against the wall in the darkness of the shadow, testing each step on the ground before he let his weight on that foot in case of noise, feeling ahead of him, with outstretched fingertips. The moon was with him, its bright light dazzling the watching policeman twenty yards away. The Negro moved back undetected.

Presently he came to a gate leading into a garden behind him. His fingers explored it and it opened. In quick silence

68

he was through and out of sight of the watcher at the end of the alley. Now he could hurry. He sped over the walls, back into the timber yard, one side of which adjoined the High Street. Creeping over the timber, he looked down into the street.

There were no soldiers to be seen, except the Military Police. Under the direction of Lieutenant Anderson they seemed to be searching houses round about the White Hart. There was a picket of two policemen fifty yards away down the street in the direction of Penzance, at the corner of Sheep Street; at the moment they were looking up that street, where something seemed to be going on.

Deserted in the street, not ten yards from where he lay on the stacked timber, there was a jeep. It stood pointing in the direction of Penzance.

Lesurier thought quickly, fighting down the panic that was overwhelming him. Although the troops were all out of the village, they could not yet have got back to the camp up at the airfield, over a mile away. If he could get the jeep out of the town, there was still a chance that he could catch up with the crowd and pass in with them through the guard, unidentified. If he could drive out on the Penzance road, there was a chance that he could work his way round through the lanes and reach the camp in time. There was the jeep, and only two policemen at the corner fifty yards away to pass.

He took a final glance around. Then he got down from the timber and strolled nonchalantly out into the street and got into the jeep. The noise of the starter made the two men turn towards him, but the light was bad and they could not distinguish the colour of the driver. Lesurier put the jeep in gear and accelerated towards them in a normal getaway, not too fast in order not to rouse suspicion.

He was only a few yards from them when they saw that it was driven by a Negro, and challenged. He jammed his foot down hard in intermediate gear and drove straight at them. They leaped to one side as he roared past; then he was driving as he had never driven a jeep before, jinking and swerving all across the street. Behind him whistles shrilled and a shot rang out, missing him by twenty feet. Then he was out of Trenarth, roaring down the road towards Penzance, four miles away.

He did not know the roads. He was a bulldozer driver, and had never driven much about the countryside, though he could handle the jeep well enough. He had thought there would be a lane leading off towards the camp, and he drove on desperately, looking for it. But there was no lane. He flung a glance behind him, over his shoulder, and there were the headlights of cars, many cars, streaming down the road half a mile behind him. They were after him, and the hunt was up.

He knew now that when they overtook him they would shoot.

Stark panic seized him, born of the lynching stories told to him in his childhood in the South. He had done the unforgivable thing, and if the mob caught up with him they would tear him in pieces, burn him on a fire, torture him in vile ways. He put his foot down hard and dashed on through the quiet English moonlit scene in a frenzy of terror. The jeep he drove was in poor condition; behind him the Command cars and the other jeeps were gaining on him. He had one hope only now, to gain the shelter of the houses of Penzance and leave the jeep, and hide somewhere, anywhere. In his agony the thought of a well came to him; perhaps there would be a well somewhere, in some yard, that a man could get down into and hide, and let the hunt pass by. They would not think of looking down a well.

He would have been safer in a British police station, but he could not be expected to know that.

He dashed into the streets of Penzance at fifty miles an hour, his speed conditioned only by the speed at which the jeep would take the bends without going over. As he drove, he swung his head desperately from side to side, seeking for refuge. He came out by the sea not far from the harbour, and that checked him. He braked heavily and swung the jeep around into a side alley, and stopped, and ran blindly up towards the shadows. A Command car drew up with a scream of tyres, and a shot rang out, and the bullet hit the wall beside him.

He leaped for a seven-foot wall and caught it with his hands, and got one leg up on it, and miraculously he was over it and in a hen run on the other side. He blundered through the wire of that and into a vegetable garden, and over another wall into a churchyard. Behind him there were lights and the voices of excited American men.

He ran through the churchyard and stopped by a wall, peering out into the street. The Military Police were spreading round the block that he was in, as they had done before. He was caught. In a few minutes he would be in their hands.

In those last moments all trace of confidence in military

70

justice left him. He was the elemental, fear-crazed nigger hunted by the whites, conditioned by centuries of discrimination. The whites were after him and murderous in their intention to avenge the insult to the colour of their skin. Rather than fall into their hands, it was preferable to fall into the hands of death.

There was an air-raid shelter built against the wall of the churchyard. Behind him the hunt was close; men were already in the far side of the churchyard at his heels. He went into the air-raid shelter and drew out his knife. It was a good knife and one that he was proud of, given to him by his father back in distant Nashville when he was on leave before proceeding overseas; he kept it as sharp as a razor.

With tears streaming down his cheeks, in the smelly darkness of the shelter, he drew it hard and unskillfully across his throat.

In the quiet moonlight of the garden, five years later, Mr Turner said to his wife, "That's what happened. That's how he come to be in the hospital with me."

His wife stirred in her chair. She was growing cold, but she was interested. "What happened to him?" she enquired.

"I dunno," he said. "I dunno only what he told me, what I've told you now. He was for court-martial when he got out, on a charge of attempted rape. That's all I know."

She said, "But what he done wasn't rape at all, was it? I mean, you said he kissed her."

"That's what he told me," said Mr Turner. "He said that's all he did."

"Well, they couldn't charge him with attempting rape for that."

"I dunno," said Mr Turner. "Maybe they can in the American Army. I dunno but what he told me may have been a pack of lies."

"It must have been," she said. "There must have been more to it than that."

He was silent for a minute. "I dunno that there was," he said at last. "I don't think he was lying. He was pretty miserable, and I think what he said was true, far as he knew it. He knew he was for court-martial, and he was kind of resigned to that."

She said, "What was he miserable about, then? Just general disgrace?"

He said, "It was the girl. He'd gone and spoilt everything

71

with his own foolishness, and made her complain against him, and he'd never see her again. He used to sit staring out of the window, hour after hour, without saying anything—wishing he was back in Nashville, I suppose. One time I saw him crying—tears running all down his black face. It made me feel sort of funny to see that."

He paused, and then he said, "I think he was in love with her. Really in love, I mean—just like he was a white lad."

CHAPTER FOUR

MR TURNER went to the London office of his firm, Cereal Products Ltd., by underground and bus next morning. Cereal Products Ltd. has a suite of offices high up in a building in Leadenhall Street. He got there about ten o'clock, and went in to see the Managing Director, Mr Parkinson. He told Mr Parkinson his position frankly, as one man to another.

"I don't want any special favour, or anything o' that," he said. "But I want what's my due, and it's only right you should know what the doctor said, so you can make your own arrangements."

Mr Parkinson told him what was his due. "On your salary scale, the firm gives three months' sick leave on full pay. Then if you are still unfit for work, another three months on half pay."

"And after that the firm's finished," said Mr Turner. "Well, that's fair enough. What about last year's summer holiday? I didn't get it then because of that Argentine deal we did—Señor Truleja. Can I have that fortnight now?"

"I suppose so," said the Managing Director. "Yes, I think we can do that."

"Can I put this year's fortnight to it 'n have a month?" said Mr Turner.

"Now?"

"Yes." He paused, and then he said, "I got things to do."

Mr Parkinson eyed him shrewdly. "Three months and three months and one month makes seven months," he said. "The firm's not going to see much more of you, is it?"

Mr Turner said, "It wouldn't see much more of you, either, not if you was in my shoes."

"No. All right, go on and take your month's holiday, Turner. I'm very sorry to hear about all this."

"Not half so sorry as I am," said Mr Turner.

He went out, and turned into a Lyons' teashop, and had a cup of coffee. He was feeling slack and unwell; the beer that he had drunk the night before and the long sitting in the garden with his wife had done him no good. He sat there moody for a time, the great wound in his forehead pulsing intermittently. He smoked two cigarettes and then got up, and paid his bill, and took a bus up to the Air Ministry in Kingsway.

"I got to try and trace an officer what served in the war," he said to the messenger at the door.

He spent the next hour waiting in corridors and explaining his requirement to a number of uninterested people. They told him to go away and write a letter about it, but he would not do that. Finally he struck a Junior Clerk (Female) who was much his type and very much in tune with the outrageous remarks that he saw fit to make to her, and who exerted herself to help him in his search.

She pulled a sheaf of cards from the immense card index. "Give over," she commanded; "here, pay attention to this. There's five Phillip Morgans here." She sorted them. "He wouldn't be the Group Captain, would he? Nor this one that got killed in April 1942? What about this one—Squadron Leader at H.Q. Bomber Command?"

"That's not him, I shouldn't think," said Mr Turner. "You're busting out of your jersey, Loveliness. Want about sixteen more stitches in the next one, round about."

"If you go on like that I won't help you any more," she said. "Now what about this Flight Lieutenant Morgan that got took prisoner by the Japs in November 1944? Released from Rangoon Jail in May 1945, and demobed."

"What was he doing before?"

She scrutinised the card. "Two tours in fighters, and then Transport Command."

Mr Turner said, "That's the boy. Got took prisoner by the Japs, did he? Well I never!"

She said, "That's right. Last job was a Dakota squadron in South East Asia Command. Supply drops, I suppose. Missing November 1944, reported prisoner in January 1945."

"How can I get hold of him?"

"I dunno," she said. "There's next of kin here. That's all the address I've got." She scrutinised the card. "There's two here, wife and mother."

"That's what'll happen to you before you're much older, Beautiful," Mr Turner said. "Specially the last. Let's have a look."

He took down the addresses in his pocketbook, and left her pleased and giggling. He lunched on a pint of beer and a snack at his favourite local off Shaftesbury Avenue, the Jolly Huntsman, and went to the address at Pont Street in the afternoon. He climbed the stairs to the tiny top-floor flat. The door was opened to him by a pleasant, plain woman.

He said, "Does Mrs Morgan live here still?" He explained, "I knew her husband in the war—I was trying to get in touch with him again."

She wrinkled her brows. "There's nobody of that name lives here now."

He said, "Pity. This was some time ago, in 1943, of course. You don't happen to have the address of the tenant before you, I suppose?"

She said, "We've been here for eighteen months. The tenant before us was a Mrs Bristow. Bobby Charmaine, the actress, you know—that was her stage name, but she was Mrs Bristow. She might know about the people who were here before her. It's just a chance, you know."

He said, "Do you know how I could get in touch with her?"

"I'm afraid I don't," she said. "There was a divorce—she divorced Squadron Leader Bristow, or he divorced her, just after they left here. Perhaps some theatrical agent could tell you how to get in touch with Bobby Charmaine—she's still on the stage. I saw that she had a small part in the Winter Gardens pantomime the Christmas before last, and my husband said he saw her in a touring company in Stockton-on-Tees last year. A theatrical agent might know."

He left, and went down to the street again. He did not feel inclined to start a round of theatrical agents to get in touch with Bobby Charmaine in a second-rate touring company up at Wigan or West Hartlepool in order that he might ask her questions about her last husband but one or two. He took a bus to Kensington to see the mother.

She still lived in Ladbroke Square. He found the house without difficulty, a tall old house, four stories high. It was set in a terrace, each house with a basement, and the stucco peeling off a little. Once it had been a smart residential neighbourhood; now it was a bit down at the heels, still proud, but poor.

He rang the bell. After a long time the door was opened

to him by a young woman, plainly, rather dowdily dressed. A glance at her and he knew from the likeness to the pilot that he had come to the right house.

"Excuse me," he said, "does Mrs Morgan live here?"

She looked him up and down, wondering what he wanted to sell. "She does," she said. "What do you want?"

He hesitated. "It's like this," he said. "I met a man called Flying Officer Morgan in the war, right back in 1943, and I was trying to get in touch with him again. Phillip Morgan, the name was. I went and asked at the Air Ministry and they told me this address."

"I see," she said. "You want my brother Phillip?" She did not seem to be particularly enthusiastic in the matter. She hesitated. "I think you'd better come in," she said at length. She led him into the narrow hall, and showed him into the room on the right, which was the dining room. "If you wouldn't mind waiting a few moments," she said, "I'll go and tell my mother." She hesitated. "What's the name?"

"Turner," he said, "Captain Turner." He had not the slightest right to use his military title, but that never worried him.

She left him, and he stood in the dining room, hat in hand, staring around at the depressing scene. The room was furnished in the most doleful late Victorian style, with heavy mahogany furniture of an uninspiring design. On the walls there were engravings of "The Stag at Bay" and of a lion and of a collie dog with a Scots shepherd, all very genteel. On the black-marble mantelpiece there was a black-marble clock with tarnished gilt pillars, stopped at twenty-three minutes to eleven. On the table was a white linen cloth, slightly soiled, and such tablespoons and cruets as would be needed for the next meal and could be conveniently left on the table. Mr Turner thought nothing of it at all, in comparison with his cheerful little villa at Watford.

"Fair gives you the creeps," he thought. And then, as he waited minute after minute, "I bet something's happened to him that they don't want to talk about. She wasn't a bit keen." The idea stiffened him to go through with the matter.

After a long ten minutes the girl came back. "Would you come upstairs and see my mother?" she said.

He went up with her to the first-floor drawing room usual in such tall old houses. It was furnished in the same Victorian style as the dining room had been, with mahogany furniture and heavy plush curtains. Although the day was warm, all the windows were closed and a small gas fire was burning at the grate. Seated in a chair before this was an invalid lady, not very old, but soured and unpleasant.

The girl said, "This is Captain Turner, Mother, who wants to know about Phillip."

Turner advanced jauntily into the room. He said, "Afternoon, Mrs Morgan. I used to know your son Phillip in the war, and I wanted to get in touch with him again, talk over the old days, and all that, you know."

She said, "Sit down." He sat down in a chair before her, and beamed at her expectantly, his hat upon his knee.

She said, "Did you know my boy well?"

"Not well. We were in hospital together."

"Did you know his wife?"

Mr Turner knew thin ice when he saw it. "I never met her," he said carefully. "From what he told me, she was a very lovely girl."

She said vehemently, "He was a fool—oh, such a fool. But then, men are. They never know when they're well off. Always running after someone new—even the lowest of the low, Captain Turner, even the lowest of the low. Joyce was very patient with him—nobody could have had a more *angelic* wife, perfectly *angelic*. But you can't expect a girl like that to wait forever. She has her pride, you know."

"I suppose so," said Mr Turner vaguely. "Can I get in touch with him? I'd kind of like to see him again."

"If you met him now, after having held the King's commission with him, you would be very disappointed, Captain Turner. A mother has a right to speak frankly about her son; you would be very disappointed that an officer and a gentleman could have fallen so low."

The girl said, "Mother, don't excite yourself."

The invalid said, "No." And then there was a long silence. Mr Turner said, "Is he in London?"

His mother raised her head. "He is abroad, in Burma somewhere, I believe. We do not correspond with him. If I were you, I should forget about him, Captain Turner. My son has not had a very satisfactory life."

He said, "I see." If Morgan was in Burma there was not much point in going on with this. He said, "Well, I'm sorry to have troubled you, Mrs Morgan. I just kind of thought if he was around about we might have got together for a glass of beer or something."

She said, "My son came home for a fortnight only, in 1945, and then went back to the East again. I am sorry that I cannot give you better news of him, but there it is."

"Oh well, can't be helped," said Mr Turner. He got to his feet. "Sorry I troubled you, but it was just a thought I had, that he might have been about somewhere."

He went downstairs escorted by the girl, leaving the invalid mother sitting over the gas fire in the sunlit room. As the girl opened the front door, he was glad to see the light and breathe fresh air after the close confinement of the house.

On the front steps he turned to the girl. He was out of the house now, and had no further need for courtesy. "What did he do?" he asked bluntly.

The girl hesitated, and then said, "He left his wife, Captain Turner. I'm sorry to have to tell you this, but you'd better know about it, in case you ever meet him. He just walked out, and left her, and went back to Burma."

"He did?" said Turner. His first reaction was that Morgan had shown more pluck and initiative than he would quite have expected. "Well, these things happen to people," he said. "Sometimes there are faults on both sides."

She said quickly, "Oh, do you think that? Did you ever meet her?"

"I never did," he said. "He showed me her photograph and he talked a lot about her in the hospital. I saw her once in a play, but only on the stage."

She said, "It's so difficult to find out things, living alone here, like we do. What did you think of her, Captain Turner?"

He was well out in the street by that time; after the constrained atmosphere of the house it was pleasant to speak freely in the clean, fresh air. "I thought she was the most bloody awful bitch God ever made," he said. "She was giving him the hell of a time, though he wouldn't admit it. He must have been crazy ever to have married her."

She stared at him, dumbfounded. "You don't think that?"

"I do think that, and a lot more," he said.

She said, "But she was always so sweet with Mother."

"I dare say." He thought for a moment. "Did your mother give her any money?" he enquired.

She stared at him. "However did you know about that? You've been talking to her, Captain Turner."

"Never met her in my life," he said, "and I don't want to, either."

They stood in silence for a moment. "I'll walk down to the end of the street with you," she said at last. They turned and walked along the pavement together. Presently she said, "You could write to my brother, if you want to, Captain

77

Turner. He writes to me sometimes, and I write back. I don't tell my mother, unless there's anything very important, and that's not often. It only upsets her."

He stopped on the pavement in the sunlit street and got out his notebook and pencil. "Where is he?" he asked.

"He's living at a place called Mandinaung," she said. "The address is Mandinaung, Irrawaddy, Burma. If you write a letter there, it will get to him all right."

He replaced the notebook. "I got that," he said. "You never know—I might be out there one day, and look him up." For the moment he had forgotten that his future was not long.

She said, "Oh." They walked in silence for a few paces. "In that case, I think I ought to tell you something, Captain Turner. My brother—" she stuck for a moment, and then said, "—my brother's living in rather a poor way, from what we can make out. He lives entirely with the natives, in this native village, Mandinaung. He is living with a native woman in a small palm shack, and he has two children by her. It practically broke my mother's heart when we heard that."

Mr Turner said quietly, "That's a bad one," and walked on in silence for a moment. This, then, was what happened to R.A.F. pilots who could do nothing but fly aeroplanes. They drifted to the East and sank to living with the natives, and were lost, submerged in the vast sea of colour. A word occurred to him. "Beachcombers," he thought. "That's what he'd be, a beachcomber."

At the corner of the street she stopped and held out her hand. "I'll say good-bye," she said. "Let me know if you hear anything of Phillip, will you? But don't write to my mother, write to me." She paused, and then she said, "We were good friends, when we were children, and we are still, even after this." She sighed. "Poor Phillip—he always made a mess of things if it were possible to do so!"

Mr Turner went back to his home at Watford by underground, for tea. He got there at about five o'clock, tired and depressed. Surprisingly, his wife was there and tea was laid for him.

"I thought that maybe you'd be back," she said. "I'll put the kettle on—it won't be long." She paused, and then she said, "I got a kipper, if you'd like it."

Kippers were his favourite delicacy; in his fatigue and his depression he felt that he could fancy a nice kipper. She cooked him two, and he ate them, and a slice of bread and jam, and two pieces of cherry cake, and drank three cups of tea, and felt a great deal better for it.

It was not his habit to discuss with his wife what he had been doing during the day; it was a long time since they had been on such terms as that. While she gathered up the tea things and began washing up, he took a chair out in the garden and sat looking at the flowers and smoking, thinking intermittently of what he wanted to do.

He was rather shocked at what he had heard of Phillip Morgan. He had fully anticipated that the boy would not make a success of life, that he would drift into some little dead-end job at four or five pounds a week; so much he was prepared for. He was not prepared to hear that he had gone completely native in a Burmese village, and he was distressed to hear it. Poverty in England in a little trivial job was one thing. Poverty in the Far East was quite another.

He stared at the flowers, and smoked cigarette after cigarette. This was what he had suspected, this was what he had set out to find. Of all the three who were in hospital with him in Penzance, Phillip Morgan had seemed least fitted for the battle of life. He had wanted to find out about him in these last months of activity ahead, in order that he might help if help should be required. Help was required all right— the boy would get no help from his mother or his wife, and very little from his sister. There was some sort of job to be done there—Mr Turner did not quite know what. The only thing was, Burma was such a hell of a long way away.

His wife came out to him presently, and brought another chair with her, and set it up beside him. "I went to the Commercial College and found out about courses," she said quietly. "I could do six weeks' shorthand and typing, and brush up the bookkeeping as well, for ten guineas. That's mornings and afternoons too. The only thing is," she said, "if I did that, I couldn't get you dinner in the middle of the day."

"I shan't want that," he said. "I should get on with it while we've still got the salary coming in. Maybe after that you could get a job half time, kind of keep your hand in."

"I believe I could do that," she said thoughtfully. "Mornings only. It'd make a bit more, too."

She turned to him. "I been thinking about this," she said. "Don't you think you ought to see another doctor, or something? I mean, surely they can do something."

He shook his head. "I wouldn't think that way," he said. "I mean, you can go on messing and messing about, and it don't do no good. They done as well as anybody could for

79

me. I've had it, and that's all about it. I don't want to go on arguing."

She said, "Did you tell them at the office?"

He told her what had happened. "I got a month's leave now," he said. "After that, I suppose I go back to work, and then go on till I have to start and take sick leave. After that, I got six months on pay, and then finish."

She said, "There'd be a war pension, or something."

"So there would," he said. "I better get Dr Worth to write a letter to the Board. Maybe you'll get something out of it as well. I better see him in the morning."

They sat together on the deck chairs in the narrow little strip of garden, and presently he was telling her about Phillip Morgan. "Well, that's the way of it," he said heavily at last. "He's made a bloody muck o' things, the way I knew he would. If he was in England I'd do what I could to see him, 'n see if one could help. But out in Burma one can't do that."

She said quietly, "Why not?"

"Too bloody far away," he said impatiently.

"I don't see that," she said. "You can fly out ever so quick, they say. Three or four days it is."

He stared at her. "You mean, fly out to Burma?"

"That's right," she said. "I don't see why you shouldn't, if you want to go."

He said ironically, "Don't talk so soft. What d'you think it'd cost?"

"I dunno, Jackie," she said quietly. "But you've got the money."

There was a long silence. It was true, he had enough money for anything that he was likely to require in his lifetime, though what he spent now would mean the less for her when he was dead. Actually, he had the time, too; he had a month's holiday to run before he had to go back to the office. It was possible to go to Burma if he wanted to, and as the thought occurred to him he knew that he wanted to go very badly.

His wife spoke again. "Look at it this way," she said. "I been thinking about things a lot. We neither of us had much fun since we got married, with the war and that. Well, I've got all my time to go, but you've only got a year, or maybe less than that. After you're dead, if that must happen, I'd not like to think you never had no fun at all, travelling and seeing places and that. Why don't you take a trip out there, and see if you can find him, Jackie? It's what you're interested in, and it won't cost all that."

"Me go to Burma?" he said thoughtfully.

"That's right."

"Well, I dunno," he said.

There was another silence. He became resolved that he would go on this trip. Whether he found Phillip Morgan or not, whether he could do anything for him if he did find him without encroaching further on the little store of money he could leave his wife, did not weigh greatly with Turner. He wanted to seize this opportunity to leave the office, and leave Watford, and go off to see new places, meet new people, and to sort out his ideas. Abruptly, he was very conscious of the generosity of Mollie in making this suggestion.

"If I was to go," he said, "would you come, too?"

She shook her head. "I did think of that," she said. "But I'd as soon stay here. I got to brush up at the College, 'n it'd all cost more. I'd like us to have a holiday together sometime—Devonshire or something. But Burma's too far off."

"Be a bit lonely for you, staying on here all alone," he said.

"I dunno," she replied. "I might go and stay with Laura for a bit. She wants help, with the baby coming and all that."

"Well," he said, "it all wants a bit of thinking about." He searched his mind for something he could do for her to match her generosity in some small measure. "Like to go to the pictures tonight?" he said. "I see there's Cary Grant on at the Regal."

Four days later he left Poole on the flying boat for Rangoon.

CHAPTER FIVE

MR TURNER enjoyed his journey in the flying boat. For practically the first time in his life comfort wrapped him round, so that it was unnecessary for him to do anything but read and rest. All day the aircraft droned on across the mountains, the deserts, and the seas. He read a little, slept a little, ate a lot, and looked out of the window at the slowly moving panorama of the world. The journey did him a great deal of good; the great wound in his forehead ceased to trouble him with its throbbing, and though he sweated profusely each time they landed, he reached Rangoon rested and refreshed.

He had not come empty-handed. He brought with him from England a few small packages of Crispy Wheaties, a breakfast cereal that his organisation was marketing in a big way, and he brought some samples of an older product, Mornmeal, which was full of vitamins and roughage. With these gifts from the West to the Far East he landed in Rangoon early in August in monsoon weather, and went to the hotel on the Strand.

He was adaptable, and though the climate in that month was trying, with alternate rain and sun, he did not find it insupportable by any means. He had bought ready-made clothing from a tropical outfitter in London, and his suits were adequate. He was a man accustomed to fending for himself and finding his own way around; the Eastern atmosphere did not impede him. He behaved in Rangoon exactly as he would have done in Manchester, and he got along quite well.

He had an introduction to the agent for his firm, a Mr S. O. Chang; he rang him up from his hotel bedroom on the first morning, and within half an hour Mr Chang was sitting with him in the hotel lounge. Mr Chang was a Chinaman, and he had represented Cereal Products Ltd. for some years in Rangoon. In Rangoon Mr Chang had a finger in every pie that would accept his finger; he was always up to something. His interests ranged from upholstery materials for railway carriages to foundation creams for ladies, from cast-iron sluices suitable for septic tanks to breakfast cereal from England. He lived modestly in a small house up towards the jail behind the Chinese quarter; he may or may not have been wealthy, but he knew everybody in Rangoon.

They talked cereals for an hour or so. "I come out here on sort of personal business, you might say," said Mr Turner. "Mr Anderson, he'll be along to see you in March. But as I was coming here, Mr Sumner said to stop and have a chat with you, and show you these."

Mr Chang beamed. "Mr Anderson, he very welcome in Rangoon. My wife, she always ask when Mr Anderson coming. My son Hsu, he asks always also, when Mr Anderson coming. Very nice man, Mr Anderson."

"Aye," said Mr Turner, "he's a proper card. Tells a good story, don't he?"

"Oh yes. Mr Anderson, he very funny man. My wife laugh

and laugh." He explained. "My wife does not know English, so I translate stories for her. She laugh very much."

Mr Turner split open one of the little sample packets of Crispy Wheaties on the table, and put two or three flakes in his mouth. "Say, tell me what you think o' these, Mr Chang. I kind of like them myself, so does my wife. Sort of malty flavour, isn't it? They're going very well at home. We'll have nearly half our whole production on these by next year."

An hour later they were finished for the time being. "There's just one other thing," said Mr Turner. "I got a friend out here somewhere, chap I used to know back in England in the war, in 1943. I don't know what he's doing, but he lives in a place called Mandinaung. Mandinaung, Irrawaddy, that's the address. Is that far from here?"

Mr Chang said, "Mandinaung is large village on the Irrawaddy River. It is about hundred, hundred and ten miles. You go by river, past Yandoon. Take two days now in the steamer, because river running very fast. One day to come back. You want to go and see your friend?"

Mr Turner hesitated. "Is it easy to get there?"

"Very easy. Steamer all the way, twice each week, Monday, Thursday, all the way up to Henzada. Next Thursday is next steamer. You arrive Mandinaung Friday afternoon." He looked up at Mr Turner. "I book passage for you—leave to me. You go Thursday?"

"Hold on a minute." He had no objection to Mr Chang earning his commission on the passage, but he did not want to be rushed. "This chap doesn't know I'm coming, and I don't know how he's living. Would it be possible to find out anything about him—what he does, or anything?"

"Sure," said Mr Chang. "I have good friend who do business in Mandinaung—cheroots. Mandinaung cheroots very good, good as Danubyu. You like cheroots, Burma cheroots?"

"I wish you'd find out something about this chap," said Mr Turner. "Phillip Morgan, his name is. I'd like to know what he's doing, how he's living, you know, before I write to him or go up there."

"I find out for you," said Mr Chang. "I ask my friend, he go there every month. Phillip Morgan. I find out for you."

He insisted that Mr Turner should dine with him the following evening at his home, and would take no refusal. They arranged that he should fetch Mr Turner from the hotel at half-past six, and then he went away. Turner sat down and wrote a cable to his wife in Watford to tell her of his safe arrival, and then, most unusual, he sat down and wrote her a long letter. He was not very good at writing, and much of his letter was concerned with a description of the plot of the detective story he had read in the aircraft on the way out; but it pleased her when she got it.

He went out presently and walked along the streets at a very slow pace, keeping well in the shade. He bought a solar topee for twice its value in a Chinese shop, and he bought a guidebook for three times its English price from a very black Chittagonian who kept a stall, and he bought a bunch of bananas in the fruit market for almost its proper price, because he smiled and was friendly to the young Burmese woman who sold them. Then he was tired, and his head was beginning to throb; so he went back to his hotel and lay down on his bed to read the guidebook. Presently he went to sleep, and when he woke up, it was afternoon. He got up and had a shower and ate some of the bananas, and went down and had a cup of tea in the hotel lounge. He spent the evening sitting in a long chair in the shade, watching the native life of the city as it moved by in the street.

Next day he went to the great shrine that dominates the city, the Shwe Dagon, and walked around the pagoda in his stockinged feet, mystified at the profusion of strange images.

That evening Mr Chang came in a very decrepit old open motor car to fetch him to dine. They bounced erratically along to the other end of the town, with Mr Chang clinging to the wheel in grim concentration and changing the worn gears with more ferocity than skill.

Mr Chang lived in a small suburban house, that stood in a garden that was unkempt, by Mr Turner's Watfor standards. It was suffering from the peculiarity that it had few walls, and those were constructed only of Venetian blind material. Outside, the jungle rats, that Mr Turner knew as squirrels, played in the trees, and sometimes came into the rooms.

In the main living room there was a long table; one end was laid with a white cloth for the meal; on the other end was a jumble of well-worn Mah Jongg ivories. Mrs Chang came forward to meet them, a little woman, with a wide, smiling face. She was dressed in sandals, black satin trousers, and a very beautifully embroidered white silk shirt that reached down almost to the knees. She said something, smiling.

"My wife speaks no English," said Mr Chang. "She very pleased you come to our house."

Mr Turner, in the course of a varied business life, had

84

acquired some experience with wives who could speak no English. He had no knowledge of any language but his own, but he had made himself pleasant in the past to French wives, German wives, Dutch wives, Polish wives, Hungarian wives, and many others; a Chinese wife presented him with no problem. He worked on the theory that all foreign wives were exactly and precisely similar to English wives, and that if you got someone to translate exactly what you would have said in Watford it worked out all right. Certainly he had always given satisfaction. Within ten minutes Mrs Chang had produced her seven-year-old son and five-year-old daughter and Mr Turner was playing "Paper wraps stone, scissors cuts paper" with the little boy.

Dinner came presently, served by a Chinese Burman girl; a curry which Mrs Chang ate with her fingers, Mr Chang with chopsticks, and Mr Turner with a spoon and fork. Mr Chang produced a bottle of rice spirit flavoured with burnt sugar, which he called Black Cat whiskey; in support of that statement he showed the black cat on the label. A glass of this set Mr Turner's head throbbing and buzzing; he refused another with some difficulty, and told them all about his head wound. Then Mrs Chang told him all about her operation for appendicitis, Mr Chang translating, so that by the end of the meal they might have been nextdoor neighbours in Watford.

The brown girl came and cleared the table, and Mr Chang produced a large paper packet of cheroots. They were very black, and Mr Turner took one with some apprehension; unexpectedly it turned out very mild.

"You like my cheroots?" asked Mr Chang.

"Aye," said Mr Turner with appreciation. "Makes a nice smoke."

"From Mandinaung, where your friend lives. Mandinaung cheroot."

"It's very nice," said Mr Turner. "Did you find out anything about Phillip Morgan?"

"Oh yes, I find out for you. Mr Morgan very important man in Mandinaung. He just made Sub-divisional Officer."

Mr Turner stared at him in astonishment. "What's that —Sub-divisional Officer? What does that mean?"

Mr Chang said, "Sub-divisional Officer, he is Government official. Like Judge and Tax Collector and Registrar. Mr Morgan is Sub-divisional Officer for five villages, but he live in Mandinaung."

Turner said, bewildered, "I thought he was quite poor."

Mr Chang smiled tolerantly. "Oh no, Mr Morgan never poor. Mr Morgan, he is owner of three motor boats, trade up and down the Irrawaddy, carry passengers and goods. Now he sold those boats, and now he is Sub-divisional Officer."

Mr Turner stared at the Chinaman. "Is he a well-known man, then?"

"Oh yes—Mr Morgan very well known in the Irrawaddy; people like him very much. He marry nice girl, Ma Nay Htohn daughter to Maung Shway Than. Maung Shway Than is important man in Rangoon. His brother, Nga Myah, is Minister for Education in the Burma Government. All very good people."

"Well, I'm damned," said Mr Turner. He sat in silence for a minute, trying to re-adjust his ideas. "This girl he married," he said presently, "—Ma something, you said—is she a native? I mean, a Burmese girl?"

"Oh yes," said Mr Chang. "Ma Nay Htohn educated at Rangoon High School; she speak very good English. Very nice girl, very clever. She have two children now, one boy, one girl. They very happy."

Mr Turner said mechanically, "That's fine," and sat trying to think out what this meant to him. It was not in the least what he had been led to expect.

Mr Chang went on to add to his information. "Ma Nay Htohn has brother, colonel in the Burma Army, Burma Independence Army in the war. His name, Utt Nee. Utt Nee, he fight against the British in 1942 to make Burma independent. Later he fight against the Japanese also to make Burma independent, but he fight more against Japanese than against the British. He very important man also, colonel in the Burma Army."

He grinned at Turner. "You want to go up river to Mandinaung to see your friend? I arrange it for you, very easy."

Mr Turner said slowly, "Yes, I think I do want to go. I'd better write him a letter first, though. How long does a letter take to get there?"

"One week to get answer. Why not send telegram?"

"Can one send telegrams to Mandinaung?"

"Oh yes, I go to Danubyu, and then boy run with the message. You get answer same day. I send it for you."

Mr Turner said, "Got a piece of paper?"

He thought for a moment, and then wrote:

86

MORGAN, MANDINAUNG, IRRAWADDY. WE MET IN HOSPITAL PENZANCE 1943 STOP I AM NOW IN RANGOON WEEK OR TWO ON BUSINESS AND WOULD LIKE SEE YOU AGAIN STOP CAN WE MEET EITHER RANGOON OR MANDINAUNG. TURNER, STRAND HOTEL, RANGOON.

He got an answer the next day at his hotel:

SORRY CANNOT GET DOWN TO RANGOON BUT GLAD TO PUT YOU UP HERE FOR A FEW DAYS IF YOU CAN SPARE THE TIME STOP DELIGHTED HEAR FROM YOU AGAIN. MORGAN.

Mr Turner stood looking at this thoughtfully, in front of the mirror in his bedroom. "Made a bloody fool of yourself," he said to his reflection. "Come all this way for nothing. He don't want your help."

He hesitated, half minded to abandon the adventure and go downstairs and book a passage back to England on the next aircraft. This young man that he had thought of as a beachcomber was a government official, and one with very good connections in the country. Out here, where white faces were few, the fact that he was married to a Burmese girl did not seem quite so shattering as it had seemed in England; Mr Turner had already seen a number of girls in the street that he would not have minded being married to, himself.

"Might as well go straight back home," he said disconsolately. "He's all right."

He did not go. The fascination of a strange scene was upon him; he had never been to the East before, and though the purpose that had brought him there was obviously void, he might as well see everything there was to see before going home. He had said nothing to anybody, fortunately, of his desire to help Phillip Morgan make his life anew; he had described himself as on a business trip, and he could stick to that story. This journey up the river to this Burmese village would be interesting, an out-of-the-way adventure, something to tell Mollie about when he got back to Watford, something to tell buyers from the Provinces when he lunched with them at the Strand Palace Hotel. He decided that he would go, and spent some time in thinking up corroborative lies about his business in Rangoon to tell to Morgan if he showed much interest in his presence in Burma.

He set out for Mandinaung the following morning on the paddle steamer. He travelled in some comfort in a cabin with a good electric fan, and he enjoyed every minute of the journey. The Irrawaddy delta is a smiling, fertile country of tall trees and rich farm land. Between the showers of rain Mr Turner sat in a deck chair on the upper deck of the steamer, watching the dugouts and sampans on the river, the women decorously bathing with two longyis wrapped about them, the domestic life in villages and bamboo houses that they passed, the monkeys playing in the trees. Each minute of the day was an interest and an amusement to him, and though he was still worried that he had come on a fool's errand, he was glad that he had come.

The steamer reached a fair-sized town called Yandoon in the evening, and berthed there for the night. Mr Turner went on shore and walked a little through the lines of bamboo and mat houses, wondering at everything he saw. He had thought that women in all Eastern countries lived in purdah and seclusion, but here the girls walked around in pairs, chi-hiking with the young men just as they did at home. He found a well that seemed to be a social centre and sat watching for a long time a very merry scene as girls and women came down for the water and the young men drew it for them. From time to time he saw a monk in bare feet and a heavy robe of a coarse yellow cloth, and wondered. He went back to the ship to dinner, rather thoughtful. There was in Yandoon an atmosphere of business, good humour, and a pleasant life that was different from his English conception of a native town.

He got to Mandinaung next day in the late afternoon. There was a little rickety bamboo jetty for the steamer to berth against, and on this jetty a white man was standing with a Burmese girl by his side, and a few natives behind. As they drew near, he saw that the man was Morgan, but a different Morgan from the one he had known in 1943 in hospital. This was an older man, who had an air of authority about him. He was very tanned. He wore an old bush hat, with a khaki shirt and faded shorts of jungle green; he had sandals on his feet. Up on the bank above the jetty an old jeep was parked, presumably his property.

The girl standing with him wore a flat, slightly conical straw sun hat, a white blouse, a green longyi wrapped around her waist and falling to her feet, and sandals. She was a pale, yellowish brown colour; she had a broad face and straight black hair which she parted in the middle and wore made up in a knot at the back of her head, usually with a flower in it for ornament. When Mr Turner came to study her at closer range, he found that she used lipstick and nail varnish like the girls in Watford, and, like them, made up her cheeks with a faint colour. Later still, he found she did it with the same brands of cosmetic that English girls used.

A native boy carried his suitcase off the boat behind him, and he went down the gangplank to meet Morgan. "I took you at your word," he said. "Seemed a shame we shouldn't meet again, being so close and all."

"I'm jolly glad you came," said Morgan. "We don't see very many people out from England, up the river here. Turner, this is my wife, Ma Nay Htohn."

Mr Turner raised his hat formally. "I'm very pleased to meet you, Mrs. Morgan."

She smiled, and then laughed a little. "Not Mrs Morgan," she said, "I am Ma Nay Htohn. We do not change our names in Burma after marriage, as you do in England. I am still Ma Nay Htohn unless we go to live in England ever. Then I suppose I shall have to be Mrs Morgan." She held out her hand. "I am very glad that you could spare the time to come and see us."

She spoke English with a lilting accent, but her choice of words was perfect.

Mr Turner was confused. "Ever so sorry," he said. "I got a bit to learn about the way you do things out here."

The girl said, laughing, "I will teach you. I hope you will be able to stay for a long time here with us."

"Just a day or two." He turned to Morgan. "You've not changed a lot."

The other studied him. "I doubt if I'd have know you again," he said. "You were all bandaged up, at the time I left the hospital. How long did you stay on after me?"

" 'Bout a month," said Mr Turner. "Bloody fed up with it, I was—just lying there day after day. After you went there was no one but the nigger to talk to."

Morgan said quietly, "I remember. How did you get on with him?"

Mr Turner said, "Well, I got on with him all right. Better 'n you'd think. We used to play a lot of draughts together, I remember. Checkers, he called it."

They turned and walked up to the jeep and got into it together with the luggage. Morgan drove along a dirt road on the track that overlooked the river, out of the village. They did not drive far. A quarter of a mile from the last bamboo house they turned the corner of a wood and came upon a clearing with a mown lawn on which stood a flagstaff; from this staff there floated a blue ensign with a peacock in the fly.

Behind the lawn there was a pleasant wooden house of two stories, with a verandah and a red-tiled roof of many gables. It stood on the river bank at a great bend, with a view over the stream nearly a mile wide.

"This is where we live," said Morgan.

"Nice place," said Mr Turner, very much impressed.

Morgan said, "We only got it built last year. You should have seen what we were living in before."

Nay Htohn rippled into laughter. "We use our old home for a garage," she said. "Show it to him, Phillip."

"All right." He stopped the jeep before the steps that led up to the verandah of the house and gave the suitcase to a manservant in a long white coat, who came out to meet them; then they drove on around the house to a small bashah made of bamboo, palm-leaf matting, and palm thatch. It stood looking out over the river in a pleasant place, but it was old now, and beginning to decay. Morgan drove the jeep into what had once been the main room, and they got out.

"This is where we used to live," he said.

Mr Turner did not know quite what to say. "Sort of country cottage," he ventured.

"That's right," said Morgan. "This was the living room, and this was the bedroom. The kitchen was that other one." He pointed to another decrepit bashah close beside. He stared around. "We lived here for two years," he said. "It wasn't bad."

The girl said softly, "We were very happy here."

Mr Turner looked around him. The place had a bare floor of trampled earth; there was a trench outside, dug around to catch the monsoon rain. He glanced into the bedroom; the bed was a platform of thin, springy bamboo slats. There were no doors, no ceiling, no glass in the windows, no amenity of any kind.

He smiled, puzzled by the contrast between the new house and the old. "Sort of rough, living here," he said warily.

Morgan said, "It was rough all right."

Nay Htohn said, "It was as we wanted it to be. My father, when we married, wanted to build us a good house. But Mandinaung itself was so much ruined that we did not want to live like that. It would not have been right."

Comprehension was beginning to dawn on Mr Turner. "What ruined it?" he asked.

Morgan said, "We did it a bit of no good one day with the Thunderbolts and Hurribombers, early in 1945, when we were coming down this way. It was a Jap headquarters. These places burn like fun, you know—there wasn't much left of the town when we'd done with it."

"I suppose they do burn pretty easy."

"They do that. When I got back here afterwards and we got married, all building materials were in short supply. Well, you see how it was. We didn't kind of fancy building a brand-new slap-up house with all modern conveniences while the rest of the bloody place was flat—especially with my R.A.F. record. So we made do with a bashah for the time." He glanced around. "They're really quite comfortable, these places, but they get old pretty soon. This one's just about had it."

The girl said, "These are very good houses while you can live simply, with just the two of you. Later on, when the babies come, it is more difficult. I was glad when we could build the new house last year, with a bathroom. But I do not regret the years we spent in this small place. And the people liked it, too, when they came to understand the reason why we lived here."

They turned, and walked up to the house. They passed through the garden, a few beds full of flowering azaleas, and strange flowers that Mr Turner did not recognize, and that he learned later were orchids. He was diffident about asking questions. They moved in a scent of flowers, brought out by the rain; beside them the azaleas and the orchids, beyond those the mimosa and the great orange and red glory of a flame tree. Mr Turner walked through these wonders in a daze.

"When did you leave England?" Morgan asked.

"Only last week—I come out by air."

The girl walking between them said, "Has Rita Hayworth made a new film, after 'My Gal Sal'?" She laughed. "I am a terrible fan."

Mr Turner scratched his head. "I dunno," he said. "I don't go much, myself. You want to ask my wife; she's always going to the pictures." He glanced at the pale brown girl beside him curiously. "Where do you go to see a film out here?"

"Sometimes they are shown in Danubyu," she said. "But every two or three months we go down to Rangoon for a few days, while Phillip does business." She laughed. "Then I am in the picture house all the time."

Mr Turner said, "Cary Grant made a good one that I saw just before I come out," and he told her about it.

They went up the steps on to the wide, shady verandah and into the house. There was a hall with rooms that opened out of it; the hall itself seemed to be the living room, and there was a table laid with afternoon tea, and long cane chairs with leg extensions.

Presently they were sitting down to tea. A large white cat walked slowly into the room from the verandah and walked straight to Mr Turner, as he lay in the cane chair, and jumped up on to his lap.

Mr Turner said, "Hullo, puss," and stroked its ear. Then he noticed Morgan and Nay Htohn staring at it.

"Well, I'm damned," said Morgan. "Never saw it do that before. You're honoured, old boy."

The cat stood, kneading, on his stomach for a moment, then settled down and began to purr. In that tropic heat its presence was uncomfortable, but Mr Turner liked a cat and was prepared to put up with it for a time. "Took a fancy to me," he said.

The girl said something softly to Morgan in Burmese. He smiled at her gently, and said a word or two in the same language.

"What's his name?" asked Turner.

Morgan glanced at the girl; she nodded slightly. "I don't call him anything," he said. "Nay Htohn calls him Maung Payah." He hesitated for a moment. "That means, Your Reverence."

"Strewth," said Turner, comfortably. "What a name to call him!"

"As a matter of fact, you're very much honoured," said Morgan. "He's a most unfriendly cat in the normal way. Won't have anything to do with me or Nay Htohn. Catches a lot of rats, though."

He turned the subject. "How did you get to know I was out here?" he asked.

It was a question that Mr Turner had some difficulty in answering; the lie, when it came, was not very convincing. "I kind of wondered what had happened to you," he said. "Then one day I met a chap in the Air Ministry who said he could find out easy—put his girl on to look up in the records. Well, he did that, 'n wrote and told me you were out in Burma, 'n give me your last address, Ladbroke Square. Well, I didn't think no more about it—stuck the letter in the file and forgot about it till the question of this trip come up at the office. Then I got to thinking if there was anybody that I knew out here, and looked out the letter. And I went 'n had a talk with your mother and sister. Week before last, that was."

The meal was over, and they were smoking. Nay Htohn got up and went into an inner room, to the sound of children. Morgan said, "Let's go and sit out on the verandah. It's cooler there."

They went out, and pulled other long cane chairs together, and reclined, smoking and looking out over the wide river. There was still sunshine, and it was very hot; on the far side of the river over in the direction of the Pegu Yoma thunderheads were massing for another storm.

Morgan said, "How was my mother?"

"She didn't seem very well to me," said Mr Turner. "'Course, I don't know her. Sort of invalid, is she?"

"Yes." Morgan hesitated, and then said, "I suppose she didn't give you a very good account of me."

Mr Turner was silent for a moment. "Seems kind of different out here to what it did in Ladbroke Square," he said at last. "What she said was right enough, but it had got a twist, if you get me. Not like things really are."

The other said quietly, "I know. I've tried to make her see it, but it's no damn good. We don't write much now. I had to make a choice between England and Burma, and—well, I chose Burma." He paused, and then he said, "England wasn't very kind to me, you know."

"How did you come to get out here?" asked Mr Turner. "I mean, settled in like this, and knowing everyone?"

Morgan said, "I'll tell you."

When he left the hospital at Penzance he went up to London to that lovely girl, his wife. She flew into his arms directly he opened the door of the little flat in Pont Street, and in her close embrace all doubts slipped away from him. Then they broke away, and she said, "Did you bring my parcel?"

He said, "I'm terribly sorry—I'm afraid it's gone. They've cleared away the wreck and everything."

She said sharply, "But it can't be gone! I mean, it's part of your luggage. It must be somewhere, if you look for it."

"I don't know what to do about it now," he said. "I think it's a write-off."

She said petulantly, "Oh, it can't be. I mean, it had perfume in it, and silk stockings. I *need* stockings. I haven't got a thing to wear."

Thinking to please her, he said, "Those are lovely ones you've got on now. Your legs look wizard in them."

She said, "Oh, those are a pair Bill gave me, but they're *literally* the only ones I've got. You must be able to find that parcel. Can't you write to somebody about it?"

He shifted uneasily. "You aren't allowed to bring that sort of stuff into the country, you know. Makes it a bit difficult."

She said, "Oh, nobody pays any attention to that."

She did not think to ask him how he was, or to explain why she had not been able to get down to Penzance to see him or to answer his letters. She was nice to him in a distracted sort of way, but her mind was utterly engrossed with her theatrical job, and with her clothes, and with the cabarets and night clubs that she went to, usually with Bristow. Flight Lieutenant Bristow had a job at the Air Ministry which kept him in London; Morgan found himself an intruder in a pleasant little friendship. Whenever he went out with Joyce, Bristow was likely to go with them, and they seldom sat at home.

"It was difficult," said Morgan, staring out over the wide river to the dim hills beyond. "You don't know what to do when things get like that. I didn't make a song and dance about it, because I wanted to go on ops and, well, there's always the risk, you know." He paused. "Anyway, Bristow usually paid the bill. I hadn't got nearly enough money for all the things Joyce wanted to do."

He sat silent for a moment. "I suppose I was a bit of a coward," he said. "I was afraid to start a row."

He was posted to an aerodrome near Exeter for ground duties after his leave, still in Transport Command. From there he could get up to London pretty frequently on a week-end pass, and each time he returned from leave distressed and worried. Bristow was very much in evidence, and it was clear to Morgan that his wife went out with Bristow almost every night. They had little secret jokes from which he was excluded, and though the girl was still kind to him, it gradually became clear that she was bored by his visits. Morgan became morose and unhappy, too inexperienced to know what to do about such things, too much tied by the R.A.F. to do very much about it anyway.

In the spring of 1944 he was put back on flying duties and sent for a short conversion course to fly Dakotas. From there he was sent to a Dakota squadron forming up in Yorkshire for supply-dropping duties; while he was there he saw very little of Joyce, who now called herself Bobby Charmaine. In July 1944 the squadron was ordered out to India, and Morgan saw his wife for the last time on his final leave.

It was not very different from his other leaves. He was going out to the war in the Far East; he would be away for three years or so, if he came back at all. His last leave left little impression on his mind but a series of wild parties after the theatre with his wife and Bristow and various officers of the U. S. Air Force—and a series of hangovers next day that lasted till the evening party started up again. During that fortnight he thought he was having a marvellous time and that everything would be all right, and that Joyce would write to him every week while he was away; he had bought her a very expensive fountain pen, and she had promised to use it. Sometimes he wondered if they couldn't do something in the country, like sailing a boat or riding a horse, which might be rather fun, but the theatre intervened, or the hangover. Then the evening party would start up, and he would have a marvellous time all over again.

The squadron left England in August 1944 and flew by night over the French battles to land at Malta in the dawn. From Malta they flew on to Cairo West, from Cairo West to Shaibah in Iraq, from Shaibah to Karachi, from Karachi to Barrackpore in Bengal. They rested at Barrackpore for a fortnight after the flight out, while defects in the aircraft were made good and the crews became acclimatised. Then, as a fully operational unit, they flew down to the dirt airstrip of Cox's Bazaar, a little place on the Bay of Bengal, on the edge of Burma.

From there they began to operate down the coast of Arakan to support the Army battling in the vicinity of Buthidaung. Each Dakota carried a load of four tons for relatively short hauls such as that; they flew in everything the Army needed, from field gun ammunition and petrol to sausages, and hair oil, dropping the loads by parachute from three hundred feet on ground marked out with white cloth strips by the Army, and returning immediately to Cox's for another load. They had more crews than aircraft, and the machines were worked very intensively. It was usual for the same crew to do two or even three trips in one day, flying for as much as twelve hours; then they would have two days of complete rest.

Morgan lived with the rest of his squadron in tents immediately beside the airstrip and the aircraft. There was no shade, of course; the fierce September sun beat down on the tents and on the blazing sand that made the strip. There is surely no place hotter in the tropics than an unpaved airstrip, except perhaps a paved one. At times it was so hot that it was possible to fry an egg on the metal tail plane of the Dakota, and this was about the only recreation the trip provided. From time to time they would take one of the squadron jeeps and drive down to the beach, and bathe in the lukewarm Bay of Bengal from the grey, dirty sand. The water was too warm and sticky to refresh them.

He lived in a continual grit of dust blown up from the surface of the strip as the aircraft took off or ran up engines on test. It got into his food, into his cigarettes and his drink, into his blankets; it formed a gritty mud on his body, with the sweat that poured off him all day. He lived dressed in a bush hat and a dirty jungle suit, which is like a battle-dress made of thin green material. Usually he wore the trousers only, and the top half of his body became tanned deep brown. In three months of this strange life of supply dropping he matured considerably; he grew more self-reliant in this mode of living, stripped down to the elementals of the job.

At the beginning of November Phillip Morgan got a letter from his wife, the first to reach him since he had left England. Thrilled and excited, he carried it off to his tent, and sitting on the charpoy in the sweltering shade, he opened it. It read:

PHILLIP DARLING,

This is going to be a dreadful letter to write and I really don't know how to begin but it's not as if we ever had been married really is it I mean had a home and all that. I know when Jack was killed you were too sweet in looking after me and of course he *wanted* it and so we simply had to and it's been marvellous and I'll never regret one minute of it will you?

Well now I've found somebody at last who can provide for me properly just what Jack would always have wanted for me it seems *too terrible* that he couldn't have been there first of all but that's the way things happen isn't it?

I wonder if you can guess who it is? Jack Bristow isn't it funny that his name should be Jack too it came on me like a thunderclap the other morning that this was what my first Jack would have wanted for me and of course I thought of you at once and my dear I was *miserable* and Jack and I talked it over last night when he came round after the show and he said I must write and tell you my dear I felt terrible I couldn't sleep. I asked him again this morning and he said I must and if I didn't he'd never see me again so I said I would and he said I ought to ask you to give me evidence a hotel bill or something so that I can divorce you and get the whole thing straight and then we can be married.

I feel this is a stinking mess but it's the only way I expect you can fix up something in Calcutta or something much better get it all settled up before you come home only please be quick because Jack has only another two months at the Air Ministry and it's horrible being sort of neither one thing nor the other in spite of it having been all a mistake to start with hasn't it? I do hope we'll be frightfully good friends for dear old Jack's sake.

Ever your loving,

BOBBY

Phillip Morgan sat for an hour in the sweltering tent turning this *cri du coeur* over and over in his hands. He sat on the charpoy, naked to the waist; the tears made little streaks in the damp mud of dust on his cheeks and mingled with the stream of sweat from his temples, and ran down his neck and into the sweat beads on his chest, and were lost in the steady stream that ran down his body. At the end of the hour he lit a cigarette with hands that trembled a little. Then Flying Officer Scott, who shared his tent, came in from a trip over the mountains into northern Burma, and Morgan showed him the letter, dumbly. Scott had the best part of a bottle of Indian gin, and sympathy, and he gave both to Morgan, and a bottle of the Wing Commander's beer ration. Presently the sharp pain eased to a dull ache, another ache among the many aches and pains and itches that made up life on the airstrip of Cox's Bazaar.

There was, of course, nothing that he could do about the question of divorce. There were only five European women, nurses, in the district at that time, and about seventy thousand men, and there were no hotels to provide him with a bill even if there had been any women. He was too far from England, and too much strained and occupied with war to do anything about it. He did not answer the letter. He stopped writing home. He sank into an apathy of heat and dust and sweat, and joined the morose ten per cent of men in South East Asia Command whose wives had let them down.

He had one relaxation for his long hours of leisure that was denied to the other pilots of his squadron. Along the strip there was a squadron of Spitfires commanded by a squadron leader who had served with Morgan in Africa. These Spitfires operated on long-range tanks right down into the south of Burma, bombing a little, dropping parachute supplies a little, shooting up a lot. Morgan had done two tours in Spitfires, and in times of little pressure he could borrow a machine and get up into the clean, cool air at ten or fifteen thousand feet in something that would really fly. Once or twice, when one of the Spitfire squadron pilots was sick, he substituted and flew with them on an operational sortie; he did that for the last time on November the 23rd, about a fortnight after he had received the letter from his wife.

The job was at extreme range for the Spitfires, to strafe Japanese river boats and shipping on the Irrawaddy River between Prome and Yandoon.

The accident, when it came, was almost unbelievably stupid. The Spitfire that he flew was old and battered, maintained for six months in the open air in the pouring rain and blazing sun of the airstrip, with only improvised appliances. Everything on it worked after a fashion; nothing worked with the mechanical reliability that Morgan was accustomed to in Spitfires. Still, he was glad of the chance to fly it, and took off with the squadron and flew into Burma. He flew on the belly tank until, not far from Zalun, as he was flying down the Irrawaddy with the squadron at two hundred feet, his engine coughed and spluttered. He zoomed up and turned on the wing tanks, but the engine did not play. Instead, it went on coughing for a little, and then stopped for good.

Phillip Morgan spoke on the radio to the squadron leader. He said: "Orange calling Charlie. Sorry, Pete, but this thing's packing up on me. Out of juice, I think. Looks like I'll have to put it down. I say again, I'll have to put it down." He switched off, and gave all his attention to the landing.

He was then at about a thousand feet, and his propeller had stopped; it stood diagonally across his view; most unusual. There were a few woods below him, the wide river, and a range of paddy fields, small areas separated by earth walls a foot or so in height. There was nothing for it but these paddy fields. He swept around in a great turn in a very flat approach glide with his wheels up for the belly landing, came in across the river, dropped off height with a little flap, and put the Spitfire down in a great smother of dust on the dry fields. She bumped from wall to wall, wrecking herself considerably, and came to rest.

Phillip Morgan was unhurt, and he jumped out with his emergency pack and his revolver in his hand. A quick inspection showed him that the wing tanks were quite dry, not having been filled up before the machine took off. The petrol gauge in the cockpit, however, still showed FULL when switched to the wing tanks.

His situation was a bad one. He was in the middle of a country occupied by the enemy, and he could speak no word of the language. If he had been a hundred miles nearer to Cox's Bazaar, his proper course would have been to stay near the wrecked Spitfire in the hope that an attempt would be made to land a light aeroplane near it, an L-5, to get him away. A quick calculation showed him that the range was too great for an L-5 to reach him. He must depend upon himself entirely if he was not to surrender tamely. He took his pack and his revolver and ran for the nearest wood, three hundred yards across the paddy fields, and reached the shelter of it, and lay down panting.

As he rested, he considered the position. He would at any rate make an attempt to get away and back to Cox's, though he knew that his prospects were not good. Nearly five hundred miles of enemy-held country separated him from the front line, a country lightly held by the Japanese, but a country of mountain and tropical jungle. He had in his emergency pack a good kit of drugs, and rations sufficient for two or three days but nothing like sufficient for a journey such as that. Moreover, the country that he was now in was relatively thickly populated and well farmed; his forced landing must have been observed by many of the natives if not by the Japanese. Still, he would walk on to the west and see what happened; he could not make his situation any worse. He could surrender at any time.

He pressed on westwards through the woods, using a jungle track; he could not have got through the undergrowth. It was early afternoon and very hot; the flies tormented him. He went on for about an hour, covering perhaps three miles, and sank down for a rest in an exhausted sweat. He was so blind with fatigue that he did not notice men creeping up behind him, did not know of their presence till he heard a voice say, "English," and he swung around. There were four Burmans, with rifles in their hands, and fierce, scowling faces. They were not in any uniform.

Dispassionately, Morgan wondered if this was to be the end of it.

He knew from his briefings that these men could be one of several categories. They could be dacoits, who would murder him immediately for his clothes and his revolver. They could be Japanese supporters, who would murder him and take his head and give it to the Japanese as evidence of loyalty, and earn a few rupees by doing so. They could be members of the Burma Independence Army, who had fought against us when the Japanese invaded the country and now were rumoured to be fighting for us. They could be just a pack of frightened farmers, uncertain of what to do for the best. He could not know, and since he could not talk the language, he had no means of learning.

He asked them in English who they were. Either they could not or they would not tell him. They held him covered by their rifles and took his revolver from him, but left him his haversack of rations and emergency kit. Two of them got behind him and prodded him with their rifles, and made signs for him to walk; two went ahead of him in single file. They took him, along the same jungle path, deeper into the country, in the same general direction, westwards.

They marched him for about two hours. He was quite unaccustomed to marching in the tropics, and it was a very hot afternoon. He moved blindly, with sweat pouring down him, utterly exhausted at the end. He lost all sense of the direction of their march; he did not know where they were going to, and did not care.

They walked into a village, in the dusk, a little place of only fifteen or twenty houses. He was bundled at once into what seemed to be the village lock-up, a small hut of very stout bamboos, with no window, and with a rough iron hasp and padlock on the door. He sank down on the floor in exhaustion. After a quarter of an hour, his perceptions returned to him, and he could take some interest in his surroundings. His lock-up stood in the garden or compound of a native house. Between the lock-up and the house there were men camped, and cooking over a wood fire. Presently the door opened and a steaming bowl of boiled rice with a little fish on the top of it was shoved in to him, with an earthenware chatty of water.

An hour later the door was opened again, and he was taken to the house by an armed guard. It was quite dark by that time, and the main room of the house was lit by two hurricane lamps. It was a native house of wooden posts and palm-leaf thatch, with the floor raised about four feet from the ground; but in it there were a table and two chairs. The place was full of young men, all armed with rifles and revolvers or automatic pistols of one sort or another; many of them also wore their dahs, long straight steel blades with clumsy wooden handles.

There was a man seated at the table, a young man, with short cropped hair and a lean brown face, dressed in a longyi and a khaki jacket. On one arm he wore a white brassard with a large five-pointed red star on it. Behind him, on the ground, a young woman sat, cross-legged.

He said in quite good English, "Sit down there." Morgan sat down on the chair before the table; his guards took their places behind him. He looked at the red star and thought, Communist. That had him foxed; there had been nothing about Communists in his briefing. He did not know what that might mean for him.

The man asked him his name and rank, and what aircraft he had been flying. Morgan told him these things freely. By that time, in Burma, the regulations about prisoners giving information to the enemy had been greatly relaxed. Cases had occurred of prisoners who had been tortured by the Japanese to give information which would not have harmed the Allied cause a great deal if it had been disclosed, and who had died bravely and unnecessarily. Now it was assumed that codes and radio wave lengths were all compromised immediately a prisoner was taken, and an organisation had been set up for changing them without delay. Prisoners threatened with torture were allowed to talk.

The man asked, "Where did you fly from?"

Morgan said, "From Cox's Bazaar."

He was asked about his mission, and he told them, to destroy Japanese military shipping on the river.

Then, "How many aeroplanes have the British got at Cox's Bazaar?"

So far, Morgan had seen no sign of any Japanese. He said, "Before I answer that, will you tell me who you are?"

The man said, "Answer the question. How many aeroplanes have the British got at Cox's Bazaar?"

Morgan said, "It varies every day." And then he said, "I want to ask you formally to take me before an officer."

The man said, "You are before one now. I am a captain in the Burma Independence Army, Captain Utt Nee." He paused, and then said, "I have no time to waste. If you do not answer the questions, it will be bad for you."

The pilot said, "I'll do my best, but it's not easy to answer that one. Aircraft move about very quickly. One day there might not be more than fifty on all the airstrips at Cox's. Another day there might be three hundred or more. It varies so."

There was a stir among the men in the room. Utt Nee said, "You are lying, Englishman. You never had three hundred aeroplanes on the whole Burma front."

Morgan said, "I'm not lying at all. I'm counting in the transport machines as well as the first-line aircraft. If you take in all the aerodromes in Bengal, the total of aircraft on

101

this front would be more like three thousand. There's the American Strategic Air Force that's as large as ours." He went on to tell them more about the figures, judging the information to be valuable in making an impression on these Burmans.

They asked about the number of tanks and guns, but although he had some idea of this he professed ignorance; the figures were not so impressive. "I'm in the Royal Air Force," he said. "We see tanks and guns about in parks and on the roads, but I've no idea how many there may be. I'd only be guessing if I told you any numbers."

The man said something in Burmese, and Morgan was taken back to the lock-up. There was no bed or furniture of any kind; clearly he would have to spend the night on the bare earth, and that was not too clean. In the semi-darkness, in the few gleams of light that came in through the bamboo walls from the lighted house, he sat down in a corner, leaning up against the walls, his feet stretched out along the ground, to wait for sleep.

Half an hour later the door opened again, and he got to his feet. His guards were there, but with them was the young Burmese woman whom he had seen sitting on the floor behind Utt Nee. She had two blankets in her arms.

She said in English, "I have brought you some blankets. This is a very poor place, and you will have to sleep on the ground. If you have to stay here another night, my brother will have a bed built up for you."

He said, "I say, that's very nice of you." He took the blankets. "I'll be perfectly all right with these."

"Have you had enough to eat and drink?" she asked.

He said, "I got some rice—I don't want any more to eat. I'd like another jug of water."

She spoke in Burmese to the guards, one of whom went off to get it.

He said, "Tell me, are you people fighting the Japanese?"

"You must ask my brother that," she replied.

He said in wonder, "You speak English very well."

She laughed. "I ought to. I worked for Stevens Brothers in Rangoon for three years. I was Mr James Stevens' personal secretary. Before that I was at Rangoon High School."

He said, "What are they going to do with me?"

"They are talking about that now," she replied. "Probably they will hand you over to the Japanese."

"The British will give you a good reward if I am taken back

102

to them unhurt," he observed. "It's all written in Burmese on a sort of handkerchief in my haversack."

She said a little scornfully, "We know that, Mr Morgan. They will not pay much attention to your ransom money—there are more important things than that which will determine what they do with you."

"I didn't mean to be rude," he said awkwardly.

The guard came back with the chatty. "Here is your water," she said. "Is there anything else you want?"

"I don't think so."

"Good night, then," she said, and went out. The guards locked the door behind her.

Morgan was left standing in the hut with the blankets in his arms, wondering. The girl had spoken to him just like an Englishwoman, though she was indubitably Burmese. She had a lilting accent to her voice; she had a broad, yellowish face, with slanting eyes, and straight black hair done in a knot behind her head. She was dressed in native costume, with bare feet thrust into sandals.

He turned, and made a rough bed of the blankets on the ground and lay down, wrapping himself around as a protection against mosquitoes; and presently he fell asleep.

Next morning he was taken out at dawn and allowed to wash in a bucket of water, and to go to a latrine, and given more rice. An hour later he was taken to the house again. There were fewer people in the room this time. Again Utt Nee, the Burman with the red star on his arm, interrogated him, the girl sitting on the floor behind.

Utt Nee asked, "How many soldiers have the British at Cox's and near by?"

Morgan said, "I don't know—quite a lot. Not many English troops, but a great many I.O.R.s—the Indian Army. I should think there might be three or four divisions."

"You mean forty or fifty thousand men? It will go badly for you if you tell us lies."

"I should think that's about it. I don't know much about the Army, though."

There was a quick interchange of sentences between the men around him in Burmese.

Utt Nee said, "If the British have so many men as that, why do they not attack?"

Morgan said, "They are attacking in the north, and on the Chindwin. Now that the war with Germany is pretty well finished, masses of stuff are coming out here. By the spring we ought to be advancing all over Burma."

103

The Burman eyed him steadily. "What do you mean, the war with Germany is finished?"

Morgan said, "Well, we've got up to the Rhine."

"You mean, the river Rhine? The river between Germany and France?"

There was a buzz of excited conversation in Burmese. They questioned him very intently, seeking to trip him up and make him contradict himself. They produced a small school atlas and made him show them the position of the Rhine and the areas occupied by the British and American forces. Presently the questions ceased, and he sat on almost unnoticed while a debate took place between the men, speaking in Burmese.

Once Utt Nee turned to him, "Do you know Major Williams?"

Morgan shook his head blankly. "Never heard of him."

Presently Utt Nee made a sign to his guards, and they took him out of the room; the debate in Burmese went on hotly behind him. At the door of his lock-up the guards checked; Morgan turned round, and the girl was there.

She said, "Mr. Morgan, I want to ask you a few questions myself."

He said, "Of course."

"First," she said, "I want to warn you to speak nothing but the truth to us. It is important to us that we should know the truth of what is going on outside Burma; we have heard nothing for three years except what the Japanese chose to tell us. It is important to you, also, because if my brother finds that you have told one single lie he will have you killed. He changed his name last year. He is now called Utt Nee, which means the Red Needle. Do you know why he is called that?"

Morgan grinned at her. "Well, I can guess."

She hesitated. "You seem a brave man," she said at last. "I want you to be careful, too, and tell us nothing but the truth."

"A prisoner of war doesn't have to talk at all," said Morgan. "You're a civilised people; you know that. If you mean to kill me if you think I'm telling you lies, I'd better keep my mouth shut."

She was silent for a moment. "I believe you," she said at last. "I think that what you have been telling us is the truth. Some of the men in there"—she indicated the house—"think that you have been telling us a pack of lies to try and save your life."

Morgan said, "I can't help that. I've done my best to answer truthfully, but they asked me a great deal that I don't really know about."

She said, "How soon do you think the English will attack? How quickly will they get down here, into the delta?"

He replied, "I don't know. If I told you anything at all, it would only be my own opinion. If it turned out wrong, you would say that I told you lies and have me killed."

"But we must have something to go on. How else can we tell what to do?"

He paused for a moment, and then said slowly, "Your brother told me that you are the Burma Independence Army. If you're the lot I'm thinking of, you fought against us when the Japanese drove us out of Burma; you killed a great many of our chaps. Some of them were tortured."

She faced him. "That is true," she said firmly. "We fought to make our country free; we have been exploited by you foreigners long enough. I do not know about the tortures, but we fight our wars more bitterly than you do yours. You are kind to all prisoners, no matter how bad and treacherous they are. My people are not so gentle."

The pilot glanced at her. "Are you still fighting with the Japanese against us?"

She said vehemently, "Never again with the Japanese." There was a pause, and then she said, "We are what we say, the Burma Independence Army. You British ruled us simply to make money out of us; you took away our teak and rice and sold them for a high price, and took the money for yourselves. The Japanese promised us independence, so we fought with them to turn the British out." She smiled cynically. "After that we found that the Japanese only meant to turn us into a colony for their own benefit. They took everything, even the sewing machines out of the villages, and sent them to Japan. They pay our coolies in paper money made in a note machine on the pay desk. Our country is ruined, and we are worse off than we have ever been."

Morgan asked curiously, "Would you like to have the British back again?"

There was a long pause. "For myself, I would," the girl said. "We have learned one thing: we are not strong enough to stand alone against great nations. If we have to have foreigners in our country at all, I would like it to be either the British or the Americans, and we know the British better. We have no quarrel with the British people— most Burmans get on very well with most British. But to be

105

governed by your English sahibs who think themselves superior to us simply because of the colour of their skin—that is unbearable. We will not have it any longer. If you try to impose it on us again, we shall murder every Englishman in the country."

Morgan said, "Starting with me."

The girl broke into laughter. The guards looked at her uncertainly, with wrinkled brows; they had not understood one word of this English talk. "It is a long time since we have had an Englishman near enough to kill. Perhaps we shall keep you as a curiosity."

Morgan said keenly, "What about the Japanese? Have your people killed any of them?"

The girl said, "A few. When we hear of a very small patrol in the jungle, my brother leads a force out to surround them; then we kill them all and take their arms. In that way we are getting a few weapons for our secret army."

She glanced up at him. "How long will it be before the British reach here? We must know that."

He rubbed his chin. "I can't tell you," he said. "I don't know. I can only tell you that something will be starting very soon—I think it has already started in the north. When it does begin, it may go very quickly." He paused, considering. "This is November, and the monsoon breaks in June. I doubt if we shall get as far as this before next June—but we might."

"What makes you think that you will advance so quickly?"

He said, "The numbers of aircraft, and guns, ships, and machines. They are simply pouring out here now, now that the war in Europe is coming to an end. Men, too. Look at me. I was in England only four months ago. Now I'm here. And there are hundreds of thousands like me in Bengal."

She said, "Oh . . . you were in England four months ago?"

He said, "That's right."

She said, "How is Mr Churchill? Is he all right? He is a very great man."

Morgan said, "He's all right. He's still Prime Minister."

She thought for a minute. "How is Deanna Durbin? Is she well?"

He blinked, and then said, "I think so. I saw her in a picture not long ago."

She said, "I like her pictures very much, ever since 'One Hundred Men and a Girl.'" She laughed. "And Rita Hayworth—is she all right still?"

He replied, "I saw her in a film called 'Cover Girl,' just

before I left London. She was simply lovely. She dances awfully well now."

The girl sighed. "Here we see nothing but Japanese propaganda films, all about people looking at cherry trees and going away to war to die for the Emperor. They are very dull."

He said, "Never mind. It won't be long now."

She turned to him. "Do you know Major Williams?"

He shook his head. "I'm afraid I don't. Who is he?"

She said, "You are quite sure?"

"I don't know him. Who is he—is he here?"

She dropped her voice a little. "I remember him—he was in Rangoon—he was the buyer for Everett and Fraser—a young man with red hair. They say that he is in Bassein, and that he is trying to get men to join what he calls a V Force—V for Victory, in English. My brother saw him ten days ago. He said the same as you have done, that the English would sweep forward very soon. Utt Nee did not believe him, but now you are here and you have said the same things as he did. That is why they are arguing so long in there. They do not know what to do."

"I see," said Morgan thoughtfully.

They stood together in silence for a minute. The guards stood patient beside them; to these men time was of no importance.

He said, "How did this Major Williams get into the country?"

She said, "They say that a small aeroplane brought him, and flew away again, by night. I do not know if that is true."

Morgan nodded; it was probably true enough. There was a flight of L-5s, he knew, that worked on missions such as that, but it was a long flight for an L-5 to come right down from Cox's to Bassein. If this man Williams was in touch, however, it might well be that he could get him out by air.

He said, "Well, it's in your hands. If you're going on playing with the Japanese, you'll give me up to them, dead or alive. If you decide to turn and help the British, then you'd better hand me over to this Major Williams."

She said, "That is what I should like to do, myself."

He laughed. "I'm an interested party, so I'd better not give my opinion."

She laughed with him; beside them the guards stirred uneasily. "Go back in there," she said. "I am going in to see my brother."

Morgan lay all day in the lock-up. Peering between the bamboos he could see the house. There was a continuous sound of voices from the room where he had been examined, and twice he heard voices raised in passionate argument and declamation. Once or twice he thought there was going to be a fight. From time to time Burmans came to the house and went in, or departed from it; they were all men, and all incredibly young. Some of them seemed hardly more than fifteen to his inexperienced eye, and all were certainly under twenty-five. It was hot in the little hut, and flies tormented him all day.

He was fetched out again at dusk, and taken to the house. Utt Nee received him, standing beside the table.

He said, "You have been talking to my sister."

Morgan said, "Yes. I answer questions from anybody who asks them. I tell them the truth, so far as I know it." Instinctively he was terrified of seeming to show interest in a native woman.

The Burman nodded. "She has told me. You know how—how we are placed. There is this Major Williams of your Army, near Bassein. He wants us to do . . . to do certain things, and he has told us beautiful stories of what the English are about to do. When I met him I did not believe a word of it."

Morgan was silent.

"Now you have come, and you tell us the same beautiful stories, and we do not know what we can believe. So I am sending you to this Major Williams as a proof of good faith on our side. On his side, I am saying that he must provide us with five hundred hand grenades and fifty light machine guns, with two hundred rounds of ammunition for each gun. We cannot do what he wants us to do without grenades and guns. If he trusts us, he will give them."

He paused. "I send a present for a present. I give you to him as token of our good faith. As token of his good faith he must give us the grenades and guns. I will not work for him on empty words alone from an Englishman. I have had some of that before."

Morgan said, "How far are we from Bassein?"

The Burman said, "About fifty miles. I shall send you to this Englishman with a small patrol under my lieutenant, Thet Shay. They will take paths that keep you away from the Japanese. I cannot go with you myself, though I should like to. I must report this to my colonel, in the direction of Pegu."

Morgan said thoughtfully, "You have no signals—no field telephones or radio?"

"None that we can use. That is another thing this Major must supply if we are to fight with the English. We must have small radio sets, and men to work them."

Morgan said, "What do you want me to tell this Major Williams? Do you want me to give him your messages, or will your man, Thet Shay, do everything you want? I'll help in any way I can."

Utt Nee sat in silence for a minute. "Thet Shay speaks no English. I do not know how well this Englishman speaks our language. When I met him, we spoke English all the time. I know he speaks Burmese a little."

Morgan said, "You speak English perfectly. What were you before the war?"

"I was a student at Rangoon University. I was studying to be an engineer. I suppose you are surprised at that. You English people think of us as naked savages. But our religion and our culture are much older than yours. In your country you have only taught the common people to read and write in very recent times. In Burma, for over a thousand years every boy has learned to read and write in our religious schools. And yet you have the impudence to think yourselves superior to us. You only ever were superior to us in one thing. Do you know what that was?"

Morgan said, "No." He had the good sense to put up with this tirade.

Utt Nee said, "Gunpowder. You learned the use of firearms before we did, and conquered our country."

Morgan said, "Well, you managed to kick us out in 1942."

Utt Nee laughed. "And now, you will say, these crazy people are talking of co-operating with this Major Williams to help the British come back again."

"I don't know anything about politics," said Morgan. "All I know is that it's a bloody crazy world."

Utt Nee said, "I have lain awake night after night wondering who is mad, the British, or my countrymen who want the Japanese to stay in Burma, or myself." He laughed cynically. "If we help the British to come back again, do you think that they will hang us all for fighting against them in 1942?"

Morgan rubbed his chin. "I don't know," he said. "It depends how well the sense of humour's worn."

Utt Nee said, "For myself, I am prepared to take the risk. I see no better chance of any sort of independence for my people now. I think, too, that we are strong enough to force a decent compromise between your way and ours."

Morgan said, "Looks as if our Government'll have to pull the finger out and do a bit of thinking."

There was a step behind them. Morgan turned, and saw that the girl had come up into the house. Utt Nee said, "I have told him that I have decided to send him with Thet Shay to the Englishman."

The girl nodded. "It is the only thing to do."

Morgan said, "Let me get this straight. I see what you want; you will do nothing for this Major unless he sends you five hundred grenades, fifty Tommy guns or Sten guns, and two hundred rounds for each. That's what you want to tell him?"

"Radio sets and operators," said Utt Nee—"we shall need those too."

The pilot nodded. "Radio sets and operators as well. Now, do you want me to tell the Major this, or is Thet Shay going to do the talking?"

Utt Nee turned to the girl. "Do you remember, does this Major speak our language?"

The girl wrinkled her brows. "I don't know. He worked in Rangoon all the time. If he speaks any, it will not be very much."

Utt Nee said, "Thet Shay will do all the negotiation on our side. I do not think that you can help us, Mr Morgan." He turned to the girl and said in Burmese, "Can we rely on Thet Shay and the Englishman understanding each other?"

She said in the same language, "You had better ask Thet Shay that."

Utt Nee got up, went to the opening in the house that served as a front door, and called for Thet Shay. A young man in a longyi and a khaki tunic came; there was a long three-cornered conference between the leader and his lieutenant and the girl. Presently they turned and came into the room, to Morgan still sitting at the table.

"This is Thet Shay," Utt Nee said in English. Morgan half rose from the table; the Burman bowed towards him stiffly. "We have decided this. You are to take no part in the negotiation; that will only make confusion. My sister will go with Thet Shay to interpret with the Englishman. If he says he will give us arms, then I will come to see him with Colonel Ne Win, and we will arrange the details."

"If he says he won't give any arms," asked Morgan, "do you take me back and hand me over to the Japanese?"

Utt Nee laughed. "I do not think we should do that. We

110

are not on speaking terms with the Japanese at the moment."
He laughed again.

"Well, I hope this Major Williams sees it your way," the
pilot said. "I'll do what I can to help."

Utt Nee said, "I have told Thet Shay that you are to start
at dawn. It will take you two days to get near Bassein, and perhaps another day to find this Englishman." He walked over
to the steps down to the ground, and then turned before going
out. "You can bring your blankets up and sleep here in the
house," he said. "There will be a meal presently."

The pilot said, "That's very good of you. Can I have my
revolver back?"

Utt Nee said, "No," and went out.

Morgan turned to the girl and to Thet Shay. He said to
the girl, "Please, would you interpret for me a little? I want
to tell Mr Thet Shay that I understand he is in charge of this
party, that I will obey his orders, and that I will try to make
no trouble."

The girl spoke in Burmese; the young man smiled and
spoke. The girl replied, "He says that he hopes that you will
get back safely to your countrymen."

Thet Shay went away, and Morgan went to get his blankets
from the lock-up. When he came back, the girl was sitting
on the steps. He passed her and put down his bundle in a
corner of the house. He took a drink from a ewer in the
corner, then he searched his pockets for a piece of paper. He
had only an air letter, but the back of the sheet was large and
fairly clean, and he had a pencil. He went hesitantly to the
girl.

"If you're doing nothing," he said, "would you tell me a
few Burmese words?"

She said, "Of course. What do you want to know?"

He said, "Just a few words, useful things, you know. One
feels such a fool if one can't say anything at all." He hesitated, pencil in hand. "To start with, would you mind telling
me your name?"

She said, "I am called Nay Htohn. You should call me Ma
Nay Htohn—that is, Miss Nay Htohn."

He wrote it at the top of his paper; she helped him with the
spelling. He said, "Now, what's the word for water?"

"*Ye,*" she said. He wrote it down.

"Food?"

"There is no word quite like that," she said. "We
speak of things. The word that everybody understands is
Htamin, which is boiled rice. If you ask for Htamin you

111

will get something to eat—unless you are with starving people."

He wrote it down, and went on to man, and woman, and latrine, and was greatly surprised when she laughed at that, just like an English girl. When he had written about twenty words he stopped. "I'll learn these tonight," he said. "If you are coming with us to Bassein, will you tell me some more tomorrow?"

She said, "I will think of some that will be useful to you if you stay here long." And then she said, "Is this the first time you have been in Burma?"

"It's the first time I have been away from England," he replied, "except that I was in North Africa last year."

"How do you like it?"

He laughed. "How would you like it if you were a prisoner and not quite sure how you were going to be treated?" He sat down on the steps, with the whole width of the flight between them. "I must say, it's a lovely country. I'd like to come back here in peacetime and see it properly."

She said, "I wish you would. The only English people who come here are the ones who want to make money out of us—Government officials who come here for their job, or traders who come to buy things from our people as cheaply as they can, and then sell them for a high price in the outside world. Those are the only sort of English that we ever see. We never meet the ordinary English people—people like ourselves."

"I suppose you get missionaries out here," he said.

"Oh, we get a lot of those. Some of them are very kind and good, especially when they start hospitals and schools, and do not try to teach us their religion."

He said hesitantly, "You aren't Christians, then?"

She smiled tolerantly. "No. In Burma we are Buddhists. Surely you knew that?"

"I know that most of the people are Buddhists," he replied. "I thought that educated people like you and your brother might be Christians."

She nodded. "Some of my friends are Christians, but not very many. I studied your religion very carefully when I was at school, but I didn't like it nearly so well as ours. I don't think it is a very good one."

He asked curiously, "What's wrong with it?"

She smiled. "I'm not going to start a religious controversy with you, Mr Morgan. When I was at school they told us that some Englishman once said that it does not matter much

112

what one believes so long as one believes in something. I think that's very true. For ordinary people who are not concerned with dogma there's not much difference between Buddhism and Christianity in the way that we are taught to live, only our way is much stricter than yours."

He was a little intrigued. "In what way?" he asked.

She said, "Well, for one thing, you are allowed to drink wine and to kill animals. I don't like that much. We have five elementary commandments; if you break them you will be reborn into a lower scale of life. You must not kill any living creature at all, you must not lie, you must not steal, you must not commit adultery, you must not touch any intoxicating drink. Those are the minimum commandments, the ones that everybody must observe if he wants to avoid being reborn as an animal. If you want to go forward you must do much more than that."

"You really think that you can become an animal in your next life?" the pilot asked. "You mean, like a pig?"

"You make your own destiny," she said. "Everyone does that. If you choose to live like a tiger or a pig, if that's the sort of life you like, you will attain your desire in your next incarnation. If you strive earnestly for wider mental powers and a better life, then next time you will be reborn higher upon the Ladder of Existence. That is what we believe."

"I see." He thought for a moment, and then asked, "What happens when you get to the top of the ladder? What happens when you are as good as you can be?"

She said, "You can only reach that point after countless thousands of lives. But ultimately, if you receive the Final Enlightenment, so that you are wholly good and completely wise, so that everything you say or do is the perfection of truth and wisdom, you are then the Buddha."

"That's the statue in the pagodas, isn't it?" he asked.

"The statue that you see in the pagodas is the last Buddha," she replied, "Prince Shin Gautama. Twenty-eight souls have attained this perfection in the history of the Universe, and only four in this world; you see, it is not very easy. Prince Shin Gautama was the last, the twenty-eighth, and it is his example that we try to follow in our daily life."

"Rather like our Christ," he said thoughtfully.

"Exactly like your Christ," she said. "But you believe that your Christ was a God, the son of a God who lives somewhere in the outer realms of space and who created you for this one life. I don't quite understand that part of your religion. We have the same idea of a supremely perfect Being, but we believe that any one of us can reach that same perfection if we try hard enough to live a holy life, in age after age. We have the statue of Prince Shin Gautama in our prayer houses as an example, to remind us of what any one of us can attain to. Frankly, Mr Morgan, I like our idea better than yours, though for practical purposes there's not much in it."

She paused, and then she said, "I think our religion is rather less debased than yours in some ways, too."

He did not feel able to embark on that one. He asked, "Is everybody in Burma a Buddhist?"

She said, "Not everyone. Nine people out of ten are Buddhists, I should think, but the Karens are sometimes Christian, and the uneducated country people still believe in Nats, the spirits of the woods and trees, and they build little houses for them. I will show you on our way, tomorrow. But when men get educated and begin to think more deeply, then they come to the pagoda."

Utt Nee passed them, going up the steps into the house. The girl said, "I have been telling the Englishman about our savage religion."

The young man laughed. "My sister is very religious," he said to Morgan. "Women think more deeply about these matters than most men. You must not let her offend you."

The pilot said, "She's been very kind in telling me about it. I didn't know a thing about all this before."

The girl said, a little wistfully, "Don't they teach anything about our country in your schools?"

Morgan said, "We learn a little, I suppose, but only facts. The names of rivers, and about rice coming from Rangoon, and things like that."

Utt Nee said, "Rice will be coming here in a few minutes. You will eat with us."

Turner watched Morgan get up from his long chair. Three men in longyis had appeared, and they squatted down on their haunches on the path at the foot of the steps. He left Turner in his chair, and went and spoke to them in Burmese. A slow conversation developed, evidently punctuated with jokes and repartee. After ten minutes there was a final sally, and the three got up and went away. Morgan came back to Turner in his chair. "Sorry about that," he said. "Have a drink?"

Mr Turner hesitated. "Got any beer?"

The other shook his head. "It doesn't keep out here. Whiskey?"

"No thanks—I got to be careful. Got a lemon squash, or anything o' that?"

"Fresh lime squash, with a bit of ice in it?"

"That'll do fine."

Morgan called an order in Burmese back into the house, and came and sat down. "What did them chaps want?" asked Mr Turner.

"Those? Oh, that was the headman from one of the villages and two of his pals, sort of shop stewards. I want some coolies to make up the road out to the rice mill. He came to fix the rate for the job."

The glasses came, borne by the barefooted Burman servant. Morgan sat, glass in hand, looking out over the river.

"I was telling you about that evening before we started for Bassein," he said. He sat in silence for a minute. "It's a damn funny thing," he said at last, "but you can usually tell when there's something wrong. I couldn't speak a word of Burmese at that time, but I was pretty sure that some of those chaps were against me. Utt Nee was for me all right, and Ma Nay Htohn. Thet Shay, I think, was very doubtful if it was a good idea to turn me over to this Major Williams; some of the rest of them I'm pretty sure were hostile to the whole thing."

He paused, "I got an idea into my head that Utt Nee sent his sister with the party, not so much to interpret as to see that I got there all right and wasn't murdered on the way. I'm pretty sure that was behind it in his mind. I asked him that straight out once, but the old devil wouldn't tell me. Anyway, we pushed off before dawn the next day for Bassein."

They went in single file along field paths between the squares of paddy—eight men, Morgan, and Nay Htohn. The arms the party carried were not very impressive. Thet Shay and one other man carried Japanese rifles, and Thet Shay wore Morgan's revolver in its holster. One of the other men had an old muzzle-loading rifle with a very long barrel, and one had a very modern twelve-bore sporting shotgun; the other four were armed only with their dahs. None of them wore brassards or any sort of uniform. Morgan hoped that they knew sufficient of the movements of the Japanese about the countryside to keep out of their way.

They marched all morning until nearly noon. They were

then in a teak forest following a barely noticeable track; they halted and lay down, and boiled rice on a little fire of leaves and twigs, extinguishing the fire immediately it was done with. Morgan was very tired, although he was marching light, with only his blanket to carry; he was unused to marching in the tropics and was drenched with sweat. Utt Nee had given him a conical straw hat to wear and this had been a comfort in the sun; but he was very, very tired. Nay Htohn and the Burmans seemed as fresh as daisies.

They ate their rice, and curled up for a sleep, leaving one man on watch. At about three o'clock they moved off up the path again, and marched till dusk.

They camped for the night in a bamboo jungle, in a small clearing by a little stream. Again they made a little fire and extinguished it immediately their simple meal was cooked; then there was nothing to do but lie down, wrapped up in blankets, and wait for sleep. Nay Htohn directed the positions of their sleeping; it did not escape Morgan's notice that the girl arranged matters so that he slept between Thet Shay and herself.

Lying upon the grass, wondering what bugs would bite him in the night, watching the fine tracery of the bamboos against the starlit sky above him, Morgan heard the girl say, "What will happen when you get back to your Army? Will they send you back to England?"

He replied, "I shouldn't think so. I'll probably get leave up in the hills, or something, for a week or two. But I'm not back yet."

"No. How do you live in England? Are you married?"

He said, "Yes, I'm married."

"Is your wife very beautiful?"

He said, "She's the most beautiful girl I have ever seen."

"Have you got children?"

"No." He did not expand on that point.

"What will you do in England when the war is over? What did you do before you became an airman?"

"I didn't do anything," he said. "I joined the R.A.F. straight from school, when I was eighteen. I don't know what I shall do. I was going to be an architect before, but I'd only just started. I don't know."

"Will you do that in England?"

"I don't know—I suppose I shall. I hadn't thought about it much." He turned his head towards her. "What will you do?"

She said, "I might go back and be a shorthand typist in a Rangoon office, as I was before. I don't know, either."

"Have you lived in the country for long?"

"My father moved up to Henzada when the Japanese came in, and I went there with him. That is a fairly large place. For the last year or so I have been mostly with my brother in the country districts. One cannot sit still and do nothing."

"You must find it pretty slow, after Rangoon," he said.

She laughed. "I miss the pictures dreadfully. Apart from that," she said, "I rather like the country. Rangoon is quite dead now, and not pleasant if you do not want to go about and dine with Japanese officers."

Presently their voices died down, and they slept uneasily on the hard ground.

At dawn they got up, cooked another meal, and marched on. That day took them to within five miles of Bassein; they camped for the night in a small spinney. They made no fire, eating the cold porridge-like remains of rice that they had cooked at lunch. Thet Shay and one other man went out along the path they were following to find a near-by village, to enquire how the land lay regarding Japanese, and to find the man who knew where they could make a contact with Major Williams.

They came back an hour later in a state of agitation. The Burmans and the girl clustered round Thet Shay; he had urgent and important news for them, and it was not good news. So much was obvious to Morgan. They squatted down together in an earnest conference; from time to time the men threw anxious glances in his direction. He waited for enlightenment with all the patience he could command. Something had happened to upset their plans; so much was evident. He took the surmise fatalistically; it had been too good to be true, that he would get away from Burma easily.

Presently the girl left the group, and came and squatted down beside him. "It is bad news," she said quietly. "A Japanese patrol has caught this Major Williams. They surrounded the village and took him while he was asleep. Now he is dead."

The pilot nodded; he had been prepared for some news of the sort. "That's a bad one," he said quietly. "What is Thet Shay going to do now?"

She said, "He has sent out scouts." Morgan glanced at the group and noticed that three men had melted away into the darkness. "It is very dangerous here. There are Japanese patrols everywhere in these villages." She hesitated. "They are

117

on the lookout for parties such as ours, who may be trying to make contact with the Englishman."

"Do they know anything about us?" the pilot asked.

"I do not think they do. The Englishman said nothing, according to the village people, although the Japanese soldiers were very cruel to him. He took fifteen hours to die."

Morgan bit his lip. No man is immune to fear, though he may be able to control himself. "Nice story," he said quietly.

She stared at him, and then laughed shortly. "I suppose that is an English joke."

He grinned at her. "Well, one's got to make a joke of something."

She said, "You must stay very quiet. We are going to wait here until the scouts come back and tell us which way we must go."

She went back to the group of men. Morgan sat a short distance from them, his back against a tree, watching them and thinking. It seemed to him that they were in a most colossal jam. The Japanese had tortured this Major Williams to make him reveal his connection with the Independence Army. If they caught any members of the Independence Army they would certainly be tortured, too—men or women —to make them reveal the extent of the conspiracy. Thet Shay would be tortured without doubt. Nay Htohn would be tortured.

If the party were taken with himself amongst them, it would be clear evidence that they were members of the Burma Independence Army. That meant torture and death for the lot of them. Nay Htohn, also, would take fifteen hours to die.

"Well, that's the way it was," Morgan said. He set down his glass and called the bearer for another couple of drinks. "The only one who might have got away with it if the Japs had caught us as a party was me. I could always plead I was an enemy in uniform doing what I could to get home— they couldn't have much against me for that."

Mr Turner said, "You was in a spot all right." He paused. "What did you do?"

Morgan said, "Oh, I skipped off out of the party and lay up in the bushes for a couple of days to let them get away; then I walked into Bassein and gave myself up to the Japs. I mean, it was the only thing to do."

CHAPTER SIX

IT was about three in the morning, when the scouts had been back for an hour, that the pilot decided to act. The news had been altogether bad. Japanese patrols were moving on all the paths; they had closed round behind them, and no direct return along the path that they had come by was now possible. They had decided to get a little sleep, and to send out scouts again at dawn to try to find a safe escape route backwards from the trap.

There was one safe escape route which was obvious to Morgan, and it was obvious to him that several of the men would like to take it. That was, that he should be murdered there and then, and buried under a tree; without him the party could split up into twos and threes and appear as peaceful villagers going about their business in the normal way. That was the safe way out for them, the way in which they could get back unquestioned and so join up with Utt Nee again. From time to time as they squatted around in conclave there was a hot argument between Thet Shay and Nay Htohn on the one side and certain of the men on the other, and in these arguments bitter, hostile glances were thrown at him. It was clear to Morgan that in the party things were moving to a crisis; that their new-found loyalty was being put to an unbearable test.

They lay down presently to sleep, with Morgan placed carefully between the girl and Thet Shay. He waited till he had heard the regular, even breathing of the girl for half an hour, to indicate that she was deeply asleep; then he shook the Burman gently by the arm.

He could not talk to him in any language, but Thet Shay was intelligent and caught on to the pilot's sign language readily. Morgan said "Bassein?" in enquiry, and pointed to each path in turn in the dim light. The Burman understood him, and showed an alley between trees, with wonder and suspicion on his broad face.

The pilot nodded, pointed to himself, then to the path. He held both hands above his head in token of surrender, and said again, "Bassein." Then he glanced at the sleeping girl and made the sign for silence.

The next part was more difficult. He got very quietly to

his feet; the Burman got up with him; they stood together in the dim starlight beneath the trees. Morgan pointed to himself and to the path for Bassein; then he pointed to the rest of the party and to the path in the opposite direction, and made a comprehensive gesture with both hands. Thet Shay nodded. Morgan went on to an elaborate pantomime of sleeping twice, and hiding in the bushes, and surrendering. He could not get that through to the Burman, and repeated it; but he was very doubtful if Thet Shay understood.

He thought for a moment, and then reached for his pencil. He had only the paper on which he had made his list of Burmese words; he wrote on this at right angles to the list,

> I have gone in to Bassein to surrender to the Japs; don't try to follow me. I shall try and hide for two days before surrendering so that you can get away. The English will send another officer to replace Major Williams; tell him about me. I will try and see you when the war is over if I get away with it. Don't think too badly of us. We may be stupid but we do our best.

He gave this note to Thet Shay, and indicated that he should show it to Nay Htohn when he had gone. The Burman nodded. Morgan picked up his haversack and turned to him, and held out his hand. Thet Shay took it, smiling, and they shook hands, and Morgan turned and walked off softly up the path towards Bassein. He never looked back at the sleeping girl.

Mr Turner said in wonder, "Must have took a bit of doing, that."

Morgan laughed. "Never been so frightened in my life. I tell you, I was simply pissed with fright. I was banking everything on getting right into Bassein before surrendering, and not meeting a patrol." He turned to Mr Turner. "It was the junior officers and N.C.O.s who did most of the torturing. If you had to surrender to the Japs, you wanted to try and pick a senior officer, and give yourself up to him. You wanted to keep clear of sergeants out on a patrol . . ."

"My Christ," said Mr Turner, "I'd want to keep clear of the whole bloody lot, myself!"

The two days of waiting were a bad time for Morgan. He went up the path about a mile, and then turned into a thicket and made his way into the woods. After a hundred yards or so he came out in a little glade, and he sat down there on a fallen tree. He had no food with him, and no water.

With his intellect he did not regret these omissions. The tale that he had formulated for the Japanese was that he had been hiding and walking across country by night, guided by the stars, from where he had forced-landed the Spitfire to Bassein. His story was that he had been told at the briefing before taking off that this Major Williams was in the neighbourhood of Bassein, and that after his forced landing he had marched by night across country to get in touch with him, hiding in the woods each day. He had finally asked a group of Burmans to lead him to the Major; they had told him that the Englishman was dead, and had then run away. With nothing else to do, he had walked in and had given himself up.

The more he thought about this yarn the more it seemed convincing; he could not see how he could be tripped up on it in interrogation if he kept his head. It was important, however, that he should not be in too good a physical condition if his story was to be that he had lived in the jungle for five or six days without much equipment. If he was half starved, crazy with thirst, and mercilessly bitten by all kinds of bugs, it would be better for his story. In the next two days in the forest he suffered all three torments. He stuck it out.

At dawn, two days later, he found the path again, and wandered down it in the direction of Bassein. He went carelessly, with a raging thirst and with the high temperature of a fever on him. He was bareheaded, for he had thrown away his conical straw sun hat as not being in the part, and he was dressed in the soiled green blouse and trousers of a jungle suit. He wore no under clothes. He had canvas Wellingtons on his feet, muddy and somewhat torn, and a soiled white scarf around his neck. He carried his haversack still with the remains of his emergency kit in it, and he had a five-day growth of beard on his face. In that condition he walked straight into Bassein.

It was not until he was actually walking down the main street of the town that a Japanese officer arrested him, a heavy automatic pistol in his hand.

He was taken to the military headquarters in a villa and given a drink of water, and then interrogated. He was interrogated again at the headquarters of the Kempeitai, who took all his papers from him. He played his part well, as if crushed with disappointment at his failure to escape. They did not bother a great deal about him; the arrest and imprisonment of airmen who had forced-landed in the country were a normal routine to the Japanese. The only feature which made this case unusual was that he had wandered for six days about the countryside, and that was satisfactorily explained by the presence of the English Major, now liquidated.

In a couple of days he was taken by river in a landing craft to Rangoon, and put in the jail there with other prisoners, mostly R.A.F.

In Rangoon jail there was no torture but a great deal of indignity. Minor infractions of the regulations were disciplined by the Japanese kicking the shins or slapping the face, the same treatment that was meted out by Japanese officers to privates in their own Army. The food was a revolting mess of boiled rice with a few vegetables occasionally as flavouring; it was deficient in every sort of vitamin because the bulk rice supply from which it came had been more than two years in store. Old rice eaten in this way causes beri-beri, and the prisoners in Rangoon jail suffered a lot from this progressive disease.

The cells were not unpleasant in that tropical climate, if prisoners had to be kept in cells at all. The jail was a fairly modern building. Morgan was put into an empty cell on the first floor of a long building that radiated with six others from a central hexagonal building which contained a well. His cell was thirteen feet long and nine feet wide, with a grating door and a grating window which permitted the cool air to blow straight through it, in itself a comfort in that climate. The walls were white washed, and the only furniture was a plank bed.

The cell had housed a succession of previous occupants, some of whom had been moved down to the communal prison on the ground floor after an initial period of solitary confinement, some of whom had died. There were calendars and messages written on the wall, half erased by the Japanese guards—"F/O J. D. Scott R.A.F. 698443 shot down near Prome in a Hurricane 7.2.43. I shall stay in this bloody hole until the bugs carry me out they are big enough." Behind the door where it was not easily seen from the corridor there was written on the wall a little dictionary of a dozen elementary words necessary for prisoners, with their Japanese equivalents—Water, Food, Doctor, Cold, Hot, Latrine, Good, Bad. Below was a verse:

Attached to it was the signature of F/O J. K. Davidson, of Kilburn. Morgan wondered grimly what had happened to F/O Davidson.

Morgan had a pencil and he immediately made a calendar on the walls to cross the days off, the first act of the prisoner in solitary confinement. Later on he added a little to the Japanese dictionary, and for a mental exercise wrote down all the counties in the United Kingdom. He also wrote down all the Burmese words that Nay Htohn had told him, with their English equivalents, in case he should forget them.

He stayed in that cell from November 29, 1944, until the Japanese left Rangoon before the advance on April 29, 1945.

His life was monotonous, and his health gradually deteriorated with deficiency of vitamins. But he was not very unhappy. He used to lie for long hours on the plank bed, thinking, and what he thought about was principally Nay Htohn. His idea of women became focussed about Nay Htohn. Bitterly hurt by the treatment he had received from his wife, he clung to the idea of the Burmese girl, so much more intelligent and so much wiser than any woman he had come in contact with in his short life. He wanted to see her again when he got out of prison, wanted to find out what had happened to her after he had left them, wanted her assurance that she had escaped the Japanese. He never had much doubt about it, but he wanted to see her again to make quite sure. He wanted to talk to her again, to be with her, to see her move and hear her lilting voice. It came to him, queerly, that he had been happy on that day that he had spent mostly in the bamboo lock-up in that nameless village in the jungle.

As the months passed, the Royal Air Force gradually faded from his mind. He was still desperately interested in air operations, and when the massed flights of Mitchells and Thunderbolts, Liberators and Spitfires, came raiding military objectives in Rangoon, he used to stand glued to the grating of his window, his heart with the air crews, well aware from his own briefings that they would be particularly careful not to hit the jail. But as time went by, he gradually became accustomed to the thought that he would never fly again, that by the time he was released, new air crews would have superseded him, that the very war might be over. The tropical and Burman scene became more real to him than his life in the Royal Air Force; England itself seemed very far away, a place of bitter hurt that he did not particularly want to go back to. He wanted to get back and see Nay Htohn, and listen to her talking, and watch her smile.

April 29, 1945, was a Sunday. In the few weeks before, with the Fourteenth Army driving down past Mandalay towards Rangoon, and with the Fifteenth Corps advancing down the coast of Arakan, the Japanese had grown much less severe in Rangoon jail; food had improved, and the surveillance was relaxed. A large proportion of the prisoners were suffering from dysentery, and for this reason the Japanese at night had fallen into the way of leaving the cell doors unlocked in order that the prisoners might visit the latrine, keeping guard only on the block compound. In the middle of the night an R.A.F. officer, thin and wasted and trembling, hurried from his cell to the latrine outside. There was a paper pinned to the door, unusual. He could not wait to look at it, but presently, when he came out, he raised his hurricane lamp to look at it. It read:

English and American prisoners, you are now free. By order of the Emperor the Japanese Army has withdrawn from Rangoon, and so we have left you to regain your liberty. We shall hope to meet you again honourably on the field of battle. The keys are on the table in the guardroom.

He stared at it amazed, and hurried back to the cells and woke the others in his building. Two senior officers ventured out of the block compound into the walled lane outside that led down from the central well towards the guardroom, half expecting to be met by a sharp squirt of submachine gun fire. But there were no Japanese. They walked down to the guardroom, and there the keys were, lying on the table, three great bunches of them. It was all quite true.

For half an hour there had been a growing clamour from the town. They unlocked the main gates and walked out into the street. From the centre of the town there was a roar of crowds rioting, and shots were going off continually. Over the houses they could see the glow of fires. It was all rather alarming to weakened, totally unarmed men isolated in a tropical city. The prisoners went back into the jail and locked themselves in. It could be a matter of only a very few days now before the Fourteenth Army marched in to relieve them.

At dawn they set about communicating with the R.A.F.

aircraft on patrol above the city. Morgan and others got a long ladder and climbed to the roof of their block, and with limewash painted in huge letters—

JAPS GONE

They were rewarded by a Mosquito which came down to a thousand feet and circled round, photographing what they had done. Later in the morning they became apprehensive that the High Command might think their sign a Jap ruse. They searched their minds for a code message which would carry conviction, and in their impatience for release they had no hesitation in framing a rude one. They got up on the other side of the pitched roof and painted in large letters—

EXTRACT DIGIT

A Thunderbolt came by and waggled its wings at them.

Firing was easier in the afternoon, and there was less noise from the city. The prisoners were urgently in need of better food; fresh meat and vegetables and fruit were probably available in the city. Under the command of a young major in the Indian Army, Morgan and three others left the jail as a compact little group and walked into the town; they were quite unarmed, and went very warily. They went slowly, for they were all suffering from swollen legs due to incipient beri-beri. They came first to the Chinese quarter and were welcomed heartily. They found that the Chinese had erected barricades across the streets to protect their shops and go-downs from the looters who were ravaging the remainder of Rangoon. They got everything they wanted in the Chinese quarter in a couple of hours without the slightest difficulty, including a few automatic pistols stolen from the Japanese. They made arrangements for the delivery of two lorry loads of fruit and vegetables to the jail. Curiously, there was plenty of petrol left behind in the town, which was damaged only by our own bombardment and by looters.

When the question of payment arose, they offered chits drawn against the paymaster for the Fourteenth Army, and these were accepted gladly by the Chinese banker they dealt with. In the office he beamed at the tattered scarecrows of men in stained jungle suits facing him across the table. "I am very glad to assist English prisoners," he said. "But also, this is better money than the Japanese paper money we have now. In helping you I help myself, gentlemen. Do not thank me."

The major asked, "Is the currency situation very bad?"

The Chinaman laughed. "I cannot describe it. During the occupation the inflation was twenty times—not less than that —twenty times at least. But last night when the Japanese left, the mob broke open the banks down in the English quarter and stole all the Japanese notes. A friend of mine who has been there this morning says that notes of fifty and a hundred rupees are lying piled like dead leaves in the gutter. If that is true, then this Japanese money is completely worthless. I would rather have your chits."

He made them drink tea with him from fine cups without handles, and then showed them out with every courtesy. In the street outside, surrounded by the crowd, the major said, "Like to take a walk up town and see if what he said about the banks is true?"

They went, walking in the middle of the street, the automatics ready to their hands. The streets were indescribably filthy; great heaps of rotting garbage lay on all the pavements. They went slowly, stopping many times to receive the greetings of various brown men in native costume who spoke excellent English. Before them, rioting and crowd activity died down, and the crowds melted away; behind them a long tail of interested citizens followed. They went carefully and steadily down the middle of the street, ready for anything.

They reached the banking district, and it was as the Chinaman had said. Every bank had been broken open and the looting was still going on. The crowds melted away before them and resumed their reprehensible activities when they passed. Five- and ten-rupee notes were everywhere in the gutters and lying on the pavements; these were chicken feed, not worth the trouble of picking up. They went into several of the wrecked banks, pistols in hand, flushing the crowd before them. Great stacks of unissued paper money in bundles were standing ripped open and scattered, heaved from a burst strong room. They stood and stared in wonder at this curious sight.

"Better take a little of this back with us for current expenses," the major said. They filled their pockets and the blouses of their jungle suits; then they commandeered a tonga and drove back to jail to rest their swollen legs. When Morgan got back to the jail he found that he had 12,860 rupees, about £950 at par, in his possession. He gave a good deal of it away that evening.

He lay awake for a short time that night before sleep,

thinking deeply. The better food that he had eaten during the day, and the rice wine that he had drunk, had revived him, had increased his clarity of thought. Within a day or two now the British and Indian troops would reach Rangoon; messages of encouragement had been dropped into the jail by aircraft flying low that evening. When that happened, the prisoners would be evacuated by air at once to India, and from there they would be sent back to England, probably to be demobilised. The last thing that Morgan wanted to do was to go back to England, into the sordid mess that was his marriage. What he wanted to do was to get up into the Irrawaddy delta and find out what had become of Nay Htohn, and to meet her again. To hell, he thought, with going back to England— at any rate, for a bit. He wanted to stay in Burma.

In the circumstances, discipline was very lax in Rangoon jail; parties of prisoners walked in and out of the town freely next morning. Morgan took stock of his possessions. He had his one worn jungle suit, his haversack with a few small articles of kit, his boots, his scarf, a blanket, about 5600 Japanese rupees, and a good automatic pistol with fifty-three rounds of ammunition. He felt foot-loose and free. He went down to see the Chinese banker who had helped them the day before, and asked him the best way to get to Henzada. He said that he had to get in touch with a man called Utt Nee.

The Chinaman knew all about Utt Nee. "He is Colonel in the Independence Army," he said. "You will be able to find somebody at Henzada who can direct you to him, if you can get there. His father is very well known in Rangoon, Maung Shway Than. He is at Henzada, or he was last month. If you find Maung Shway Than, give him my very kind regards."

The pilot asked, "You know him, do you?"

"Oh yes. Maung Shway Than had many important business interests in Rangoon. He has several children; Utt Nee is the eldest son. He was at Rangoon University."

They turned to the consideration of the journey. "You will have to go by river," said the Chinaman. "I do not know the situation with regard to the Japanese, but I think there are very many up by Henzada still. You can go to Yandoon in a sampan fairly easily from here; I can arrange that for you. At Yandoon you should ask for Mr Liu Sen, who is a banker we have dealings with. I will give you a letter to him, and he will help you if he can. I do not know what conditions are from Yandoon up to Henzada."

Morgan did not go back to the jail. The Chinaman was as

good as his word; he bustled around and produced a letter in Chinese for Mr Liu Sen at Yandoon. He left his office and they walked down to the waterfront. From the hundreds of sampans he picked one and they made their way from boat to boat to reach it. It was manned by a family of Chinese Karens, a man, his wife, and two small children. They could not speak a word of English, of course.

The banker talked to them for some time, then turned to Morgan. "These are people of my Kong," he said. "You can trust them. They will take you to Yandoon for two hundred Japanese rupees; it will take two days, or a little longer. I have arranged that you will pay one hundred rupees at Yandoon, but give them a hundred and twenty. The other hundred I will pay them when I get a letter from Liu Sen that you arrived there safely. Now we must buy food for the journey."

He bought rice and vegetables and fruit for Morgan and had it taken down to the waterfront by the woman. For payment for his services the banker wanted a letter to the officer commanding the Fourteenth Army, saying that he had given the prisoners great help. Morgan guessed that he had had many dealings with the Japanese during the occupation and was uncertain of his own position and anxious to establish credit. The pilot gave him a note of gratitude willingly, and left Rangoon by water at about three o'clock that afternoon.

By all civilised standards the discomfort of the sampan was extreme; to the prisoners just out of Rangoon jail it was delightful. So much do standards change. The Chinese Karens took little notice of him, treating him mainly as a piece of cargo, as they laboured at their sweeps to bring the sampan up the river in the slack water by the river banks. Morgan sat playing with the children and watching the unaccustomed scene. He kept his money out of sight and his pistol very much in sight, and he had no trouble. The river was thronged with sampans, but when they left the main stream and entered the narrow chaungs to reach the Irrawaddy, the natives motioned him to stay inside the bamboo mat shelter, in case a roving band of Japanese seeking to escape towards the east should notice him and take a shot at him.

He slept two nights in the sampan, lying on the bare boards, and eating with his hands out of a common bowl, with the family. They got to Yandoon on the third day, without incident. He found Mr Liu Sen, and paid off the Chinese Karens. Mr Sen introduced him to a young man called Maung Boh Galay, who held an indeterminate rank in the Independence

Army and who spoke a little English. This man sent the pilot on by sampan up to Henzada, with two armed Burmans, as a bodyguard, with instructions to deliver him to Utt Nee. Morgan arrived in Henzada six days after leaving Rangoon, having experienced no special difficulty on the journey.

On the way up river he had learned from various people that Henzada had been bombed, but he was distressed and saddened by what he found there. It had been a Japanese Headquarters; sometime in April the Royal Air Force had been turned on to it. In two or three sharp raids they had practically obliterated the town. Once it had been a thriving place of close on to twenty thousand people; now fire had swept across it, more devastating than in Europe since so much was built of wood and bamboo mat. A native town destroyed is sadder than a British city, for there is so little help for the people. These people were stricken by a clash of greater nations than they in their land, and little could be done to help them in their trouble. Here were no army doctors and nurses to help them; here were no gifts of clothes and food from other prosperous communities. A native town blitzed means an end to civilization in that district for the time; the survivors must disperse, to live as best they can from the wild fruits of the jungle; or if fortunate, to work as labourers in the paddy fields.

Morgan's bodyguard made enquiries from the local people, and hearing that no Japanese were in the town, took the pilot to the headquarters of the Independence Army, a native house that stood undamaged in a palm grove on the outskirts. A young officer received him here with sullen suspicion; amongst considerable coming and going in the little house, Mrgan was put through a sharp interrogation. The Independence Army at that time was worried and not a little frightened. They had been fighting for the British after fighting against them, and now that the British were back in the country, the Burmans were by no means sure if they would think in terms of 1945 or 1942. Morgan was the first Englishman to reach them in the district, with the exception of transient guerrilla officers, and they were distrustful of him till the policy of the British became known. They were by no means sure in Henzada that they would not have to turn and fight the British all over again, and if so, here was Flying Officer Morgan for them to make a start on.

In the middle of all this a young Burman passed by them.

Morgan glanced at him, and he at Morgan. The pilot said, "Thet Shay?"

The other stopped and stared, then broke into a beaming smile, and came and shook him by the hand. In the babel of Burmese that followed, the interrogating officer melted and became genial. "Everything has been explained," he said. "I have heard of you from Colonel Utt Nee, and from Maung Thet Shay. The Colonel is away up the river; we expect him back here tomorrow."

The pilot said, "Can I stay here till he comes? I want to see him before I go back to England."

The Burmese talked together for a time. Then the interrogating officer turned to him again. "It is very uncomfortable here," he said. "Maung Thet Shay will take you to the father of Utt Nee, who is here in Henzada and has a good house. He will be glad to put you up. His name is Maung Shway Than."

Morgan nodded, "I want to see him, too. I have a message for him from a business friend in Rangoon."

Thet Shay took him through the ruined town, a place of miserable desolation and burnt posts, to a residential district out beyond what had been the railway station, to the west of the town. Here they came to a large Burmese house surrounded by a fairly well-tended garden. Thet Shay escorted him up the steps on to the verandah, and paused at the entrance to the main living room, furnished in European style, with cane chairs and tables. The pilot saw an old man with grey hair sitting there smoking a cheroot, a brown old man, clad in nothing but a longyi. There was a very young man, or boy, reading a book.

Thet Shay said something in Burmese. Morgan stood hesitant at the entrance, feeling rather a fool. The grey-haired old Burman got to his feet, listened to Thet Shay for a minute, and then turned to Morgan. "I am very pleased to meet you," he said in good English. "I remember my eldest son spoke of you."

The pilot said, "I'm afraid this is a bit of an intrusion, but I didn't want to leave Burma without seeing your son again. He was very kind to me when I forced-landed last November, and he did his best to get me back across our lines. It wasn't his fault that I got taken by the Japs. It was just one of those things."

Shway Than said, "Are you free to leave Burma now? Is the port of Rangoon taken by the British?"

Morgan told him what the situation had been in Rangoon when he left. The old man said, "So you have been in Rangoon jail. I am very sorry. You must need rest now, and good food. Come in and sit down."

Thet Shay slipped away. Morgan dropped his haversack in a corner, and sank down into one of the cane chairs. He was already tired. "I'm very sorry to turn up like this," he said, glancing down at his soiled, threadbare jungle suit, and feeling the stubble on his chin. "I've been travelling since Monday."

The old man said, "You will want clean clothes and a bath. I can provide what you need." He spoke a few words in Burmese to the boy, who went out to the back of the house. The old man turned to Morgan. "I am beginning to understand this now," he said. "You are the Englishman who surrendered to the Japanese at Bassein after the English Major had been killed, are you not?"

The pilot said, "That's right."

The old man said, "You saved my daughter and Thet Shay from a bad situation."

"It was the only thing to do. I didn't want them to get into a mess with the Japs on account of me."

The old man wagged his head. "Some men would not have seen it in that light. In this house we are very grateful to you." He struggled to his feet. "I do not show great gratitude by keeping you talking when you are tired and dirty. Come with me."

He took the pilot into a cool bedroom with a bathroom opening out of it, with water in a great red chatty. On the string bed a Burman servant was laying out clothes—fine drill trousers and a shirt, and a longyi. Shway Than said, "There are both English and Burmese clothes for you to choose from. Here are towels and soap—only Japanese soap—very bad—I am sorry. But we have English tea; it will be ready when you are."

He went out, and the pilot stepped gratefully out of his clothes and sluiced himself with water. He thanked his stars he was not verminous. After the jail and the sampan, the bedroom with the huge chatty of cool water was utter luxury; he stood about, wet, with the water drying on him as he shaved, and sluiced himself again. It was nearly an hour before he could tear himself away from it, till he appeared in the living room in the shirt and trousers. He had not dared experiment with the longyi; he did not know the knot that keeps it up around the waist.

There was no sign of the old man or the boy when he

131

looked around, but the table was laid as if for afternoon tea in England. In the entrance leading out to the verandah, with her back to him, Nay Htohn was standing. She was dressed in a green longyi and a little short cream-coloured jacket over a white shirt; she had a dark red flower in her hair. He stood silent, watching her for a moment; he had not known before quite how badly he had wanted to see her again.

He made a movement, and she turned at the slight sound, and saw him. She smiled, and moved towards him quickly, and took his hand. "My father said that you were here." And then she stooped before him in a sort of curtsy, and kissed his hand.

He touched her on the shoulder, half blinded with a sudden watering of the eyes. "I say, you don't have to do that," he muttered. Then they had separated, and were staring at each other in wonder, and laughing.

She said, "Were they cruel to you?"

He grinned at her. "They had me in the bloody prison up till now. Not crueller than that. Nothing like—like they are sometimes. Nothing like that."

She said, "We had them here—they only went away last week. They lived like pigs."

He said quickly, "Did they trouble you?"

She shook her head. "They were quite correct—actually, we saw very little of them. But in their officers' mess! When first they came, they were short of plates and crockery. They used to mix up all their rations—tea and flour and sugar and meat and jam and vegetables and salt and biscuit—they used to mix this all together into a sort of swill—and they served it on the table in a bedpan!"

He laughed. "No?"

She laughed with him. "It is absolutely true. For weeks they ate out of the bedpan. They saw nothing wrong with it. But that was the Army. The civilians were more civilised. Still, we were very glad to see them go."

He said, "You got back from Bassein all right?"

She said, "Thanks to you we did. We walked back in twos and threes, as local villagers. I carried a basket of mangoes on my head until we were past the Japanese patrols, with the revolver and all the rifle ammunition underneath the mangoes. It was terribly heavy. We had to bury the rifles, but we got them all back later on." She glanced at him. "You will stay with us for some days?"

"If it won't be too much nuisance, I should like to," he

132

replied. "I'm a bit groggy still. My ankles keep on swelling up."

She made him sit down in a chair, and knelt at his feet, and pressed the swollen flesh with her slim fingers. Her touch was infinitely soothing. She said, "They gave you very bad food in the jail."

It was a plain statement of fact, competent and comforting in its efficiency. He nodded.

"Beri-beri, isn't it?" he asked.

She said, "It is in an early stage; it will get well soon, with better food and rest. Our people get this sometimes when the crops are bad and they have to eat the old rice. But you must stay with us till you are well."

He said, "I don't want to be a nuisance."

She said gravely, "How could you be that!"

She called out in Burmese, and a manservant came in from the back quarters; he exclaimed when he saw Morgan's feet. The girl spoke to him for a time in Burmese and he went away; later he came back with a steaming brew in a jug on a tray, with a cup, and set it down by Morgan.

"You must drink a great deal of that," the girl said. "It will do you good."

He discovered later that it was an infusion of fresh limes and rice husks, the vitamin-bearing portion of the rice. It was a country remedy for beri-beri known to the people long before the vitamin was known to anybody.

He had a long talk that evening with the girl and her father. From time to time other relatives drifted in and out. He learned that there were still roving parties of Japanese about the countryside, up to three hundred strong; they were avoiding the towns and roads, which were patrolled by the Independence Army. These roving bands were short of food, and cut off from their retreat towards the east by the advance of the Fourteenth Army down the middle of the country to Rangoon. A number of them were escaping down river every night in power landing craft, in an attempt to gain the sea and make a sea crossing eastwards to Tavoy. Others were trying to make their way across country, usually by night, to break through the Fourteenth Army's narrow salient in sorties to the east.

The evening meal came, and they sat down, seven in number, to the table. The meal consisted of a great platter of boiled rice, with little bowls of curry in the middle of the table. Nay Htohn arranged special dishes for Morgan. These foods were eaten with a spoon by all except for one old lady, who used chopsticks. The meal over, Morgan sat with a cheroot on the verandah, in the dim light, utterly peaceful and at rest in a long chair. Nay Htohn came and knelt down on the floor by his feet; it was more natural for her to squat down on the floor than to sit up on a chair.

She had something in her hand. She said, "I have a paper of yours here. I think perhaps you want it back."

He said, "A paper of mine?"

It was a very dog-eared, grubby piece of paper that she gave him. He held it up to the light that streamed from the room behind. It read, in his handwriting,

Ma Nay Htohn.   Water—YE.
                    Boiled rice—HTAMIN
                    Man—

He smiled, and turned it sideways to read again what was written across the paper:

> I have gone in to Bassein to surrender to the Japs; don't try to follow me. I shall try and hide for two days before surrendering so that you can get away. The English will send another officer to replace Major Williams; tell him about me. I will try and see you when the war is over if I get away with it. Don't think too badly of us. We may be stupid but we do our best.

He smiled gently, thinking back to the tenseness of that bad time from the ease and friendship of his chair on the verandah. He was touched that she should have thought it worth while to keep so trivial a scrap as a memento. He said, "You must teach me some more words while I'm here."

She hesitated, and then said, "Have you looked inside?"

He turned the paper over, and saw that it was an old air letter, addressed to him; the sprawling, unformed handwriting gave him a great shock. He opened the tattered folds in silence, and read,

PHILLIP DARLING
This is going to be a dreadful letter to write and I really don't know how to begin but it's not as if we ever had been married really is it I mean had a home and all that. I know when Jack was killed you were too sweet in looking after me and of course he *wanted* it and so we simply had to and it's been marvellous and I'll never regret one minute of it will you?

He read on in silence, in a wave of sudden misery.

. . . and it's horrible being sort of neither one thing nor the other in spite of it having been all a mistake to start with hasn't it? I do hope we'll be frightfully good friends for dear old Jack's sake.

Ever your loving,

BOBBY

"My Christ," he said quietly. "I thought the Japs had got this one!"

He glanced down at the girl beside him; she was gazing up at him, and there were tears in her eyes. "This is an old letter from my wife," he said. "Did you read it?"

She said, "I read it, but I did not let anybody else read it. It seemed so private. I thought you would not like people to see it."

He said, "That's terribly nice of you. I wouldn't like other people to see this. I didn't realise what it was when I wrote that message on the back of it."

She gazed up at him. "It meant so little to you?"

"Yes." He thought for a moment, and then said, "We didn't match up very well, my wife and I. And then other things happened that were more—more sort of real, like crash-landing the Spit, and getting taken by your people, and all that. I just didn't think about it. The Japs took all the papers in my wallet when they searched me at Bassein, and I thought they'd got this one, too."

She took the letter, and turned it over curiously, holding it between the very tips of her fingers. "Did she really write this filthy thing to you in India—when you were so far from home, and fighting in the war?"

"I got it a few days before I crash-landed the Spit," he said. "She wouldn't have thought of it like that, of course."

She looked up at him and met his eyes. "It is a vile letter!" she said. "I should like to see it burnt."

"Burn it, if you like, Nay Htohn," he said gravely. "I'm through with all that now. My wife and I—we're all washed up."

She smiled suddenly. "I have taken a copy of the message that you wrote for me. I am not going to lose that." They laughed together, and she went and fetched a hurricane lamp from the table in the living room, and they watched the letter shrivel and turn black and burn till there was nothing left of it.

She came and knelt beside him, up against his knee, and they talked about Henzada and the Irrawaddy, and of her

135

life in Rangoon, and the shorthand typing she had done for Mr Stevens in the office. And presently his hand dropped to her shoulder and caressed her; she looked up at him quickly, and smiled.

He went to bed, presently, and slept for the first time in six months upon a yielding bed; to him the string charpoy was the acme of luxurious ease. He slept well, and woke in the cool of the morning infinitely refreshed. From where he lay he could see the trees in the garden, and beyond them the glorious deep orange masses of a flame-of-the-forest tree, over sixty feet in height. The bright flowers, the blue sky, the first shafts of the sunlight, and the jungle rats running up and down the trunks enchanted him. He felt that he was in a lovely place, a feeling not diminished by the thought that Nay Htohn was sleeping in the same house, probably not very far away. He was suddenly convinced that if he had had a nightmare of the prison and had cried out, she would have been with him in an instant. On that thought he drifted off to sleep again, and slept another hour.

Breakfast consisted of a repetition of supper, being rice and various curries, with a pot of tea for Morgan. He sat for an hour on the verandah afterwards, smoking another cheroot, and then, feeling comparatively full of beans, he walked out into the road to look at the town.

Nay Htohn came running after him, and he turned to meet her. She said, "You ought not to walk; you should rest your legs."

"I've got to rest my behind, too," he pointed out. "Besides, I want to see things."

She said, "May I come with you?" She hesitated. "Some of our people are doubtful about what the British will do when they come back. You should have someone with you who can speak our language, just for a day or two."

He said, "Come on. What's the Burmese for a road—this road that we're on now?"

They walked through the desolate, burnt-out middle of the town. Men, women, and children were living and sleeping in the charred ruins. Some of them had set up little stalls to sell a few vegetables or fruits. The pilot was distressed at the sight, nothing was being done to help these people, for there was nobody to do anything. It was no hardship for them to sleep out while the fine weather lasted, but the monsoon was due to break in a fortnight. He spoke about this to Nay Htohn.

"What will they do?" he asked. "Is there any shelter for them?"

The girl shrugged her shoulders. "None," she said. "They will try to build bashas—look, there is a man building one. But there is very little bamboo or palm left within walking distance of this place. And it is too crowded here. There will be a great deal of fever when the rains come and the people have no shelter."

"That's bad. Can't they get bamboo and stuff from up the river?"

The girl said, "There are no boats left."

That, Morgan knew, was very true. The river banks had been lined all the way up from Yandoon with holed and sunk sampans, some sunk by the Japanese and others by the R.A.F.

"There are over thirty tons of corrugated iron sheets at Taunsaw, but there is no means of bringing them here," she observed. "There are no lorries left, and the Japanese took most of the bullock carts."

"Where's Taunsaw?"

"Forty miles from here, down the railway to Bassein. There is a wide chaung there, with a bridge which was blown up by the R.A.F. in January."

"What is the matter with the railway?" the pilot asked.

"I do not know. It has not run for three years, since the British went away."

The pilot asked, "Is the track still all right? I mean, surely to God there must be just one truck left that will roll. If there are corrugated iron sheets at this place Taunsaw, couldn't we get a gang of coolies and let them push a truck down there or something, and get a load?"

She glanced at him curiously. "There may be Japanese down the line."

He grinned at her. "There may *not*—or there may be the Burma Independence Army to look after them. Let's have a look at the railway."

There were trucks standing on the weedy, grass-grown rails of the metre-gauge line, mostly riddled with cannon fire by the R.A.F., mostly still capable of use. In the engine shed there were three tank locomotives, rusty and forlorn, sad-looking little engines. Each showed two gaping holes on the sides of the boiler, with a loose pipe leading to it where the feed-water clacks once had been. It was obvious that parts were missing, but the pilot did not know what the parts were, or what their function was. Steam locomotives were a sealed book to him then.

"Someone's had a nibble at them, there," he said.

A Burman in a longyi and a vest had followed them into the shed, and said something. Nay Htohn asked a question, and commenced a little conversation with the man while Morgan waited. Presently she turned to him and said:

"He says these parts were taken off when the British went away, and that the District Engineer told the Japanese the British had taken them away to India with them. He says that was not true; the District Engineer took them away and hid them himself."

"Where's the District Engineer?"

She asked the man in Burmese. "He is dead. He was working in the repair shops at Insein and was killed in an air raid."

"Too bad." The pilot thought for a minute. "Does he know what the parts were, or where they are now?"

She asked, and then said, "He does not know anything more. He is only the man who cleans the carriages."

"Are there any drivers left in Henzada?"

She asked again. "He says that all the drivers were sent down to Rangoon to work on the main line."

Morgan said again, "Too bad." There was nothing to be done about it, and they turned and went back to the house. His legs were considerably swollen again by the time they got there, and he was glad to put them up in a long chair on the verandah. Nay Htohn said, "It is a very good chair, that. It is the Japanese Commandant's chair."

He grinned. "Well, that's an honour."

She brought him a cheroot, and then she settled down on the floor beside him with some needlework. He glanced at it, and saw that she was working on the faded, threadbare trousers of his jungle suit, now washed and pressed. She was repairing a small tear with delicate, fine stitches, using thread of the same material frayed from a seam.

He thanked her, and she turned over the blouse. It had been carefully washed, and the wings and ribbons stood out almost smartly on the faded cloth. "Tell me," she said, "what do these things mean?"

He told her about the wings and how you got them, and about flying.

"And—" she said, "—these are medals, are they not?"

He showed her the 1940 star, and told her what it meant. And then she put her finger on the other one.

"And this?"

"That's the Distinguished Flying Cross," he said. "That doesn't mean a thing. They send them round with the rations."

She looked up at him uncertainly. "Does everybody get it?"

He was suddenly aware of the great pleasure that he was withholding from her. "Not everybody," he said awkwardly. "You get it if you're lucky."

She was puzzled. "How, lucky?"

"Lucky enough to get away with it," he said. "Lucky enough to come back home again."

She said slowly, "Is it given for something very brave?"

He shifted uneasily. "Not quite like that. You get it for doing something rather difficult."

"And dangerous?"

"And dangerous. But you don't think much of it when you've got it. So many people do much more and don't get anything."

"Tell me," she said, "what was it that you did?"

He told her, and she listened to him wide-eyed, kneeling by him, the sewing on her knee. In the end she said, "Who gave it to you? Is there a ceremony?"

"You get it from the King," he said. "You go to Buck House for it."

She breathed, "You mean, from the King Emperor? Did you see him?"

"See him? He pinned it on, and he couldn't get the pin in. He said, 'Sorry to be so damn clumsy.'"

She stared at him. "The King Emperor said that to you?"

"Yes. I thought it was decent of him."

"What did you say?"

"Oh, I said, 'That's okay, sir,' or something."

She was silent for a minute. Then she said, "Would you mind if I tell my father?"

"If you want to." He hesitated. "Don't spread it round the whole place, though. I mean, it doesn't mean a thing, really, you know. Honestly, it doesn't."

She stared at him, smiling a little. "I believe it does," she said. "I believe it means a great deal."

He changed the subject. "I'd like to put on those clothes when you've finished them," he said. "It's better to be in uniform."

The girl said, "I will not be very long."

He sat thinking, watching her deft grace as she knelt

139

beside him, sewing. "About that District Engineer," he said. "Did he live here? I mean, before he went to Insein and got killed?"

Nay Htohn said, "I suppose he did."

"Do you think his wife would be here still? I mean, the parts that he took away are probably in Henzada, if we could find them."

She said, "I will find out."

That evening found them talking to an elderly Burman woman standing in the middle of a blackened heap of ashes that had once been a house. The woman was garrulous and distressed; Nay Htohn was sharp with her, and several times cut short her long meanderings.

"The box was buried somewhere here," she said to Morgan, "underneath the house. That is, between these posts."

They marked the place, and left the woman and walked back to the house. Presently they returned with two coolies carrying a shovel and a pick. In half an hour they had found the wooden box buried a foot down; it was decayed and eaten by ants, but the six feed-water clack valves in it were all wrapped up in sacking, and were in good condition.

They returned to the house in high spirits, the coolies behind them, with the box. They set it down in the verandah. Nay Htohn went and fetched her father.

"This is very good," he said. "But now we have to find a man who knows about the railway and can drive the engines. I do not think that will be very easy."

Morgan said, "Well, I can put these valves in—that's easy enough. I should think you just screw them in and put a bit of paint or something on the threads, and away you go."

Shway Than said, "Do you understand railway engines?"

The pilot said, "No. But if you can't find anyone who does, I'll bloody soon learn. After all, it's only a sort of kettle with a piston and a cylinder attached. It ought not to be difficult to get the hang of it."

The old Burman said, "Not difficult for you, perhaps. It would be very difficult for me."

Morgan thought for a moment. "One thing," he said. "It's going to be filthy dirty on those engines, and I've only got the one uniform. Is it possible to get an overall, or anything like that?"

Shway Than laughed. "He will keep you busy," he said to his daughter. "You will have to get up early every morning now to wash his clothes." She coloured a little.

Morgan turned to her. "Did you wash this uniform yourself?" he asked.

Her father said, "She would not let any of the servants touch it."

The pilot said, "That was very kind of you. It was so dirty."

The girl laughed awkwardly. "I will see what I can find for an overall."

All the next day the pilot worked in the engine shed. He picked the one of the three locomotives that seemed to be in the best condition, and fitted the two clack valves without difficulty. Then he spent some time in tracing out the lead of the various pipes and pumps, and thinking deeply; he did not want to ruin everything by making some stupid mistake and burning out the boiler. The news got round that he was working on the engines, and a few Burmans arrived to watch the progress of the work. One lad in the Independence Army turned up. Nay Htohn talked to him for a little and then brought him to Morgan. "He says he knows all about these engines," she said.

The pilot looked him over. The boy did not seem to be much more than fifteen years old. "Did he work on them?"

She said, "No. He was only a little boy then. But he was interested in the engines and he used to play in here and watch the driver and the mechanics. He says he could drive one."

"I'm not interested in that just at present," said the pilot. "Ask him if he knows how the water gets into the boiler in the first place."

He professed to do so, and Morgan, tracing out the run of the pipes to the mechanical feed pump, discovered what appeared to be a hand pump; the boy's suggestion seemed a likely one. He turned to the girl, "What's his name?"

He replied, "Maung Bah Too."

Morgan elevated a thumb. "Okay, Maung Bah Too, we'll try it your way." Nay Htohn translated that, and the lad grinned. "Now, what about getting us a few tons of water?"

This proved to be a major difficulty. The water tower had been thrown down and shattered by a bomb; there was no running water in the place at all. They left the engine shed and went together to the headquarters of the Independence Army and saw the officer who had interrogated Morgan on the first day. After some negotiation by Nay Htohn, the officer detailed Bah Too to round up thirty coolies with a bullock cart to bale water from the river into casks and carry it to the locomotive. It took the remainder of the day to get the tanks half filled.

They went back wearily to the house at dusk. Utt Nee was there, having arrived from up country an hour before. He had grown in stature and in poise from the young man that the pilot remembered six months before; he now seemed more self-confident and more mature. He was very glad to see Morgan.

Later in the evening, as they sat together in the verandah after the evening meal, he was quite candid. "It was a great help to me when you surrendered to the Japanese," he said. "I had quite made up my mind that we should turn and co-operate with the British again as the best way to work towards our freedom, and that was the policy of our leaders, too. But in a loose army such as ours, you understand, it is not always easy to persuade people to do what you think right, even if you are in command. When we took you, there were many of my people who thought the British were all treacherous and selfish, who would have liked to give you to the Japanese, or perhaps to do something else with you. It had a great effect upon my people when you surrendered yourself to save the party from trouble. I tell you, the British suddenly became quite popular. I had no difficulty after that in getting my own way, and now we have been fighting side by side with British troops for the last five months, and we have gained the victory." He grinned. "We are quite friendly with the British now, so friendly that they will probably hang us all as traitors."

The pilot said, "If they do that, you can take it out on me."

Utt Nee laughed. "I am not very much afraid. I am twenty-five years old, and nobody has hung me yet."

He said that there were reports that British naval vessels were operating in the delta down below Yandoon, and that there had been one or two engagements with Japanese in landing craft escaping down the rivers to the sea. He had no information as to when the British troops were to be expected in that district; he thought the Fourteenth Army were too busy for the moment in maintaining their line down the middle of the country, and so keeping the broken Japanese army trapped, to start mopping-up operations for a time. "You are very far ahead of your own forces," Utt Nee said. "When they get here in the end and find you here, and learn that you came up here in a sampan, they will be very cross."

"They'll be bloody cross anyway," the pilot said. "I've probably been posted as a deserter by this time. But what the hell."

Utt Nee said, "They will hang both of us, then, side by side." He translated this sally to one or two of his friends sitting in the house; it went as a very good joke.

Next day, while the coolie gang laboured to carry water to complete the filling of the tanks, Morgan, with Maung Bah Too to help him, oiled and lubricated the engine in every hole that seemed designed to take it. There was no shortage of lubricants, although Bah Too asserted that the Japanese soldiers had eaten some of the engine grease as butter, and liked it. There was plenty of coal and wood. Utt Nee came in with several other officers about midday; they were impressed with the progress of the work, and set another gang to improvise a more efficient water supply. Later that afternoon they discovered a small motor pump belonging to the fire brigade, and thereafter they had little trouble with getting water.

Next day, early in the morning, they manhandled the small locomotive to the extension smoke stack and clamped it down onto the funnel, and lit the fire in the fire box. They had some trouble in getting it to burn, knowing none of the tricks of firing a stone-cold engine. But by the middle of the morning steam pressure was mounting on the gauge, and Morgan, with sweat running off him in a steady stream, was anxiously experimenting with the feed pump controls in the cab.

Finally he turned to Nay Htohn, always at his side. "She should go now," he said. He pulled the valve control over to reverse, and unwound the handbrake. Then he showed her the regulator. "Pull that over just a little bit, and see what happens," he said.

She hung back, laughing. "You do it."

He said, "You do it. Go on."

Below them, on the ground, the Burmans rocked with laughter at the dispute. The girl put her hand up and moved the regulator handle an inch, gingerly; nothing happened. Urged by Morgan, she moved it a little more. With a sigh and a clank the locomotive stirred and moved backwards, giving a great puff. Nay Htohn dropped her hand from the regulator in a panic. Morgan closed it, and the engine rolled out of the shed and came to rest a yard or two outside. There was a cheer from the crowd.

He pulled the whistle twice, the signal that he had arranged with Utt Nee, and the crowd cheered again, and Utt Nee and his officers arrived, and they all had a ride on the engine, up and down the track. They found three trucks in good condition, and greased the axle boxes. With these trucks they did a little shunting practice, forming up a train. By evening the locomotive seemed to have settled down and to be running reasonably well; they put it back in the shed and banked the fire. Bah Too was detailed to look after it, and they went back to the house, very satisfied with the day's work.

They held a conference that evening, sitting on chairs around a table in the living room, in the light of a couple of hurricane lamps. Maung Shaway Than was in the chair; Utt Nee was there with two of his officers, and Morgan and Nay Htohn. The old man said, "Now that we have this railway running, we can go down to Taunsaw, if the track is good enough. Does anybody know for certain if the bridge is broken?"

One of the officers said in Burmese, "It is down and lying in the river. I was there six weeks ago, and saw it."

Nay Htohn, squatting by Morgan's chair, translated in a low tone.

They went on to discuss what they could do by going as far as Taunsaw. Corrugated iron was lying in a dump there, and there were bamboo and palm groves which would provide housing materials. It was by no means certain that the country along the line was free from Japanese, however. But they decided to run what amounted to an armoured train next day.

They left next morning about an hour after dawn, the little engine pushing one truck in front and pulling two behind. These trucks were filled with armed soldiers of the Independence Army, about two hundred of them. They took with them a supply of water and fuel, breakdown gear, and food. Utt Nee would not allow Nay Htohn to come with them, fearing action with the straggling Japanese, and he rode with Morgan and Bah Too on the footplate of the engine.

They went slowly, at about fifteen miles an hour. The track was rough but adequate; in places it sagged ominously down beneath the train, to spring up again when they had passed. They were not greatly troubled about this; they had with them several platelayers accustomed to track maintenance who had remained in Henzada; as soon as it was known that there were no enemy about, these men would get on with their job and make the track sound where it needed attention.

They moved along cautiously, stopping every few miles to

144

enquire about the Japanese. Everywhere they were told that there was a band about three hundred strong in the vicinity. Over and over they heard this, but always the band was somewhere else, never very close at hand. So they went on cautiously, and reached Taunsaw at about midday. Before them lay the bridge, a fine steel girder structure, broken and collapsed into the river.

They set to work there to re-water the engine and to load the corrugated iron. It was evening by the time all this was done; they decided not to risk a night journey back to Henzada. So they formed a lager around the train, put pickets out, and cooked a meal before nightfall, extinguishing the fire at once.

Morgan sat smoking with Utt Nee in the evening light, sitting on the sill of one of the trucks, looking out over the river and the wrecked bridge. He felt in some way responsible for that bridge, and sorry about it. It had been a fine structure; that had cost somebody a lot of money. The railway that it carried across the river had not functioned since 1942 when the Japanese had driven us from Burma, but in 1945 the bridge had been made a target for the R.A.F., and they had smashed it up, and it now lay broken in the river. As one of the R.A.F., and seeing things from a different angle from his usual view out of the cockpit, Morgan was sorry about the bridge. It seemed, now, a wanton bit of senseless damage, rather like the nine or ten bridges on the line from Toungoo to Pegu that we had thought it necessary to destroy to put that railway out of action. One would have been sufficient; or perhaps one at each end.

Voicing his thoughts, he said, "There's the hell of a lot of patching up needs doing in this country."

The Burman by his side, "Are you thinking of the bridge?"

The pilot nodded. "Got to be rebuilt. I don't see why we had to go and knock it down."

Utt Nee said, "It is a great pity. This railway was useful in this part of the country. It will be difficult for people in Bassein to trade with Henzada until we get that bridge again."

"How long do you suppose it will take to rebuild it?"

"How long? I do not know. If some of you British soldiers stay and help us get things right, it should not be many years before this country is running again like it was before. But if you all go home and leave us to the pukka sahibs, it will take a very long time."

The pilot said, "We've not got very many engineers out here."

"Engineers are necessary," the Burman said. "But we need people who can tell the engineers what to do." He glanced at Morgan. "People like you," he said, and laughed.

The pilot was astonished. "I couldn't tell an engineer what to do."

Utt Nee said, "You got this railway going."

"Oh well—that's different," the pilot said. "That's just been a bit of bloody good fun."

The Burman laughed with him. "All work that interests you is bloody good fun," he said. "And yet, the railway is now running, and it was broken before you had your fun with it." He turned to the Englishman. "What are you going to do?" he asked. "Are you going back to England, to live there forever as an architect?"

"I've got a sort of job to go to there," the pilot said.

"There will be many jobs here for you," said the Burman, "if you like mending railways and things that are broken."

Morgan sat in silence for a few minutes, staring out over the river in the gathering dusk. He had seen sufficient since he got out of jail to make him realise that this was not a casual approach. He had been living for the last week with responsible people; old Maung Shway Than was a man of influence in Rangoon in times of peace; Utt Nee held a high position in the Independence Army. This was an offer of a job, or something very like it; a job with people he could work with in a country that he was already much attached to.

He said at last, "You wouldn't want an Englishman in any important job here. It's Burma for the Burmans now."

Utt Nee said, "That is true, up to a point. But there are too few of us educated yet to run this country by ourselves, with no help from the British at all. There will always be important jobs for Englishmen in Burma who are not too proud to work on level terms with us and share our life, who would not think it an indignity to work under a Burman if he is the better man. I do not think you need worry about that."

There was another long silence. Morgan said at last, "There's another difficulty. If I were to stay here, I should ask Nay Htohn to marry me. I expect you'd rather I went back to England."

Utt Nee shrugged his shoulders. "I do not want to see my sister with a broken heart. You must know she is very much in love with you."

146

"You wouldn't mind about a mixed marriage?" Morgan asked.

"Why should I mind if that makes her happy? I should be very glad for her. I know several Englishmen who married Burmese girls and made them very good husbands. This is not India, you know. Our girls marry whom they like. Just as in your country."

"What about your father? Would he mind?"

"I think he would be very pleased."

"Do you know I'm married already? That I've got a wife, back home in England?"

The Burman said, "I know a little about that. Nay Htohn said that she was not faithful to you."

"That's about right." The pilot told him briefly what had happened, and answered a few questions. "So I'm a bit shop soiled, you might say."

"I do not think my sister thinks of you like that. So why should you think it of yourself?" He turned to Morgan. "Think it over," he said quietly. "I know a few Englishmen that I would like to see stay in our country, and I know many that we must get rid of at all costs. You have all the vigour of your people, and you are not too proud to learn our ways. If you marry Nay Htohn she will make you a good wife, and both my father and myself would like to have you with us."

That night Morgan slept on the floor of one of the trucks, covered by his blanket, his head on a gunny sack. Around him lay the Burmese soldiers that were not on guard. He could talk to them a little about very simple things, and understand them if they spoke to him slowly upon simple matters. He had become accustomed to their brown skins and their way of life. They did not seem strangers to him any more, did not seem to be incalculable creatures to be treated with distrust. He found them understandable, thinking along the same lines as he did and laughing at the same brand of joke. They treated him with genuine liking and respect, the man who could fly aeroplanes and make the railway go.

He lay, before sleep came to him, watching the stars beyond a cauliflower-like banyan tree against the deep blue sky. England to him was represented by school life, war hardships, blitz and death, and a sordid and unprofitable marriage. Burma to him meant fun and games with railways and broken bridges and smashed boats, with people who already liked him and respected him for his achievements; it meant love from a clever girl who, in her own country, was of his own social class, or better. There was no doubt in his own mind which he would do. He snuggled closer in his blanket on the hard plank floor, shifted the gunny sack beneath his head, and drifted off to sleep, thinking of Nay Htohn.

They steamed into Henzada about midday, having dropped off the platelaying gang halfway down the track, and loaded up with bamboos and palm thatch. They had been careful to announce their arrival by whistling at intervals for the last five miles, and a considerable crowd was there to meet them. Nay Htohn came forward to greet Morgan as he got down from the footplate of the little engine, grimy in his old jungle suit. Maung Shway Than was with her.

The old man said, "Did you meet any Japanese?"

"Not one," the pilot said. "The line is clear right down to Taunsaw; if it wasn't for the bridge, we could have gone all the way to Bassein."

He turned to the girl. "It was a joy ride."

She smiled. "I was imagining . . . all sorts of things."

He smiled with her. "I was imagining things, too. I was thinking that we had most of the Army with us on the train, and that perhaps the Japanese would have come back here while we were away."

She laughed. "We are still quite all right. They say that one of their motor landing craft went down the river last night full of Japanese soldiers, and that your British gunboats sank it, south of Danubyu. I do not know if that is true."

He said, "Are the British as close as that?"

"So they say."

He went back to the house with her, and washed, and had a meal, and slept a little on the charpoy; in the cool of the evening he got up and found that while he had been sleeping she had washed and pressed his jungle suit again. He went out to the verandah; she was there, sitting in the evening light and sewing something, with a flower in her hair. He thanked her for washing his clothes, and then said, "Has anything been heard of the British gunboats?"

She shook her head. "Only that they are down by Danubyu. They may be here any time."

He nodded. "I shall have to go on board and report when they come."

She said, "Will you have to go away with them?"

"I think I shall," he said. "I think if I don't I shall be posted as a deserter."

Her lip trembled, and she said, "It will be very sad for us when you go."

He said, "It's better that I should go. I've got this matter of the divorce from my wife to attend to, and I'll have to go to England for that." He glanced down at her, squatting down upon the mat beside his knee. "But I could come back."

She glanced up at him quickly. "When you are at home with your own people, you will not want to come back to Henzada."

"I don't know about Henzada," he said. "I should always want to come back to you."

She said softly, "I could make you very happy."

He dropped his hand on to her shoulder, and caressed her neck; she turned quickly, and laid her head against his knee. Then she looked up at him and said, "This is very bad. People can see us from the road." But she did not move away.

He said, "When I come back, will you marry me, Nay Htohn?"

She looked up at him, laughing. "I would marry you now. You know that very well."

He said, "I've got a wife already."

She tossed her head. "I do not call that being married. She has not given you a child, and when you are away fighting she goes with other men. You are not married at all, really. I would be a better wife to you than that."

He stroked her hair. "I know. But I am married all the same, and I've got to get that straightened out. After that, Nay Htohn, I want to come back, if you'll have me."

She breathed, "Have you . . ." and rubbed her cheek against his knee again. And then she said, "It is eight thousand miles from here to England, and she has another man. Why must you go away at all? I think that you could just forget about her, and stay here with me. We could be married very soon."

He said, "No."

He got to his feet, and raised her up. She stood up obediently and went and stood with him at the verandah rail. "I want you to understand," he said. "I like this place; I like your people and your country, and I love you, Nay Htohm. I think we could be frightfully happy together, living here in Burma. And because of that, I want to start off properly, without any mess in the background. I want everything to be all tickety-boo. I want to marry you properly according to the English law so that your people will know that I'm playing straight with you. If we just married now it wouldn't be legal, and I could beat it any time and leave you flat, and Utt Nee would know that, and so would Maung Shway Than. That's not the way I want to start in Burma. I'll have to go back to England." He thought for a minute. "Besides, there's a war on. I think they'll probably demobilise me now, but if they want me to go on in the R.A.F. I'll have to do that till the war is over. But after that I shall come back to Burma. I shall want you very badly then."

She said softly, "I want you very badly now." He took her hand and held it, and they stood together for a minute in the dusk.

Presently she said, "I think that you are right. Our people are suspicious of all Englishmen, and rightly so, and although I would marry you tonight and be very happy, I think that you would get on better with my people if it was a legal marriage by your laws. And there is another thing." She hesitated. "I think you ought to go back home to England and think carefully about this. You Westerners are brought up differently from us, and many of you have very strange ideas about your colour, and mixed marriages. I do not want to rush you into anything. If when you have been at home in England for a little you come back to me in Henzada or in Rangoon, I will marry you the day you land, Phillip. And I will make you a good wife."

He grinned down at her. "Nay Htohn, would it be all wrong by your standards if I was to give you a kiss?"

She glanced up at him, eyes dancing. "You mean, in the Western fashion, as they do on the movies? I have never done that."

He said, "Like to try?"

"Not here." She hesitated. "We do not do that in Burma. Even married people do not kiss in public. We could go into your bedroom."

"Does that make it all right? It would make it all wrong in England."

She said demurely, "It would be perfectly all right." So they went into the bedroom and shut the door, and she came into his arms, and he kissed her mouth and neck, feeling her slim body lissom in his arms. And when at last he let her go, she said, "I understand why we do not do this in Burma. It is too exciting." And they smiled together, and kissed again more gently, and went out again to the verandah, and sat talking quietly in the dim light of the stars over the flame tree. The fireflies flickered about them, and the great noise of frogs made a continuous background to their talk, and they talked on for hours.

At about ten o'clock at night a man came to the verandah and asked for Utt Nee. In the dim light they could see that he wore the brassard of the Independence Army. Nay Htohn said that her brother was down at headquarters.

The man said, "Five British gunboats have arrived."

The girl translated this to Morgan. She asked, "Where are they?"

He said, "They have not landed. The ships are lying in an ambush by the ferry, anchored close under the bank, in the shadow. We have a picket out around them. Utt Nee has sent a party two miles up the river, to the paddy mill, to watch for Japanese boats coming down the river. Then we are to warn the British by the little radio."

She said, "You will find Utt Nee at the headquarters." The man slipped off into the darkness.

Morgan said, "How far off is the ferry where the gunboats are?"

She said, "About a mile."

"Like to walk down and see if we can see anything?"

She agreed, and they set out together by the shadowy paths towards the railway terminus on the river bank. They went rather slowly, hand in hand; it was about a quarter to eleven when they reached the place. Standing on the bank by the wrecked railway trucks they could see the gunboats just below them, not a hundred yards away, five Fairmile B type motor launches, anchored and silent, their guns trained up the river, without a light of any kind showing. They gave the pilot a great thrill, the first British forces he had seen for seven months. It was with difficulty that he restrained himself from hailing them.

He squatted down on the bank, with Nay Htohn by his side, watching the ships. They stayed for half an hour, and were about to walk back to the house when things began to happen. There was a movement on the vessels, and a faint jangle of bells, and then a deep rumble, as the engines started up. Ship after ship started engines, all down the line. The leading two weighed anchor and moved silently out into the middle of the stream; the other three also weighed and moved a little way upshore, keeping close in to the bank. All five lay there silent, just stemming the stream, making a great L across the river.

"Christ," breathed the pilot, "they've given us a grandstand seat!"

They waited tensely. There was a faint rumble of engines from up river. From the farthest of the Fairmiles a

151

searchlight blazed out, swept a little, and focussed on three landing craft about a thousand yards away, and coming down the river. A spurt of small-arms fire came from them, and the heavier beating of a 37 millimetre automatic gun. Morgan pressed Nay Htohn down on to the grass beside him and they lay flat, watching a naval battle. It was over in a couple of minutes. The Fairmiles turned their broadsides to bring all the guns to bear, and opened fire with Oerlikons and Bofors in the glare of their searchlights. One by one the landing craft were hit and went on fire, and headed for the shore. Two came to the Henzada bank and one to the far side. At Henzada the Independence Army were lining the bank. There was much shooting, which presently died down; the fires died out upon the craft, and the Fair miles slipped back and anchored in their old stations, to watch again.

Morgan and Nay Htohn walked back to the town, tense and alert. The walk was not without danger, for the pilot was in his jungle suit and might have been mistaken in the darkness for a Japanese or fired at by a fugitive from the boats. They went to the headquarters and found Utt Nee there, in the centre of a group of officers. He detached himself to talk with Morgan.

"What happened to the Japs?" the pilot asked.

"We have two prisoners," the Burman replied. "Two who were so badly wounded that they could not do their hara-kiri. The rest were either killed, or else they killed themselves. I do not know anything about the other boat; that landed on the other shore. They have got away."

The pilot said, "Mind if we walk down and see the boats?" An idea was already forming in his mind.

Utt Nee sent a young officer with them, and they walked down to the shore with a hurricane lamp. There were many bodies of dead Japanese where the battle had taken place. Morgan looked at them with curiosity; these were the first dead Japanese he had seen. They picked their way between them, going warily, with pistols in their hands in case any of the corpses came to life and took a shot at them, as Japanese will do.

The boats were separated by about three hundred yards. They were twin-hulled, flat-bottomed landing craft, with a ramp forward and a Diesel engine aft. They mounted one 37mm. gun as their sole fixed armament apart from small arms and mortars carried by the troops. The first one they went on board smelled badly of stale food and excrement and burning oil. Casks of Diesel oil on her deck had been on fire, but the fire had not reached the engine, which was flooded. She was holed in three places by the Bofors, and considerably punctured by the Oerlikon fire.

Morgan said quietly to Nay Htohn, "We could repair this one."

She stared at him in wonder. "Repair it and use it?"

"That's right. The engine hasn't been hit. It's probably full of water, but we could get it going again. And we could patch up the hull with concrete until we can get it done properly."

She said, "Could you do that?"

The pilot said, "I'd have a stab at it."

They went on to the other landing craft. This one was in a worse state than the first, for the engine compartment had been on fire, and that engine was probably done for. The hull, however, was not so bad as the first one.

Morgan said thoughtfully, "I wonder what the one over on the other side is like?"

In the morning he sat in conference with Maung Shway Than, Utt Nee, and Nay Htohn. "This is good-bye for the moment," he said quietly. "I've got to go and report myself on board these gunboats now, and go down to Rangoon with them; from there I shall be sent to England. I want to come back here as soon as ever I can. I want to come back and marry Nay Htohn, if she'll have me."

Maung Shway Than said, "I should be very glad for you to do so. How long do you think it will be before you can get back to us?"

"I don't know—it may be three months. It should not be longer than a year. But I shall write every two or three days, and let you know what is happening with me." He paused. "Before I go, there is one important matter that we must discuss. These Jap landing craft can be repaired. The one down the river is the best of the two, but they must all be pulled up out of the water, and above high-water level at the monsoon. If you can get them going, they'll be something to replace all the sampans that have been sunk."

Maung Shway Than said, "I will take them over and see that they are salvaged as much as we can. We can use the sampan builders on the work."

The pilot said, "Get somebody to go up and down the river and look at every one of them that you can find. Get the engines taken out and kept in a dry place, and greased; there's plenty of grease up with the locomotives, in the shed.

Get the sampan builders to patch up the hulls if they can do it. I shall hope to be back here directly after the monsoon, and I'll get down to it myself then. I'm quite sure we can get some of those boats running again if we tackle it the right way. Out of the lot we might get two or three going, putting the best engines into the best hulls. If you find that we need tools, write to me in England by air mail and tell me what we need, and I'll bring it out with me."

The old man said, "It would be very profitable if we could get one or two of those boats running. There is no transport on the Irrawaddy now. All the river steamers have been sunk."

Nay Htohn said, "I will see that it is done. I will make Maung Bah Too go down the river and see every boat. I will go myself and see that it is done. Every boat shall be pulled up out of the water and the engine shall be dried and greased, and then when you come back we will go and see them, and you can decide on each boat which parts we can use."

Morgan thought for a moment. "If you find any boat mechanics, or men who have run Diesel engines at any time, get hold of them."

Utt Nee said, "There are not many of those in Burma. But our people are good with machinery; they only need to be shown how."

Maung Shway Than said, "I will take over every boat, and I will pay whatever costs may be necessary. I think it will be a very good business."

Two hours later Morgan was with Nay Htohn on the river bank. "This is not good-bye," he said, holding her hand. "You need not be afraid; I shall come back. This is a happy place, and I shall be back here as soon as ever I can make it."

She said, with brimming eyes, "I have no fear, but make it very soon."

He went out to the leading M.L. in a dugout paddled by a little boy, and climbed on board her. An R.N.R. lieutenant commander met him on the deck.

"I was in Rangoon jail," the pilot said. "We've got the railway running halfway to Bassein, if that's any good to you."

CHAPTER SEVEN

THE first raindrops of the storm plashed on the path below the verandah; a cool breeze drifted around Mr Turner as he sat with Morgan in the darkness. The latter stirred. "Be time for supper in a minute," he said. "I told Nay Htohn we'd have an English meal."

Mr Turner said, "You come back here pretty soon, then?"

"Lord, yes. I shot back to England and out here again like a scalded cat." He smiled. "I had an advantage, of course, because I knew everybody in Transport Command. I saw the A.V.M. in Calcutta and told him I wanted to take my discharge in Burma, and about the landing craft and everything. I got flown to England in a Liberator and back to Calcutta again in a York, as part of the air crew. I was only seventeen days in England."

"Fixed up your divorce, then?"

"Yes. There wasn't much difficulty about that. I got the solicitor cracking on it before I left England. It wasn't legal for about two years, but we didn't wait for that. I got back to Henzada in seven weeks, seven weeks to the day from the time I left, and we got married right away. Our first kid was nearly a year old before we could get married properly, but we did it then."

Mr Turner grinned; it was all very deplorable, but in the circles that he moved in in England he had heard of similar doings. "What about the boats?" he asked.

Morgan said, "That turned out pretty well. Nay Htohn had seen to that." He turned to Turner. "You know, Burmese girls are very good businesswomen, better than the men. There're no flies on any of them. Nay Htohn had got all the boats pulled up out of the water, seven of them, some of them pretty badly shot up. Maung Shway Than gave them to us as a wedding present. One down by Zalun was practically undamaged, and I got that going in a week. I got another going a month later, and the third sometime after that. That's all we salvaged, just the three of them."

"What happened to them?"

"I ran them for two years," Morgan said. "We ran a regular service from Rangoon right up to Prome, and made a packet of money out of it. You see, the Irrawaddy Flotilla

Company was short of vessels and it was some time before there was much competition; we got in on the ground floor." He mused for a moment. "God, they've done some work, those boats!"

"Are you still running them, then?"

"No, I sold out last year. They're still running—you'll see one of them go down tomorrow about midday. But I sold out." He turned to Turner. "I'm in the civil service now. I stayed out for some time, because I thought an Englishman wouldn't be very welcome—Burma for the Burmans, and all that, you know. But I got mixed up in a lot of local things. Then last year Shway Than's brother, Maung Nga Myah, had a long talk with me and persuaded me to take this job—he's in the Government, you know—Minister for Education. He said they wanted me, so I said I'd give it a crack. I think it may pan out all right."

Mr Turner wrinkled his forehead. "I don't get that. I thought they wasn't taking English people now."

"It was a kind of compliment," Morgan said. "They've spent the last two years getting rid of all the pukka sahibs from the civil service as quick as they could, and then they came along and wanted me to join it. They sort of count me as a Burman now, I think."

"Funny sort of set-up," said Mr Turner in wonder.

Morgan got up from his chair and collected the glasses. "I've got my roots deep in this country," he said. "Wife and kids and work and friends. I'd never want to go back and live in England again, after this. When this country gets Dominion status, I'll probably take out naturalisation papers. Make a job of it."

They went into the house to dinner, a meal served by candlelight, with silver on the table; a meal of soup and casseroled chicken, and a savoury. Morgan and Ma Nay Htohn were genuinely glad to have a visitor from England. In the friendship of their interest Mr Turner expanded, and talked fairly lucidly to them about conditions in London. He talked so much that he became very tired, and was glad to sit quietly after the meal, with a cheroot, in a long chair. The white cat, Maung Payah, walked in as soon as he sat down and jumped up on his lap, kneaded a place for himself, and settled down to purr.

Nay Htohn looked at it in wonder, and spoke again to Morgan in a low tone, in Burmese.

He laughed. "My wife can't make out about that cat,"

he said. "He never does that with anyone. He won't sit with her, or with me, either."

Mr Turner was pleased, and rubbed the cat's ear; it pressed its head against his hand in pleasure. "Took a fancy to me all right, he has," he said. "What was that you said you call him?"

"Maung Payah," said Nay Htohn. "In our langauge that means Mr Holiness, or 'Your Reverence.' "

"Why d'you call him that?" Turner asked the question with sincerity.

The girl hesitated, and then laughed shyly. "My people have a superstition," she said. "Just like in your country, if you spill salt you throw it over your shoulder to avert bad luck. You do not really believe it, but you do it. Well—like that, the country people here say that a white animal—any white animal—is a very beautiful soul on its path up the Ladder of Existence; so fine a soul that it will one day be the Buddha." She smiled. "It is not part of our religion, that one—you will not find it in our holy books. It is just what the country people say. My nurse told me, when I was a little child."

Mr. Turner grinned. "That's why you call him Mr Holiness?"

She laughed softly. "It is a kind of joke."

He stroked the cat's ear. "We think black cats are lucky in England," he said. "Just the opposite."

He was desperately tired. The strange scene and all the talking he had done seemed to have exhausted him; he was confused by all the new impressions he had taken in, and the great wound in his head was throbbing painfully. A heavy weight seemed to be pressing on the nape of his neck. He made an excuse as soon as his cheroot was finished, and Morgan showed him to his bedroom, a pleasant, spacious room, with a fan and a mosquito net. Outside, the rain was pouring down in sheets; Mr Turner threw off his few clothes and fell upon the bed in heavy sleep.

He woke next morning unrefreshed, and feeling slack and tired, and with a headache. He took an aspirin and lay for some time watching the glory of the dawn over the river; the air was fresh and cool after the rain, and the sky cloudless. He got up presently and went down to breakfast.

He found, rather to his surprise, that quite a heavy meal of curry and rice had been provided; his previous breakfasts in the country had been light affairs. He said, "I see you stick to the old English custom of eating hearty in the morning."

Morgan said, "Me? I don't usually have more than one cup of coffee and a little fruit." And then he said, "Oh, I see what you mean. Nay Htohn—it's her duty day. She always eats a big meal that morning."

Mr Turner said, "What's a duty day?"

The girl smiled at him. "One day in each week all good Buddhists keep a duty day; it is like your Sunday. On that day we must not eat after midday, so I eat plenty for breakfast." She laughed.

Turner said, "Do you go to church?"

She said, "I go to the pagoda in the morning. It is just like the Christian Sunday, but I think our duty day is rather more strict than yours. I may not use any cosmetics on my face or fingernails." He glanced at her and noticed that she had no make-up on. "We do not play the gramophone or have any music, and I must not touch gold or silver." She raised her hand, and Mr Turner noticed that she was eating with a wooden spoon.

Morgan laughed mischievously. "She used to sleep on the floor, too, before we were married, but I struck at that."

The girl laughed with him shyly. "If you keep the duty day properly you should sleep on the floor," she said. "That is for humility. But I do not think that that is meant for married women who have husbands to look after."

Mr Turner said to Morgan, "Are you a Buddhist?"

"I'm not anything," Morgan said. "Just a heretic, or an agnostic, or what-have-you." He paused, and then he said, "If I was to be anything, I guess I'd be a Buddhist."

"I suppose so," Mr Turner said. "Religion of the country and all that. Like what you were saying last night, about making your life in Burma."

"In a way," said Morgan. "But I wouldn't bother about that angle to it. A good many English people out here turn Buddhist when they get to know the ins and outs of it. It's a very pure form of religion."

"Well, I dunno," said Mr Turner. "The one I was brought up to's good enough for me."

Nay Htohn said, "There is very little difference for ordinary people like ourselves."

Mr Turner did not eat much at breakfast; the feeling of oppression was still heavy at the nape of his neck. Nay Htohn vanished into the back quarters, from which came the occasional sounds of children.

Morgan excused himself. "Do you mind looking after yourself till lunch time?" he said. "I've got my court sitting this morning. After lunch I've got to go out to a village in the country; you might like to come with me, in the jeep."

"I'll be all right," said Mr Turner. "I'm feeling a bit washed out today. I'll just sit here for a bit. Be all right if I take a walk down in the village later on?"

"Of course," said Morgan. "They'll be glad to see you. Take off your shoes if you go into the pagoda."

"I know about that," Mr Turner said. "I saw the Shwe Dagon last week."

He sat for an hour in the long chair, smoking and looking at the sampan traffic on the river. A brown girl came out of the house and set up a play pen in the shade and then went back and fetched a little yellow boy in a short pair of pants and put him in it, and sat sewing by him on the grass. Mr Turner got up and walked over and spoke to them. The girl stood up and smiled, but as she could speak no English and Mr Turner could speak no Burmese and the little boy was too young to speak much of anything, they didn't get very far.

Being on his feet, he went and fetched his sun hat and strolled out towards the village. It was only half a mile along the river bank; he took it slowly, and found the walk pleasant. He spent some time in the village, looking in the shops and smiling at the people. He found three men building a sampan on the bank, which interested him very much. He was interested, too, in the samples of rice and millet in the shops.

He passed the pagoda, but did not go in. He paused at the gate and looked in. Before the calm statue of the Buddha there were many flowers arranged in vases. On the paving before the image there were two or three rows of women kneeling in prayer; he looked at them curiously, and saw Nay Htohn. She was kneeling devoutly, with a long spray of gladiola held between her hands; salmon pink it was, and fresh and beautiful. Her lips moved in prayer; she was utterly absorbed.

Mr Turner walked on, rather thoughtfully.

He found the walk back trying. The sun was higher, and it was very hot; the road along the river bank seemed very long before he reached the shade of the trees by the house, and the pressure on the nape of his neck grew unbearable. He reached the steps leading up to the verandah and walked halfway up them towards his chair; then everything went red before his eyes, and he staggered, and grasped at the balustrade beside him, missed it, and fell heavily, and rolled down the steps that he had mounted, onto the path in the sun. The nurse saw him fall, from where she sat beside the play pen on the lawn, and called the bearer, and came running.

They found Mr Turner quite unconscious, and with some difficulty, and with the cook helping them, they carried him upstairs and laid him on the bed. The bearer fetched cold water and began to bathe his face, and the nurse went running to call Nay Htohn from the pagoda.

Mr Turner remained unconscious for three hours, lying on his back and breathing with a snoring sound. Morgan got back half an hour after Nay Htohn. Beyond loosening all his clothes and bathing his head with cold water, they did not know what to do. This illness was like nothing they had ever experienced. At that time there was a great shortage of visiting doctors in that part of Burma. There was a hospital at Henzada, thirty-seven miles away, but the jeep track to it was very bad, and it did not seem wise to attempt such a journey with the man in his condition. By river, in a sampan, it would take a day, but there was no motor vessel going up till the next day.

After an hour of vain effort to get him round, Nay Htohn said, "We must have help, Phillip; we are doing no good. I think we ought to ask the Sayah to come over."

Morgan thought for a moment. He knew the Sayah fairly well, the Father Superior of the local Buddhist monastery. He knew him for an honest old man, but privately he considered him to be a bit simple. Still, there was something in what his wife had said. The Sayah was the nearest approach to a doctor that Mandinaung could provide; moreover, if Turner were to die on their hands it would make matters easier all round if someone else with a position in the community had seen him. He said, "All right. I'll go and see if he can come along, if that's what you'd like."

She said, "I think he ought to come. Will you go for me?"

She could not go herself. When the monk arrived, she would have to keep hidden out of his sight, and ensure that he saw no female servants. When a man has taken to a life of continence and placed the world behind him, it is both rude and unkind to flaunt young women in his sight.

Morgan got into the jeep and went to the monastery. He knew the polite routine, and was shown in to the old man, sitting on a mat, in quiet contemplation. He explained his business and asked for help. In a few minutes he was in the jeep with the Sayah beside him, holding his coarse yellow robe about him in the wind of their passage.

The bearer met them at the door and made obeisance; there were no women in sight. Morgan took the Sayah upstairs to the bedroom. Turner was lying as the women had left him a moment before. A bowl of water by his side and a wet cloth on his head showed their most recent ministrations.

The old man went up to the bed and laid two fingers on his temples. Then he turned to Morgan, speaking in Burmese, "He will recover very soon," he said. "He will be normal before sunset. I do not think he has very long to go."

"Is he dying, then?"

"Not now. I do not think that he has very many months to come." The old man glanced at Morgan. "I will draw his horoscope."

"All right. What will you want to know, Payah?"

"The date and hour of his birth, and in what part of the world. He will recover before long. I will wait till he can tell me." He retired to a corner of the room and squatted down in meditation.

Morgan sat bathing Mr Turner's face and head. He had not expected any more from the Sayah, but his presence was a comfort and an assurance against any trouble. From the door there came a whisper from his wife, and he went out to her. She had been listening from the next room.

She whispered to him, "Maung Payah. Tell him about Maung Payah."

He smiled at her tenderly. He knew her very well. He knew that with her intellect she derided the divinity of the cat; he knew that with that which was still childlike in her, which he loved, she believed in it. It had not been wholly as a joke that she had called the cat Maung Payah. He said, "Would you like me to do that?"

She said, "Please do."

He touched her hand and she smiled up at him, and he went back into the room.

"We have a cat," he said simply, to the old man, "a white cat that my wife calls Maung Payah." The old man nodded his shaven head in understanding, and Morgan went on to tell him of the liking that the cat had shown for Mr Turner.

The old man sat in meditation for a time. At last he asked, "Is he a Christian?"

"As much as he is anything," Morgan replied in Burmese. "In the country that he was born in, as I was, there is not much religion in the life of ordinary men. He would

161

have been christened as a child, and confirmed when he was a boy, I suppose."

There was another long silence. The Sayah said at last, "Virtue is measured from the knowledge that is given to the soul in the beginning. Even if a man has kept no one of the Five Precepts for the reason that he did not know about them, he may still attain the dwellings of the Dewahs if his progress in this life has been sufficient."

He relapsed into silence, sitting cross-legged on the floor in the corner of the room, dressed in his coarse yellow robe, his bald, shaven head bowed in meditation. Morgan turned and went on bathing Turner's face. In the house there was silence but for his slight movements.

Gradually, the heavy breathing of the man upon the bed grew easier, and presently he stirred, as if in sleep, and rolled over a little.

At last he woke, and stirred, and sat up on the charpoy. He saw Morgan standing with a sponge and basin by his side, and a queer old Burmese monk beside him. He said, "I fell down."

"That's right," said Morgan. "You've been unconscious for three hours."

"Christ!" said Mr. Turner. "That's a bloody sight longer than what it was before." He relapsed into a depressed silence.

"Better lie down a bit and take it easy," Morgan said. "I couldn't get a doctor. Is there anything you ought to have done?"

"I'll be all right," Mr Turner said heavily. "I got one of these turns before." He paused, and then he said, "I didn't want to make myself a bloody nuisance."

"Don't bother about that," said Morgan. "I got the Sayah here to come and have a look at you; he knows more doctoring than I do. Like to tell him one or two things?"

"Sure," said Turner heavily. "What does he want to know?"

Morgan exchanged a few words in Burmese with the old man. "He wants to know when you were born, what day and at what time, if you know that."

"June the 16th, 1908," said Mr Turner. "Must have been about seven or eight in the evening. I know Ma was took bad at tea."

"And the place?"

"No. 17 Victoria Grove, Willesden Green."

Morgan transmitted this information to the Sayah, who gathered his robe about him to depart.

"That all he wants to know?" Mr Turner asked in surprise.

"That's all."

"Bloody funny kind of doctor."

Morgan took the Sayah back to his kyaung in the jeep, and returned to the house. He found that Nay Htohn had ordered the patient to stay in bed; they kept him there for the remainder of that day. He told them a little about his attack, sufficient to make them understand that it was connected with the great wound on his forehead. But he was reticent about it and told them no more than he need. When Morgan went up in the evening he found the white cat sitting on his bed. Mr Turner got real pleasure from the presence of the cat, and from the feeling that he was specially favoured.

Dawn came at about six o'clock in the morning. When Morgan came down shortly after that, in the cool of the day, he found the Sayah squatting on the verandah waiting for him. The old man produced a large sheet of paper from the folds of his garment, written all over with numerals arranged in columns under the days of the week and months of the year, the whole being roughly rectangular in form. He said, "I have drawn the zadah of the Englishman."

Morgan knew a Burmese horoscope when he saw it. Nay Htohn had one somewhat similar to this but more carefully made out, which she affected to think little of and treasured very carefully under lock and key. He said, "Will you interpret it for me, Payah?"

The old man squatted down on the verandah and spread the paper out on the ground before him. Morgan drew up a chair beside him and leaned down to see the figures that his finger indicated. A faint rustle from the room behind them told him that Nay Htohn had crept up within hearing.

The Sayah said, "I will not trouble you with that which is not important." He laid his finger on the chart. "When he was twenty-six years old he passed into the House of Saturn, to abide there for the ten years that all must abide. That is a bad age at which to enter the house of danger, and he did many foolish things. In the eighth year he offended against the laws of his country. In the ninth year he received the wound that you now see on his forehead." The old man laid his finger on a numeral. "Beside that wound, this symbol

163

shows yourself. I do not know what that may mean; perhaps you do."

Morgan said quietly, "I think I do. What year was that in, Payah?"

The old man studied the chart. "1943," he said. "In the following year, the last year of his sojourn in the House of Saturn, the man went to prison."

Morgan said quietly, "I wondered about that."

"Passing from the evil influence," the old man said, "he entered the House of Jupiter and lived there for three years, doing little good and little evil. From there, and early in this very year, he fell into Yahu under the Tuskless Elephant, here, where he received foreknowledge of his death."

Morgan glanced at the old man. "He knows when he will die?"

"He will die next year in April," the Sayah said. "He knows that, almost to the very month. This symbol is for knowledge, this one is for death, and this one is for April. It is very certain he knows about his death."

Morgan was silent for a minute. A crow flew into the verandah, picked up a crumb, and flew away. "I know very little about him, Payah," he said at last. "What kind of man is he?"

The old man studied the chart and said. "He is a good man, and will climb up to the Six Blissful Seats. He has known sin and trouble and it has not made him bitter; he has known sorrow and it has not made him sad. In these last months that have been granted to him he is trying to do good, not to avoid damnation, for he has no such beliefs, but for sheer love of good. Such a man will go on up the Ladder of Existence; he will not fall back."

The Sayah laid his finger on the last numerals of the chart. "Here is the symbol for a generous impulse, and here a great journey, and here beside it is again the symbol for yourself. I do not know what that means. Here is this illness under the gyoh of the North, which means a swift recovery." He laid the paper down. "I cannot tell you any more."

He got to his feet, offered to leave the horoscope with Morgan, and was evidently pleased when he was told to take it back to the monastery. In careful, polite Burmese Morgan thanked him at some length, and the old man shambled away down the road to his own place.

Morgan stood thoughtful, looking after him; Nay Htohn came out and stood beside him. "You heard all that about Turner?" he asked her in Burmese.

"I heard," she said. "We are honoured to have such a good man with us."

They stood for a minute in silence watching the retreating figure in the yellow robe. "We must send something," Morgan said at last. "What had we better send?"

The girl said, "Give them a bell. They can always use another bell." They turned and went into the house.

They went up together to see Turner, and found him awake. They persuaded him to stay in bed for breakfast; he stayed in bed until he wearied of it in the heat of the forenoon, and came down about eleven o'clock to sit on the verandah in his long chair. Morgan was out. Nay Htohn was watching for him, and made him comfortable in his chair, with a cheroot and a long drink of iced lime squash. He sat there at ease, watching the traffic on the river.

He felt that he must leave as soon as possible, and go back to England. The fit that he had suffered had been a sharp warning to him that his time was getting short. His journey to Burma, he felt, had been a complete fiasco. He had come out from England to locate a beachcomber and set him on his feet if that were possible; instead, he had found him a man of means, happily married, and holding a considerable position for a man of his age in the country of his choice. He had enjoyed every minute of the journey; he would have liked to stay and see more of the lovely country that he had come to, but there was no time for that. His time was very short; he would not waste it. If Morgan did not need his help there would be all the more for Duggie Brent, or for the Negro if he ever got in touch with him. He must get back to Watford and begin again.

He rested all day on the verandah. Morgan came back at about teatime and sat smoking with him, and Mr Turner told him something of what was in his mind.

"Them steamers down the river to Rangoon," he said. "I got to be thinking about getting back. The firm wouldn't half play hell if they knew I was sitting here like this with a nice drink 'n a cigar, 'n not doing a bloody thing."

Morgan said, "Stay a few days more and get yourself quite right. The firm would give you sick leave."

Turner said, "I don't think I'd better. I've not got much time. I better be getting back to Rangoon."

"There's a boat down the river tomorrow, if you really feel you've got to go."

"I better take it. I can't afford to hang around."

Morgan glanced at him. "Did you see anyone in England about these fits you get? A doctor?"

Mr Turner said, "Oh yes. I got examined by a specialist after the last time."

"What did he say about it?"

Mr Turner was silent for a minute. Then he said, "It wasn't so good."

"Is it very bad?"

"All be the same in a hundred years," said Mr Turner quietly. "That's the way I look at it."

Morgan said, "It's kind of—fatal, is it?"

Mr Turner stared at him in admiration. "You're a pretty sharp one," he said. "I never told you anything o' that, did I?"

"No. But it's right, is it?"

"Aye, it's right enough," said Mr Turner. "I got bits of shrapnel going bad inside my napper, 'n they can't do nothing about it. I got seven or eight months to go, not more. But I didn't want anyone to know."

"I'm very sorry." Morgan was silent for a minute, and then said, "Why did you come out here, really?"

"I told you. I got business in Rangoon."

"I know. Was it because you got a very bad account of me from my mother, by any chance?"

Mr Turner shifted uneasily in his chair. "I thought if I was out here I might look you up," he said evasively.

Morgan got up and walked over to the verandah rail, and stood looking out over the river. He turned presently and came back to the table by their chairs, and took another cheroot.

"When you see my mother," he said, "try and make her understand the way I live out here. Try and make her understand that Nay Htohn isn't a naked savage, holding me with Oriental wiles. Tell her I'm doing work I can do well. Tell her I'm prosperous and happy. Try and make her understand."

Mr Turner said, "I'll go and see her when I get back home next week, 'n I'll do what I can. But things look kind of different back in Notting Hill Gate, you know."

"I know." There was a pause. "You're going back home at once?"

Mr Turner nodded. "Soon as I can get a seat on a plane."

Morgan turned, and walked slowly to the end of the verandah, smoking and thoughtful. When he came back he said, "It's been very, very nice seeing you here, Turner. I've had it on my mind for some time that I should have tried to find out something of what happened to you—and the other two in that ward at Penzance. I know a bit about the nigger, but I never heard a thing about you or Corporal Brent." He stood looking down at Turner in the chair. "I felt a bit of a rotter about that," he said quietly. "'I've got on so well myself that I ought to have been able to spare time to poke around a bit and see if you and Brent were getting on all right. We were all in it together then. We ought to have kept up."

"Well, that's what I thought," Mr Turner said. "I mean, I got a nice house at Watford 'n a bit of money saved, in spite of everything and going through a bad patch and that. And then, when the chap in Harley Street said what he did, I kind of thought I ought to get and find out, case any of you hadn't been so lucky as me."

"That's why you came to Burma, really, isn't it?" said Morgan.

Mr Turner said defensively, "I got business to do in Rangoon as well."

They smoked in silence for a few minutes; then he said, "It's been nice of you 'n Mrs Morgan—I mean, your wife—to have me," he said. "I didn't know you'd be well off and settled like this, or maybe I wouldn't have come. I thought . . . well, things'd be different to what they are." He hesitated, then said, "I got in prison for ten months after leaving hospital; maybe you know about that. Over them trucks of sugar. I wouldn't have come if I'd known you were a proper magistrate, and that."

Morgan grinned. "That's all right," he said. "You didn't get away with it?"

Mr Turner shook his head. "They give me a year," he said, "but I got two months off for good conduct. I went a bit too far that time."

The pilot said, "You needed money very badly?"

" 'Course I did. I got kind of worried." He turned to Morgan. "I don't know how anybody gets along these days without they do a deal now and then to get something put by for when they can't work any longer." He paused, and then he said, "Time was, in the old days, a chap could save for his old age, or being ill, or that, out of what he earned on a salary. But now with income tax, 'n purchase tax, 'n every other bloody sort of tax, unless you do a deal now 'n again you can't get to be safe at all. Straight, you can't."

Morgan said thoughtfully, "It's like that in England now, is it?"

" 'Course it is. Chaps working on the bench, they got security of a sort. Chaps working for the Government, they got a bloody great pension to look forward to. But chaps working on their own, like shopkeepers, or chaps working in offices like me, they ain't got nothing to speak of. You got to keep your eyes wide open for a deal all the time, and some of them deals can be pretty slippery."

Morgan grinned. "Like the sugar?"

"Like that bloody sugar. I knew it was a bad un, but what's a man to do?" He turned to Morgan. "I was kind of worried," he said simply. "I mean, I'd just got married, and I thought the wife was going to have a baby. She never, but I thought she was. And I hadn't got a bean saved—fifty or sixty pounds, maybe, not more. And I got to worrying over what would happen if I got killed or badly hurt, 'n where she would be then. I mean, a chap's got to do something."

"I suppose so."

There was a pause. "Well, that's all over and done with now," said Mr Turner. "I got three thousand pounds saved up, 'n a nice house, 'n furniture, 'n all. I wouldn't like the wife to know the way some of it come, but it's better 'n leaving her stuck with nothing at all next year. And then," he said, "I got to kind of thinking about us four in that room in hospital. And I thought, the wife doesn't know how much I've got, so she won't miss a little bit of it 'n I could pop around before I go and see if you was all all right."

"I was thinking on the same lines," said Morgan slowly. "I was thinking I ought to try and find out something about you three. I don't know anything about Corporal Brent. But I do know a little bit about the nigger." He glanced at Mr Turner. "There was the hell of a row about that nigger," he said thoughtfully. "Like to hear about it?"

CHAPTER EIGHT

NAY HTOHN came out of the house on to the verandah with her sewing in a flat rush basket. The men got to their feet. "I was just starting in to tell Turner about that nigger at Penzance," Morgan said.

She smiled. "I like that story. I wish we could find out

what happened to him in the end." They sat down again, and Nay Htohn knelt down by her husband's chair, and began sewing.

Morgan said, "I must try and get this straight—it's rather a long time ago. But I was interested at the time, of course —and it was damn funny, because when I was at Exeter after Penzance we shared a mess with some Americans, and we used to pull their legs about it."

He paused, looking out over the wide river. Over the Pegu Yoma in the far distance the great thunderheads of the monsoon were massing for another storm; a little wind blew past them on the verandah, cool and refreshing. Jungle rats scampered up and down the trunk of the banyan tree, their tails held high; on the river beneath them sampans drifted by.

"There was an American lieutenant in the Army Air Corps who'd been stationed at this place Trenarth," Morgan said at last. "He came in one day in a B-25, and at lunch I heard him telling the other goddams all about it. I guessed it was our nigger when I heard him telling them."

Mr Turner asked, "What did he say?"

The American had said, "Colonel McCulloch sure has got himself a mess of nigger trouble down at Trenarth. It's got so the boys down there don't just know who they're to take orders from, the Colonel or the landlord of the pub."

It had been just before closing time when Sergeant Burton blew his whistle as he raced around the corner of the White Hart in pursuit of Private Dave Lesurier. In the bar Mr Frobisher had already said, "Time, gentlemen, please," to a room full of Negroes, beaming at them as he did so. He used the words that he had used for twenty-seven years each evening to warn his patrons at five minutes to ten that they must drink up and go, at the conclusion of his licensed hours. He beamed, because he was well aware by now of the simple pleasure that the Negroes got from the words which were his common use. They would grin back at him, and drink up, and go quietly on the stroke of ten o'clock. The bar of the White Hart was therefore reeking with Anglo-American goodwill when Sergeant Burton blew his whistle and the jeep came screaming to a standstill in the street outside and the fun started.

The Negroes went tumbling out into the street to see what was going on, and because they had to go anyway. After the last had left, Mr Frobisher walked slowly round the bar, wiping it down with a rag. Then he walked to the front door, to bolt it for the night, and stood for a minute looking out into the street.

In the moonlight he could see the street was full of American soldiers, white and black. There was whistling and the arrival of more cars with Military Police; somebody was standing up in the back of a Command car and ordering the troops back to their camps. There was a good deal of confusion, but the doings of the military did not interest Mr Frobisher very much. He bolted the door and retired into his parlour, and put on the wireless and lit his pipe, and sat down for a quiet smoke before bed.

Within five minutes the U. S. Military Police were hammering on his door. He heaved himself out of his chair and went to open it; he was faced by a sergeant with a couple of soldiers at his back, all armed to the teeth.

The sergeant said, "We got to search this house for a nigger. You got any niggers in here?"

"Nobody in here but me," said Mr Frobisher. "Not unless my daughter's upstairs in her room."

"Well, we got to search this house," the sergeant said, and made as if to come in.

The landlord said slowly, "Here, steady on a minute. What's all this about?"

"One of your village girls got raped or near raped by a nigger," said the sergeant. "The lieutenant said, search all the houses in this block."

Mr Frobisher said, "You got a search warrant?"

The sergeant stared at him nonplussed. "We don't need no warrant."

Mr Frobisher said, "Well, you can't go searching houses in this country without you've got a warrant. You ought to know better. There's no nigger in this house now, anyway. They all went at ten o'clock."

"For crying out loud!" the sergeant said. "You going to let us in here, or not?"

"You got to have a warrant if you're going to search my house," said Mr Frobisher firmly.

One of the men behind pushed forward. "Let me see if I can do it, Sarge." The sergeant gave place to him. Private Graves had lived and worked in England for five years.

"Mr Frobisher," he said, "we've got no warrant to search your house. But one of your young ladies has complained that a nigger stopped her and did something to her in the street, and he's run away. We thought maybe he might be hiding in your back yard or some place. Mind if we come in and have a look?"

"Sure," said the landlord, "go ahead. Why didn't you say that first of all?"

Slightly bewildered, the sergeant led his men into the house. They spread out quickly, looked in all the ground-floor rooms, and went out into the yard. Mr Frobisher said to Private Graves, "Take a look upstairs if you want to." He went with him and knocked on his daughter's door.

She answered from inside, "Who's that?"

"Come on out a minute," her father said.

She appeared in a kimono, and saw her father standing with an American soldier. He said, "This gentleman wants to know if you've got a nigger in there."

She said, "Why, Daddy, what a thing to say! You'd better go to bed."

He was quite unmoved. "Well, that's what they want to know." In a few words he told her what was happening. "You'd better let him take a look."

A very much abashed military policeman put his head in at the door and looked around, while Bessie regarded him as so much dirt. He went downstairs again with Mr. Frobisher, and the girl slammed her door.

The sergeant left one military policeman in the yard and moved on to the next house.

A few minutes after that there was the noise of a jeep being started up, a challenge, and two shots. In the street outside there was turmoil. Cars filled with running men and roared off in the direction of Penzance. Quite suddenly the street was quiet again, still and deserted in the bright moonlight.

Mr Frobisher shut the street door carefully, and shot the bolts, one by one. Then he turned, and Bessie was standing halfway down the stairs, in her kimono.

"Was that shots fired?" she asked, and there was wonder in her voice.

"Aye," said her father heavily. "It won't do no good, that."

The girl said, "Lor'! . . ." And then she asked, "Who was it got assaulted, do you know?"

"I dunno."

"Do you know which of the boys did it?"

"I dunno. One o' them called up from the cotton fields, I should think. Some o' them don't seem ever to have been educated at all, not to speak of."

She tossed her head. "Even so, a girl what's got her head

171

screwed on right doesn't have to get assaulted, not unless she wants to."

"Aye," he said, "that's right."

They went to bed.

Lieutenant Anderson of the U. S. Military Police did not get a great deal of sleep that night. He was a decent man, and secretly concerned at what he had found in the air-raid shelter. Easing his way cautiously around the buttress, gun in one hand and torch in the other, with a sergeant back of him carrying a submachine gun, he had found a young Negro sitting on a seat, his head bowed down on his knees, and drenched in his own blood. He put away his gun in favour of a first-aid kit, and rushed the lad in a Command car to the nearest hospital, in the next street, and left him there under guard. He had then an awkward five minutes with a British police sergeant who turned up and wanted to know all about it. Lieutenant Anderson was well aware that the British civil police had funny ideas about shooting. They went unarmed themselves, and seemed to have no difficulty in dealing with the pansy British criminals that way.

This police sergeant was a man of fifty, unimaginative and difficult. "Was that your men shooting in the street just now?" he asked.

"That's right," said the lieutenant.

The sergeant said ponderously, "Well, you can't do that here." He reached for his black notebook. "Can I have your name and unit?"

"Say, what is this?" said the lieutenant unhappily. "We're the Military Police. We don't have to make any report to you."

"Maybe not," said the sergeant equably, "but I got to make a report about you. You can't go shooting off guns in the street like that, not in this country you can't. You might ha' killed somebody."

Lieutenant Anderson realised that some explanation was required from him. "Maybe you wouldn't know about the color difficulty," he said patiently. "It's kind of different when you are dealing with a nigger. They don't react until you show a gun."

"Was this Negro armed when you found him?" asked the sergeant.

"Only just his knife," said the lieutenant. "But the boys wouldn't necessarily know that."

The sergeant wrote it all down laboriously in his note-book. Again he demanded the lieutenant's name and unit, and got them and wrote them down. "It doesn't seem to be anything to do with us," the sergeant said at last. "I'll have to make out a bit of a report because of the firing, but I don't suppose you'll hear no more about it." He went away at last, leaving Lieutenant Anderson irritated and slightly worried.

He drove back to his camp and, before going to bed, questioned Sergeant Burton rather closely. The sergeant, fat and forty, did not know the name of the girl, but he had seen her in the street several times, and knew where she lived.

It seemed to Lieutenant Anderson that before he made out his report to Colonel McCulloch he should make the matter water-tight by getting evidence from the girl, and at half-past eight next morning he was knocking on her cottage door, with Sergeant Burton at his side.

Mr Trefusis, signalman on the railway, had already gone to work. Mrs Trefusis opened the door to them full of feminine indignation. Gracie had come in crying shortly after ten o'clock and had been closely questioned by her mother. She had told her mother that she had been grabbed and kissed by a Negro soldier, and that she had screamed, and a sergeant of the U.S. Military Police had come running up and saved her. In her confusion and distress she thought that this was true.

"And let me tell you," said Mrs Trefusis, arms akimbo, "if you think you can bring them black savages into a decent town like this and let them run amuck, you're very much mistaken. It's just the mercy of Providence the poor girl isn't lying in her grave this very minute, and a lot any of you would care about it. But you ain't heard the last of this, you mark my word. Fine goings on, when decent girls can't go out after dark 'n come home safe! Fine goings on!"

Lieutenant Anderson's spirits rose; this was just what he wanted. If there was any difficulty about the charge or the shooting he could bring the Colonel down and let him listen to the mother of the victim. "I guess we're all real sorry this has happened, lady," he said meekly.

"And well you might be, young man," she replied indignantly. "This is a decent town; we don't have them goings on here, you know, however you may carry on at home where you come from. We don't want any o' your Wild West manners here. What do we have to do? Keep our girls in of an evening 'cause the niggers get them? I never did hear such! The poor child hasn't slept a wink all night and didn't eat no breakfast, and now late at the shop and all. I told Mr Trefusis, I did, I said we ought to have a doctor to her, that we did. That's what I told him. But he didn't pay no attention to me."

She stopped for breath.

The lieutenant said, "You don't have to worry any more. We got the nigger, and you can depend upon it there won't be no more trouble of that sort, no ma'am. He'll be up for court-martial, that nigger will. He'll get sent up for about ten years. As for your daughter, ma'am, I'm here to tell you that we're real sorry in the U. S. Army this thing had to happen. I guess there's nothing we can do will ease the little lady's feelings, but if there's anything she needs, or anything that we can get her that'd take her mind off it, I'd be real glad if you'd tell me."

Mrs Trefusis said, "I dunno. If you've got him and he's going to be court-martialled . . ."

The lieutenant laughed shortly. "Don't you worry about that. We're going to make an example of that nigger. This isn't going to happen again." He hesitated. "Could I see the little lady for a minute? I'd like to know if she can identify him."

"Come in." She showed them into the parlour, and went to find her daughter, who was hurrying to go to work.

"There's a couple of American officers come in about last night, dearie," she said. "Ever so nice they are. Come on in for just a minute and talk to them."

The girl said, "I don't want to see them, Ma."

"Come on, dearie—they won't hurt you. It won't take you long. They just want to know if you can identify the nigger that they've caught."

"I don't want to identify anybody. Why can't they leave it be?"

Her mother said firmly, "The guilty have to take their punishment. Now come along. It won't take but a minute."

"Oh, Ma!"

When she appeared behind her mother in the parlour she was practically inarticulate with embarrassment and fright. The lieutenant glanced at her, pretty and blushing and very young, and a momentary wave of fellow feeling with Lesurier swept over him; she certainly was a lovely little piece of work. This conviction was succeeded by a virtuous resolution to make very sure the Negro got the limit.

He said, "I'm here for the U. S. Army, Miss Trefusis,

to apologize for what happened last night. We're all real sorry about it, and we hope you won't think too badly of us over it."

The girl blushed, and was silent. Her mother said kindly, "She don't bear no ill will, do you, Gracie?"

The girl whispered, "No."

The lieutenant said kindly, "Did you ever see this man before, Miss Trefusis?"

Her mother said, "Speak up, Gracie, and tell the gentleman."

She whispered, "I see him in the shop."

"Did you ever go out walking with him, Miss Trefusis?"

She shook her head. Her mother said, "She don't go out with boys. Gracie's always been a very good girl, Captain."

The lieutenant thought, but a darn sight more backward than some. I could teach her plenty.

Aloud, he said, "Do you know his name, Miss Trefusis?"

She shook her head, and whispered, "I heard someone call him Dave once, in the shop."

Sergeant Burton said, "That's right, Lieutenant—Dave Lesurier."

"You're quite sure it was the same one that troubled you last night?" the lieutenant asked.

She nodded.

"Did you ever speak to him outside the shop," he asked.

She shook her head.

Her mother said, "Speak up, Gracie, and answer the gentleman when he speaks to you." To the lieutenant she said fondly, "She's lost her tongue."

The girl cleared her throat and said, "He used to come in and buy Players. I never spoke to him except for that."

The lieutenant said, "Just tell me in your own words what happened, Miss Trefusis."

She said, "I come out of the Hall and went along the pavement, and he was there, all alone. There was no one else about, 'n he said something, I forget what he said. And then he put his arms round me and kissed me."

Lieutenant Anderson asked, "Did you know he was going to do that?"

"Oh no, sir."

"What did you do?"

"I struggled to make him let go, and cried out. And then"— she indicated the sergeant—"he come running up and the nigger let go, and I ran away."

The sergeant was about to say something, but the lieutenant checked him. "You never gave this nigger any encouragement?" he asked.

"Oh no, sir. I only see him in the shop."

Lieutenant Anderson began to take his leave, well satisfied that he had got a cast-iron case to give the Colonel.

In the jeep as he drove off, the sergeant said, "There's just one thing about all that, Lieutenant. I heard her cry out to let go when I was round the corner, and the next I knew she come running flat out into me. She got away from the nigger before ever he saw me."

"Shucks," said Lieutenant Anderson. "He'd have caught her again, easy enough, if you hadn't been there. Good thing for her you was." They drove back to the camp.

The identity of the victim percolated through the village in the course of the morning. Bessie Frobisher, who went out every morning to do the shopping for the White Hart, came back and reported to her father that Gracie did not look very much the worse for her assault. "Doing up the rations like she does every day," she said. "She hasn't got no bruises on her face, or anything."

Jerry Bowman came at midday with a load of beer. He parked the lorry and rolled down the casks, with Mr Frobisher to help him, and came into the bar for a plate of bread and cheese and a pint of his own cargo.

"Had some trouble here last night, they tell me," he said affably.

"Aye," said Mr Frobisher. "Just outside here by the gate into the back yard, round the corner. They got the nigger, did they? In Penzance?"

"They've got him in the hospital," said Mr Bowman. "You know he cut 'is throat?"

Mr Frobisher stared at him. "No!"

Mr Bowman told him what he had learned at the Sun in Penzance, which was not a lot. Private Dave Lesurier had got through the night with the help of a transfusion, and would live; he had not at that time developed septicaemia. In the White Hart at dinnertime the case made a first-class sensation; it made a bigger one that evening when the Negroes came down after work.

Sergeant Lorimer was worried and distressed. He leaned over the bar, his great black hands clasped round a tankard, talking to Mr Frobisher and Bessie. "It don't seem to make sense, any way you look at it," he said. "If it was some of these sharecropper boys, now, it'd be different because some of them might not know better. Even so, colored boys have been treated real nice in this place; I don't think even the sharecropper boys'd do a thing like that. But Dave's got education; he's a mighty nice sort of boy, is Dave. I can't see that he'd ever do a thing like that, no, sir."

Mr Frobisher said, "Well, what did he do, anyway? I haven't heard that yet."

."They say up at the camp he's being charged with an attempt at rape. That's a mighty serious offense to charge a decent boy with, Mr Frobisher."

Bessie said, "It must have been something pretty serious, Sam, or he'd never have cut his throat. A boy don't go and do that for nothing."

"I dunno. That boy acted mighty high-strung now and then. He's got education."

"Well, anyway," said Mr Frobisher, "I'd like to know just what it was he did."

He thought about it for an hour or two while he served beer across the bar and listened to the Negroes as they discussed it. He found that, one and all, they took it cynically. They linked it with the conduct of the Military Police.

"They been waiting for a case they could go to court-martial on," one said. "They hate like hell to see us walking with white girls. Now they got one, and they'll make it plenty tough for that nigger. Yes, sir, they been out to get a colored boy on a color charge for a court-martial, 'n now they've got one. That boy's certainly going up for a long stretch." There was sullen agreement in the bar with this view.

They displayed complete revulsion from the war. When the nine o'clock news came on the radio, one said, "Aw, turn the blame thing off. Let the white men get on with the white man's war 'n leave us be." Nobody wanted to hear the news, and after an uncertain pause Mr Frobisher turned the knob to the light programme and got dance music for them.

The landlord's mind worked rather slowly, but along fairly straight lines. This thing concerned the village, and anything that concerned the village concerned him. At nine o'clock he said to Bessie, "Slip up and see Ted Trefusis, 'n ask him if he'd care to step over for a pint in the back parlour."

Mr Trefusis came, a lean, grey-haired man, responsible and serious as a signalman must be. Mr Frobisher took him into the back parlour and brought a jug of mild in from

177

the bar. Mr Trefusis said, "Glad to get out of the house, straight I am. The way the wife's been going on you'd think the end of the world was come."

Mr Frobisher said, "Aye?" And then he said, "Well, I dunno that it's what one would choose to have happen in the family."

Mr Trefusis lit a cigarette. "No," he said, "but it might ha' been worse. After all, there's no harm done."

Mr Frobisher cocked an eye at him. "Gracie all right?"

"Be all right if her mother'd stop putting a lot of fool notions in her head. After all, many a girl's been kissed in a dark corner before now, and will be again."

"Aye," said Mr Frobisher. "That all that happened?"

"Aye. Chap come up 'n said something to her, 'n put his arms round her, 'n give her a hug and a kiss. Then when she started struggling, he let her go."

"That's right, is it?" said Mr Frobisher. "He let her go?"

"Aye, and she run round the corner and bumped into an American policeman. 'Course a young girl gets a bit upset about a thing like that, specially when it's a black man. But some of these things, least said soonest mended. I told her mother, I said—after all, it's not as if she come to any harm."

"Seems to me," said Mr Frobisher slowly, "the man's come to more harm than Gracie has."

"Is that right what someone told me, that he cut his throat?"

"Aye," said Mr Frobisher, "that's right enough. They got him in the hospital."

"Whatever did he want to do a thing like that for?"

Mr Frobisher told him what he knew, and they discussed it for some time. "He's for court-martial soon as he comes out o' hospital," he said.

"What's he charged with, then?" asked Mr Trefusis.

"Attempted rape."

"O' my Gracie?"

"That's it."

"But that ain't right. He let her go."

"That's what he's to be charged with, all the same."

Mr Trefusis sat silent for a minute or two, smoking and thoughtful. At last he said, "There was a couple of Americans come to the house soon after I went to work this morning, an officer and a sergeant. God knows what the wife told them." There was another long silence. At last the railwayman said, "They're kind of hard on these black fellows, aren't they?"

Mr Frobisher drew thoughtfully at his pipe. "Well, it does seem like it," he said at last. " 'Course, we dunno what they may be like in their own place back in the States. They may have a lot of trouble with them that we don't know about. But I must say, at times it seems as if nothing they can do is right."

Mr Trefusis said, "D'you know the one they've caught, the one that cut his throat?"

"Aye, he comes in here. Decent enough sort of lad, he seemed to be, like most of them are. Always willing to lend a hand with shifting casks, or that. His sergeant was in here just this evening, speaking up for him."

They could reach no conclusion in the matter; indeed, it seemed to be clean out of their hands.

Next day it became known in the village that Dave Lesurier was being held under guard in hospital and was to come before court-martial on a charge of attempted rape as soon as he was well enough. In the streets the Military Police redoubled their vigilance; every Negro seen to be walking with a white girl was followed by an armed military policeman, to the sullen fury of the Negro and the blazing indignation of the girl. The Negroes took to walking in the streets in bands of ten or fifteen, looking for trouble, and fights with similar bands of white American troops took place on two occasions. One night Jim Dakers was set on by a gang of Negro soldiers and cruelly beaten up.

Mr Frobisher watched these developments with grave concern, and discussed them discreetly with the traveller from his brewery, with the Vicar, and with various men of Trenarth in the forces, home on leave from various parts of the country. He learned of pitched battles with firearms between American white troops and American Negroes at Leicester and at Lancaster, reports of which were censored from the newspapers. He thought about these stories gravely while he stood behind the bar, or tapped new casks down in the cellar, or sat and smoked in his back parlour when the bar was closed. He did not think quickly, and it took him a week or two to decide upon a course of action; but when he did make up his mind on the line that he was going to take, it was not a bad one.

He sat down in his shirt sleeves one Sunday afternoon after dinner and, breathing heavily with every word, he wrote a letter to General Eisenhower. It ran:

DEAR SIR,

I take up my pen to tell you things are not as they ought to be here in Trenarth on account of there being trouble between your coloured soldiers and your white soldiers. It is not my place to say which is right but if things are not put right I think there will be shooting here like other places because there are fights and things are getting very bad. We don't want that to happen in Trenarth because in all the twenty-seven years I have held this licence we have had nothing worse than an affiliation order.

I think if you could see your way to do something about Pte David Lesurier, coloured, now being held on a charge of attempted rape of one of our young ladies it would assist and stop things getting worse because the black fellows are very sore about this charge and we think it is a bit of humbug too because the young lady struggled and he let her go at once. It is very kind of Colonel McCulloch to see that men who interfere with our young ladies get punished as they should be, but between you and me the young lady come to no harm and it would be better to forget about it because the black fellows say this is a trumped up charge.

Pardon me writing when you will be very busy, but we don't want things to be let go and get so bad that there is shooting here like other places.

Yours respectfully,
JAMES FROBISHER, Landlord

He sealed this in an envelope and addressed it to General Eisenhower, Headquarters of the U. S. Army, care of G.P.O., London, and posted it.

Three days later Major Mark T. Curtis arrived in Trenarth from the office of the Staff Judge-Advocate. He came nominally in connection with the application for court-martial filed by Colonel McCulloch, and announced that he had come for a preliminary examination of the evidence. According to the book this seemed irregular to the Colonel, but he was not one to question any officer from the Staff Judge-Advocate, and laid the whole matter before Major Curtis.

"You see the way it is," he said at last, "these colored boys have been alone here too long, and they've got uppity."

"Yeah," said the Major. "Had any other trouble of this sort here, Colonel?"

"No," said Colonel McCulloch. "They haven't needed to go raping. I don't know what to make of these darned English girls. You just can't keep them away from the niggers. I tell you, in this place the girls seem to prefer going with a colored man to one of our white boys. The whole place is plumb color crazy. The landlord of the pub down in the village here, he'd rather have the niggers than the white boys in his bar. Can you beat that?"

Major Curtis said casually, "Does he stir up trouble?"

"I wouldn't say that," said the Colonel. "He's made a packet of trouble for me because he won't have the white boys and I've had to find alternative accommodation for them. But I don't think he makes any trouble between whites and colored."

The Major said, "You think this attempted rape is part of the same picture, that the colored boys got swelled heads?"

The Colonel said, "That's right. If you treat the colored boys too well, they'll start thinking about white women right off. That's always the way."

The Major smiled. "I come from Maine," he said. "I wouldn't know about a thing like that."

"I come from Georgia," the Colonel said. "I do."

"You're pretty sure about the evidence?" the Major asked.

"Oh, sure. Lieutenant Anderson, he's interviewed the girl —you've got it all in his report there, in that file." He turned the pages and picked out a paper. "This one."

The Major read it through again. "I'd like to have a talk with her myself," he said. "And with the colored man in hospital. The Staff Judge-Advocate, he's very anxious not to get anything irregular in these mixed cases with the British. We've got to be right all along the line."

"Sure," said the Colonel. "The man is in hospital in Penzance, and I'll give you a driver who knows how to contact the girl. You like anyone to go along with you?"

The Major shook his head. "Guess I'd better see them alone. They'll talk more freely."

"Any way you like," said the Colonel.

He put a jeep at the disposal of the Major, driven by a sergeant in the Military Police who knew the district.

That afternoon Major Curtis drove into Penzance. He went with an open mind, realising the limitations of his knowledge and wondering a little why the Staff Judge-Advocate had picked him for the job. He knew very little about Negroes. He came from Portland, Maine, and had been

181

through the law school at Harvard; he had practised for a time in Albany, New York, and later had become junior partner in a firm of attorneys in Boston. Once he had defended a colored janitor on a charge of stealing coal, and got him off; he could not recollect any other occasion in his legal life when he had been in contact with a Negro. It seemed to Major Mark T. Curtis that in all the Staff Judge-Advocate's department there were few officers less suitable than he for this assignment; but he was an open-minded man and quite prepared to do his best with it, working from the elementary first principles of law. It never struck him that this was why he had been sent.

He found Private Dave Lesurier sitting up in bed, with a dressing round his throat; he seemed to have boils all over him, and he was looking thin and ill. The guard on the door arranged with the sister for a screen around the bed, for there were other men in the ward. The Major sat down on a chair, by the Negro, behind this screen, and said, "I'm from the Staff Judge-Advocate's office, at Headquarters. You know there's been some talk about court-martialling you, Lesurier?"

The Negro said, "Yes, sir."

"Well, that's all in the future," the Major said. "If you have done anything very wrong, you will not get away with it without being punished. If it comes to a court-martial, you will have a couple of officers who know the law to help you. Before it gets that far, we've got to make up our minds if you've done anything so bad as to make it worth while putting you on trial. That's why I've come to see you, to get your story of what happened. Do you understand me?"

The Negro said, "Yes, sir."

"Well, now, would you like to tell me what it's all about?"

The Negro said, "I guess you know that already."

The officer was silent for a moment. "Maybe I know some of it," he said. "I've seen a statement Miss Trefusis made. I've seen nothing from you."

The boy said, "If you've seen what Miss Trefusis said, I guess you've seen everything, sir."

"There are two sides to every question, Lesurier. I want you to tell me yours."

There was a long silence. The Negro sat studying the grey blanket spread over his bed, with the red lettering on it, PENZANCE GENERAL HOSPITAL. "I guess there's nothing much to say," he said at last. "I don't want to deny it. I just grabbed a hold of her—'n kissed her. That's all there is to it."

Major Curtis said unexpectedly, "Have you got a girl back home?"

Lesurier looked up in surprise. "No, sir. Not one regular one."

"How long have you been over here?"

"Four months, sir."

"Got to know many girls since you got over here?"

The Negro shook his head.

"None?"

The boy hesitated. "Not unless you count Miss Trefusis," he said.

"Apart from her, Lesurier, have you been out with any girls at all since you got over here?"

"No, sir. I haven't spoken to one since I left Nashville."

"How old are you, Lesurier?"

"Twenty-two, sir."

The Major thought, a mighty long time for a boy of twenty-two to go without speaking to a girl. He said, "What were you doing before you got drafted?"

He sat patiently, asking a question now and then, building up the background to the case. He heard all about the Filtair Corporation and the James Hollis School for Colored Boys back in distant Nashville, and about the garage, and the truck driving, and the bulldozer. He had very seldom probed into a Negro's life before. In his home in Portland the help had all been white. Except in sleeping cars and shoeshine parlors he had not come much in contact with the coloured people. He sat patiently making the boy talk, realising the imperfection of his own knowledge, anxious to learn.

At last he said, "Well, now, tell me about Miss Trefusis. Where did you first meet her?"

The boy said, "In the store."

"I see." The Major glanced at him, and there was humour in his eye. "Like to tell me what you said to her?"

"Sure," said the Negro. "I asked her for ten Players."

"That all you said?"

"That's all, sir."

"Well, what happened next time you met her? Where was that?"

"In the store again, sir. I asked for another ten Players."

For an instant Major Mark T. Curtis felt that he was being trifled with; then, suddenly, he was almost sure he wasn't. He said, "Apart from asking her for cigarettes, when did you first speak to her?"

"I never did, sir. Only to buy Players."

The officer stared at him. "Do you mean you never said a thing to her before you grabbed hold of her and kissed her, except to ask for ten Players?"

"That's right, Major. I know it sounds mighty dumb, but that's right."

"I'll say it sounds dumb." The Major sat in silence for a moment, conning the evidence so far. Amongst white folks there were nuances in these affairs; sometimes the spoken word did not count for so much. He had not known before that coloured folks knew anything about nuances, and he was incredulous now. But his duty was to ascertain the truth.

He thought very deeply for a moment, and then said, "Was she nice to you?"

Lesurier said evasively, "She never spoke to me except to give me change and that."

"I know. But when she did that, was she nice to you?"

Their eyes met for an instant; the Negro dropped his glance down to the grey blanket with the red lettering. "She was mighty nice," he said quietly.

"I see." There was a short pause. "Well, now, Lesurier, what happened in the street that night? You'd arranged for her to meet you?"

"No, sir. I told you, I never said a thing to her except to buy things."

"Well, were you waiting for her?"

"That's right, Major."

"What for?"

"I wanted to ask her if she'd care to take a little walk with me one evening."

The Major felt that he was getting on to firmer ground. "You could have asked her that in the store," he pointed out. "Why didn't you?"

"There was always other folks around," the Negro said. "I didn't think she'd like it if I asked her that with other folks around."

"I see. So you waited for her in the street to ask her. Why did you pick ten o'clock at night, though?"

"I didn't pick it, Major. I started waiting for her around six, when I came down from the camp."

"You hung around from six o'clock till ten to try and get a chance to speak to her alone?"

"That's right."

"Have you got any way of proving that, Lesurier? Did you tell anyone what you were doing?"

"No, *sir*." The Negro thought for a minute. "I walked down from the camp with Corporal Booker Jones," he said. "He said to come on into the White Hart and have a little drink, but I said I guessed I would stick around outside. That was around six o'clock or soon after. He might remember."

Major Curtis made a mental note of the name. "Well, now," he said, "in the end she came along. Was she alone?"

"Yes, sir."

"What happened then?"

The Negro hesitated. "I went up to her to ask her," he said at last, "and then I thought it was kind of late to ask her if she'd like to take a little walk, and I didn't know what to do—after waiting all that time, and that . . ."

"What did you do?"

The boy said, "I give her a kiss, Major. That's all I did."

"Kind of sudden, wasn't it?"

The Negro said wearily, "I guess so. It sounds mighty silly now. The only thing I got to say is that it didn't seem so silly then."

"I see. What did she say about it?"

"Called me a beast, 'n started struggling," the boy said heavily. "I let her go."

"You let her go as soon as she struggled?"

"Of course, sir," the boy said. "I wouldn't want to do nothing she didn't like."

Major Curtis sat with him for some time longer, drawing out the rest of the story. He questioned the Negro very closely over the attempted suicide, feeling that it must have some connection with a guilty conscience over Miss Trefusis. All he got was, "I was just plum scared of what those M.P.'s would do if they caught me after messing with a white girl, sir."

In the end, Major Curtis said, "You realize that what you did was very wrong, Lesurier? You just can't go around treating women that way, any women, white or colored. And especially a British girl over here. You realize that?"

The boy said, "Sure I done wrong, Major. I know that. Will they send me up for a court-martial?"

"I don't know. I'll have to see Miss Trefusis and the Military Police and then write the whole thing up, and make out a report. The Staff Judge-Advocate decides if you're to be court-martialled, not me."

"I don't want to make trouble," the boy said. "I did wrong and I can take what's coming." He hesitated, and then said, "Would I get a chance to tell the little lady I'm real sorry about what I did?"

"I don't know," said the Major thoughtfully. "That might help."

He went down to his jeep and drove out to Trenarth. He knew from his own experience, as every soldier knows, that sex-starved men may not be altogether normal; that justice is not served by trying to apply civilian standards to conditions they were not set up to govern. It seemed to him that Miss Trefusis was a casualty of the war. If she had lived in one of the big cities of Great Britain, she might have been shattered by a bomb; as she lived in the country, she had been kissed against her will by a Negro soldier. Both were very unpleasant experiences, and both were due entirely to the war. The landlord of the pub had described this case as a bit of humbug; Major Mark T. Curtis was inclined to agree with him.

He said to the sergeant driving him, "Take me to the White Hart."

"It ain't open yet, Major. Not till five-thirty."

"That's okay—take me there. I want to see the landlord."

His ring at the creaking bell wire roused Mr Frobisher from his afternoon nap. He came slowly to the door and shot the bolts back. He stepped aside when he saw a strange American officer, who said, "Mr Frobisher? My name is Curtis, Major Mark T. Curtis, from the Staff Judge-Advocate's department at Headquarters. Mind if I come in and have a talk with you?"

Mr Frobisher took him into the back parlour.

"You wrote a letter to the General," the officer said, "about the situation here, and about Private Lesurier. That's right, isn't it?"

"Aye," said Mr Frobisher. He figured for a moment in surprise. "Monday I wrote it. What's this—Thursday. I didn't think they'd act so quick as that."

"We don't like to leave things to get worse," the Major said. "I've got nothing to do with the general situation between whites and colored in this place. I'm here to look into the evidence for this court-martial. I want to see Miss Trefusis this afternoon, if I can, but before doing that I thought I'd come and have a talk with you. I'd like to know about the background of this girl, what sort of family she comes from, what they say about her moral character. It all adds up, you know."

"Aye," said the landlord. "Well, sit down 'n make yourself comfortable. Can I get you anything? I got some whiskey, Major."

Major Curtis was not the man to refuse a Scotch; he gave Mr Frobisher a Lucky Strike and they settled down to talk. "What sort of girl is this?" he asked the landlord. "What does her father do?"

Mr Frobisher told him.

"Run around with boys much?" asked the officer.

The landlord shook his head. "She isn't old enough," he said. "I know they start young these days, but not so young as Grace Trefusis is."

"How old is she, then?"

"Let's see," said Mr Frobisher thoughtfully. "She was going to school when war started, 'cause she used to pass this window every morning with the other children. Yes, 'n she was still going to school when we started the Home Guard, the L.D.V. we called it then, because I remember seeing her pass when we was drilling with pikes 'n shotguns out in the Square. Summer of 1940, that was. Well, now, she was under fourteen then. She'd be sixteen-and-a-half now, at that rate. Maybe just on seventeen."

"Some of them get going by that time," the Major said.

"Aye," said Mr Frobisher, "but not this one."

"Anyway, you wouldn't put her down as a girl of loose character?"

Mr Frobisher was rather shocked. "Nothing like that," he said a little curtly.

Major Curtis felt the situation needed easing a little. "I wanted to be sure of your reaction to that," he explained. "There have been cases, not very many, but a few, of British women of loose character blackmailing our colored soldiers by threatening to charge them with assault. It's pretty serious with us, you know, when colored men assault white women."

"Aye," said Mr Frobisher, "you'll likely get a bit o' that in the slum parts of the big cities. But not here in Trenarth."

They discussed the girl a little more, and then the Major said, "Say, Mr Frobisher, just what did you mean in that letter by saying that you reckoned this case was a lot of humbug?"

"Well," said Mr Frobisher, "she come to no harm."

"Isn't that because there was a military policeman there?"

"Not according to what her father said to me. He said the Negro let her go as soon as she struggled."

Major Curtis eyed him keenly. "That's not what she said next day when Lieutenant Anderson went to see her."

"Aye?" said Mr Frobisher. "Well, she was with her mother then. You'll have to sort the truth of it out for yourself."

Major Curtis made a mental note to do so. "You've got no strong feelings about colored men associating with white girls, then?" he asked.

"Wouldn't be no good if I did have," said the landlord comfortably. "If a girl takes a fancy to a black fellow and likes him, well, there's nothing you or I can do to stop it." He turned to the officer. "One thing about these black fellows o' yours," he said, "they're ever so kind and considerate to the girls that go with them. Everybody's been remarking about that. Not spending money—I don't mean that. But doing things for the girls, putting themselves out for them, thinking ahead of ways to make them happy. That's the reputation that they've got in this place, and there's no good blinking it."

"Have there been any attempts at marriage?" the Major asked. He felt he'd better know the worst.

"Not yet," said the landlord thoughtfully. "I dunno that there may not be some, though. The way your coloured fellows go talking in the bar of an evening, a lot of them would like to come back here to live when the war's over."

Major Curtis got up to go. "Well, thanks a lot for what you've told me, Mr Frobisher," he said. "And thank you for writing to the General the way you did. We certainly did appreciate that very much. Say, where would I find Miss Trefusis now?"

The landlord glanced at his watch. "You'd catch her at the shop, if you're quick," he said. "Robertson's grocery shop, just up the street towards the cross. On the left-hand side. He shuts in five minutes, but you'll find her there if you go now."

The officer said, "Which had I better do, see her there or see her in her home?"

Mr Frobisher said, "If you see her in her home, you'll have her mother to deal with."

"I see," said Major Curtis. "I'll go to the shop. Well, thanks a lot, Mr Frobisher."

He went out into the street, and telling the driver of the jeep to wait for him, he walked towards the shop. He felt himself to be in very deep water. Even in Portland, where he had been brought up, no white girl would go out with a coloured man; a marriage would have been incredible. In this village things were different. Probably never very strong, the colour bar in Trenarth had collapsed entirely with the influx of large numbers of coloured Americans. According to the landlord, marriages of black men and white girls would certainly be tolerated and the girls would not lose much in social caste. In some respects the villagers seemed to find the coloured men desirable.

He entered Robertson's grocery shop with the feeling that he must be very careful not to offend. His duty was to get a fair statement from the girl of what had happened that he could put in a report for the Judge-Advocate; it would not help him to secure the truth if he showed revulsion from the standards of the village. He felt at a loss in another respect. He was there to question a very young girl, a good girl by all accounts, on a very intimate matter. He knew practically nothing about British girls; he had very seldom spoken to one in his life. Certainly he had never spoken to a British village girl like this; he had no idea how she might react to any of his questions. He felt that quite unknowingly he might defeat his object by his ignorance and clumsiness, fail to secure the truth, and make the matter worse. Still, he must do his best.

He went into the shop. Most of it was given over to groceries, but there was a sub post office in one corner, behind a wire grille. At the grocery counter there were a middle-aged woman and two girls, all dressed in rather soiled white overalls, serving two or three customers. Behind the post office grille was a middle-aged man.

The officer went up to the grille. "Mr Robertson?" he asked.

The man looked up. "That's me."

"I'm looking for a young lady, Miss Trefusis," the Major said quietly. "Is she here?"

The man nodded with understanding. "That's her at the end," he said in a low tone. The Major turned and saw a very pretty, dark-haired girl at the other counter.

He said, "I want to have a talk with her about this trouble that she's had. Could I do that here?"

"Well, if you like," the man said. "I'm just shutting up. It'll be quiet in here in a few minutes, if you like to wait."

Major Curtis waited. Mr Robertson came out of the post office section and closed the street door. One by one the customers were shown out. He saw the shopkeeper go to his wife and say a word to her quietly; they glanced at him and at the girl. He crossed over to the counter and said to her, "Miss Trefusis? Could I have a word or two with you?"

She said nervously, "With me?"

"Yes," he said. "I guess you know what it's about. I've been sent down from Headquarters over this court-martial there's to be about your trouble. Would you tell me a few things?"

She said, "I told one officer about it the day after, when he came. I don't want to talk about it any more."

"I know that," he said. "I don't like worrying you, Miss Trefusis. But that colored boy, he's in a very serious position. He can go to prison for five years or more on a charge like this. Well, that's fair enough and quite right if he did what he's charged with, but we want to be sure there isn't any doubt about the matter. Five to ten years in prison is a mighty long time if there was any mistake."

She was silent.

"We all want to do what's proper and what's right," he said. "We've got to stop things like this happening, so that you girls can go about your own streets safe at nights. But we've got to be fair all round, fair to you and fair to him. There are just one or two things I want to ask you, to check up with his own story. Will you tell me?"

She said, "All right."

He smiled at her. "How long have you worked here, Miss Trefusis?"

She looked up at him in surprise. "Here? I come here about three years ago, after school."

"Live in Trenarth all your life?"

She shook her head. "We lived at Wadebridge first of all; my Dad, he works on the railway. He got moved here when I was about seven."

Major Curtis nodded. He knew Wadebridge, another little town in Cornwall, not much bigger than Trenarth. "That about ten years back?"

"That's right."

He glanced down at the little packages she had been making up, of butter and of cheese. "Are they the day's rations?" he enquired. "Do you spend all your time doing up those things?"

She stared at him. "Week, you mean. We don't make up rations by the day." She took one up. "That's butter for a week, that is."

"Gee," he said. "It doesn't look like much."

"It's not much," she retorted. "Two ounces."

"Do you get bored with it?" he asked. "Making up those little packets all the time?"

"Well, I dunno," she said. "You've got to do something."

He leaned casually against the counter; she was beginning to talk freely. "Do you get many of our soldiers in here?" he enquired. "Americans, I mean?"

She said, "Not very many—just a few. I don't think there's much for them here. They aren't allowed to buy the rationed foods. Some of them come in to the post office."

He asked, "Do any of them get fresh?"

She tossed her head. "Some of the white ones try and be funny. I think they're awfully silly."

"Don't the black ones ever get that way?"

She said, "Oh no. They've got ever such good manners."

Major Mark T. Curtis laughed within himself and thought, that's one for you. Aloud, he said:

"Tell me, you knew this boy you had your trouble with a little bit, didn't you?"

She said, "I wouldn't call it knowing him. He used to come in here for cigarettes."

"Did you wait on him?"

"If I was about. I do the cigarettes and Maggie does the sweets. It's easier for one person to remember all the different prices of them things."

"What did he usually buy?"

"Players."

"How many? Fifty or a hundred?"

"Oh no. We couldn't sell that many to one customer. He used to buy ten."

"Just a little packet of ten Players?"

"That's right."

"They couldn't have lasted him long."

"They didn't. He was in here almost every day."

"How long did he keep on coming in like that?"

"Oh, a long time. Nigh on to three weeks, maybe."

"He didn't get fresh?"

"Oh no, sir—the black ones never do. I was telling you."

Major Curtis said, "Ever strike you, Miss Trefusis, that he came in to see you?"

She dropped her eyes. "I dunno."

The officer said, "Be fair to him. He's in a great deal of trouble over this. If he kind of admired you, Miss Trefusis, well, there's nothing wrong with that." He stopped rather suddenly, in mid oration. He had been about to say that a cat could look at a king, but it occurred to him that that might not apply to a Negro and a white girl.

She said in a low tone, "Well, it did seem sort of funny that he came here so often."

The Major veered off on another tack, fearing to dwell too long upon a delicate point. "Do you go to the movies much?" he asked.

She looked up, surprised. "Oh yes, I think they're ever so nice. We close Saturday afternoons, and we go then."

"To Penzance?"

She nodded. "There's two lovely picture houses there, the Empire and the Regal. They get ever such good pictures."

"Whom do you go with?"

She said, "Nellie Hunter, or Jane Penlee, mostly. Sometimes I go with Ma."

"Are those girls that you mentioned school friends?"

"That's right."

He smiled at her. "Ever go with a boy?"

She shook her head. "Not alone."

He smiled more broadly. "Ever been asked?"

She laughed shyly. "Not yet."

"Oh well," he said, "I guess there's plenty of time." And still smiling at her, he asked, "Suppose this colored boy had asked you to go to the movies with him, would you have gone?"

The smile died from her face. "I dunno. You mean, before he done what he did?"

"That's right, Miss Trefusis. Suppose he'd brought a colored friend along with him and suggested that you bring one of your friends, and you all make a party and go to the movies together, would you have gone?"

She said, "I wouldn't now, not after seeing how he could behave. I might have done before, when I didn't know."

"You weren't afraid of him before this happened?"

She shook her head. The golliwog was forgotten.

"Was it a great surprise to you when he behaved so badly?"

The girl said, "Well, yes, it was. I'd never have expected him to do a thing like that. He always seemed so quiet."

The Major said, "I had a talk in hospital with him this afternoon. He told me he wanted to ask you something that night, but things kind of went wrong. Would you like to know what it was he wanted to ask you?"

She nodded.

"He wanted to ask you if you'd like to take a little walk

with him one evening. He was very lonely, and he wanted somebody to talk to. He didn't like to ask you in the shop, because he didn't want to embarrass you in front of other people. So he waited for you outside. He began waiting at six o'clock that evening, hoping he'd meet you alone and be able to ask you without other people hearing. He didn't get his chance till ten o'clock at night, and he thought it was too late to ask you. I guess he got kind of confused then, and just naturally kissed you. He's mighty sorry now."

"So he should be," the girl said indignantly, "doing a thing like that!" And then she said, "Why ever didn't he say if he wanted me to go for a walk with him? I wouldn't have been cross."

Major Curtis said, "It must be very difficult for a colored boy to ask a white girl that. He wouldn't dare to do it back in his home town."

"Because of his colour?"

"That's right. That's one of the things that got him all confused."

The girl said thoughtfully, "I wouldn't have minded. I might not have gone with him, but I wouldn't have minded him asking."

The Major said, "There's just one thing, Miss Trefusis, where his account doesn't check up with what Lieutenant Anderson says you told him. What happened when you started struggling? Did he let you go, or did he hang on?"

She said, "I was ever so frightened. I don't really know." She thought for a minute. "I ran round the corner and bumped right into another man, that fat policeman."

"That's not what the lieutenant put in his report. He said that the Negro didn't let you go until the policeman came. It makes a big difference," he explained, "whether he let you go at once or not until the policeman came."

She said, "I think he must have let go. I think he must have done. He wasn't all that bad."

"It's not quite what you told Lieutenant Anderson."

She said, "I don't remember what I did say. Ma did most of the talking."

"The boy himself says he let go at once."

"I was ever so frightened," she repeated. "I think maybe he did. It's kind of silly to be frightened of things, isn't it?"

"I don't know about that," the Major said. "What he did was quite enough to frighten anyone. He acted very wrongly. But he's taken a good deal of punishment, one way and another. Do you want us to go on with this court-martial, Miss Trefusis?"

She looked up at him. "I never asked you to start no court-martial," she said. "You did that yourselves. No one ever asked me anything about it."

He smiled. "I guess that's so. Would you be content if we just drop the charge against him and let the matter be?"

"I don't want you to charge him with anything," she said. The mother flared up in her. "If ever I see him again I'll give him a piece of my mind, acting like he did. But you don't have to send him to prison, not on my account."

The Major said, "I think that's very generous of you, Miss Trefusis. It's in your hands. We're over here and in your country, and we want to do right by you Britishers. If you say charge him, then he'll go for a court-martial, and he'll get what he'd get if he behaved that way back in his own State, and that's plenty! If you say let him off, why then we'll feel that he's had sufficient punishment for discipline already, and just let the matter rest."

The girl said, "Well, I'd say let him off."

He said, "Well, that's what I think, too." He felt mentally refreshed by the mere fact that he himself had been talking to a girl for the last twenty minutes; it was a long time since he had done that. "These boys when they're a long way from home, they get so darned lonely, Miss Trefusis, they'd give just anything to sit and talk a little with a girl. Maybe you wouldn't know about that, but it's true. You don't want to be too hard on them when these things happen."

She said, "It must be terrible to be so far away from everything you know."

The Major put his thumbs in his belt, and straightened up to go. "Well, that's the way things are in wartime, and we can't change it." He paused for a minute. "There was just one thing," he said. "Lesurier said to tell you he was very sorry he did that to you. He didn't mean to frighten you. It just kind of happened."

She said, "Did he say that? I'm sorry I got frightened." And then she hesitated, and said, "Will he be coming back here, after he comes out of hospital?"

The Major shook his head. "Not after this. He'll be drafted to another theater of war altogether probably."

He said good-bye to her and walked out and down the street to where the jeep was waiting for him in front of the White Hart. He looked in to see Mr Frobisher, and found the landlord at his tea. He refused an invitation to join the meal.

"I just looked in to say it's all okay about that court-martial," he said. "I had a talk with Miss Trefusis. She doesn't want us to go on with it. I'll have to make out my report in those terms for the Staff Judge-Advocate. I'd say he'll wash it out."

"Aye?" said Mr Frobisher. "Well, that's a good thing, to my way of thinking."

"And to mine," the Major said. "I just stepped in to let you know."

He got into the jeep, and drove up to the camp. Mr Frobisher went back to his tea, gratified with the success he had achieved, and told his daughter Bessie about it. Half an hour later Bessie was telling Sergeant Lorimer; an hour later it was all around the village.

Up in the camp Major Mark T. Curtis sat with Colonel McCulloch, facing him across the office desk. "I guess we'll have to drop the whole thing, Colonel," he was saying. "We haven't got a case."

"Not got a case against a goddam nigger when he catches a white girl in a dark street and kisses her against her will?" the Colonel asked indignantly.

"No, *sir*. If she'd been six months older, she wouldn't have taken it so seriously. As things are, she won't give evidence against him."

Colonel McCulloch started in and told the Major just exactly what he thought of British girls. It lasted for ten minutes, till the Major had to leave to catch his train.

Down in the White Hart the Negroes were jubilant and, curiously, much more interested in the war; they listened to the nine o'clock news in almost complete silence. During the evening a Negro hand pulled the cardboard placard out of the window. With furtive laughter they added three words to it, and put it back again. It stayed there all next day till somebody called Mr Frobisher's attention to it, reading:

THIS HOUSE IS FOR ENGLISHMEN AND
COLOURED AMERICAN TROOPS ONLY
AND GENERAL EISENHOWER

Mr Frobisher took it out of the window and stuck it down beside his chair in the back parlour. It seemed to him that it had served its turn.

Next evening when the Negroes came down to the White Hart, they came with long faces. They had spent all day packing up; they had received surprise orders for a move to some new and unknown location. In any case, their work was practically finished; they would move along and make another airfield somewhere else.

They brought a present of a ham and a box of cigars for Mr Frobisher, and a huge box of candy and a dozen pairs of sheer silk stockings for Bessie. "We been treated mighty nice since we been here," said Sergeant Lorimer. "The boys all say they never liked a place so much as this."

At closing time they left for the last time. Exhausted with all the leavetaking and handshaking, Mr Frobisher stood with his daughter waving to the last of them as they went up the street towards the camp. They vanished out of sight, and Mr Frobisher moved slowly to shoot the bolts of the street door.

"Eh, well," he said, straightening up, "that's the end o' that."

His daughter said, a little wistfully, "Do you think we'll ever see any of them again?"

Her father shook his head. "Soldiers come and go in times like these," he said. "We'll never see them no more."

Morgan finished and no one spoke for a long time.

CHAPTER NINE

MR TURNER slept quietly and well that night, his last night in Mandinaung. Morgan had sent a boy running to Danubyu with a telegram reserving for him a passage on a plane for England. Mr Turner slept in the knowledge that in a week or so he would be back home in Watford telling Mollie all about it. He felt that he would like to do that. He had parted from his wife on different terms from those which were his custom; he wanted to get back to her, to see her again and tell her all that he had done. And he was very anxious to get home to Watford before he had another fall. He knew that would happen sometime. He wanted to be with someone who would look after him when it did happen.

He woke at dawn, turned back his net, rested and at ease, and lay and watched the light creep up over the wide river. The white cat, Maung Payah, walked in at the doorless entrance to his room, jumped up on to his bed, and lay down beside him. Mr Turner said, "Hullo, puss," and lay stroking its head and tickling its ear. He was a little saddened at the thought that he was leaving Burma so soon after his arrival; he would have liked to stay longer, to see more. Nay Htohn had pointed out the ridge of the Pegu Yoma on the far horizon and told him it was lovely there; she had urged him to stay a little longer and get up into the hills of the Shan States. Others would see these places, but not he. Burma for Mr Turner was a thought of loveliness. He had seen a fringe of it and knew that it was there; he would carry that knowledge back with him to Watford, enlarged and enriched by it, content if not satisfied.

He was with Nay Htohn alone for a few minutes after breakfast, on the verandah, as they waited for the steamer to come in sight around the bend of the river.

"When you see Phillip's mother," she said quietly, "try and make her like me. I know she does not like me now. That is curious, because we have never met. I know that it is difficult for old people in England to understand a mixed marriage like ours. It's difficult here, too. Some of my aunts think that I have done a dreadful thing in marrying an Englishman. But we have been very happy so far, and I do not fear the future. Try and make his mother understand."

Mr Turner said, "I'll try. I'll go and tell her just how you live, and what you have for dinner, and how you run the house, and that. But you mustn't expect too much. She's old, and she's an invalid, too. I don't think she ever goes out."

Nay Htohn smiled. "That is the trouble with the English," she said. "They so seldom go out, to see for themselves."

He sat talking to Morgan and his wife until the steamer came in sight up the river; then they got into the jeep and drove down to the jetty. The steamer came in and berthed for her few minutes' stay. Morgan carried Mr Turner's suitcase on board and found his cabin. They went out on deck, and found the captain waiting for Morgan to go ashore before casting off.

Morgan held out his hand. "Well, this is good-bye," he said. "Thanks a lot for coming, Turner. If ever you get a chance, come out for a longer stay and I'll take you up country for a tour." He said that because it is the sort of thing you do say, even when you know, or perhaps because you do know, that it can never happen.

Mr Turner shook his hand. "You've seen the last o' me," he said simply. "I'd like to have seen the Shan Hills, 'n all

197

that, but I won't now. Still, I've seen things I never thought to see when I was working in the flour business. I'll go 'n see your mother soon as I get back."

Nay Htohn said, "Good-bye, Mr Turner. We are very proud to have had you staying in our house."

He smiled, thinking that at last her perfect English had betrayed her. "Wish I could have stayed a bit longer," he said. "But I got to be getting on." He grinned. "I haven't got much time."

Morgan and Nay Htohn went on to the jetty; the moorings were cast off, and the steamer pulled out into the stream. They stood close together, waving. Mr Turner stood on the upper deck, waving to them in turn until they dwindled in the distance, and were gone.

The captain, a Burman, paused by him, and said, "You have been staying with Mr Morgan?"

"Aye," said Mr Turner, "just for a day or two. I haven't seen him since the war."

The captain said, "He is a very fine man, and he married into a very good family. One day he will be a member of the Government."

Mr Turner settled down in a deck chair, smoking his cheroot and figuring the cost of it as the river scene passed by him. Cheroots in Mandinaung cost two rupees twelve annas for a hundred, or about three a penny, a price which Nay Htohn considered to be gross extortion and nearly double what they should be. They were good big cigars, mild and satisfying, with a filter tip of pith; Mr Turner considered that in a London shop they were worth a shilling of anybody's money. He had no intention of returning to London out of pocket by this journey. He travelled thoughtfully down river, and when he reached Rangoon he telephoned to his Chinese agent, Mr S. O. Chang, from his hotel bedroom, sitting on the bed as he would have done in Birmingham or Hull. He said:

"Afternoon, Mr Chang—I just got back from Mandinaung. Yes, I had a very good time. I'm leaving for England day after tomorrow, but before I go I thought it would be kind of nice to ship a few of these Burma cheroots back home, and see what I could do with them. You know, the Danubyu ones with the filter tip. Suppose a chap wanted to buy a little parcel of them, say about twenty thousand, how would he set about it?"

Mr Chang told him, thrusting his own finger deep into the pie. Mr Turner pulled it out a bit next day, and left for

198

England at the end of the week, having seen the packing cases sealed and delivered to the shipping company. He travelled home by air, as he had come, in a great flying boat from the Rangoon River. For four days he dozed across the world, rested and relaxed in the cool air as the burning deserts of Sind and Arabia passed slowly far below and gave place to the Libyan sands, the blue wastes of the Mediterranean, and the small fields of France. He ate a good deal and slept a good deal, and he got back to England at the beginning of August, just a month from the day he left.

He had not told his wife which day he was arriving because he did not know himself. From the airway terminus he took a taxi to the underground, and travelled out to Watford, carrying his bag, as he had done so many times returning from a business trip into the provinces. It was a warm afternoon, so he took a taxi at the station, and he opened his front door with his latchkey and walked in.

The house was empty, but there were food and fresh milk in the larder, and the kettle on the gas stove was still faintly warm. He diagnosed that his wife had been there at lunchtime and had made herself a cup of tea. "At the pictures," he said thoughtfully, "or else over with Laura." He did not resent her absence, for he had not told her when he was arriving. He prowled around the house for a short time, savouring his old familiar things, and presently he found The Daily Express, and carried a deck chair out into the garden, and sat down to read the paper. But in a very short time it was draped across his face, and he was lying back at ease.

Funny to think that Mollie was at the pictures, and Nay Htohn, she liked the pictures, just the same. The same pictures, too. Funny to think that Nay Htohn was living seven thousand miles away, right the other side of the world. Funny the way he'd sort of felt at home in her house, in spite of everything being different.

He slept.

His wife, returning from the pictures, came to the French window of the sitting room and saw him sitting there asleep on the lawn of their long, narrow strip of garden; her heart leaped at the sight of him, for she had missed him very much. The knowledge that she would not have him for much longer had given him an added value to her. She had wanted to meet him on his way home from so long a journey, and to make him welcome. He had eluded her, and here he was, as always, alseep with a newspaper across his

199

face, as though he had been no farther than the office or the warehouse at Gravesend. A momentary wave of disappointment swept over her, and a little irritation; she had wanted so much to do something special for him, and the opportunity was gone.

She walked down the garden and stood by his chair. "Well, you're a fine one," she said amiably, "slinking in like that without a word, and going off to sleep with a newspaper, after being half across the world and all. Ain't you got no romance in you?"

He opened his eyes, and brushed away the paper. "Hullo," he said vaguely. "I must have dropped off."

"I'll say you did." She smiled down at him. "You might have let me know when you were coming. I'd have come to meet you, or something."

He said, "I didn't know, myself."

"Did you have a good trip? You're home much quicker than I thought you'd be, going all that way. It's only just a month since you left."

"Aye," he said, "just about a month. There wasn't much to do when I got there, so I come home again."

She said, "Pretty hopeless, was it?"

He looked up. "Hopeless? What d'you mean?"

"This chap that you went out to see, the pilot fellow. Couldn't you do nothing for him?"

"*For* him?" Mr Turner smiled thoughtfully. "I got a bit of a surprise," he said. "It's not like we thought at all. He's got a better job than I have, and lives ever so much better, too. Great big house he lives in, with about five servants. He's all right."

She said, puzzled, "But I thought he lived with a native woman." And then, curiously, "Did you see her?"

"Aye," said Mr Turner. "As nice a girl as any that you'd find in Watford, or in Harrow, either. It's quite different to what we thought."

She looked at him doubtfully. "Could she speak any English?"

"Better 'n you or me," said Mr Turner. "I tell you, Mr Morgan done very well for himself when he got rid of the other one and married her. Two lovely little kids, they've got."

She said impulsively, "But whatever colour are the children?"

"Yellowy," he replied. "Sort of half-and-half, you might say."

"How awful!"

"I dunno," said Mr Turner. "Things look sort of different out there to what they do back here. Let's have a cup o' tea, and I'll tell you."

She studied him with some concern over tea. In the month that he had been away he had changed, and not for the better. He seemed well and cheerful, but a little shrunken, and with a good deal less energy. The disability of his right hand was markedly increased, and he had difficulty in using it for cutting his food with a knife; he made increasing use of his left hand. She realised heavily that this was one of the things that must be; from now on he would need her more and more.

She said, "How have you been yourself, Jackie? Had any pain, or any of them dizzy fits?"

He said, "I had a fall, 'n passed out for three hours."

"Three hours!" She was appalled. "Was anyone with you?"

He told her how it had happened, and what had been done. "They couldn't have been nicer," he said. "No one could have done more. There wasn't any doctor in the place, but I didn't need one. I got over it all right."

She said, "You'd better see Doctor Worth, now you're back."

"I don't want to go seeing no more doctors," Mr Turner replied. "I know what's coming, 'n there's no good belly-aching about it, wasting people's time."

They took another chair out into the garden, and sat together while he told her about his journey, what he had seen and heard. It took an hour. She listened carefully, trying to understand the changes that had taken place in his outlook.

At last she said, "Well, what are you going to do now, Jackie? Going to try it in the office?"

She had worked, herself, for several years in an office. She knew that managements are generally kind to the individual; especially where the individual is known. In asking if he was going to try it in the office, she knew that in his case there would be no harsh dividing line between employment and sick leave; so long as he showed his face now and then and did a bit of work when he could manage it, he would draw his salary all right. Sick leave for Mr Turner would begin when he had not shown up for a consecutive fortnight or so, not till then.

He said, "I think so." He thought for a minute, and then said, "I got to think about them other two, the corporal and the nigger. I'm not so much worried about the nigger, now; it looks like he got off all right. I would like to know about that Corporal Brent, though."

She said, "I wouldn't bother about the nigger any more, Jackie. He'll be back in Nashville, or some place like that. He'll be all right."

"Aye," he said slowly, "I think he's all right. I don't think I'll do much about him. It's just Duggie Brent now."

His wife said, "I expect he's all right, too."

"Maybe," said Mr Turner thoughtfully. "But I'd like to know."

In the distance they heard the church clock strike six. Mollie asked what he wanted to do that evening, and Mr Turner said at once that perhaps it would be nice to take a run out to the Barley Mow. She vetoed that, on the score that he was tired after his journey, and won her case. Instead, they talked about Burma, and about her refresher course in shorthand typing, and presently they moved indoors, as it grew cool, and put the wireless on and listened to "Itma" with Tommy Handley and Lady Sonly and Inspector Ankles and the Colonel and Naive, and Mr Turner, who had missed this programme very much while he had been away, laughed until the tears came to his eyes, and fifteen million other people in the British Islands did the same.

He went down to the office next day—only a day or two adrift on his holiday time—and found a little work to do, and told the Managing Director about Mr S. O. Chang in far Rangoon. Secretly they were all rather shocked to see the change in him. If Mr Parkinson had wanted any confirmation of the sentence of death passed on Turner, he found it in the change in his appearance.

He went back to the office after lunch for a short time, and then went out and took a bus to Notting Hill Gate. He walked slowly through the streets to Ladbroke Square, and then up the steps, and rang the bell. Again the door was opened to him by Morgan's sister, as it had been only about five weeks before.

"Good afternoon," he said.

The girl said, "Oh—it's you."

"Aye," he said, "it's me all right. I've been staying with your brother, out in Mandinaung, Miss Morgan. I told him that I'd come and see you when I got back home. I got some things to tell his mother."

She stared at him. "You say you've been staying with my brother, out in Burma?"

202

"That's right."

She did not move from the door, or ask him in. "You can't have been," she said suspiciously. "You were here only the other day."

He said, "I flew out, and flew back again; I was in Burma just on a fortnight. I was staying with your brother Thursday of last week."

"But that's fantastic . . ." She moved aside, still only half convinced that this was not some imposition. "Come in, Mr Turner."

She took him up to the first-floor drawing room. The mother was not there, and one of the long windows was open, letting fresh air and sunlight into the room.

"Yes," he said, "I made a very quick trip, but I got time to spend a few days with your brother, up at Mandinaung."

"At Mandinaung? You went and saw him there?"

"That's right. He gave me a fine time."

She stared at him. "But could he . . . where did you stay?"

Mr Turner said, "I don't know as you've got the right idea of how he lives, Miss Morgan. He's got a great big house, 'n servants, 'n a good job, too. It's true enough he lived in a palm hut for a while after the war, same as any young couple might live in a prefab when they start off first. But now he's built himself a great big house outside the town. Real lovely that house is," he said, a little wistfully. "He's living better than what I do, or what you do here."

She said, "He did mention something about a new house, once . . ." She glanced at Mr Turner. "I'm afraid we don't know as much about my brother as we ought to," she said. "There was—well, something of a breach when he married that native woman. We don't hear from him very often." She paused, and then asked, "Did you see her?"

"Aye," said Mr Turner, "I saw quite a lot of her. As nice a girl as any that you'd find in this country or any other."

She stared at him, incredulous, and then asked, as Mollie had, "Can she speak any English?"

He felt at a loss, not knowing where to begin. "She speaks better'n what I do, by a long chalk," he said. "She's a very well-educated girl, Miss Morgan, and come of a good family, too. I think your brother done all right for himself, marrying her, if you ask me."

She said, "But they lived in a palm hut in the jungle!"

The wheel had gone the full circle, and Mr Turner started again, patiently. He told her about the house, the meals, the furniture, the children, the servants; he told her everything that he could think of about life in Mandinaung. As he talked, there came to his mind the figure of Nay Htohn, wistful. "That is the trouble with the English," she had said. "They so seldom go out to see for themselves." He talked to Morgan's sister with the figure of the Burman girl before his eyes, and he talked for nearly half an hour, and he was very tired by the time he had done.

A uniformed nurse came into the room, hesitated at the door on seeing Turner, and went out again. Miss Morgan said, "My mother is ill, Mr Turner, or I should have liked her to see you and to hear all this. But I'm afraid she is too ill to see you now."

"That don't matter," he said. "I'll look in some other time, when she's up and about again."

The girl hesitated. "That's very kind of you," she said at last. "My mother had a stroke soon after you were here before. She's very ill. If she recovers sufficiently, I will let you know. But she's made no progress in the last three weeks and the doctor tells me I must be prepared for anything."

"Dying, eh?" said Mr Turner.

She nodded, and her eyes were very full.

"Well, there's a pair of us," he said cheerfully. "I'm dying, too." The girl stared at him indignantly. "It's a fact," he said. "This wound in my old napper's going wrong on me." She glanced involuntarily at the great wound on his forehead, red and angry. "I got till next April, not longer, and I don't reckon that I'll be in circulation after Christmas. I've had it, Miss Morgan. But what the hell? All be the same in a hundred years, that's what I say."

She said, rather at a loss, "I am so sorry."

"So am I," said Mr Turner. "I'd like to have gone on a bit longer, but that's the way it is." He thought for a minute. "I think you should go out and stay with your brother," he said at last. "After your mother's gone, that is. I think you ought to go and see with your own eyes how different it all is to what you think. It don't cost much to go, considering what you'd get out of it."

She said seriously, "I'll think that over, Mr Turner. You've given me a lot to think about."

He said, "You won't be seeing me again, Miss Morgan, I don't suppose, because of what I told you." He got to his feet to go. "So just remember this. When your Ma dies, you write out to your brother, 'n go out and spend a few months with him, 'n get to know your sister-in-law. You girls are of an age and educated much the same; you'll hit it off with

204

her all right if you can just forget what folks have told you about colour and judge for yourself from what you see with your own eyes. I don't ask more than that. Just make up your own mind from what you see with your own eyes." He picked up his hat. "Well, I must be getting along."

He left the house and travelled back to Watford on the underground, and arrived home in time for tea. Mollie was expecting him and had a kipper for him and a great slab of cherry cake and strawberry jam, all the delicacies that Mr Turner liked best. And relaxing in a deck chair after this repast, and looking at the roses, and smoking his pipe, Mr Turner felt that there was a great deal to be said for Watford, whatever the charms of Burma. And presently, when Mollie came from washing up the tea things, he said, "Like to take a run out to the Barley Mow this evening?"

She smiled tolerantly. "If you like."

So presently they got out the little seven-year-old Ford and started down the arterial road in the cool evening. They got to the Barley Mow at about a quarter to nine and parked the car with all the others, and went into the saloon bar. It was full of light and smoke and good company; all his old familiar cronies were there—Georgie Harries, and Gillie Simmonds with a new girl friend on the stage, and fat old Dickie Watson, the bookie. In that atmosphere Mr Turner drank his beer and came out like a flower.

He told them the story of the temperance lecture and the glass of whiskey and the worm, and he told them the one about the lecture on psychic research and the goat. He was a very good raconteur and told a dubious story well. Standing in the middle of the crowd by the bar, flushed with beer, with the great wound in his forehead red and pulsing he was in his element. He never thought to tell them he had been in Burma, but he told them about the schoolmistress and the little girl who lisped, and about the man who climbed up on the wall of the lunatic asylum and found out all about Hipposexology. He had an inexhaustible supply of these stories, all somewhat juvenile, all certain of a laugh when told as Jackie Turner told them. The men enjoyed his company tremendously; the women stood by, faintly bored and brightly cheerful, with one eye covertly on the clock.

He tired presently, more quickly than he used to, and stood listening to other people's anecdotes and stories, with a mug of beer clasped in his hand. A broad-shouldered young man dressed in a black coat and dark-grey striped trousers told a very legal story about a man who had half his house requisitioned as a Wrennery and went on living in the other half, which was a Roman bastion and so an "Ancient Monument," and immune, and what came of it all. Mr Turner found himself beside this young man presently, and said:

"You in the law business?"

The other nodded. "I'm a junior clerk in Sir Almroth Hopkinson's chambers, in the Temple."

Mr Turner took a sip of beer, and thought for a moment. "Suppose one wanted to find out what happened in a trial back in 1943," he said. "How would one set about it?"

"Get somebody to look it up in the register."

"Can anyone do that?"

The young man shook his head. "You'd have to do it through a solicitor." He glanced at Mr Turner. "What sort of case was it?"

"A murder."

"Murder? Do you remember the name of the prisoner?"

"Brent. Douglas Theodore Brent. A corporal he was, in the Parachute Regiment."

"Rex v. Brent . . ." The young man stared at him absently. "Wait now, Rex v. Brent . . . He got off, didn't he? Manslaughter, was it?"

"I dunno," said Mr Turner. "That's what I want to find out."

"Rex v. Brent . . ." the young man said again. "I've heard about that case. I know—Stanier, Marcus Stanier—that's right. He was defended by a chap called Carter in Sir Phillip Bell's chambers. A man called Marcus Stanier is a clerk there now. It was he who told me about it. That's right. I could find out about it if you like."

"I'd be real glad if you would," said Mr Turner. "I was in hospital with him just before. I've always thought I'd like to know."

They exchanged names and telephone numbers; Mr Turner learned that the young man was Mr Viner. He rang up Mr Viner the next afternoon from the office.

Viner said, "Oh yes. I've got a copy of the transcript of the shorthand note of the trial here, Mr Turner, taken for the Judge-Advocate General. And I've got counsel's notes for his speech. Marcus Stanier brought them over this morning. I said I'd let him have them back tomorrow. Matter of fact, I've been reading it myself—it's quite an interesting case. He got six months, for manslaughter."

206

"That all?" said Mr Turner in surprise. "It don't sound much. He reckoned he was charged with murder."

"That's right," said Mr Viner. "But he had a very good counsel, a very unusual counsel, I may say. Would you like to see the papers?"

"I would," said Mr Turner. "If I slip over now, could I have a read at them?"

He went out and took a bus down to the Temple, and found the chambers with some difficulty. Mr Viner sat him down in a little badly lit outer office full of books and packets of old briefs and coats and hats, and gave him a dusty carbon copy of the shorthand transcript, Rex v. Douglas Theodore Brent. With it there was a dog-eared, marble-paper-covered book of pencilled manuscript, now smudged and faded, labelled P. C. CARTER.

The Judge was Mr Justice Lambourn; the prosecuting counsel, Mr Constantine Paget, K.C., with Mr Peter Melrose for his junior; and the defending counsel was Mr P. C. Carter. In the opening formalities the Judge had asked, "And for the defence?"

Major Carter stood up in the front bench. He did not wear wig and gown. He wore a uniform practically identical with that of the prisoner, with the emblem of the Parachute Regiment on the shoulder of his rough serge battledress. The crown on his epaulette was the only distinction between them.

"May it please your Lordship," he said, "I appear for the prisoner."

The Judge glanced slowly from the counsel to the prisoner, and back to the counsel. A thin, wintry smile appeared on his lips. He bowed slightly. "Very well, Mr Carter. You are for the defence." He leaned back in his seat. "Proceed."

Mr Constantine Paget stood up, a sheaf of papers in his hand, and opened the case for the Crown. The case concerned, he said, a Mr Michael Seddon, a boilermaker by trade, who met his death in the Miller Hospital at Greenwich as a result of injuries sustained outside a public house known as the Goat and Compasses in Albion Street, New Cross, on the night of March 22, 1943. He would call evidence to prove a quarrel between the deceased man and the defendant in the public house, and to prove that this quarrel continued in the street after closing time, which was ten-thirty. He would call medical evidence relating to the injuries that the deceased sustained. He would call evidence to show the court that the defendant was a man of violent passions, and he would bring to the court the only witness of the struggle which resulted in the fatal injuries to the deceased, the young lady friend of the defendant. With this evidence he would show the court that here was a case of wilful murder, and he would ask the jury for a conviction in those terms.

He then proceeded to call the barman, who gave evidence of the quarrel, and the landlord's daughter, who gave evidence about the telephone call received ten minutes after closing time from an unknown caller. He called the house surgeon of the Miller Hospital for evidence of the cause of death. For the violent passions, he called a Mr Isidore Levy, a commission agent of Southampton, who deputed that in 1942 the defendant and another man had come in and wrecked his office and injured him so severely that he had to spend a week in bed, following an argument about paying out after a dog race. In cross-examination by Mr Carter, this witness admitted that he had not brought the matter to the notice of the police, for business reasons. Finally Mr Constantine Paget produced a most reluctant Phyllis Styles of the A.T.S. and put her in the box, and he examined her on her sworn deposition in the police court, proving what had taken place outside the pub.

Major Carter rose to cross-examine her. She knew he was a friend of Duggie's and greeted him with a bright smile.

"Miss Styles," he said, "what was the original cause of this quarrel in the public house? What happened first of all?"

"He started saying ever such rude things to Duggie," she said at once. "He'd had a bit too much."

The counsel said, "Well, let's leave that for the moment. Will you tell us, what exactly did he say?"

Patiently he extracted from her, for the benefit of the jury, all that Mr Seddon had thought fit to say about the paratrooper's fancy hat. "This hat that caused so much trouble," he enquired, "what sort of hat was it?"

She said, "His beret. You know, what they all wear now."

Major Carter reached down to the seat beside him and picked up his own maroon beret, and held it up. "To make the matter quite clear, Miss Styles, was it a hat like this?"

She said, "That's right, sir; just like yours. The Parachute beret."

The counsel glanced towards the jury, and dropped his beret back on to the seat beside him. A faint smile crossed the features of the Judge. Major Carter went on and took

er through the entire quarrel; the court heard all Mr Sed-
on's opinions of the work done by the Army and his views
n the Second Front. And after ten minutes of all this, he
aid:

"And now, Miss Styles, I want you to tell the court ex-
ctly what the deceased man last said before he was attacked
y Corporal Brent."

He turned to the Judge. "May it please your Lordship,
t may well be that the court would wish that the witness
hould write down the answer to this question rather than
ive a verbal answer."

The Judge looked at the girl, slim and erect in her A.T.S.
niform. "Would you rather write down the words that the
eceased man used?" he said.

But Private Phyllis Styles had seen two years of service
n an A.A. battery, and had few inhibitions. "I don't mind
aying it if you don't mind hearing it," she replied. "He said
was a mucking Army tart, wearing a fancy tart's hat." She
ut her hand up to the gay forage cap tucked under the
paulette of her tunic, and glanced at the jury, as Major
Carter had before. "This one, he meant. Then he give Dug-
ie a terrible kick up his behind and Duggie went for him."

Mr Constantine Paget leaned back in his seat, stifling a
mile. He was going down on this case, he could see, all on
ccount of these blessed hats; he did not greatly care. He
oubted if the jury would give murder after what the girl
ad said. He did not really want them to. His duty was to
resent the case for the Crown but not to strive for victory
t the expense of what was right. He rose slowly to his feet
or re-examination of the witness, and said:

"Now, Miss Styles, what happened after the deceased man
sed the words that you have told us, and before he kicked
Corporal Brent? The corporal said something, didn't he?"

The girl said reluctantly, "Well, yes, he said he was the
cum of bloody Dublin, and one or two things like that."

"Thank you, Miss Styles. And then what happened, after
hat?"

"Well, he kicked Duggie, like I said."

"Thank you." He turned to the Judge. "My Lord, I have
o further evidence to offer."

Major Carter rose to his feet. "May it please your Lord-
hip," he said, "I have no witnesses with the exception of
he accused man, Douglas Theodore Brent, whom I propose
o bring forward as a witness on his own behalf. I have no
esitation in proceeding in this way because I am convinced

that he has nothing to conceal from cross-examination b
my learned friend, and because by doing so I shall convinc
the court not only that no question of murder is involve
but also that the deceased man met his death due solely t
the circumstances of the war in which this country is en
gaged."

The Judge raised his eyebrows. "Very well."

Major Carter said, "Call Douglas Theodore Brent."

Duggie Brent was taken from the dock by the escort an
put into the witness box; he was in uniform and bare-headed
He moved with the quick grace of perfectly developed mus
cles; his red curly hair was as untidy as ever. In spite o
his serious position he looked tolerably cheerful.

He took his oath, and his counsel started to interrogat
him. He gave his age as twenty-two, and the court hear
that he had joined the Army at the age of seventeen, i
1938. After the preliminaries, his counsel said:

"Now, Corporal Brent, when you were called up in 1939
were you fully trained?"

"No, sir," the corporal said. "I didn't know hardly any
thing."

"I see. What weapon were you taught the use of firs
after you were called up?"

"The rifle, sir."

"Yes. Were you taught to shoot with it?"

"Yes, sir."

"What at?"

"Targets, sir."

"What sort of targets?"

"Pictures of men advancing in open order, or behind
tank, or that."

"Yes, pictures of men." He paused. "Now after that, Co
poral, what did they teach you to do next?"

"To attack with the bayonet, sir."

"Yes. What did you attack?"

"Dummies, sir. Dummies representing enemy soldiers.

"Yes. What did you have to do with whese dummies?"

"Run at them, 'n run them through with the bayonet, sir.

"As if you were trying to kill them?"

"Yes, sir."

"I see. How long did this bayonet training go on for?"

Brent hesitated. "About three months, I think—off and on.

"And at the end of it, were your instructors satisfied th
you could kill a man easily and quickly with the bayonet?"

"Yes, sir. I passed out top of my platoon."

The counsel said drily, "They must have been very pleased with you. How old were you then?"

"Eighteen, sir."

Mr Justice Lambourn raised his head. "Mr Carter, is all this relevant to your case?"

The Major said, "If I may have the indulgence of the court, my Lord, I shall show presently that all this is extremely relevant to the case that is before us."

The Judge leaned back in his chair. "Very well, Mr Carter."

The counsel said, "Now, Corporal Brent, what did they teach you to do after that?"

He took the corporal step by step through his whole military education, with a furtive eye on the jury, watching for the first signs of boredom. For twenty minutes he displayed to them the processes by which the corporal had been trained for four years to kill men, to kill them with grenade and flame thrower, to kill them with the Sten gun and with the beer bottle that went off. And when at last the jury began shuffling and coughing, he said:

"Now, Corporal Brent, you volunteered for the Commandoes, did you not?" Mr Constantine Paget sat up in sudden protest at the lead, and sank back again, watchful of his colleague. It was all wrong, but it would save time.

"Yes, sir."

"When was that?"

"In June last year, sir."

"What unit were you sent to?"

"Number Eleven Commando Training Unit, sir."

"What was the first thing you were taught to do there?"

"Fight with knives, sir. You remember that—you taught the course."

The Major said smoothly, "Well, yes."

Mr Constantine Paget rose to his feet; he could not let the defence get away with that. "My Lord," he said, "I really must protest. The actions of my learned friend in another place and in another capacity can have no bearing on this case."

Mr Justice Lambourn raised his head. "Mr Carter?"

The counsel said, "My Lord, I did not seek the evidence to which my learned friend objects. But since the matter has been mentioned, it is right that you should know I serve the King in two capacities. I assist in the discovery of the King's justice in these courts. In another capacity and in another place, by order of the King passed to me through his officers, I teach men such as Douglas Theodore Brent to kill other men with knives. I cannot dissociate my two responsibilities to the Monarch, and it is right that this court should know the full extent of the duties that I carry out for him. Moreover, if I may have your indulgence, I shall show my learned friend that this evidence is not irrelevant to the case before us, in its wider aspects."

There was a long, slow silence in the court. The jury sat tense and alert; there was no boredom now. At last the Judge inclined his head, smiled faintly, and said, "Yes, Mr Carter?" Mr Constantine Paget shrugged his shoulders testily, and sat down again.

The counsel turned to the prisoner. "Yes, I taught you to fight with knives. Were you taught to do this noisily or quietly, Corporal Brent?"

"Quietly, sir."

"Yes. Were you taught to approach your victim from the front?"

"No, sir. We was to creep up behind him in the dark and stick him in the back."

"How many ways of doing this were you taught?"

"Three ways, sir."

The counsel said, "Yes. I taught you three different ways of creeping up behind a man in the darkness to stab him in the back." There was dead silence in the court. "How old were you then, Corporal Brent?"

"Twenty, sir."

The counsel with supreme artistry bent down and shuffled with his papers, searching for a document; there was a long, painful pause. The foreman of the jury whispered something to the man next to him. Mr Constantine Paget whispered to his junior, "Fancy letting him go on like this! Lambourn is just giving him the case." Presently the Major straightened up, a paper in his hand.

"Now, Corporal Brent," he said, "when you left that course, what course did you go on?"

"Unarmed Combat, sir."

"Yes, you went on to a course in Unarmed Combat. What did they teach you to do there?"

"We was taught how to attack an armed man just with our hands and feet, sir."

"Yes. Were you taught to treat him gently?"

"No, sir. We was taught how to kill him."

"Yes, you were taught how to kill a man with your bare hands, assisted by your feet. How did you get on, Corporal?

212

What grade did you receive on passing out from this course?"

"I was graded 'satisfactory,' sir."

"Who signed your grading certificate?"

"Captain Willis, sir."

The counsel held up the paper in his hand. "My Lord, I have this grading certificate here, signed by an officer who holds the King's commission, stating that he has trained the prisoner in the form of attack that you have heard described, and that his progress was satisfactory. If my learned friend desires, I will call Captain Willis tomorrow morning to prove this document in evidence, but on account of his urgent military duties I am anxious to avoid that course. If my learned friend can consent to treat this document as if it had been proven, it will assist the progress of the war."

It was passed up to the Judge, who glanced at it and passed it down to the prosecution. Mr Constantine Paget glanced at it, and nodded. The Judge nodded to Major Carter, who turned to the prisoner, and said:

"Corporal Brent, did anybody ever teach you boxing?"

"No, sir."

"Apart from this course in Unarmed Combat, did anybody ever teach you how to fight with your hands, at any time?"

"No, sir."

"Was this course the only sort of instruction you have ever had in fighting without a weapon?"

"Yes, sir."

"Now, Corporal Brent, take your mind back to the night on which this man, Mr Seddon, met his death. When you attacked him on the pavement outside the public house, what were your feelings towards him?" the Major asked.

The corporal hesitated. "I was kind of blind mad," he said at last. "I just went for him."

"You were very angry with him?"

"Yes, sir, I was."

"Why was that?"

"Well, sir, on account of what he said about my young lady, and picking on me all evening, and then kicking me up the arse."

"Yes. Now, after he kicked you, did you stop and think what you were going to do?"

"No, sir. I just went for him."

"How did you go for him? What exactly did you do?"

213

"I went at him the Unarmed Combat way, sir, like we had been taught."

"Yes, like you had been taught. What did you do first?"

"Well, sir, he was facing me, so I gave him a kick in the—in the lower stomach, you might say."

"Yes, you kicked him in the lower stomach. What happened then?"

"It worked all right, sir, and he bent up double, so I could get behind him and get him up against the wall, with my elbow under his chin and my knee in his back."

"Yes. Where did you learn to do this?"

"On the Unarmed Combat course, sir."

"Yes. Now, when you applied the pressure with your elbow and your knee to pull his head back, what did you mean to do to him?"

The corporal said, "Just give him a bit of a tweak, sir. That's all I meant to do. Just hurt him a bit, for saying that about my girl."

"Yes, you just meant to hurt him slightly. In your instruction at the School of Unarmed Combat, had anybody told you when to stop the pressure if the man's back was not to be broken?"

"No, sir. We was taught to use all the strength we'd got and finish it."

"Did you use all your strength on this occasion?"

"No, sir."

"Are you quite sure of that?"

"Yes, sir. I could have pulled him a lot harder than what I did."

"Was he struggling?"

"Yes, sir. He was a big chap and much stronger than me. I don't think I'd have stood much of a chance against him in the ordinary way."

"Now, Corporal, when you applied the moderate pressure that you did, what happened?"

"Well, he kind of collapsed, sir, and stopped struggling, so I let him go. And he fell down."

"Were you surprised when he collapsed?"

"Yes, sir. I couldn't hardly credit it."

"Why were you surprised?"

"Well, he was a great big chap, sir, about three stone heavier than me. And I wasn't pressing very hard."

"After he fell down, what did you do next?"

"I went to see if he was all right, and he was sort of breathing hard and groaning."

"Did he say anything?"

"No, sir. He didn't say nothing that I heard."

"And what did you do then?"

"I went off to a telephone box and rang up the pub, 'n told them there was a man ill on the pavement outside."

The counsel turned to the Bench. "My Lord," he said, "I have no more questions to ask the witness."

Mr Constantine Paget got briskly to his feet. He had little hope now of a murder verdict, and he had no intention of prolonging his cross-examination so that the case would stretch out and occupy another day; he was too busy a man for that. At the same time, he had his duties to perform, and one of those was to make quite sure that if this corporal got away with it he would at any rate remember the case. He said:

"Now, Corporal Brent, when you kicked this man in the lower stomach, did you know that that was a very dangerous thing to do?"

There was an uncertain pause. "I can't rightly say," the corporal said at last. "I didn't think."

"You didn't think! Do you know that such a kick could quite easily kill a man, in itself?"

"Yes, sir. We was told that on the course."

"You were told that on the course. You knew before this fight that such a kick could kill a man?"

There was another pause.

Mr Constantine Paget stared at the prisoner. "Will you please answer the question. Did you know before you had this fight that such a kick could kill a man?"

"Yes, I did. I told you."

"When you kicked him in this way, then, did you mean to kill this man?"

"No, sir. I didn't think."

"Why not?"

"Well, sir, he kicked me, and I kicked him."

Mr Constantine Paget shifted his papers. "There must have been an interval between these kicks, was there not?"

Major Carter rose to his feet. "My Lord," he said.

The Judge said, "If you please, Mr Paget."

Mr Constantine Paget said testily, "I will repeat that question in another form. Corporal Brent, was there any interval of time between these kicks?"

The corporal said hesitantly, "I don't really know. I don't think there was."

"Why don't you know?"

"I was sort of mad, I suppose."

"Corporal Brent, remembering that you are giving witness upon oath, do you really mean to tell the jury that when you kicked this man you had no idea of killing him?"

"Yes, sir. I didn't go to kill him."

Mr Constantine Paget wrapped his gown around him and sat down. Major Carter got up.

"Now, Corporal Brent, when this man kicked you, did it hurt?"

"Yes, sir. He got me right on the spine."

"Were you in pain, then, when you went for him?"

"Yes, sir. It was hurting something cruel."

"Is that why you cannot remember quite what you did?"

"Yes, sir."

"How long did this pain go on for?"

"I dunno," the corporal said. "I remember it was pretty fierce when I was telephoning."

Counsel glanced at the Judge. "My Lord, I have no more questions."

Mr Justice Lambourn glanced at the clock, and left his seat, murmuring, "Till two o'clock," and vanished through a door behind his chair.

The clerk said in a loud tone, "The court is adjourned for one hour and ten minutes."

After the lunch adjournment the defending counsel addressed the court. He said:

"My Lord and members of the jury, very few of the facts in this case are matters of dispute. We have heard evidence from a number of witnesses that there was a quarrel between these two men, and we have heard from the witness Phyllis Styles the words which the deceased last uttered, which brought the stinging repartee from the defendant, which caused the deceased man to launch the kick which was the first blow in this fight. If I may have the indulgence of the court for a very few moments I should like to speculate on what would have happened if this matter had occurred in peacetime, if Douglas Theodore Brent had never learned the terrible crafts that we have taught him to use against the enemy."

He glanced up at the Judge a little anxiously, to see if he would be allowed to go on with this line. The grey wig inclined slowly. He went on with more confidence.

"I have little doubt in my own mind that a return blow would have been struck, and normal reasonable men might well agree that such a blow would have been merited. But

I have little doubt also that it would have been an unskilled blow, a blow with the hands directed at the face or body. It would not have been the terrible blow that in fact occurred, the fierce, well-directed kick at the lower stomach that disabled the deceased. We have heard evidence to the effect that the accused man has had no training whatsoever in the art of fighting other than that provided by the Army. In peacetime, any blow that he might have struck would have been a feeble blow, unlikely to maim or even seriously to inconvenience his powerful opponent, more than three stone heavier than himself."

He paused. "I want you to imagine that scene, quite a common one in certain parts of our great cities. There would no doubt have been a return blow from the deceased; there would have been a fight outside the public house that night. There might have been a black eye, a nose might have bled, and both parties might well have appeared before the magistrate next morning on a charge of disturbing the peace. If that had happened, the accused, who now stands before you in the dock on a charge of murder, might have been fined five shillings, though in view of certain words of provocation which have been repeated in this court it might well be that he would have been convicted and bound over to keep the peace."

He looked up. "Members of the jury, I have done with speculation now; the matter did not take that course because at the time of Munich, at the age of seventeen, Douglas Theodore Brent joined the Territorial Army to submit himself to military discipline and training. This very young man volunteered and joined the Army before he was called up because he deemed it was his duty, being vigorous and strong, to serve his country in a time of need. The Army seems to have accepted him without any very great enquiry, and they proceeded to train him in the duties of a modern soldier."

He paused. "Well, now," he said at last, "we have heard in this court today something of these duties. All soldiers are trained to kill men quickly and efficiently; we cannot overlook that this is the very substance of war. Corporal Brent was trained as an infantry soldier; he then volunteered for Commando service, and later for service in the Parachute Regiment. In those units of the Army it is necessary to teach men certain ways of killing the enemy, certain deadly and ruthless ways of ending human life, which are beyond the education of the ordinary soldier. For many

217

months, by the delegated order of the King executed through his officers, this immature young man has learned these deadly crafts."

He stood in silence for a minute, staring at the foreman of the jury, marshalling his thoughts; in the court there was a long, tense pause. "I speak of what I know," he said quietly. "I have come here to defend this man for other reasons than because I want to take the fee marked on the brief. You have heard it stated in the evidence that I myself taught Douglas Theodore Brent to creep up in the darkness behind an unsuspecting man, and stab him with a knife, and kill him. I taught him to do that in three different ways, so that whatever method of approach was forced on him by circumstances he could kill his man immediately and without noise. I taught him more than that. With other instructors I endeavoured to secure that Douglas Theodore Brent, the man on trial before you, would act instinctively to choose the one of the three methods he was taught which would serve him best in his assault. We reasoned, we instructors, that in desperate circumstances he would have no time to stop and think. He must know his craft so well, the knife must be so familiar in his hand, that he would act instinctively in what he had to do, without the least hesitation, without any thought. Members of the jury, those are the principles that I have endeavoured to instill into the man before you."

He paused again. Mr Constantine Paget whispered something in disgust to his junior.

The Major said, "I have dwelt on my own association with the accused because it is a prototype of the unarmed combat instruction which he subsequently received, and which resulted lamentably in the death of Michael Seddon. Again, I ask you to consider for one moment what would have happened in peacetime if I and others like me had taught these deadly crafts to this young man before you. I do not think we should have escaped the censure of this court. We should have been involved in this matter with him, very rightly, as aiding and abetting in the crime of which he is charged. If I had taught Brent in time of peace to creep up behind a man and stab him in the back, and if he had done so in a private quarrel, I should have been implicated in his crime."

He raised his head and faced the jury. "I am not implicated in this crime, nor is Captain Willis, who taught him the deadly methods of unarmed combat which he used, inadvertently, with such terrible effect. Why is not Captain Willis charged in this court with Corporal Brent as aiding and abetting in his crime? It is because Captain Willis did what he did by order of the King, passed indirectly to him through his various officers. The Crown protects Captain Willis, and myself, from the consequences of our acts, of our instruction to innocent men in these terrible crafts. Are we to say, then, that the Crown throws a cloak of immunity around myself and Captain Willis, but leaves Corporal Brent unprotected to face a trial for murder, for doing what we have taught him to do by instinct and without thought?"

He smiled thoughtfully. "No; justice cannot be served in that way. If Douglas Theodore Brent is held to be guilty of the crime of murder, then Captain Willis must be held guilty of aiding and abetting in his crime. Alternatively, if Captain Willis is held to be immune from censure because he taught these things to Corporal Brent by order of the King, then that immunity must cover Corporal Brent, who in a struggle did by instinct what he had been taught. Members of the jury, this is the truth of it. The accident of war has taught this young man to do certain things by instinct. The accident of war has turned what would have been a simple brawl into a lamentable homicide. In your deliberations you cannot escape the fact that the real and fundamental cause of this man's death was the accident of war."

He paused. "Members of the jury, I have nearly done. In your deliberations you may well ask—where is this thing to end? You may say, the Army is training men in the dire arts of homicide, and training them to kill at sight without thought, mercy, or compunction. The Army euphemistically describes this as a 'toughening' process. You may well ask, how are these killers that the Army has created to be controlled if the Law be not strained and twisted to convict them? It is a reasonable question that, and one that must be answered. Upon the evidence you have no option but to find this man innocent of murder. But you may well ask —how, then, is the public to be protected from the homicidal crafts that he has learned in the years following the war?"

He smiled faintly. "I cannot look into the future, but I can, perhaps, see further than you. I, too, have been through this toughening process. In civil life I serve these courts as barrister, but in recent years I, too, have been trained to

219

kill men without mercy or compunction, instinctively, and without thought. But unlike Corporal Brent, I am thirty-seven years of age, and unlike him I have known another life, a life of peace. And I can tell you this. When the war ends and Corporal Brent puts off his uniform and puts on his civilian clothes and walks out into Civvy Street, all these dread arts will be sloughed off like his uniform. In three months after that you will find him thinking only about motorcycle races or the wallflowers in his garden, and when at times he is reminded that he once killed men in brutal physical assault, he will be filled with wonder that that same man was he. Innocent men are not so easily diverted from the life of innocence as many people think. There will be trouble with a few criminal types, who by virtue of their army training have enlarged their repertoire of crime. Such men are few in number. The many thousands who have learned these deadly crafts for use against the enemy will soon be thinking of them in wonder and distaste, letting their knowledge sink into oblivion as soon as may be. I say again, innocent men are not easily diverted from the life of innocence."

He gathered his papers together. "Members of the jury, I have finished now. Upon the evidence before you, you have no option but to find the prisoner Not Guilty of the crime of murder. And, gentlemen, I do not think that you need fear for the consequences of that verdict."

He sat down, and the Judge began to speak. The summing up of Mr Justice Lambourn came like a breath of clean, cold air into the court. He told the jury to put out of their minds the somewhat novel interpretation of the Law that they had heard from counsel, and to listen to him. It was not disputed by the defence that the deceased man, Michael Seddon, had met his death at the hands of the prisoner. Three verdicts were therefore open to them—murder, man-slaughter, or homicide in self-defence. If on the evidence that they had heard they came to the conclusion that the prisoner intended to kill the deceased man when he went into this struggle, or at any time in the struggle, that would constitute malice aforethought, and it would be their duty to find the prisoner guilty of the crime of murder. Alternatively, if they should think that there was no such malice, but that the deceased met his death through carelessness or negligence on the part of the prisoner, then they should return the verdict that the prisoner was guilty of manslaughter. If they should consider that the prisoner was convinced during the struggle that Mr Seddon intended to kill him and that the only way in which he could avoid death was to kill Mr Seddon, then the proper verdict for them to return would be homicide in self-defence. No other verdicts were open to them. No other considerations should be allowed to enter into their deliberations.

The jury retired for a quarter of an hour, came back into court, and returned a verdict of guilty of manslaughter. Mr Justice Lambourn sentenced the corporal to six months' penal servitude.

Mr Turner finished reading the dusty, faded carbon copy and sat down for a few minutes in the dim lobby, turning it over in his hands. Duggie Brent had got away with it, thanks to a counsel with a sense of the dramatic who had made the most of an indifferent case. Presently Mr Viner looked in on him. "Finished?" he enquired.

"Aye," said Mr Turner. "Pretty lucky, wasn't he?"

Mr Viner took the transcript and the counsel's notebook from him. "I suppose you might say so," he said thoughtfully. "Of course, it was in the middle of the war and, say what you like, the emotional aspect does come in, even with the Judge—the counsel who was a Commando and a paratrooper himself, and all that. But really, you know, simple people doing the best they can haven't got much to fear from the Law."

"I suppose that's right," said Mr Turner conventionally. He thought otherwise himself and from his own experience, but he did not say so. "Very interesting, it was," he said. "Thanks for letting me have a read at it."

The young man was pleased. "I thought you'd like to see it," he observed. "It *is* an interesting trial. A bit out of the ordinary."

"Aye," said Mr Turner. He turned towards the door, and then stopped. "There's just one thing," he said. "I'm trying to find out what Duggie Brent is doing now. Do you think this counsel that he had, this Major Carter, would have kept in touch with him?"

Viner stared at him. "I thought I told you," he replied. He glanced down at the dog-eared, dirty manuscript book in his hand. "This was the last brief Carter ever took. He dropped with his parachute party at Arnhem and held out at the bridgehead with his party for several days. Then he was taken prisoner. He was shot next day while trying to escape. Too bad that had to happen. He had a great future before him in these criminal cases."

"Aye," said Mr Turner heavily. "Too bad!"

CHAPTER TEN

THE months of August and September slipped past without incident for Mr Turner. He went and showed his face in the office most days, but Cereal Products Ltd. got little value out of him. Most of his time was spent in peddling samples of his cheroots in various tobacconists' shops around London. He was obsessed with the idea that his extravagance in going out to Burma must not leave his wife the poorer; whatever else he did, he must cover the cost of that journey before strength failed. And strength was failing, patently and rather fast. He was plagued with headaches and with fits of dizziness. He was beginning to find reading difficult, but it seemed hardly worth while bothering with glasses now; it was pleasanter to sit and listen to the wireless. He had increasing difficulty with his right hand, and it was a relief to him when Mollie started to do up his collar for him every morning, and to tie his tie. And he was losing weight.

He was still interested in his search for Duggie Brent, but he did not get on very well with it. With Mr Viner's help he made contact with the solicitors who had briefed Major P. C. Carter for the defence of the paratrooper, and learned from them, after much searching of old dusty files of letters, that Brent's father had been a butcher in Romsey. He set out one Saturday morning in the little car, with Mollie driving, and went to Romsey, where he made enquiries first at the post office and later at the police station. He came back empty-handed. Duggie Brent's father had died two years previously, and there were no relatives in the district. Nobody knew anything about Duggie Brent; it was a long time since he had been seen in Romsey, though his trial was remembered well enough. His paternity order had not been paid for a considerable time, for the girl had married and had suffered it to lapse. Mr and Mrs Turner had a nice drive down into the country, but returned to Watford very little wiser.

Over supper that evening Turner said, "There's one thing we never did. We could have got on to the solicitor what

222

settled up the father's will, and that. He must have been in touch with Brent at the time."

His wife said, "Why not leave it be? He'll be all right. He got off from his trial, so he's just the same as any other man, now."

"He didn't get off," Mr Turner said. "He got six months. But anyway, I'd kind of like to know."

"Seems like a waste of time, if you ask me," she said.

He was annoyed, because he knew that what she said was true. "Well, what of it?" he enquired. "My time's my own, 'n if I like to spend it this way, why can't I? I got little enough to come."

She said quietly, "Okay, Jackie—please yourself. Like me to do a letter for you, then?"

She was falling into the habit of doing all his correspondence for him on the typewriter, and her sister Laura was seeing a good deal less of her in consequence. Writing for Mr Turner was becoming a matter of increasing difficulty as his infirmity progressed.

He could still sign his letters, but his signature was getting very bad. Taking his letters was for her an exercise in shorthand typing, and this itself was useful to her for practice.

She wrote a letter for him to the police at Romsey, reminding them of their visit, and asking if they could find out the name of the solicitor who had wound up the estate of Mr Brent, butcher. In a few days they got an answer, and wrote again to Messrs Haslett and Peabody, asking for the address of Mr Douglas Theodore Brent. The reply they received read:

Haslett and Peabody,
Romsey,
Wilts.

DEAR SIR,

We regret we have no knowledge of the present whereabouts of Mr Douglas Brent. The last address we have, dated April 1946, was,

c/o Badcock's Entertainments Ltd.
Rising Sun Hotel,
Edgware, Middlesex.

Yours truly,

H. O. HASLETT

This brought the matter well into the sphere of Mr Turner. Edgware is a satellite of London not very far from Watford, and though Mr. Turner did not know the Rising Sun, he had no objection whatsoever to making the saloon bar of that house the object of a journey. His wife drove him there one evening early in September, two days after the arrival of this letter, resigned to an evening of forced cheerfulness and beer.

The Rising Sun Hotel proved to be an old house on the outskirts of what once had been a small country town. It was now surrounded by a great area of modern little houses, dormitories for a part of the huge mass of London workers. Amongst these modern shops and houses the Rising Run stood gaunt and shabby in old dirty brick, soon to be pulled down, no doubt, to make place for a more streamlined hostelry. Behind it was a field, or parking place, now empty and dirty. One or two small caravans, some piles of timber, and a circus trailer jacked up, with one wheel off, showed that an entertainment business might have its headquarters there.

"Aye," said the barmaid presently. "Badcock's Circus. They come here in the winter. They're out on the road now, of course. Come in for the winter about the end of October they do, and go out again about Easter."

Mr Turner said, "I used to know a chap was with them one time, chap called Duggie Brent. Is he with them still?"

She wrinkled her brows. "I don't remember . . . I've only been here eighteen months, you see." And then she said, "Oh, wait now. Was he one of them that did the Wall of Death?"

"I dunno," said Mr Turner. "I dunno what he did with them. I knew him in the war."

"There was a Brent . . ." she said. "That's right. Duggie Brent. Married he was, wasn't he? Chap with red hair, short and stocky, like?"

"That's the boy," said Mr Turner eagerly. "Is he with them still?"

"I dunno," said the barmaid doubtfully. "I don't think so. He hasn't been in here for a long time. Over a year, I'd say."

Mollie asked, "What was his wife like?"

The girl said, "Dark—slight—wore her hair in a bang. Used to take the money in the box for the Wall of Death. Phyllis, her name was."

Mr Turner said, "This Wall of Death—that what they do with motor bikes?"

"That's right," she said. "Going round and round. He was one of the riders. But I don't think he's doing it now." She called across the room. "Eddie, is that red-headed boy, Duggie Brent, still on the Wall of Death?"

"Nah," said Eddie. "Left at the end of last season, 'n never turned up for this. Monty Burke and Dick Fletcher are doing the riding now."

"How do you think I could find out where he went to?" asked Mr Turner. "I'd like to see him again."

The girl asked shrewdly, "He been doing anything?"

He shook his head. "I'm not a copper. I live over at Watford, and a pal told me this was his address. I just slipped over for a beer, 'n to try and see him. We was together in the war."

"That so?" she said. "Well, I dunno, I'm sure. Mr Badcock might know."

"He here now?"

She shook her head. "They're out on the road now, won't be back before the end of next month." She raised her voice. "Eddie, where they playing this week?"

"Thame," said Eddie. "Abingdon on Monday. Newbury after that."

Mollie had become strangely patient with Mr Turner, and raised no objection to another day spent in the little car, bouncing at forty miles an hour, hour after hour, down the long arterial roads in search of Mr Badcock. They found him after lunch in a grass field outside the small Oxfordshire town of Abingdon, among the hurly-burly of his swings and roundabouts and flip-flops and dodgem cars, and the Wall of Death, and Sawing Through a Woman, and the many tables on which you roll a penny for a girl to pick it up and drop it in a bucket by her side. Mr Badcock was a small, harassed man in a bowler hat, but he was affable enough.

"Brent?" he said. "Duggie Brent? I know —Wall of Death. Left last season he did, when we shut down for the winter, never come back for this." Mr Turner asked if he knew an address. The little man shook his head. "I got a couple o' letters waiting for him, been waiting for months. I been meaning to give 'em back to the postman some day, but I put 'em away somewhere."

"Eh," said Mr Turner, "it was just a thought I had. I knew he was with you, one time."

"That's right, up till last October. He didn't show up in March for his job."

Mr Turner asked, "Did you expect him?"

"Well, not really. Wife was going to have a baby, and the ladies, they get funny when they get like that. Oh, thanks." He accepted a cigarette; Mr Turner lit it for him. "Funny thing about that Wall of Death," he said. "Best attraction I've got. The public, they think all the time he's going over the top, see? The riders' wives, they get all of a twitter, even the real hard pieces—straight they do. But the riders themselves, they just get bored. Round and round, a quarter of an hour, six times a day. They get proper fed up with it." He turned to Mollie. "You've seen it, I suppose?"

She shook her head. "I'd like to."

He pulled out a heavy watch from his waistcoat pocket. "One starting in about ten minutes," he said. "Sorry I can't help about your friend. If you see him, say I've got a couple o' letters for him."

They went and stood on the little gallery overlooking the vertical track of the Wall of Death, watched the riders start their motorcycles in the basin-shaped arena down below and ride up on the wall in a crescendo of open exhausts. Round and round they went, weaving in and out together, up and down the wall. Between the turns Mr Turner studied the performers. They were rather florid, beery-looking young men, professionally reckless, well aware that their performance looked a great deal more alarming than it really was. It was a job that a Commando or a paratrooper would have turned to naturally, Mr Turner thought, full of bravado and noise and glamour. It was a job that a Commando or a paratrooper soon got tired of, if Mr Badcock was to be believed. Studying the performance with a critical eye, Mr Turner did believe him. Duggie Brent had been there and had gone, nobody knew where.

They came down from the gallery at the conclusion of the act, dazed with the noise and rather tired. There was nothing left to stay for. They went to a café and had a cup of tea, and drove back to Watford.

Mr Turner was very, very tired when they got home. He had a couple of sausages and a pint of beer for supper, with some bread and cheese, and went to bed at ten.

In the middle of the night his wife woke up with a start. In the dim light she saw him sitting upright in his bed; he seemed to be shivering. She was instantly awake, and said, "What's up, Jackie?"

He said, "Bloody bed's been turning over and over. Each time I lie down the bloody thing turns over." He sounded infinitely tired.

She slipped out of bed, pulling on her dressing gown. "I'll get you one of them powders."

She gave him his powder, with a drink of water, and talked to him a little; presently he lay back on his pillows. She lay down then herself, and kept awake until the regularity of his breathing told her that he was asleep; then she, too, slept.

In the morning she woke up at seven o'clock. Jackie Turner slept on in a heavy coma, breathing irregularly and rather fast. For a time she tried to wake him by sponging his face with cold water; then she went downstairs and telephoned to Dr Worth.

Mr Turner stayed in his coma till about eleven o'clock, the doctor with him for the last hour-and-a-half. He woke with a splitting headache, which the doctor mitigated for him, and he lay for the remainder of the day, drowsy with drugs, in the little sunlit bedroom. Downstairs in the sitting room the doctor had a word with Mrs Turner.

"I can't hold out much hope that there will not be more of these," he said. "It's going exactly as Mr Hughes told us it would."

Mollie nodded. "How long should he go on working, doctor?"

He shrugged his shoulders. "As long as he feels he can. He couldn't go to work today or tomorrow, of course. But it's better that he should have an interest as long as he can manage it. We don't want him to get depressed with having no occupation."

She said thoughtfully, "I don't believe he'd go like that." And then she said, "How long do you think it will be before he has to go into a home, or something?"

He said, "I think by Christmas he will be permanently in bed, at this rate. Of course, you could keep him here, if you feel able to take on the work. The nurse can look in every day and do anything that might be necessary." He hesitated, and then said, "I don't imagine it would be for very long."

She raised her head. "I'd like to do that, doctor. If there's no reason why he should go into a home, he'd be much better off in his own house here while it lasts."

He said, "It will tie you down, you know. He ought not to be left alone."

"I know," she said. "But I've not been such a good wife to him that I've not got a bit to make up, like."

He thought for a minute. "Mr Hughes said he wanted to

227

see him after four months. I think that takes us to about the end of October. I'll write to Mr Hughes and make an appointment for him then."

He gave her a few instructions about nursing and medicines, and went away. She took The Daily Mirror up to Mr Turner and he took it gratefully, and turned at once to the cartoon of "Jane," who once more had got herself into a predicament that involved the loss of much of her clothing, and he chuckled over it, and laid the paper down. They had a wireless set that required no aerial or earth, and Mollie brought that up into the bedroom and plugged it in for him to listen to a talk on "Laying the Car Up for the Winter," which interested Mr Turner very much, while she went down and cooked a bloater for his lunch.

He slept a little in the afternoon, and she brought his tea up to him as he lay in bed. And over tea he said, "I been thinking about laying up the car, like it said on the wireless. It's quarter day next week, 'n we can turn the tax in and get something back on the insurance. I reckon we ought to save the money, 'n we shan't want it till the spring."

She thought, they would not want it then, but did not say so. The car was his adventure. It would be reasonable to sell it, but she did not suggest that. Instead, she said, "I dunno about that. What would you think if we went off in it first, 'n had a kind of holiday together, driving round? It's ever so long since we had a holiday together."

He considered this. He liked driving in the car, and a holiday touring round and staying in hotels entirely for pleasure was a thing that he had never done since he was married. He said, "I had my holiday this year. I got to think about work sometimes."

She said, "You've got your sick leave coming, Jackie."

"Aye," he said. "Does Dr Worth think I ought to start that now?"

"Not really," she admitted. "But I think it would be fun if we went off and had a bit of holiday together like. I mean, after all," she said, "what's the use of just going on working till you've got to stop? You've got to have a bit of fun sometimes."

He felt that he could not have agreed with her more. "It'd cost an awful lot," he said, "staying in hotels every night, and that."

"It wouldn't matter for a fortnight," she said. "We've got that much money. Then we could come back here and put the car up like you said. We'd only lose a little bit if we did that. And the weather's lovely still."

He said, "Where would you want to go?"

She thought for a moment. "Devonshire," she said. "And Dartmoor and places like that. The heather gets ever so pretty on the hills this time of year."

Next day she wrote a letter for him to Mr Parkinson, the Managing Director of Cereal Products Ltd. They got an answer back two days later; Mr Parkinson was very sorry to hear such bad news of his illness, and had arranged with the secretary to put Mr Turner on sick leave, commencing at the end of the month. The additional ten days of full pay and commission was a gracious little act that pleased them very much.

They spent a few days planning with their maps while Mr Turner recuperated, and started off for Taunton on a Monday. They stayed the night there, after a long drive in the little car, and went on to Minehead next day, and after that across Exmoor to South Molton, where Mr Turner found an old friend in the saloon bar travelling in ladies' underwear, and had a glorious time with him, and learned two new stories, and got a rayon slip for Mollie very cheap. From there they went to Dartmoor and spent a couple of nights at Two Bridges, stared at the prison, and then went on through Launceston across Bodmin Moor to Bodmin.

In the hotel that night, over dinner, Mr Turner said casually, "I see we're only about forty miles from Penzance, here."

His wife said quietly, "Like to go there, Jackie?" She had seen the point of his manoeuvres westwards for some days.

"Well, I dunno," he said. "It might be nice to go on to the very end, now we've come so far. I never seen Lands End yet."

They decided that it would be nice to go on and see Lands End, and came to Penzance the next day in time for lunch. They took a room and went out after lunch in the small car and drove out to Lands End, and stood on the cliff looking out towards America. The sea looked very cold and grey and unfriendly, and they were glad to get back to Penzance for tea in the hotel.

Over tea Mr Turner said casually, "We're only four miles from that place Trenarth where all that happened about Dave Lesurier, the Negro I was telling you about. Like to take a run out and see what the beer's like at the pub?"

This was his holiday, and probably his last. She knew

that he had been distressed that he had only located one of his companions in the ward so far, that the quest still lay very near the surface of his mind. She was not in the least deceived by his dissimulation; he wanted to go there, she knew, in the faint hope that he might glean something from the landlord of the pub. She said quietly, "It'll probably have changed hands by this time, Jackie." She did not want to see him suddenly disappointed. "There'll be another landlord after all these years."

He said, "Well, I dunno; it's not so long as that. Anyway, I'd kind of like to go and see the place."

She got up. "I'll just run up and put my things on."

They drove out to the little town Trenarth and parked the car in the small square outside the White Hart Hotel. Mr Turner stood for a few minutes looking round, while Mollie waited for him. This was the place that he had heard so much about in hospital in 1943 from the young Negro, and in Burma recently, eight thousand miles away, from the young man who had married a brown girl. Nay Htohn in Mandinaung had known about this place, though she would never see it. Negroes in Memphis and New Orleans, in Nashville and St Louis, remembered this small town with pleasure. This unconsidered place, these slate-roofed, unimposing houses, and these unassuming people had formed themselves into a little thread in the weave of friendship and of knowledge that holds countries together. Mr Turner felt that Trenarth had done something for the world; it was impossible to feel otherwise when he had heard so much about it in Burma.

It seemed incredible, looking at this quiet little place, that it had once been full of Negroes from America. It seemed incredible that the landlord of this shabby little pub had once sat down in his shirt sleeves to write a letter to General Eisenhower, and had got a hearing.

It seemed incredible that all that could have happened here.

He went into the bar with Mollie. There was a stout man of about sixty behind the bar, in shirt sleeves; a common man, but a man of authority and poise. At the first glance Mr Turner knew that the White Hart had not changed hands; he glanced at Mollie and she glanced at him in the same knowledge. Mr Turner ordered a pint of bitter for himself and a gin and French for Mollie.

The landlord served them across the bar. They stood at the bar for a moment; Mr Turner gave his wife a cigarette, and offered one to the landlord, who accepted it. "Just passing through?" he asked.

Mr Turner blew a cloud of smoke. "Staying in Penzance the night," he said. "Matter of fact, I been down here before. Not in this place. I was in hospital in Penzance for a time, back in 1943."

"Aye?" said Mr Frobisher.

"Bit different now," said Mr Turner.

"Aye," said Mr Frobisher. "1943—that's when we had all them Americans in camp here, turning the place upside down."

"That's right," said Mr Turner. "I was in the ward with one of them, got into trouble here. A young Negro soldier he was, Dave Lesurier."

"Aye?" said Mr Frobisher with interest. "You was in hospital with Dave Lesurier?"

"That's right," said Mr Turner. "We used to play draughts together. Checkers, he called it."

"He calls it checkers still," said Mr Frobisher. "He comes in here now and again; Saturday nights, mostly."

There was a momentary pause.

"Is he about here, then?" asked Mr Turner. "I reckoned he'd have gone back to America."

"He did," said Mr Frobisher. "And he come back again. He lives just up the road. Works over at Camborne as a draughtsman—goes there every day. It's only two stations up the line."

"Well, I'm damned," said Mr Turner. "You say he's living here now? I'd like to see him again."

"Aye," said Mr Frobisher, "you'll find him up the road. House called Sunnyvale, four doors up past Woodwards' store, just past the church. You can't miss it. On the same side as Robertson's."

Mr Turner thought for a minute. "Does he live alone?" he asked. "In digs, like?"

"No, he's married," said the landlord. "Married a Trenarth girl last year—Grace Trefusis that was."

From Penzance Hospital, in 1943, Dave Lesurier had been sent to Northern Ireland, where he had joined a draft for Iceland; in Iceland he had driven a truck till V-E day, when he had been sent back to the United States and demolised. He had got back to Nashville in the late summer of that year, a free man, to find that the Filtair Corporation

231

was laying off hands strenuously and that his old job in the garage was a thing of the past.

He did not regret it. It had been a dead-end job at best, one which would never lead him further than the maintenance of trucks. He did not know what he wanted to do, except that he wanted more than that; as a first step he wanted to design things, to make drawings, on a drawing board, of engineering parts, and watch them come to life on the fitter's bench. And he wanted to meet Grace Trefusis again, to say that he was sorry.

If there had been work for him in Nashville of a sort that he could settle down to, both these vague ambitions might have faded. In the turmoil of reconversion there was nothing for him at the time that he got home but those jobs which are traditional for the Negro—domestic or hotel service, work on a farm or on the roads, or in a shoeshine parlor. His travels had made Dave Lesurier despise these things. He was resentful of the land of opportunity that gave so small an opportunity to him. While he was living on his Army money in those first few weeks at home, his mind turned back to England. Compared with the glittering, streamlined prizes of a white man's career in his own country, the rewards that England had to offer seemed drab enough and poor, but they were more accessible to him.

He talked the whole matter out with his father, who had been laid off due to reductions in the drafting staff at Filtair consequent on reconversion, and was doing casual tracing for a local architect, for irregular payments at the wage rate of a girl. Money was tight in the Lesurier household, but his father advised him objectively.

"If you reckon you can make a living better over in Europe, son," he said, "you go ahead and don't you worry about Ma and me. We'll get by all right. There'll be plenty trouble in this country before colored folks get equal opportunities with whites, at any rate down South. If they ever do, you can come right back home and slip into a good job. But in the meantime, if you got a hunch you can do better over there—well, son, you go ahead and try it while you've got some money left."

Dave Lesurier did try it. He hitchhiked to Charleston and went to the United States Shipping Board with his Army discharge papers, and after three days got a job as a mess boy in a freighter bound for Durban with machinery. He washed dishes from Charleston to Durban, from Durban to Sydney, from Sydney to Calcutta, and from Calcutta to

New York. He landed back in the United States after seven months without having made much progress towards England, but with a little money saved. He shipped again then in another freighter from New York to Buenos Aires. From Buenos Aires his ship sailed for Avonmouth, with a cargo of hides.

He drew his pay and left the ship at Avonmouth, only a hundred and fifty miles from Trenarth, eleven-and-a-half months after setting out from Nashville. He was twenty-five years old then, more fully developed and self-confident than he had been when he was last in England, still anxious to become a draughtsman, still anxious to see Grace Trefusis once again, if only to say that he was sorry for his lapse three years before. A long scar, somewhat blacker than his choc-olate-coloured skin, reminded him of it each time he looked in a mirror.

He travelled down to Penzance by train, staring out the window at the little fertile fields, immersed in memories of his previous journeys in troop trains about this coun-try. At Penzance he parked the suitcase which held all his property in the station cloak room, and went and asked a policeman where he could spend the night; he spent it in a common lodging house.

In the morning he walked out to Trenarth. It was Sep-tember, and the weather was fine and warm. He had a good suit in his bag, but he wore his seaman's clothes—blue linen slacks, a khaki shirt, and a windcheater. On his head he wore an old soft hat. He turned up in the bar of the White Hart at opening time, and the first person he saw was Bessie Frobisher, behind the bar.

She greeted him warmly. "We've wondered ever so many times if any of you boys would come back here and see us," she said. "We hear of some of them. Sam Lorimer, he wrote at Christmas; ever so nice it was to hear from him. He's married now and living at a place called Detroit, where they make motor cars or something." She smiled at him. "You married yet?"

He shook his head. "No ma'am!"

She laughed. "Won't nobody have you?"

She asked him what he had been doing, and heard all about his wandering. "Fancy!" she said. Then she went to the parlour door and called her father. "Dad, here's Dave Lesurier come back!" And he had to tell his story all over again. And then Mr Penlee, the farmer, came in, and he had to tell it a third time.

Mr Frobisher took him into the back parlour and gave him dinner, while Bessie served the bar; she had had her meal before opening time. After the pudding, Dave gave his host a cigarette, and said:

"It's been mighty nice of you to give me dinner, Mr Frobisher." He hesitated. "If I wanted to stop over for the night, would you have a bed? I've got money to pay for it."

"Aye," said the landlord, "I can fix you up somehow. You staying for a few days?"

"I dunno, Mr Frobisher." The Negro hesitated. "There was quite a mite of trouble last time I was here," he said at last. "Would folks remember that around these parts?"

"Aye," said Mr Frobisher, "they remember it all right. Proper rumpus that set up, that did."

"If that's the way it is," said Lesurier, "maybe I better move along."

"Not unless you want to," said the landlord. "The feeling here was you'd been treated pretty bad."

"There wouldn't be no more trouble if folks saw me here, on account of what I did?"

"I shouldn't think so," said the landlord slowly. "Not unless Grace Trefusis or her mother cut up nasty, and I don't see why they should."

Lesurier asked, "Is Miss Grace still here?"

"Aye," said the landlord. "She works up at Robertson's just the same. Been there all the time."

There was a long, slow pause.

"Well, thanks a lot," the Negro said at last. "I'll be back around five or six tonight, Mr Frobisher, 'n let you know if I'll be wanting to stay."

"Aye," said the landlord, "please yourself. The bed's there if you want it."

Dave Lesurier went out and stood on the street corner, smoking, till the church clock struck two. Then he turned, and walked slowly up the road to Robertson's grocery shop, and went in, and walked straight up to Grace Trefusis behind the counter, and said quietly, "Ten Players, please, ma'am."

She looked up quickly, and met his eyes. Between them, for an instant, the world stood still. She was three years older now, nearly twenty. Her figure had filled out, making her more mature and prettier than the frightened adolescent he had known before. She was more knowledgeable about men, too; she had been to the pictures many times and with a number of young men, and had been kissed by several in a dark corner since the Negro had initiated her into that

234

deplorable pastime. She met his eyes, and the old fear flickered in her own for an instant, but then she smiled.

"Oh . . ." she said, "it's you!"

In that instant all his old shyness swept back over him. He coloured hotly, and wished desperately for eloquence, that he might make some flip and smart rejoinder, but no inspiration came. Instead, there was an awkward pause, and all he could find to say to her at last was to repeat, "Ten Players, please, ma'am."

The last trace of fear of him left her forever. In her more adult experience she knew that she would never be in any danger from this shy young man, coloured though he might be. The words of an American officer came to her mind, secretly treasured and remembered for three years—"If he kind of admired you, Miss Trefusis, well, there's nothing wrong with that." That admiration had brought nothing to him but attempted suicide, hospital, and disgrace; and now, after three years, he had come back for more. She reached mechanically to the shelf for a packet of cigarettes, and said gently, "Are you out of the Army, now?"

He swallowed, and said, "Yes, ma'am."

She had the packet in her hand, but she did not give it to him. "What are you doing then?" she enquired.

He raised his head, and looked at her, and she was smiling at him in the way that she always had smiled at him when she gave him cigarettes, but she was prettier than he had ever remembered her. Courage came back to him, and he said, "I got a job on a freighter, with the steward, and we docked in at Avonmouth. I thought as it was pretty close, I'd kind of come along down here." He met her eyes again. "I thought I'd kind of like to see if you was anywhere around here still, and tell you I've been mighty sorry about that time."

She coloured and laughed awkwardly. "Oh, that's all right." And then she asked curiously, "Did you come all the way from Avonmouth just to say that?"

"Yes, ma'am," he said simply.

She had once been as far as Exeter, nearly a hundred miles away, but Avonmouth, she knew, was much farther than that, and it seemed a very long way to her. She said weakly, "Fancy . . ." And then she said, "You didn't have to come all that way, just to say that." She did not know that he had come from the United States to say it, in eleven months. "There was an officer here once, about that time," she said. "He said you didn't mean nothing by it."

"That's right," he said. He looked at her, and she was

235

smiling, and a slow smile spread across his own face. "I reckon it just kind of happened."

"Well," she said, "you just look out it doesn't happen again." But she was still smiling as she said it, and he took more courage from her smile.

"I was wondering—" he said, and stopped. "I got a lot I'd like to tell you about that time—" he said, and stopped again. And then he managed to get it out, after three years. "If I stopped over for the night," he said, "I was wondering if you'd care to take a little walk with me this evening."

She said gently, "That's what you wanted to ask me before, wasn't it?"

"Yes, ma'am."

"Just for an hour?"

He nodded.

She smiled at him. "I don't mind if I do. Six o'clock, by the gate into the churchyard?"

"I'll be waiting for you, Miss Grace."

She laughed. "None of your tricks, now."

He said in horror, "No *ma'am!*"

"All right," she said. "See you then." And as he turned to go, "You're forgetting your cigarettes!"

Dave Lesurier did not go down the street turning cartwheels, but he felt like it. He went and waited for the bus, went into Penzance and got his bag, and took it back to the White Hart Hotel, and spent the rest of the afternoon dressing for the party. When he walked out of the White Hart that evening for his date he wore a blue suit that was a little too blue, with a very marked waist, and pointed light-brown shoes rather too tight for his feet, and a bright yellow tie with spots on it, and a green silk shirt and collar, and a magenta handkerchief. Grace Trefusis, when she saw him coming, thought he looked ever so smart, and wished she'd put on her best frock instead of the one she'd been wearing for three days.

He had bought a large bunch of violets for her in Penzance, and he gave her these when he met her by the churchyard gate. "They looked so pretty, right there in the shop," he said diffidently, "I thought maybe you'd like them."

She buried her face in the little blossoms. "Oh, they're ever so nice. Just take a smell!" He sniffed them, laughing, and they turned and walked past the churchyard wall together, out towards the hill, and old Mrs Polread, the sexton's wife, who had seen the whole thing from her cottage

236

window, had a fine tale to tell Mrs Penlee when they met an hour later.

"That black boy that assaulted Grace Trefusis when the Americans were here, you know, the one that there was all that trouble over? Believe it or not, he's back here, and she's walking out with him this very minute! And he give her a bunch of violets, too, big as a plate!"

Most of that first walk they spent in talking of his plans. "I kind of thought maybe there'd be a chance of something over here," he said. "Drafting, or that. It's not so easy for a colored boy to get a chance at drafting in my country." She did not really know what drafting was, but she was impressed by his sincerity of purpose. "I thought maybe I'd take a look round a little before I get to looking for another ship. I don't want to go on as mess boy."

He brought her back to the churchyard gate exactly at seven o'clock; she had never been treated with such courtesy and such consideration by any other young man.

"How long are you stopping here?" she asked.

"I d'know," he said. "Tomorrow, maybe."

She said with studied carelessness, "I got a half-day Saturday, but I suppose you'll be gone by then."

He said, "I might not be, Miss Grace. If I was still here, would you like to go to a movie in Penzance, or something?"

She said, "There's ever such a good one on. Ginger Rogers, all in Technicolour. I do think she's ever so nice, don't you?"

He had seen Ginger Rogers all in Technicolour before he left New York; what he wanted to see now was Grace Trefusis. He said, "I think she's swell, Miss Grace. I'd be real honored if you'd let me take you."

She said, "Well, look in at the shop tomorrow and say if you'll be staying over the week-end. I'd like to see that picture ever so."

"Okay, Miss Grace."

He lifted his hat, showing his short, kinky hair, and stood bareheaded while she walked away from him towards her home, to make what explanation of her conduct that she could before her parents.

In the White Hart that evening Dave Lesurier consulted Mr Frobisher about work as a draftsman. Mr Frobisher knew something about draftsmen, only he called them "draughtsmen." His wife's brother had been one. Habitually, too, he kept his ear close to the ground and gathered all the gossip of the district. "I did hear that Jones and Porter, over Camborne way, were taking on draughtsmen," he said thoughtfully. "That was some time back. You might try there, perhaps."

"What kind of work would that be, Mr Frobisher?"

"Electric switches, mostly—time switches and that, special ones to shut off under water, 'n that sort of thing. They got a lot of draughtsmen working there, that I do know."

Lesurier did not let the opportunity pass by. Next morning at eleven o'clock he was at the office of a Mr Horrocks, chief draughtsman of Jones and Porter Ltd., outside Camborne. Mr Horrocks was a thin, dark man, a little at a loss with the young Negro before him. He wanted junior draughtsmen and he was naturally inclined to take a man who came after a job, but he had never engaged a Negro, and Dave's ability was difficult to assess. On his own confession the young man had had no experience in draughtsmanship except his course at school, which might mean nothing at all.

Mr Horrocks picked a bolt up from his desk and gave it to the Negro. "What thread is that?" he asked.

Lesurier took it with a sinking heart, and turned it over in his fingers. "It's a quarter bolt, of course," he said at last, "but what the thread is I don't rightly know. It's a British thread," he explained. "Back home a standard fine thread on a quarter bolt would be twenty-eight to the inch, but this looks coarser to me." He said, "I'm real sorry, sir, but I don't know the British standards. But I'd soon pick them up."

Mr Horrocks took the bolt back. "That's a B.S.F.," he said. "Twenty-six to the inch." He stood for a moment in thought; the young man's answer had not been unintelligent. "Tell you what I'll do," he said. "You can start on Monday for a week on trial, if you like, at two pounds ten. At the end of the week I'll have another talk with you."

Lesurier said, "I certainly will do my best to please you, sir." He hesitated, and then said, "There wouldn't be any trouble with the other men?"

"Trouble? What about?"

"On account of the color."

"Colour?" The chief draughtsman was puzzled for an instant. "Oh, I see what you mean. No, of course there won't be any trouble. I'd like to see them try it on." He made a note of Lesurier's name and temporary address. "Are you a British subject?"

"No, sir. I'm a citizen of the United States."

238

"Oh well, we'll cross that bridge when we come to it. Monday, nine o'clock."

Dave Lesurier walked back to the station bursting with pride and apprehension, pride for having got a job as a draughtsman, and apprehension that he would not be able to hold it. He went past Trenarth in the train and on to Penzance. There he bought a British engineer's pocket book, a fat little volume, full of concentrated information, and a few drawing instruments, and an elementary book on electricity. He had learned the rudiments of electricity at the James Hollis School for Colored Boys back in Nashville; enough to warn him that his knowledge was lamentably deficient for the work he had to do, or thought he had to do. It never struck him that Mr Horrocks did not really think that he was getting an experienced electrical engineer for two pounds ten a week.

He walked rather shyly into Robertson's that afternoon and waited while Grace served another customer. Then he said, "Ten Players, please, ma'am." It had become almost a joke between them by that time. She reached for the packet, and said, "You staying tomorrow, or have you got to go?"

He said, "I'd be real honored if you'd let me take you to the movies, Miss Grace. I've got something to celebrate. I've got a job. A job as draftsman."

She stared at him. "Not already? Wherever to?"

"Jones and Porter Limited, at a place called Camborne, up the line a ways. I got taken on this morning; start on Monday."

Another customer was waiting to be served. She said, "Oh, I am glad!" She shoved the cigarettes into his hand. "I can't stop now. See you tomorrow, two o'clock, at the bus stop outside the church?"

He said, "Okay, Miss Grace. I'll be there."

He was there a quarter of an hour early, having spent the morning studying the comprehendible hardware detailed in his engineer's pocket book, and the incomprehendible abstractions of his electrical textbook. She thought again as she walked up the road towards the bus stop that he looked ever so distinguished; his brown skin and his bright blue suit and his green shirt and collar made a colour scheme that she admired very much. Whatever people might say about going out with a coloured boy, she thought, there were very few men in Trenarth who wore clothes like he did—and in that she was about right.

He was carrying a little parcel unobtrusively, and when they got into the pictures, in the friendly darkness, he offered it to her shyly, and it was a pound box of chocolates, which she called sweets and he called candy. None of her other swains had ever bought her chocolates in a beautiful box like that, all cellophane and green ribbon, and she knew that he could ill afford it, and that made the little present valuable to her. She said, "It's ever so kind of you to think—they're lovely. Here, have one." A woman behind leaned over and asked if she would mind not talking.

They had tea in a café after the picture, and went back to Trenarth in the bus. And at the bus stop in Trenarth he raised his hat to her, and said, "I better say good-night, Miss Grace. It certainly has been one swell day for me."

She said, "Oh no. Come on, 'n see me home. I want you to meet Dad and Ma."

He hesitated. "Maybe they wouldn't care so much about that, Miss Grace."

She said, "They got to meet you some time, if you're only going to be up at Camborne. Come on, just for a minute." She smiled at him. "They won't eat you."

He laughed. "I d'know about that, Miss Grace. Maybe they will." But he went with her to the cottage where she and her parents lived, and to which Lieutenant Anderson had come three years before.

Grace Trefusis had inherited all the vigour of her mother. She took him in and said, "Ma, this is Mr Lesurier that I was telling you about. Dad, this is Dave."

Mr Trefusis got up and said, "How d'you do?"

Mrs Trefusis said, "Well!"

Grace Trefusis said, "Now don't you start that, Ma. If Dave and I can let bygones be bygones, so can you. We've been in to see Ginger Rogers at the Regal. Ever so lovely, it was."

Her mother said with an effort, "How long are you staying for, Mr Lesurier?"

"I got a job here, ma'am," he said shyly. "At Jones and Porter, up at Camborne. I got taken on for a draftsman, starting Monday."

Mr Trefusis said, "A draughtsman?" He looked at the young Negro with a new interest. To the signalman there was some social standing in a draughtsman's job; it was an office job that might lead to management. It was true that most draughtsmen of his acquaintance had ended up in a little sweet and tobacco shop, but some had not. "I didn't know you was a draughtsman," he said.

Lesurier smiled. "I d'know as I am, sir," he said candidly. "I guess I'll need to work plenty hard to hold it down. But it's something to have got a start."

"Sit down," said the railwayman. He offered a cigarette out of a packet. "Where d'you say you come from now?"

Lesurier left them an hour later, having promised to go back to tea next day. The Trefusis family were very thoughtful when he left them on Sunday. By that time they had grown accustomed to the milk-chocolate colour of his skin, which was not unhandsome when you got accustomed to it. He was more widely travelled and better educated than any of the young men Grace had brought to the house before, for in Trenarth there was not a wide choice for her. He seemed to be infinitely considerate and kind, and they remembered this as characteristic of Negroes in the mass three years before. Moreover, Mr Trefusis, when Lesurier went away on Sunday, had a shrewd idea that he would hold his job.

Mr Horrocks began to have the same idea on Tuesday afternoon, five minutes before the drawing office knocked off, when Lesurier came to him. The drawing office was on normal hours of work, but the shop was working overtime till eight o'clock at night.

"I took a little walk around the shop last night, sir, after hours," Dave said. "There's a whole raft of things here that I have never seen before. Would I be able to work down on the bench for the overtime hours, sir, on the assembly of the switches? I wouldn't want no money. I reckon it would make things easier to see the way the drawings go if I knew more about the job down on the bench."

Mr Horrocks thought this was a very reasonable proposal. "You can't go down tonight," he said. "There's the union to be considered." He made a note on his pad. "I'll see the shop steward in the morning about it, Lesurier. I think that's a very good idea."

Lesurier started work down on the bench on Wednesday evening and found to his surprise and pleasure that the shop steward had insisted that he should be paid, which put another twenty-seven shillings in his pay packet at the week's end. He moved into very cheap lodgings in Camborne, and got down to his work in earnest.

He did not find the office work particularly exacting. He was put under an old grey-haired draughtsman called Mr

King. His work consisted principally of copying drawings that had become torn and dirty in the print room. Mr King said severely on the first morning, "Are your hands clean?"

The Negro replied meekly, "Yes, sir. This don't come off." The little joke went round the drawing office, directed against Mr King, who was felt to be a fussy old man, and it spread down into the shop, where Mr King was regarded as an impractical obstructionist and the arch enemy of production. He may have been both of these, but he could teach Lesurier a great deal, and the Negro was wise enough to realise it. Under the stern eye of the old man Dave developed a neatness of drawing and a classic style of printing which were fully up to standard, and with this he began to have some inkling of what the many drawings were about, and why the radiuses and gauge thicknesses were made so.

He became quite popular in the office. His diversity of experience made him interesting to talk to, and he was always willing to help in tiresome jobs like entering in the part number book or checking details. He gave a cosmopolitan air to this small Cornish drawing office which the draughtsmen rather liked, and which was certainly no hindrance to the management.

This was apparent one day when the Managing Director, showing a buying delegation from the Turkish Government around the works and walking them through the drawing office, was asked, "You use Africans for draughting in this country?" He replied grandly, "We use anybody in this company who has the brains we want, white or black. As a matter of fact, that man is an American. He's a very clever young designer."

It was not, of course, because of this that Jones and Porter got an order for three thousand time switches from the Turkish delegation, but Mr Porter felt that his reply had been, perhaps, a small contributory factor.

Gradually, Dave Lesurier became absorbed into the life of the community in which he moved. He spent much of his spare time with Grace Trefusis, and generally had tea with her family on Sunday afternoons. They very soon discovered that he could play the flute, and in the overfurnished little parlour of the Trefusis home he would play hymn tunes for them on Sunday evening. On wet days they sometimes got him to go to church with them, on Sunday mornings, but he was no great churchgoer and preferred to take his exercise at that time. He bought a bicycle, and put it on a Jones and Porter truck that was going up to London, one Saturday, and drove to Plymouth in the truck. He spent two hours there going round the drapers' shops with a snippet of the dress that Mrs Trefusis wore on Sundays, to find a scarf that matched it, for a birthday present for her, and rode home in the evening, fifty-five miles, on his bicycle. He was always doing things like that.

Before spring Dave Lesurier and Grace Trefusis decided to get married; it was a point of dispute afterwards between them which asked which. They did it on the sea front at Penzance after a British Legion dance. Lesurier felt secure in his job with Jones and Porter by that time; he had been advanced to the full rate for his age, four pounds ten a week, and he had joined the Draughtsmen's Association. He felt that he was in control of his job, able to do the work expected of him, and a bit more. Practically the whole of his spare time had been spent with the Trefusis family while he had been in England; they had lost all sense of strangeness at his colour, and thought of him only as a very courteous and pleasant young American with whom Grace went out every Saturday.

The two walked out of the dance hall arm in arm at midnight, reluctant to break away to fetch their bicycles and ride home. They stood on the sea front looking out over the moonlit seascape. Presently the Negro said:

"You know, it still seems darned funny to me folks don't get interfering when they see you and me dancing together."

The girl said, "Why should they? It's got nothing to do with them what either of us do. You got this colour business on the brain, Dave."

"Maybe," he replied. "It's how you've been brought up. I know we couldn't go on like this back home."

"Well, this is my home, and we can," she said. She pressed a little closer to him. "You'd better make it yours, 'n give up worrying."

"You mean, stay here for good?"

"That's right. You like it here, don't you?"

"I like it fine," he said. "I'd like nothing better than to stay right here for good." And then he hesitated. "But I guess there're other things to think about as well."

"What's that?" she asked.

"Place of your own," he said quietly. "Being married, and having kids, and that. You've got to settle where you can do that."

She said softly, "Well, what's wrong with doing that here, Dave?"

He stared out over the sea. "I guess no English girl would want to marry a black man."

She said, "You haven't asked one, Dave."

They were standing arm in arm in their heavy coats; he took her other hand and drew her closer to him. "Do you reckon you could ever get around to thinking that you'd like to marry me?" he asked.

She did not answer, but he knew her silences. "I know it's mighty difficult for a white girl to say yes to that," he said quietly. "Color's color, and nobody can get away from it. When you marry I guess you'll want babies, or you wouldn't be you. And if you marry me, they'll be black ones; not quite so black as me, perhaps, but mighty black, all the same."

She said gently, "You aren't all that black, Dave. You don't want to go exaggerating things."

He said, "I don't reckon that I'd pass for white, though, even in the dark." There was a rueful hint of laughter in his voice. "I guess you know the way I feel about you, ever since those first times we met, in the store. There's never been another girl for me, not after that. I got enough now with this last raise to ask you, Gracie. If you kind of feel that you can't fancy it, I wouldn't blame you. Back home in some States, even saying this to you would likely get me in trouble."

She asked, "Do you think I'd have come out with you all these times if I cared about things like that?"

"I d'know," he said. "I never did know rightly what girls care about, Gracie. But getting married to a nigger is a mighty big thing for a white girl, seems to me."

She said quietly, "Getting married is a mighty big thing anyway, Dave. There's such a sight of things that can go wrong in a marriage, 'n I don't think colour's as important as some others—getting on all right, and respecting one another, and that. You wouldn't have asked me if you didn't think them things were right. And I think they're right, too."

His grasp tightened on her hand. "You mean that?"

"O' course I do. I'll marry you, Dave, if you want me."

"Do I want you?" And then he said, "You do know what it means? We'll be all right in England, maybe, but it could be mighty awkward for you if we ever had to go to the United States."

"Who's talking about going to the United States?" she said. "You don't want to go back there, do you?"

"It's my country," he said. He stood for a minute, thought-

244

ful, filled with nostalgic regret for the things that might have been. "I don't reckon that I'll ever want to go back there," he said at last. "I've got a good job here, and a darn sight more opportunity than ever I'd get at home. I don't reckon I'll ever want to go back to the States."

Mr Turner and Mollie waited in the White Hart till half-past six, to give Lesurier time to get back from his work and have his tea. Then they walked up the road and found Sunnyvale. It was a drab little slate cottage, but the window frames were freshly painted, and some care seemed to have been taken over the front garden. Mr Turner walked up to the door with his wife at his elbow, and knocked.

The door was opened by a young Negro. Turner said, "Mr Lesurier, isn't it?"

"That's right." It was nearly dark, though the room within was brightly lit by a paraffin lamp. The Negro peered at them.

"You won't remember me," said Mr Turner, "but I was in the White Hart, and the landlord told me you lived here. We were in hospital together back in 1943, Dave. My name's Turner."

Lesurier exclaimed. "Say . . . Captain Turner?"

"That's right. Not 'Captain' any longer, though—just Mister."

"Come right in, Captain." He led the way into the room, half parlour and half kitchen. "Think of meeting again, after all this time!" He was introduced to Mollie. "Sit right down and make yourselves at home a minute, while I tell the wife." He explained, "She's bathing the baby."

They sat down, and he vanished up a flight of wooden stairs contained in a cupboard-like structure at the side of the room; there was a murmur of voices from above.

Mr Turner and Mollie looked around them. The room was fairly spacious for the size of the house, being practically the whole of the ground floor. The furniture was aged but adequate; a bright fire burned in the small kitchen range; the room was cosy and cheerful, with bright, rather gaudy colours in curtains and loose covers. The lamp stood on a large kitchen table still littered with the remains of tea, but the tea things had been pushed to one side, and a pencil and cheap exercise book, and a thin book of trigonometrical functions, and a slide rule, and a copy of a book called *Transient Phenomena* by Steinmetz, with a library tag on it, showed that the draughtsman was learning the oddities of alternating-current circuits. Then there was a clattering down the stairs and Dave appeared again.

"She'll be right down," he said. "Say, I'm mighty glad to see you, Captain. You know," he said, "it's been bothering me quite a bit I never got to know what happened to you, with that wound you got, and everything. It seemed to me sometimes that we was all in a bit of a tough spot, even the pilot, with his fancy wife, and we ought to have kept up. But I never heard no more of you, nor of the pilot, either." He laughed. "The way I was fixed myself, I didn't get much chance to make enquiries."

"Well, I can tell you what happened to Flying Officer Morgan," said Mr Turner comfortably. "He . . ." He checked himself, and looked up at the Negro. "I met him out in Burma," he said quietly. "It'll interest you, this will. He got rid of that wife of his and married a Burmese girl."

"No!"

"Fact. I met him out there, only a couple o' months ago."

"A colored girl?"

"That's right."

Lesurier burst out laughing, and slapped his thigh. "Well, what do you know about that! Say, Captain, do you think there could have been something 'catching' in that ward? You know, I married a white girl?"

"So Mr Frobisher told me," said Mr Turner. "Maybe it *is* catching. For all I know, it may be going on all over the world. If so, I shan't lose any sleep about it."

Lesurier said, "Tell me more about Mr Morgan, Captain. How did he come to meet this colored girl he married?"

"He met her out in Burma," Mr Turner said. He settled down on the worn settee to tell the Negro all about it. In the middle of their discussion Grace came downstairs, and they all stood up and were introduced. She said, "I'm ever so pleased to meet you. I've heard Dave talk about you, Captain Turner, ever so many times when Mr Brent was here, and they were wondering what happened to you." She turned to Mollie. "I just been putting down the baby. Like to take a peep at him before he goes to sleep?"

"Oh, I'd like to do that." The two women went upstairs, and Mr Turner turned to the Negro. "Did your wife say something about Brent?"

"That's right," said Lesurier. "Duggie Brent. He's the only one of the four of us that I knew anything about, till you came in this evening."

"What's he doing now?" asked Mr Turner.

"Got a job at Camborne, with a butcher," said the Negro. "Drives all round this end of Cornwall in the van, selling in the villages. I'll tell you about him. But go on about Morgan."

Mr Turner went on talking about Flight Lieutenant Morgan and Nay Htohn in far-off Mandinaung.

Upstairs in the little bedroom, the two women bent over the cradle. The face of the baby showed as a yellowish-brown patch on the white pillow.

"He's ever such a darling," said the mother softly. "He knows us both already, and he's ever so intelligent. Got all his father's brains, he has. He's going to have a little brother or sister in May."

"Fancy," said Mollie. "My dear, I am so glad."

Grace said, "Well, we thought as he was kind of dark that it'd make things easier if he had two or three brothers 'n sisters of his own sort along with him, besides our wanting them as well." She straightened up over the cradle. "I dunno how you think about these things," she said. "Lots of folks, they think I done something terrible, marrying a Negro. But they never talk that way after they get to know Dave." She laughed. "Most o' them say then he's exceptional, 'n not like the others. But I dunno. I never had no regrets."

Mollie stooped over the baby. "He is a darling little chap," she said, wistful at her own childlessness. "Do you suppose he'll have much trouble at school, when he gets older, with the other children?"

Grace shook her head. "Not if we keep him to school here," she said. "There's one or two more like him in Trenarth, sort of souvenirs of the Americans." She laughed, and then she said, "Of course, Dave says he will have trouble on account of his colour. Like he has himself. But I dunno—I don't think trouble hurts people so much. I think it kind of brings out what's the best in them, don't you? I know it has with Dave."

Mollie nodded. "I expect that's right."

Grace said, "My dear, I must tell you what the Vicar said about him—it was awful! He's ever such a queer man, Mr Kendall—says the queerest things, right out in the pulpit, sometimes. I suppose that's why he's only vicar of a little place like this, they wouldn't give him a bigger parish. Well, I asked him to come and see baby here before the christening because I thought he might not like it about the colour, and he came, and I asked him. And he said, he was about the colour of babies in the Middle East, in Palestine

and that, and then he said, 'about the colour of Jesus Christ.'
My dear, wasn't that a terrible thing to say? He's ever such
a queer man, Mr Kendall. I shouldn't think he'd ever get
to be a bishop."

Downstairs, Mr Turner was again asking about Duggie
Brent. "He's getting on all right," Dave said. "He comes by
here with the van Mondays and Thursdays, and always saves
us a nice joint. Grace gets all her meat from him. It's better
meat, and cheaper too, than any she can get in Trenarth or
Penzance. Of course," he said reflectively, "I dare say he
goes out of his way with us, because it was through us he
kind of got the job, you see."

Mr Turner asked, "How was that, then?"

It seemed that Badcock's Fair had come to Penzance in
the previous autumn, and Dave had taken Grace to it, and
they had been to see the Wall of Death, and there was Duggie Brent, red-headed, dashing round and round on a motorcycle, and when it was over, standing, bowing, at the bottom
of the saucer, while the audience, encouraged by the com-
père, showered pennies down on the riders. They had met
him after the show and had been introduced to his wife in
the pay box, who was evidently going to have a baby pretty
soon. They had all gone to the local for a drink, and had
got on so well together that on Sunday when the show was
closed down for the day, the Brents had come out to Trenarth for tea with the Lesuriers.

"That was soon after our baby was born," Dave said.
"They were kind of envious of us having a home like this,
although it's not much. Phyllis didn't want to go on in the
show business, with the baby coming and all that, and Duggie—say, that boy certainly was fed up with the Wall of
Death. But there wasn't anything else he could do except
butchering, and his father's shop in Romsey, that was sold.
Well, they went on with the show, but we kept thinking
about it and how nice it would be if they could be neighbours, because Grace and Phyllis, they hit it off all right.
So then I got to hear that Mr Sparshatt over at Camborne
was starting his van round again—and say, was it wanted!
The meat supply around these parts has been just terrible,
for all that it's a country district. Well, Grace knows Jane
Sparshatt through being at school together. And Jane spoke
to her father, and I wrote to Duggie at some hotel in Edgware saying that there was a job there if he wanted it, and
he came right down, and Mr Sparshatt took him on for the
van round. So now he drives the van around all week, selling

248

the meat, getting back to Camborne every night, of course. He says it's a darn sight more fun than the Wall of Death, or the Parachute Corps, either."

"Got a house at Camborne, has he?"

"That's so. Got a little girl, too, Julienne Phyllis. Got another coming pretty soon, too. He's fixed up all right. Take over the shop someday, after Mr Sparshatt's time, I'd think."

"Well, that's fine," said Mr Turner. "We all come out all right then, all the lot of us. You'd never have thought it, back in 1943, would you?"

"No," said the Negro. "We certainly did seem a no-good bunch of bums around that time." He glanced at Mr Turner. "You got on all right, then?"

"Oh, I done fine," said Mr Turner. He hesitated for a moment, and then said, "I had a bit o' trouble after I left hospital, but after that I went ahead in business, 'n never looked back. I got a nice house now in Watford, paid for, too, 'n a good job. I been mighty lucky, taking it all round."

"Say, that's great," said Lesurier. "You don't ever get no trouble from the wound?"

"Not so's you'd notice," said Mr Turner briefly. "Throbs a bit, now and then, but nothing to signify."

Lesurier did not feel that he could ask for more detail. To him, his visitor looked to be a very sick man indeed; there was a thin grey look about him that Dave did not understand but which seemed menacing, and he seemed to have only partial use of the right hand. He said, "You made a mighty fine recovery, you know. Back in the hospital, one time, they didn't think you'd live."

"Born to be hanged," said Mr Turner comfortably. "That's what it is."

The women came downstairs, and Grace Lesurier made a cup of fresh tea while Dave and Mollie washed the old tea things and they sat talking for an hour. At last the Turners got up to go.

"It's been real nice seeing you again, Captain Turner," said the Negro. "It's a pity Duggie Brent couldn't have been here, too."

"Don't matter," said Mr. Turner, "s'long as I know he's all right; that's all I care about. I never did see him, you know. I was all bandaged up. All I ever did was hear his voice. I wouldn't know him if I met him, now."

"Fancy . . ." said Grace.

"I'll tell him about you and Mr Morgan when I see him next," Dave said. "I reckon he'll be mighty glad to hear you're going on so well. We got kind of worried, him and me, thinking we ought to try and find out what had happened to you. It didn't seem right when we was both fixed up so nice that we shouldn't try and find out about you and Mr Morgan. And now, you're better fixed than either one of us!"

"The pilot out in Burma," Mr Turner said, "he's better off than all the lot of us together."

They said good-bye at the door. "Let us know when you're down in these parts again," Dave said. "That likely to be soon?"

"Oh, aye," said Mr Turner. "I get down here once in a while. Next summer, maybe."

Grace said, "Be sure and let us know."

They got into the little car and drove off to Penzance. At the wheel, Mollie said, "Why did you say we'd be down here again, Jackie?"

"Got to say something," he said heavily. "You didn't tell her nothing, did you?"

"No," she said quietly. "I thought maybe you wouldn't want it."

"That's right," he said. "No good getting folks upset about things they can't do nothing about." He paused, and then came out with his favourite cliché, "All be the same in a hundred years," he said. "That's what I say."

They drove into Penzance.

CHAPTER ELEVEN

AFTER his holiday in Cornwall, Mr Turner went downhill rather rapidly. They got back to Watford without incident, but he was tired by the journey, and when his wife suggested he should stay in bed next day he made no protest. He had breakfast in bed—"like a lord," as he put it—and looked at the pictures in the paper, especially "Jane." But reading was now difficult for him except for the very large headlines, and he had soon done with The Mirror. His wife brought him up the wireless and he lay listening to that while she cleaned and tidied the house and washed the breakfast things. She went out presently to do her shopping, and on returning to the house about half-past eleven, found that he had turned the wireless off and was lying in bed doing nothing at all. As she took her coat off, she said, "Didn't you want the wireless any longer, then?"

He said, "I turned it off. Kind of stops one thinking."

She sat down on the bed for a minute before going down to start to cook the dinner. "What you been thinking about?"

He said, "Oh, all sorts of things. Seems like I never had time for any real thinking before, thinking things out, I mean. I been having a grand time. Ought to ha' got sick like this long ago."

"What sort of things, Jackie?"

"I dunno." He paused, and then he said. "I keep on being ever so glad them chaps got themselves fixed up all right, all the lot of them. And all having babies, too, right and left, every one of them. All the whole boiling of them. Sort of makes up for you and I not having any, don't it?"

"I suppose so," she said slowly. "I suppose it does."

He said, "You aren't sorry that we never, are you, now?"

"I dunno," she said. "Sometimes I kind of wish we had."

"I'm glad we didn't," he said. "Things being like they are, with you having to work again and that, I'm glad we never. But lying here and thinking, I'm glad them chaps don't think about it like we do."

"They're not so sensible," she said thoughtfully.

He grinned. "That's right," he said. "Chaps with a dud napper like I got ought to be sensible about not having kids, but they don't have to be."

She went downstairs to get on with the cooking, and presently she brought him up his dinner in bed while he lay listening to the wireless. And when she came, he turned it off and said, "I been thinking, I'd like to write a letter to Mr Morgan out in Burma to tell him about Dave Lesurier and Duggie Brent. I know he'd like to hear, 'n Nay Htohn, she'd like to hear about them, too."

So after lunch Mollie got her pad and he lay dictating a very long letter all about Trenarth and Grace Trefusis and the disease that was "catching," and about Jones and Porter, and about Duggie Brent. And, tired with the effort of so much dictation, he sank into sleep while Mollie was downstairs typing it, and slept till it was time for tea, and then got up and dressed and had his tea with her downstairs, and went out with her to the pictures. That was a prototype for many days that followed, perhaps the happiest of their chequered married life.

On his good days he would get up soon after breakfast, and walk out with Mollie to help her in her shopping, and come back and write one or two business letters. He shifted the last of his parcels of cheroots during these weeks, and on casting up his accounts came to the conclusion that he had made a profit of about £340 on them, which more than covered the cost of his trip out to Burma. That pleased him very much.

They did not lay the little car up for the winter, but kept it in commission for his outings. On his good days, once or twice a week, Mollie drove him to the Barley Mow for an hour before closing time. He no longer had the energy to lead the party, but these short evenings, drinking beer and listening to the gossip and the stories in the warmth and light of a crowded bar, were a great pleasure to him. He would talk of them next day with reminiscent pleasure, and make plans for the next outing.

He did his football pool religiously every week. He could no longer read the small print of the announcements, but Mollie read it all out to him each week and they would make out the coupons and send them in, one for him and one for her. He did not win anything, to her regret, but she won two pounds fifteen shillings one week, and this gave them both a great deal of pleasure.

On his bad days, when headache forced him to his drugs, he stayed in bed all day, sleepy and thoughtful.

About the middle of October he had a fall in the kitchen. He had walked all morning, shopping, with Mollie. On coming into the house the vertigo seized him; he reached for the kitchen dresser and missed it and fell, hitting the back of his head heavily on the fender. He brought down the soup tureen with him and three plates, and Mollie, hurrying downstairs to the noise, found him lying unconscious on the floor in a litter of smashed china.

She called Mrs Pocock from next door to help her, and together they managed to carry him upstairs and put him to bed. He had come round by the time Dr Worth arrived, two hours later, but after that he did not walk out in the street again.

Mrs Pocock was devoted to good works. For want of someone to confide in, and for help in getting Mr Turner up the stairs, Mollie told her the facts of his illness; she relayed them to the Vicar. They were not regular churchgoers by any means—indeed, neither of them had very often been inside the place, but the Vicar was a kindly and broad-minded man, and called one afternoon when Mr Turner was in bed and thinking of getting up for tea to take a run out to the Barley Mow.

Mollie brought the Vicar up to the bedroom. "Here's Mr Holden come to see you, Jackie," she said. To the clergyman she said, "It's ever so kind of you to call."

She left them together, and went downstairs to get on with the ironing. Half an hour later she heard the Vicar coming out of the bedroom, and went to meet him in the hall, to open the front door for him.

Mr Holden said, "He seems to keep very cheerful, Mrs Turner."

"That's right," she replied. "Nothing seems to get him down, does it?"

"No; he seems very composed." He thought for a minute. "Of course, it's clear that he has never been what one would call a religious man," he said, and smiled. She wondered apprehensively what Jackie had been saying to him. "If I can do anything practical to help you, Mrs Turner, let me know. And if you find a little later on that he would like to see me again—that sometimes does happen, you know —I will come at once. At any time."

She said, "That's ever so kind of you, Mr Holden. I'm sure he'll like to know that."

He left, and she turned off the iron and went up to the bedroom. "I just let Mr Holden out," she said. "Like to have your tea up here, Jackie, or are you going to get up?"

"Oh, I'll get up," he replied. "I'm feeling all right now. I reckon we can go out, like we said."

She asked, "What had Mr Holden got to say?"

"I dunno—all about having Faith, and that." He paused. "I asked him straight out what was going to happen to me —'Where do I go from here?' I said. But he don't know nothing, really. He talked a lot of stuff about Judgment, 'n Heaven, 'n Hell, only he don't seem to believe in Hell himself, not properly. What it all seems to boil down to is, you just got to have Faith that God'll put you where you belong, but he don't know where that is or what happens to you there. It don't seem very satisfactory to me."

Theological discussion was a new thing between them. "I wouldn't bother my head about it too much, Jackie," she said gently. "Just take it as it comes."

He was silent for a minute, deep in thought. "I been thinking about this," he said at last. "I kind of like the idea them Buddhists have the best—what Mr Morgan and Nay Htohn believe. I don't want to be judged, not yet. I done a sight o' mean things in my life; things you probably don't know nothing about, in business and that. You got to these days, or you can't get by and build up any security at all, with taxes like they are. If I come up to be judged now, 'n it's either Heaven or Hell, I know which it would be."

"You can't know that yourself, Jackie," she said. "That don't make sense."

"Well, I've got a pretty good idea," he replied. "But these Buddhists, what they say is, if you haven't done so good in this life then you get reborn again a bit lower down, maybe as an Indian sweeper, or lower down still, as a horse or a dog. That gives you another go, like, to have another shot at it 'n try and do a bit better. And however low you get, they say, you always get reborn, and you can always have another go, and work yourself up again by living a better life. That's what Nay Htohn said. I'd like to think that it was going to be like that."

"Maybe it will be like that, then," she said quietly. "I wouldn't worry about it, anyway."

Mr Turner said, "I don't. Can't do anything about it now, so it's no good worrying. But I kind of like the Buddhist idea—that's how I'd like it to be." He grinned up at her. "So if you see a little dog about next year you haven't seen before, 'n you call 'Jackie,' 'n it comes, just give it a nice bone."

"And put a bottle of beer in its bowl, too, I suppose," she said. She turned, laughing, to the door. "Come on and get up, if you're getting up today. I'll go and put the kettle on for tea."

Another time, he said, "I had been thinking about these darker-skinned people that I got to know about, Nay Htohn and Dave Lesurier. You know, there don't seem to be nothing different at all between all of us, only the colour of our skin. I thought somehow they'd be different to that. They got some things we haven't got, too—better manners, sometimes. I reckon we could learn a thing or two from them."

His wife said, "You got to remember that those two were different to the general run of dark-skinned people, Jackie. They were educated ones."

"That's so," he said thoughtfully. "Maybe there's some sense in paying for all this schooling."

On October 30th Mr Turner came to my rooms in Harley Street, by an appointment made for him by his general practitioner, Dr Worth. I saw him at four o'clock in the afternoon on a day when I had no further appointments, thinking that I might find it necessary to take him to the hospital for further radiological examination.

My receptionist showed him in. His wife came in with him, one hand lightly guiding his arm; she seemed to be afraid to let him move a step without her. She watched him as he lowered himself into the chair, and then said, "I'll wait outside, doctor."

"No, you can stay if you want to," I replied. "That is, if Mr Turner doesn't mind?"

"Suits me all right," he said.

He spoke thickly, with a slurring of the consonants. He still possessed his jaunty air of cheerfulness, but one glance told me that I would have little need of radiological examination for him. Paralysis of the right arm was far advanced. The left eye was fixed and evidently useless to him, and the right one was already much affected. He had lost a great deal of weight, so that his clothes, once tight upon his body, hung on him loosely. He still had colour in his face, but around his eyes and temples there was a grey tinge to his skin. It did not seem to me that he had very long to go.

I have been over thirty years in specialist practice. Some men say that they get hardened to these things, but I have never overcome that sadness of compassion that one must feel for a man in his position.

I offered him a cigarette, and reached over, and lit it for him.

I said, "Well, Mr Turner, what have you been doing since I saw you last?"